MAGDALENA
MOUNTAIN

BOOKS BY ROBERT MICHAEL PYLE

PROSE

Wintergreen: Rambles in a Ravaged Land
The Thunder Tree: Lessons from an Urban Wildland
Where Bigfoot Walks: Crossing the Dark Divide
Nabokov's Butterflies (Editor, with Brian Boyd and Dmitri Nabokov)
Chasing Monarchs: Migrating with the Butterflies of Passage
Walking the High Ridge: Life as Field Trip
Sky Time in Gray's River: Living for Keeps in a Forgotten Place
Mariposa Road: The First Butterfly Big Year
The Tangled Bank: Essays from Orion
Through a Green Lens: Fifty Years of Writing for Nature

POETRY

Letting the Flies Out (chapbook)
Evolution of the Genus Iris
Chinook and Chanterelle

ON ENTOMOLOGY

Watching Washington Butterflies
The Audubon Society Field Guide to North American Butterflies
The IUCN Invertebrate Red Data Book
(with S. M. Wells and N. M. Collins)
Handbook for Butterfly Watchers
Butterflies: A Peterson Field Guide Coloring Book
(with Roger Tory Peterson and Sarah Anne Hughes)
Insects: A Peterson Field Guide Coloring Book (with Kristin Kest)
The Butterflies of Cascadia
Butterflies of the Pacific Northwest (with Caitlin LaBar)

MAGDALENA MOUNTAIN

A NOVEL

ROBERT MICHAEL PYLE

COUNTERPOINT
Berkeley, California

F
Pyl

Magdalena Mountain

Library of Congress Cataloging-in-Publication Data
Names: Pyle, Robert Michael, author.
Title: Magdalena Mountain / Robert Michael Pyle.
Description: Berkeley, CA : Counterpoint Press, [2018]
Identifiers: LCCN 2017060550 | ISBN 9781640090774 (softcover)
Subjects: LCSH: Quests (Expeditions)—Fiction. | Wilderness areas—
    Fiction. | Naturalists—Fiction. | Butterflies—Fiction.
Classification: LCC PS3616.Y545 M34 2018 | DDC 813/.6—dc23
LC record available at https://lccn.loc.gov/2017060550

Jacket designed by Kelly Winton
Book designed by Jordan Koluch

COUNTERPOINT
2560 Ninth Street, Suite 318
Berkeley, CA 94710
www.counterpointpress.com

Printed in the United States of America
Distributed by Publishers Group West

10 9 8 7 6 5 4 3 2 1

For the women
who made this book possible:
JoAnne, Sally, Thea, Mary Jane, Jan, and Florence
~they know what they did~
and, of course,
for Maggie May

MAGDALENA MOUNTAIN

BEFORE

Should a landing craft from elsewhere settle onto Magdalena Mountain on an early-autumn morning, the visitors might arrive at two conclusions. First, this world is a golden one; the denizens must have monochromatic vision. Second, this world is harsh; the citizens must be tough. Upon leaving, they would jot field notes such as "inhospitable, but rather pretty in a raw sort of way" in their intergalactic log.

On both counts they would be partly right. The rockslide and its environs indeed glitter in September's dawn. On the fellfield, all the prostrate herbage has yellowed, except for certain low shrubs that have turned red, and they only lend depth to the overall gold. Sliding up the ridges, the tongues of aspenwood range, in their clones, from cinnamon to lemon, with orange-peel and persimmon in between. Even the granite, the substance of the scene, shines with a varied patina in the rising sun and morning frost, mica catching the sun's color, feldspar pink going to peach, gray feldspar to platinum.

So, golden. And rough. But not necessarily inhospitable. True enough, humanity seldom appears on the scene. But there are lives below the surface, many of them. Now, in the chilly gilt of oncoming autumn, they come out of the rocks to bask. They suck every calorie of warmth from the cool fire of the alpenglow. For soon enough, afternoon cloud will rise, promising something rougher yet: rocks in winter. For now, frost holds off. Then the sun passes beyond its perigee, and all the gold is gone. Most of the animals retreat beneath the stones, as a minute caterpillar creeps down deep into a withered tussock of grass.

PART ONE

1

The yellow Karmann Ghia left the road at forty-five. Its tires never scored the soft tissue of the tundra. It simply flew over the edge, into the mountain abyss.

A lookout marmot shrilled at the sight. A pair of pikas, young of the year, disappeared beneath their rockpile as the strange object passed overhead. Clearing the stony incline, the doomed auto glided over the rich mountain turf. Its shadow fell across a patch of alpine forget-me-nots, deepening their hue from sky to delft, then passed over a pink clump of moss campion. A black butterfly nectaring on the campion twitched at the momentary shading. Such a shift of light often signaled a coming storm, sending the alpine insects into hiding among the sod or stones. But this cloud passed quickly, so the sipping butterfly hunkered only briefly, then resumed its suck from the sweet-filled floret. A bigger black form took flight when the bright intruder entered its territory. The raven charged the big yellow bird to chase the interloper out of its airspace, succeeded, and resettled.

As the slope fell away toward the canyon below, more than keeping pace with the glide path of the Ghia, so fell the yellow missile. Sky whooshed aside to make room for it, otherwise there was no sound but for three shrieks on the alpine air: a nutcracker's alarm scream; the whine of the engine, gunned by the foot glued to the Ghia's floorboard; and a third, muffled by the glass, growing into a hopeless wail.

The thin alpine air parted before the plummeting car, smelling of green musk, of the great high lawn that is the Colorado mountain tundra. The perfumes of a hundred alpine wildflowers filled the grille of the Ghia. Soon the sweet mingled scents would be overcome by the rank fumes of oil and gasoline mixing with the terpenes of torn evergreens as the grille split against pine and stone. But the rider smelled nothing.

The air took on a chill as the projectile left the sunny upper reaches, crossed over timberline, and entered the shade of the upper forest. Never once had it touched down since takeoff, nor could it fly much farther. Gravity never ran out, but the earth rushed up at last to meet it. All the elements of the alpine earth—mineral soil, bare stone, grass, sedge, herb, shrub, and solid trunk of ancient limber pine—mingled with the yellow metal when the Ghia went to ground. Soft parts met hard. Granite tore rubber. Branches smashed glass and pierced the cloth upholstery. The engine block escaped its mounts and flew a little farther before shattering against a boulder and coming to rest as shiny shrapnel in the streambed far below. The blow that tore the motor free, ending its long scream, ripped the driver's door from its hinges. That other shriek was loosed into the general clamor. Then nothing.

Almost nothing remained from this unplanned event to disturb the day up above, where it began. The nutcracker returned to its snag, the marmot to its post, the raven to its rock. The black butterfly nectared on, then flew. The forget-me-nots still flowered low against the ground. Not even the green verge of the road betrayed anything amiss. Only a black rubber streak in the roadway gave away the launching spot. Even the golden-mantled ground squirrel whose mad dash across the asphalt had started it all lay not dead on the shoulder, but basking on a boulder nearby in the late-summer sun, unabashed by her close call.

Of the steaming yellow mass among the trees and rocks a thousand feet below, no one knew a thing. Bumblebees investigating the yellow spatter on the slope found battered, barren steel instead of woolly sunflowers. The Karmann Ghia's aberrant track would never be repeated. And for all the difference it made to the mountain, it might never have happened at all.

2

Yellow cottonwoods left the creekbeds outside Albuquerque and boarded an eastbound cross-country bus en masse as the driver called out destinations: "All passengers for Parmalee Gulch, Raton Junction, Cambridge, and Peoria, yer on the right bus. If yer plannin' on goin' anywheres else, better get the heck off now. An' git them gol-durned 'possums offa my bus!"

It seemed to James Mead that he was indeed going somewhere else, although he couldn't quite remember where, and in any case the bus was already moving too fast and too far off the ground to jump. Besides, if he jumped, what about his luggage? God, I forgot my suitcase, he yelped, and then realized he was also absent his pants, and the other passengers were beginning to look and snicker, and he had to pee in the worst way. The rows of cottonwood trees began shedding their yellow leaves along with the possums hanging upside down from their lower boughs. The possums dropped like great gray bombs onto people's heads, exploding into storms of gray confetti like that crap in padded envelopes that gets all over everything. Mead felt the ratty tail of a possum slap his cheek and its thin gray hair go up his nostrils. This tickled, made him sneeze, and woke him up.

Mead shook his head, rubbed his gritty eyes, and tried to reconstruct the dream. "Okay, Albuquerque and the trees," he mumbled to himself. He'd boarded the bus there the day before, among the glint of afternoon autumn poplars. "I remember Parmalee from field trips, and I *do* have to pee like crazy." He assumed his bag was safely stowed below. "But what's the deal with the possums?"

"God placed the opossum on the earth for a reason," began the amateur evangelist in the seat next to him, "to serve men in the only way they know how . . ." The man had been silent for over an hour in deference to his young seatmate's nodding slumber. Now that he'd awakened, Mead became fair game again. ". . . by giving possum hounds a run for their money and by patching potholes in the mud with their poor, battered bodies. Now let me tell you, son, how we all must serve His greater purpose."

Mead made his escape by pleading his bladder's screaming need. He slung his way down the aisle toward the chemical stink of the toilet. For balance, he hung on to the luggage racks instead of the seat backs, as people of lesser height usually do. A young woman on her way to Bowdoin vetted his long-sleeved cotton plaid shirt, his khaki chinos (which he was wearing, after all), his Bass shoes. He would do for conversation. Maybe he was Ivy, she conjectured, and resolved to catch his eye on his return journey up the aisle.

Considering Mead's fine-featured face, partly hidden, partly chiseled by a short-trimmed brown beard, a matron thought, now that was a son she wouldn't mind having. The bus driver noticed him too, as he appraised everyone in the rearview mirror, especially the young women whose breasts jostled with the sway of the road. He regarded his own paunch jammed against the big steering wheel, and he envied Mead his slender, muscular frame, the youth that went with it, and the gaze of the woman on her way to Maine.

Mead, heading back to his seat, noticed the girl's glance. Eager to sit anywhere other than beside the preacher, he asked if the seat next to her was free. Her rehearsed shrug said sure, and she smiled, so Mead coiled into the seat. As he dropped down to window level, he spotted a grayish lump beside the median strip, and the source of the dream possums came clear. For miles and miles after Peoria, road-killed marsupials lay along the highway like omens, or reproaches. "Yeah, that's it—roadkill!" he said. The girl next to him frowned, pretty sure she'd made a mistake encouraging his company. Mead saw the look in her eyes and thought he'd better just go back to sleep.

He dropped off, the bus rolled on, and a new dream began to roll, in which an endless graduation march seemed to include every face he'd ever known except his own. The faculty marshals, brightly gowned and carrying ceremonial maces carved from cottonwood sticks, wore grins like the leers of flattened possums.

Mead awoke to the whine of the air brakes as the driver called a lunch stop in Akron. Outside the bus, Mead sucked in air that would have seemed marginal in New Mexico but tasted great now. He stretched, tucked in his shirt (for he suffered the curse of the long torso: his shirttails always came out, always would), and lanked off in search of lunch. The girl from Bowdoin joined him, and they scared up a sandwich and a park bench.

Twenty minutes later they dumped their leavings into the overflowing trash bin as a pigeon lady took their place on the bench and began scattering bread crumbs. They emerged from a pearly curtain of pigeon wings to find the bus driver staring in their direction.

"Where the hell have you two been?" he growled. "Eager to move to Akron, are we?" His jowls swelled and glowed like the cock pigeons' plumbeous puffs, his envy sitting like stale bread in his gizzard. His eyes crawled over Chloe as she climbed up the steps and resumed her seat. Mead plopped down beside her and glared back. The big bus pulled back onto the interstate, a traveling humidor of smoke, stale air, and overtired bodies.

Chloe definitely beat the Baptist for conversation. But truth to tell, Mead wouldn't have cared much if she were a Pentecostal bearing down with hammer and tracts, as long as she stayed put. By Buffalo, James and Chloe knew each other fairly well, the way people quickly do on long-distance buses and then forget. James knew one thing, anyway; he would never forget her scent, which did not seem to come entirely from bottles. It seemed distilled from equal parts of heather and crushed leaves, blended in a light base of sweat. How much the vapid air of the coach confounded her aroma he could not tell, but it did not mask the pheromones at play. By twelve they were asleep, her head on his shoulder. But when Mead awoke, Chloe was gone, disembarked for a visit with an aunt in Springfield. Vaguely disappointed, he went back to sleep.

A day and a night later, Mead's strange and dreamy endless idyll was shattered by the air brakes and a different driver's voice, a woman now. "New Haven," she barked as the air brakes sighed. "All passengers for New Haven."

"*That's* why they call them Greyhounds," Mead said to himself as he dropped down. "The brakes sound just like a dog at the end of its leash, and its patience."

"We're all at the end of the road," replied the preacher, stepping down too. "And soon, the End Times. Have you found your savior?"

"Found," Mead said, "and lost. But she was nice while she lasted." Hoisting his bags, he hurried off, leaving the man open-mouthed and, for once, at a loss for words.

Wandering unknown streets unlike any in Albuquerque, he dowsed a cup of coffee out of early morning in the old New England town. Soon the humidity of a late September day began to rise around his stained collar. He strode in the direction of the crocketed towers that he reckoned must signify Yale University. "Here goes nothing," he said to himself. Then, to no one in particular, "Possums or not!"

3

On Magdalena Mountain, at the base of certain boulders, the winter forage of little rock rabbits, called pikas, lies curing in the sun. Its summer green turns to the gold of haystacks. Vigilant on the rocks above, a mother pika looks grayish-tan in the shade; then, dashing into a sunbeam, her fur at its thickest and richest, she shines like her own gathered hay.

Atop another rock, a marmot basks. Unlike the winter-wakeful pika, this old boar of a marmot will hibernate deeply for months. His fat wobbles as he scrambles rock to rock with the shifting sun. As if to store a little more warmth to get him through the long night of winter, he boulder-basks throughout the long, sunny hours of September, then eats and eats some more. He plucks a paintbrush, consumes it with a few moves of his split lips and big yellow teeth, then goes for a columbine. Over inches of stored fat, his inch of chestnut and chinchilla pelt glimmers in the sunshine until the coming chill drives him and his kind understone for half a year or more.

The talus grows harsher by the night. Tough life dwells there by using the very rocks that make the place seem barren. That butterball marmot knows of a holt deep beneath the coming rime. That pika may be just a short-eared, hay-grazing boulder bunny, but she can move through the catacombs of granite at will, wandering through winter from one side of the pile to another without ever coming to the surface, safe from snow and ice and blowing, shearing wind.

Ptarmigan and rosy finches cling to the violent hide of the arctic-alpine year-round, dropping downhill only when snow forces winter birds to work the edges of the rockslides, the buried branches of the snow willows. Now, their nests only dim memories, the half-white ptarmigan nicker among the willow hems and the finches forage for early seeds and late insects. A ptarmigan fledgling, as big as its mother, makes a dash at a grasshopper, startling the sentry pika into calling *Geek!*

Though the rocks make a harsh home, these and others live here well enough, knowing and needing none but its cold and stony comforts. Many others, swarming in the sun and freezing in the chill, cannot summon the rush of warm blood to keep them from the coming cold. A bumblebee alights on an owl clover, and as a cloud covers the sun, she shivers, making a little body heat. But most of the alpine insects rely strictly on the sun to make their muscles work. For these cold-blooded ones, autumn brings death, or dormancy. That grasshopper escaped the clumsy chick only to freeze some night soon. Unless the fliers, crawlers, and spinners have antifreeze, and many do, their season of life is closing in fast. Everything is about to change.

On Magdalena Mountain, the onset of autumn is palpable. Marmots bask, feed, grow fat and somnolent. Pikas, never more awake, harrow their clippings to cure in the late sun, then store the sweet haystacks in clefts within the castle walls. Ptarmigan are getting whitewashed along with the varying hares downslope: brown feathers and fur are falling out, to be replaced by white. Most of the other birds skedaddle downhill or down south. Even the rocks seem to close ranks, preparing for the storms, whose unblunted breath only they can withstand, and even then not unscathed.

By late August, most of the butterflies have died on Magdalena

Mountain. They have left behind living legacies in various forms, but seldom in their own image. The rockslide checkerspot caterpillar has settled for the winter in a naked, hanging chrysalis in which the most marvelous changes will take place while the world about it sleeps. The lustrous copper has left her eggs, like jeweled pincushions, among rosettes of alpine sorrel. The plant will die back, but then come on again in spring, when the eggs hatch.

The butterfly that bears the mountain's name, the Magdalena alpine, spends its winters as a tiny caterpillar. The first adults emerged from their pupae in early summer, mated, and laid their eggs near clumps of grass among the boulders of the talus or in steep, broken meadows beside the rockslides. These eggs hatched while the autumn sun still shed life onto the alpage. The larvae took their first meal from their own eggshells, the next of tender, new-growth grass or sedge. A few more feedings, maybe a molt when their skins grew taut, and they ceased grazing. Crawling down among the very rootstocks of the grass clumps, the larvae spun loose, individual tents of dead grass and silk and there went to sleep, or something like it, snug within the blanket of the alpine turf.

Of one particular female's hundred eggs, ten fed ants or other foragers right off. After they hatched, twenty-six of the baby caterpillars went to spiders, beetles, and such. The rest made it to hibernation. Several settled in near their point of nascence and there perished when the mother pika harvested their grass clumps—some to eat, some to dry—on her penultimate foraging trip of the year. But one of the siblings feels a walkabout urge prior to settling down, saving him from that fate. This creature, called Erebia for his genus, wanders many times his body length. A chance left turn at a lichened cobble keeps him from a lethal head-on with a ground beetle. Finally he pauses in a tussock at the base of a great boulder, hunkers in, and shuts down but for a flicker of life in his dormant cells.

Come morning, snow covers the talus. It has fallen before, even during midsummer, but it never lasted. This time it sticks to the rocks, fills exposed clefts, and blows about with the fierceness of Boreas making Mehitabel dance, more with each new day. Clicking ptarmigan dive into powder downslope, followed by the rock-roosting ravens. Marmots sleep hard. Pikas, their rock-top vigils finished for now, curl among their faded haystacks deep beneath the glazed surface of the roof stones.

This one alpine caterpillar, Erebia, moves not at all. A minute tube of life, he sleeps on as the world of Magdalena Mountain freezes, solid and pale.

4

"So what happened to her?" Iris asked.

"What happens to all the young ones who aren't here for war shock or drug-busted brains?" Ellen said. "Head injured in a car crash."

"Who is she?"

"Her name is Mary," the doctor said. This one made him sad and uneasy, and he wanted to get away from the nursing home as quickly as he could. She was like the young women brought in after motorcycle wrecks without helmets—the few who survived—but somehow worse. He took a moment to tell the floor nurse and the attendant what he knew. "Three months ago her Karmann Ghia went out of control on Trail Ridge Road, and she fell more than nine hundred feet down into a canyon, fortunately strapped in, and no fire. She was busted up pretty bad, but reparable, except maybe for her head."

"How bad?"

"Both her legs were broken—bilateral tibia and fibula fractures, fifth through tenth ribs, punctured lung, lots of lacerations. But nothing too bad inside; she's healed well."

"Except her head?"

"The tests show little permanent damage. She had a skull fracture and no doubt bruising of the brain, but no major bleeding. Frontal lobe okay, cortex—but next to no mental activity upon admission. Autonomic functions and reflexes fine. The exact nature of her trauma is puzzling. Now that she has recuperated physically, we can't justify keeping her at C. U. Med Center any longer."

The nurse considered this information. She frowned, tsked, then translated it for herself. "So her mind is lost?"

"Oh, Iris . . . who knows? There appears to be no physiological reason, but the psyche seldom consults physiologists. She doesn't seem to know herself. It may be for life or for a month. In the meantime, we thought it best that she come here, where she can't hurt herself."

Mary Glanville, waiting in the nursing home's office, listened to the others speak outside in the hall. She heard some of the words, but they made no sense. Wreck? All she had where the memory of these months should have been was a picture of mountains upon mountains.

"But why here, Dr. Ziegler? Does she really need to be here? She looks so much younger, brighter, healthier than most of our others. Can't she recover somewhere else?"

"But *will* she recover?" asked the doctor. "She doesn't speak or respond after three months. She has no advocate, no relatives we've been able to find, and no resources or insurance as far as we could discover. Her ID was never found, by the way—we know her name is Mary only from a girl's charm bracelet she was wearing."

"What about the automobile registration?"

"Licensed in Connecticut to some fly-by-night secondhand auto dealer, since flown. The temporary registration must be with her bag, somewhere down that canyon. No one has answered state patrol's APB on her. Something will turn up eventually, I suppose, but not so far. So for now? Mary is a ward of the state, and destitute. That means here is it."

Iris tsked. The doctor went on. "CU did all they could. Fort

Logan wouldn't take her without a specific psychosis or other mental diagnosis. So it's either here, with Medicaid, or Pueblo, which I'm sure you wouldn't wish on her—they've had nothing but budget cuts, and they house the hard cases, often violent. If she were my sister, I wouldn't want her there. Anyway, if she gets better, she'll be free to leave."

"No one gets better here," Iris muttered. "I think you know that."

"Take care of her, Iris," said the doctor. "Maybe she'll be the first. Just vitamins for now; if she has any trouble settling in, give her Thorazine, one hundred milligrams, morning and night, for now." He turned and left the facility for the clear night air. He felt relieved, but not happy about it.

With nothing else to do, the nurse led Mary to an empty bed in a bare little room. There were two other beds in the room. Across one lay a confused woman in an old robe who smiled childlike at their approach. "Can I go too, Iris?" she implored.

"We're not going anywhere, Beth, we're coming in. This is Mary, your new roommate."

"Oh, goodie! Gotta smoke, Mary?"

"Mary isn't speaking now, Beth, and she doesn't smoke. Let her rest and move in in peace. Besides, I told you to stop bumming cigarettes."

"Everybody smokes," Beth said with certain sureness. She was almost right. The atmosphere was so thick with tobacco smoke that it almost masked the odors of urine and disinfectant. The residents couldn't smoke in their beds, but the hallways and common areas were filled with puffing, vacant faces.

The second bed held an ancient woman who lay babylike, whimpering, toothless. At the sight of her, Mary started and opened her mouth, but did not speak. The third bed, nearest the heavily screened window, was hers. The nurse showed her to it, then pointed out her closet. "Watch your clothes, they tend to disappear. Showers in the morning at six. I'll be back for you then to show you the ropes.

Toothbrushes kept by the bathroom sink, toilet over there. Breakfast is at eight, lunch at noon, dinner six." Iris had no idea if Mary was taking any of it in.

Then she said, "I'm so sorry you have to be here. Talk to me sometime, okay? My name's Iris." Then the floor nurse, a bulky woman with russet hair, black skin, and red lipstick, her face a mixture of weary officiousness and defeated tenderness, smiled at Mary. She squeezed her hand and returned to her station.

Mary Glanville lay upon the dorm-like bed, her back to the other four eyes in the bleak room. Until then her movements had been slow, tentative, compliant. Now she began, slowly, then gaining speed and violence, to shake. No tears came, just a dry, silent sobbing that wailed against the realization growing in her bruised brain. She shook and shook until she rolled off the bed onto the floor. Disinfectant spiked her nose, and still she shook and writhed. And then a new thing—new, that is, since the day three months before when her car left the black stripe on the mountain and arced over the falling, falling slope—her voice came.

It came first in a tiny, almost inaudible squeak, rose into a low howl, and grew to a shriek that for thirty seconds silenced the entire home. No words, just the scream, which seemed like words to Mary, demanding to know *"What is happening to me? Why am I in this place? This is no dream and I realize what it is and this is the kind of place you VISIT only when you must and don't stay any longer than you have to and then get out, and damn it I am HERE and staying behind and WHY? Get me out, oh, out, anywhere, OOOUUUT!"* All this she wailed without words until the last ones, which came again, wailed, wailed. And she screamed it so loud that her temples swelled and her hands, gripping the bed legs, turned white.

All the nurses and orderlies came, bound Mary, gave her shots, subdued her into a dull, tormented semblance of sleep. For the next three days, every time she awakened, Mary wailed and shrieked *"Why? WHYYYY? Get me OUUUUT!"* Whenever the sedatives lost their grip on her savaged larynx, Mary keened. And then, on the fourth day, when the mental health agency ordered an ambulance to take her to the state asylum at Pueblo, Mary awoke becalmed. Iris called the doctor, who canceled the ambulance.

Hoarse, but silent, Mary was permitted to remain at Mid-Continent Care Center. She settled in. She took meals with the burned-out boys from Vietnam—overflows from the VA who seemed to age more day by day. And with the brain-shattered youths, the poor and vacant with dementia or drugs, and the menacingly or mildly mad for whatever reason. In self-defense, her eyes took on a shieldlike hardness. Her mouth turned up in a demi-smile below permanent furrows in her forehead. And she no longer shrieked aloud, only within, for all the others as well as herself.

Mary was free to go outside, but there was little reason to do so. This was downtown Denver. There were no living things to be seen, felt, or heard, other than a few street trees, weeds, pigeons, and blank-faced people. Or so Mary thought at first. But then one day, when the smoke sting grew too much, she stepped out to the back for air and found a vacant lot. Bachelor's buttons, cornflower blue, bloomed profusely, and little checkered butterflies, bluish too, skipped among the green disks of cheeseweed. They intrigued her. Here was a fragment of peace and relief, entirely unexpected. She took to coming here often after that, sitting on an old aluminum-and-plastic chair from a dinette set that someone had hauled out to the alley.

Mary was afraid to venture farther into streets she heard were mean, especially after her one walk around the block got her groped. Once, an activities bus took her up into the Denver Mountain Parks, along with a few other residents. The breath of the ponderosas was heavenly after the smoke and smog below. But then Mary realized that she could see the higher peaks between the trees, and, beyond her control, that slow wail began to swell from her belly like the cold water from the pump in the picnic ground. Nurses had a needle in her arm in seconds and had her back in bed in an hour. After that

Mary remained in the home. At most she went out to her vacant lot. That she did often, until the cold came.

Then new snow dropped on Denver like a clean diaper over a dirty one. Mary withdrew even deeper into her pupa of confusion. She sat in her spare little room, barely noticing as the other beds filled or emptied. She thought little, spoke less, failed to understand anything, especially not herself. Why couldn't she just stand up, say "I'm all right now," and leave? Why did her head ache so, especially where her hair was still short above her forehead? Why couldn't she carry an idea through to conclusion? Some mornings she thought she might begin to speak with the floor nurse, and then the pill came, and the blankness.

And then Iris was transferred, the only one who had shown her any kindness, personal interest, or concern. Missing her, and hearing she was gone, Mary despaired even more. Now there was no one to talk with, even if she could.

5

James Mead had been off the bus for less than an hour, the images of possum bombs and leering lecturers fresh in his muddy mind. It was the latter that troubled him now. A couple of years earlier, as an undergraduate at New Mexico State in Las Cruces, his route had looked clear. After graduation he would take a teacher's certificate, then spend an adequate life in the ranks of the public school pedagogues—the family tradition. But Mead showed talent in research, and at the urging of a perceptive professor he took a lucky whack at a Fulbright in the U.K. After that, larger horizons seemed in order, and (again through luck, as he saw it) he was accepted at Yale University for doctoral studies in biology. Once here, he wondered whether his own ambition had outpaced his abilities.

"I doubt I'll be able to hack this place," he told his coffee.

The waitress, serving her opinion with his doughnut, said, "You wouldn't be the first," and the dishwasher winked from the kitchen. Resolving to keep his thoughts to himself, Mead set off for whatever awaited.

He walked up Prospect Avenue toward the unequal edifices of the Yale biological establishment: Kline Biology Tower and Osborn Memorial Laboratories. Osborn, a twin-turreted pile with an arched entrance, looked like a college department should look, he thought, recalling the real thing at Cambridge. Osborn was the scene of a half century's progress in ecology. But in the past twenty years, actual animals and plants had become passé, and the cell was the thing—or the gene, or the molecules. Kline Tower was the citadel of the cell. It brimmed with privilege and grant-borne pretension: stories upon stories of slag-brown bricks that shone in the September sun and positively repelled ivy, between black windows that never opened—all the looks and personality of a giant Tootsie Roll.

Happily for him, Mead seemed destined for Osborn. Some said ecology was already dead at Yale, but the recent environmental cyclone had blown fresh breath into that field in New Haven. That there was anything left to resuscitate was the result of the labors of certain torchbearers in Osborn who had never lost track of natural history in the swirl of change. One of these was Evelyn Hutchinson, who developed the now-universal concept of the ecological niche here in the 1920s. Another was George Winchester, whom Mead was about to meet—his first Yale professor, his likely adviser, a famous man of science. Mead shook a little in his mountain-states boots as he entered Winchester's outer office.

The friendly smell of thousands of scientific papers in file drawers overrode an unfamiliar scent coming from down the hall. Mead wondered what was in there, a door away, but his thoughts were interrupted by a lilting "Good afternoon." A handsome, relaxed woman of fifty or so occupied the anteroom. She removed her chained glasses and looked up from her typewriter. "May I help you?"

"Hello, I'm here to see Professor Winchester?"

She took on a guarding-the-ramparts air. "Do you have an appointment?"

"Uh, yes—I'm sorry. I'm James Mead. I believe Dr. Winchester has been assigned as my adviser, and I wrote that I would be arriving today."

The secretary's expression slid into a relaxed smile. "Of course—

Mr. Mead. We're expecting you. Dr. Winchester is with another student, but I'll let him know you're here. I'm Mrs. Pauling," she said, offering her hand. Then she disappeared into an inner sanctum, and Mead heard muffled voices, one high, one deep. He felt just as he did in any doctor's waiting room. Mrs. Pauling said, "The professor will be with you in a few minutes," and handed him a copy of *Discovery*, the magazine of the university's natural history museum. Well, he thought, it beats *Highlights*.

Under "Staff Notes" in the back of the magazine, Mead noticed that Winchester had recently returned from a summer in Colorado, where he journeyed annually for research at the Rocky Mountain Biological Laboratory. Mrs. Pauling was typing copy for what he took for specimen labels, all headed "Colo.: Gunnison Co." He relaxed a degree; at least they would have the Rockies in common. Mead asked himself, but not out loud, why he was already blaming Yale (and everyone in it) for being superior, and himself for his background.

After a few minutes the big varnished door of the inner office opened, and a young female student emerged. She was glowing. "All right, Professor, I'll read that paper and let you know what I think of it Monday," she said over her tawny shoulder.

A syllable of concurrence came from within, then a spirited, "See you then, Noni. Enjoy your weekend, but do try to get another modest number of pages of your draft ready for me to read."

The woman passed Mead, smiled, and left with a word for Mrs. Pauling and a back-glance at him. Mead noticed that her dark eyes possessed epicanthal folds. Yet she did not look entirely Asian: her long, straight hair was brown. He also noted her accent. No midwesterner she, probably straight out of the Seven Sisters, likely bound next for Harvard. His relapsing sense of inadequacy was suddenly swamped by a reddish dust devil as a large presence flew out of the inner office, halted before him, and thrust out an enormous paw. Tilting his head, grinning through his ginger beard, the professor blurted, "Welcome, Mr. Mead! Please come inside."

Never had Mead been so rapidly rid of doubts. Dr. Winchester seemed genuinely glad to see him here at Yale. He himself had come from a small midwestern college, never venturing toward the Ivy League until he was James's age. From his own swivel chair behind a massive desk, Winchester bade him sit. "So you're from New Mexico—not far south of my summer haunts. I've reviewed your transcripts, which look good. Do you prefer the lab or the field?"

"The field, for sure."

"Good—right answer. Do you know anything about butterflies?"

"I collected butterflies and moths when I was younger," Mead said. "Just locally."

"Why did you stop?"

"Same as most kids, I guess—girls, sports—embarrassed by the net, I suppose."

"We lose a lot that way." Winchester sighed. "It becomes socially penalizing. Well, you may have a chance to get back into it if you are still interested. Most of my own work involves Lepidoptera." Winchester's large head bobbed as he spoke, and the great rack of his shoulders seemed to hold up the wall of books behind him.

"Will my research project have to deal with butterflies, then?" Mead had half expected to be ushered into an amenable PhD topic, an extension of the major professor's work, as so often happens in graduate schools.

"Not necessarily, no," Winchester said. "Though you've certainly got the name for it."

"How so?"

"T. L. Mead was one of the best lepidopterists of the last century. He brought many western butterflies to light. But we'll get to him later, as we tour the collection. As for selecting a dissertation question, there is plenty of time: don't rush it. You'll have to live with it for four or five, maybe six or seven years, depending on how it goes, so you'd better choose something right for you. The only bounds are that it must be original research with a rigorous approach. And, if I am to be useful as an adviser, it should lie somewhere in the area of population biology, genetics, or ecology. Of course, funding may be easier if it relates to any of our ongoing grants."

"That's a broad menu. But preferably involving insects?"

"Preferably, but not essentially. One of my students worked on warblers recently, another on human and chimpanzee sexuality. Oh, those bonobos!"

Mead raised an eyebrow at that. Then he wondered whether, when it came down to approval, it would turn out to be like a Russian menu: lots of choices, but few of them actually available. Winchester pursed his lips for a moment or two before he spoke again.

"It is true that the committee must approve the eventual topic. But it's not likely they would veto a project that you and I agreed was worthwhile. Take your time, and take your pick—so long as we all agree on the value of the work, and funding is available, you should be able to cater to your own interests and, if you're lucky, your passion. It does happen sometimes. I'm glad you asked, by the way; too many students expect to be led by the hand from square one, which doesn't interest me."

The time sneaked by like the silverfish in the corners of the room. Now and then Winchester leaned back and caught a fly with his hand without looking directly at it or breaking pace. Then, at a certain point, his shoulders, or perhaps it was his heroic eyebrows, dropped a degree relative to the bookshelf behind. By whatever subtle signal, Mead knew the interview was over. He stood, nearly all his trepidation flushed away. Dr. Winchester's broad, high, balding brow was damp. I would hate, Mead thought later, to be on his wrong side. He'd heard too many beery tales of major professors turned into major roadblocks. As Winchester noted their next appointment in his tiny blue pocket diary, Mead remembered one more question he'd meant to ask. "Dr. Winchester, what is that peculiar odor coming from the lab down the hall?"

"Odor?" Winchester narrowed his gaze and tilted his head in

puzzlement. "Oh, I suppose newcomers might detect a slight aroma. You'll find out soon enough," he said with a leprechaun's grin. "As curatorial associate, not *everything* will be your own choice for the first year or two." It was clear that he did not mean to elaborate, so Mead left it there and made his way from the cool bastion of Osborn Laboratories into the wet heat outside.

The next Sunday, Mead awakened amazed to be a dweller beside the Atlantic Ocean. He had rented a three-room beach cottage east of the city in Branford, on Long Island Sound. It was supposed to be winterized, but he doubted that it really was. Once he became accustomed to the crescendo of the katydids screeching from the trees each night, he slept well to the tumble of waves on little Limewood Beach.

Now he strolled the crescent sand strip, stooping to pluck slipper shells from the gray strand, and let the peaceful afternoon work its way with his mind. He lay against the grassy foreshore and napped. The air was cooler by the Sound than in the city. He awoke to raindrops, scouts for a raging Atlantic thunderstorm. The rain brought more cool air and freshness and a falling of leaves; the relief of autumn was near.

The sun came out again. Mead wandered about his new habitat, which was wreathed in a thick, sweet smell he'd already learned to associate with the heavy, late-season ripeness of New England vegetation. He walked a meadow speckled with tiny white asters and big purple asters, all against a backcloth of goldenrod. Buckeyes and sulphurs nectared, and monarchs tanked up for their impending exodus. Little blue herons stalked the margins of the salt marsh at Indian Neck. Mead felt that species of refreshment that all naturalists know in new places.

His day finished with a beer or three at the Indian Neck Tavern, an old place hanging over the salt marsh on stilts, where he drank to having landed on his feet in Connecticut. Then he said, "Apparently, anyway" and raised another schooner to that, rapping the wooden table as he did. "I guess I'll survive." The bartender brought him another Schaefer just to make sure.

Mead met Monday with equanimity, which was good, as it was the day scheduled for his first meeting with his committee members. After messing about with cereal and milk in his new cottage and kitchenette, he dressed and hitchhiked the eight miles in to Yale. "Good afternoon, again," he greeted Professor Winchester as he entered the conference room and awaited introductions to the rest of his faculty committee. He noticed that Winchester's manner, while still friendly, was a little more formal.

"Hello, James. Let me introduce Dr. Phelps, whose work with sandhill and Siberian cranes you will no doubt know . . ." Mead shook the proffered hand of the handsome, white-haired wildlife biologist. He had a skeptical cant to his eyelids that suggested way too many such meetings over the years, but his grip was firm and his blue eyes were not bored. ". . . and Dr. Scotland, James Mead." The young forest sociologist, tall with a sheet of yellow hair that he shook or swept out of his eyes frequently, had an earnestness about him that suggested dedication or ambition, or both. Mead thought he saw generosity there as well.

"Ah, here comes Frank. Professor Griffin has journeyed across the hill from Kline Tower to join us."

"Hello, Mead. New Mexico, eh? Ummm." He contributed little more to the meeting, other than pipe smoke and a sermonette on the nature of "real" research. This seemed to carry a thinly veiled put-down of field studies in general and an advertisement for Kline as the proper seat of almost everything of value in biological science.

Mead couldn't tell whether these potshots were for his benefit or that of the rest of the committee, all field men connected with western institutions.

The initial meeting remained comfortably vague until the question of a dissertation topic came up. Winchester reiterated what he had told Mead about time, choice, and rigor. Phelps and Scotland nodded assent and seemed happy to leave it at that, but Griffin begged to differ.

"Gentlemen," he began. "Research today is expensive, and so is our time. The dissertation project should be directed, effective, and parsimonious—anything but whimsical. I'm sure we can find a suitable problem for you soon enough, Mr. Mead, if your lab skills are adequate, that is."

"Well, I haven't framed a research question yet," said Mead, "but my interests lie more in the field."

"Excuse me, George, I have experiments waiting. I hope when you convene us again, we'll have more to discuss. Good day!" Griffin rose and dissipated from the conference room like a bad fog blowing.

"Positive fellow, isn't he?" said Scotland after the door closed. "Please let me know if I can help in sifting your thoughts, James. I enjoyed meeting you. Dick, I think the dean's got sherry up for us next door, hasn't he?"

"Right; faculty search reception. Pleased to know you, Mr. Mead. Come over and take some classes with us in Sage Hall, or drop in for a seminar. And don't mind old Frank . . . he's a bit formal and brusque, but he's all right, and a good scientist. Glad to have you here at Yale. George, I'll see you at the gym Wednesday dawning?"

"Of course, and this time I'll squash your butt, so to speak." When the others had left, Winchester asked Mead to remain behind for a moment. "James," he said, "Frank Griffin is a rather sour man . . . different. He is abrupt, he thinks he's the only busy person with a grant and a lab to run, and he is entirely absent of humor, as far as I can see. Plus, he bears a load of resentment. For all that, as Phelps said, he's a fine scientist."

"Resentment over what, sir?" Mead asked.

"No need to air dirty laundry so soon. But in the barest terms, he was passed over for department chair twice. Both times, the deciding faculty votes came from Osborn Lab. That sharpened his basic distrust of ecology and ecologists. He knows whole animal biology is in a secondary position, and he likes to whip the underdog—kick it, too." Winchester raised one corner of his mouth. "I'm afraid he may prove a challenge for you, not to say a roadblock."

"But the catalogue states that I can dismiss committee members if I wish . . ."

"And so you may. But the department wants a diversity of faculty interests on each advisory committee—that's why he was appointed in the first place—and his replacement might be worse. Besides, to dismiss Frank would only alienate him, and he heads the departmental grants committee—a sop to him last time he was passed over for chairman. You might find you need that support. It may be better for now to try to work with the man."

"Hmm," said James.

"Who knows? His attitudes might even soften from the experience when he sees you doing good work. We can expect some pressure from him to settle on a thesis topic sooner than you might wish, and on a lab study rather than one in the field. But don't be intimidated. It's your PhD. Here, let's look over your classes."

Winchester peered over his half-glasses at Mead's proposed course of studies for the fall semester. "That Computer Methods course can't hurt; more and more students are using the mainframes, which are getting smaller and more approachable all the time. Saves a lot of time over a slide rule when you get to your statistics. They say personal computers might be next—imagine! And Evolution is my own favorite class to teach; I hope you'll enjoy it too. I'm interested to see that you've selected Runic Lit. for an elective. I'll look forward to glancing over your shoulder. And with Phelps's Advanced Population Biology, you'll have a very full term."

"Yes, I have a bad habit of taking big bites from the smorgasbord."

"One or two more like that, and you should be ready for full-time research. Here, let me sign that." Once again, George Winchester had managed to banish his new grad student's fears, at least for the time being. Then he assigned Mead a workspace of his own, an office-cum-laboratory; explained the curatorial assistantship at the museum, which was paying part of his way; and wished him good day. And by the time Mead made his way back to Limewood Beach, he almost felt as if he might make it in New Haven after all.

Mead began his coursework. At odd times he explored the wondrous Yale libraries, prowled the campus, and explored the individual colleges. Their beautiful courtyards and cloisters softened the harshness of the industrial seaboard city, with its edgeward sprawl, interior decay, and ever-present crime. The campus shone in its mellow Federal bricks and college-Gothic masonry from the 1920s. He thought the paternal gaze of the green copper weathervane, a six-foot owl perched atop Sterling Library, conveyed the intended atmosphere of Jefferson's "academical village," though the streets of poverty huddled just beyond. Mead's studies prospered, and one night on his way to one of the college dining halls he realized that he was just a face, like any other. By Halloween, he felt he belonged.

When the frosts came and the katydids didn't anymore, the nights fell strangely silent. Then a new sound took over the night—the rush of thousands of oak and maple leaves swept by wind. Never having seen a northeastern fall and its many hardwood hues, he thought of paint chips in a hardware store. The cottonwoods and aspens in the Rockies had not prepared him for an incandescent autumn in New England. When the colors faded in the shortening evenings, Mead left off tramping through the leaves and withdrew to the cellars of the museum.

His assistantship consisted of helping to curate the entomological collections in the Peabody Museum of Natural History, a resource Winchester had brought to international significance. After dinner in a nearby café, Mead worked for an hour or two, spreading, labeling, and arranging specimens, before catching a late bus to Branford. One night in late November, between mounting batches of African butterflies, he was topping up preserving fluid in glass specimen containers. More to his liking than jars full of yellowed, clenched, and bulbous-bodied spiders were trays of arthropods preserved naturally and perfectly in lumps of Baltic amber. A large body of work had been done on these gemmed sarcophagi by the great Yale spider man, Alexander Petrunkevitch. Mead saw what it had gotten him; this cozy corner in the museum's bowel was no anonymous nook nor nameless cranny, for it bore a plaque on which he read in the gloom: THE ALEXANDER PETRUNKEVITCH ARACHNOLOGY ALCOVE.

"A fine tribute," Mead announced to the general company, but no one replied, pro or con. He took down a tome on amber spiders and marveled at the many species Professor Petrunkevitch had found immured in the fossilized pitch of Baltic trees.

Reaching up to replace the book in its rank of dusty black volumes, he spied behind it a singular volume that didn't seem to fit among the rest. He gathered it down and saw that it was a blue, clothbound record book, much stained and used, with manuscript text between the covers. He spread the crackly pages and read the title page, written in a steady hand in soft pencil: "Field Book and Journal: Volume Twelve." And down in the corner, in smaller script, the name of the writer: "October Carson."

It was late, so Mead put the odd volume back in its place. In so doing, he dislodged a spider book and saw that the entire shelf was double stacked. Quickly now he pulled down the first row and found a baker's dozen of this Carson person's journals crouching there in the pale amber light. His curiosity aroused beyond his craving for sleep, he selected the first volume of the notebooks and began to read. Outside, the first snow swirled about the museum's tower.

6

<u>October 31, 1969</u>. Crossed the Columbia River into Washington State today, in a constant curtain of rain. What a very wet, green land. Conifer hills broken up by yellow maples, their leaves dropping like big floppy washcloths, ground to a brown pulp on the highway by the interminable train of logging trucks. These low hills are pretty, or would be if they weren't chopped to hell for logs. The ships down under the high bridge from Astoria are piled high with logs bound for Japan, even though the chat in the coffee shop back in Hebo was all about the local mills shutting down—go figure. These lumpy hills look like the latest load of draftees skinned by a bad barber. My last ride was with a kind log-truck driver who pulled over in the rain, so I kept such thoughts to myself.

He asked what I did for a living, and I said I was looking around. "For work?" he asked. "Good luck!"

"No, not really," I said.

"Then what for?"

"Ahh, something nothing," I replied. He stared at me strangely, and I explained. "Sorry. That's New Guinea pidgin for 'whatever.'" I thanked him for the ride when he turned off toward Longview, and I hopped down. He still looked puzzled—thought I was on something, I think. Something, nothing; <u>whatever</u>. Hemlock boughs and cedar bark blew off in his wake, their sweet smell mixing with the sour diesel exhaust as he pulled east through six gears or more. I put my thumb out for west.

<u>November 12, 1969</u>. I've been beachcombing the Washington shores of the Long Beach Peninsula for nearly two weeks. Not many Japanese glass floats, most of them are plastic now. But I have found enough, especially after the great honking storm on the sixth, to swap for food at a curio museum and general store on the waterfront in Ilwaco. The shorebirds are good company, but this state has a doltish law extending the public highway system to the beaches. I've seen pickups speed up to try to hit flocks of sanderlings and gulls, and motorbikers kick the heads of penguinlike murres, breaking their necks. My greatest satisfaction wasn't the eight-inch green-glass float I found in a wadge of kelp, but watching a pickup marooned in the wet sand with the tide coming in way out on Leadbetter Point. The driver got out; the truck did not. I tried to help him get unstuck, but it was futile. I gave him a shot of Teacher's and we drank silently to the sinking truck, his loss, the sanderlings' and clams' gain. I'm on their side, but I felt a little sorry for him in spite of myself. It was a nice truck.

My cynicism may be coming home to roost these days because other than the one glass ball, I've found nothing of value for three days other than the clean sea air, peace, and tranquillity when the beach traffic is at bay. Plus sunsets of lead and copper that no scrap dealer could ever afford. I think I'll head north.

<u>November 13</u>. My ride around Willapa Bay came in an oyster truck. When I told the driver I loved oysters, he said he hoped I like zinc. Why, I asked? "'Cuz the fishermen is turning up radioactive zinc in the oysters here," he said. "They say it comes down the Columbia from Hanford and around the bay on the outflow plume." One day

I'd walked over the peninsula to the bay side and poached a few at low tide; they were great, roasted over my campfire with a few butter clams. "And I won't eat sturgeon from the river no more," the driver went on, "not with the paper mill pumping out chlorine." Silly me, expecting this country to be wild and pristine, as the visitors' guide says. Blazers on the beach, the big cedars mostly in absentia, glow-in-the-dark seafood. Roll on, Columbia.

<u>November 20</u>, Shi Shi Beach. The Olympic Park beaches may be sandy in summer, but in winter they go largely to pea gravel and cobbles. Most of the floats I find are shattered. Backpackers clamber over the driftwood piles like crabs, sometimes finding the whole ones before me. I feel I have a prior claim; their packs, after all, are full of food. I have found a sign saying "No Smoking" in Russian, and a pig's heart (I think), as well as a coconut in its husk. I cooked its sweet meat with mussels plucked from the rocks—red tide should be over by now—and a large crayfish I caught in a back-beach pond, over a driftwood fire in a sprucy enclave, out of the rain.

Latter-day back-to-the-landers and poets have built huts by a glorious spot called Point of Arches, where horns and hoops of black basalt spill a mile out into the sea. They asked me to join them for the winter, but I declined. I don't think their company would improve upon the ravens and the black bears that nose around my camp. And besides, I don't believe anyone (since the Makah left long ago) should live here. Well, if the loggers don't roust them out, the weather will. They've built in a gully and will surely be launched to sea during some big storm to come.

<u>November 30</u>. And so they were. And so was my tent. I am cold and wet through, though never too hungry in this land that made the Makah fat in winter. Not that I've got the dried salmon, gray whale blubber, and eulachon oil that stuck to their ribs during the winter

ceremonials. But I've feasted on razor and horse clams, sea cucumber, a ruffed grouse I got with a lucky rock toss, and plenty of late evergreen huckleberries and cranberries. The none-too-adept hippies up in the ravine told me there was nothing here to eat. For the most part they seemed to subsist on canned goods and hot dogs, for which they made periodic trips out to the reservation store in Neah Bay.

But now, roofless to the elements, they've left, leaving their midden of old moldy sleeping bags and tin cans in the ruins of their campsite. I reckon I'll be gone too, soon. Even if I waited out the winter without dying by drowning or pneumonia or sheer rot—it rains a hundred inches in winter here—I doubt there would be any butterflies to catch in this dense rainforest. Now, if my clients would buy unlimited quantities of these fine big banana slugs, or the purple urchins or lavender and orange sea stars that plaster the rocks offshore—if I could emulate Doc in *Cannery Row*, financing my beer and pickling fluid with the proceeds from harvesting the tide pools—then I'd be in business.

But no, my customers want butterflies. Even the Olympic Mountains won't help, as they're just about all in the national park, where amateurs (read: professionals without degrees, like me) cannot collect. Maybe it's time to start heading for the Rockies. One of the beach survivalists shot a gull the other day and didn't even try to eat it. I asked him why he did it. "Just practicin' my survival skills, man," is what he said. Easy riding, gull.

December 3. Slow hitching along the Strait of Juan de Fuca. Passenger cars whizzed on by without a second look; can't blame them. I probably wouldn't pick me up. Fortunately, I had chestnut-backed chickadees and golden-crowned kinglets for company. Finally, a crabber gave me a lift and a couple of Dungeness crabs that I cooked in a driftwood fire at the eponymous Dungeness Spit. Then a birdwatcher took me down Hood Canal and all the way to Tacoma. I told him about the motorbiked murres, and he told me of an oil spill he'd recently been in on. "A murre with a broken neck would have been lucky," he said. "We had dozens of them all gummed up in crude." This was offshore. "We're waiting for the big one in Puget Sound," he told me, "with a governor who wants to let supertankers in. One of these days there's going to be a really giant spill in one of the bays—Puget Sound, Barkley Sound, maybe up in Prince William Sound where they still have sea otters—and then we'll see how oil and water mix." If it's down here, he told me, we can just about say goodbye to rhinoceros auklets, and marbled murrelets too—"even if they still have any big trees left to nest in." He was verging on gloomy, so I bought him an Oly at the tavern near the Tacoma railyards where he dropped me off. We drank to the birds, the trees, Robinson Jeffers, and all the other sad misanthropes like ourselves.

December 5. Caught a freight east, but the bull kicked me off at Wishram—an old-time hobo junction outside a has-been railroad town deep inside the Columbia Gorge. Hoboes don't like Dungeness crab, at least these didn't, nor did they much like me. Anyway, I didn't feel like waking up splayed, even if it had been warm enough to sleep, which it wasn't with the infamous Gorge wind screaming through like just another train. It may have been an old-time 'bo camp, but these weren't old-time 'boes. I've never known a genuine gentleman of the road to be unwelcoming around his fire. These guys were younger, harder—guys back from Vietnam with incredulous looks in their eyes, guys on drugs or wishing they were. I walked up the long grade to Highway 14 and tried the asphalt road instead. God bless that onion-truck driver! Now I sit in an all-night truck stop outside Walla Walla, a dusty dawn coming on. Will I ever get out of here, or will I become an onion grunt in the spring (as the driver suggested), planting Walla Walla sweets, maybe even sticking around to pull them up in the summer?

Waitress figures I'll never get out of here. Gum-chewing siren in a coral uniform, she saw me writing and asked me what. "Just traveler's tales," I told her.

"Not romances?" she asked, clearly disappointed. When I convinced her I was no novelist, just a vagrant making chicken scratches while waiting for a ride, and no, I couldn't write her life story for her, though I was sure it was every bit as fascinating and "weird" as she said, she told me I'd never get a ride. Coreen pouted for a while, but I was her only company, so she broke down and gave me another cup of coffee and a slice of peach pie, at the cost of also accepting a slice of her plenty-weird story. Then the morning trade began to butt in, demanding Coreen's attention and aborting the saga, which I was quite enjoying, as it made my life sound easy. Why am I writing this crap? Just to stay awake.

December 13. I've read that Friday the 13th was a lucky day in the old religions, turned around by the latecomers, just like All Hallows' itself. Anyway, the goblins smiled, and I landed from a ride with a rancher just outside Boise, Idaho. It's a dreadful cold night, and any reasonable person might consider this bad fortune. But I recognized from the topography, at a spot way down the Snake this morning, the likelihood of a Nez Percé arrowhead manufactory. By midafternoon I had gathered 47 flint, chert, and obsidian points and some excellent shards. I traded a spearpoint with the manager of a motel for two nights' lodging and four home-cooked meals. Tomorrow, I ought to make a week's wages selling the points in Nampa, Boise, or Burley.

The manager, an amateur collector, told me he's heard rumblings about new federal regulations that will ban the collecting of artifacts on public lands altogether. My first reaction, like his, was what the hell are so-called public lands for? But then, though I didn't tell him this, I remembered feeling qualms about digging into that midden today. Seems a hard world where a ranch kid couldn't pick up an arrowhead without being a crook. But maybe those times are going; maybe there won't be any more ranch kids. Maybe there will be pothunters swarming all over the public lands, not just a few like me. And maybe such a law is inevitable. All I know is it's a bloody cold gale out there. The sage is struggling to keep its roots in the ground. Where would I be spending the night without those arrowheads? It doesn't bear thinking about.

December 15. I made nearly twice what I expected, all from people who have spent their lives in the area and have never found a single point. "Where did you pick these up?" inquires a potential buyer. "Far from here, over by White Swan," I lie. If he knew they were from his own backyard, he might not buy. Or else he'd say I stole them. But they don't search. What's the matter with people who never look beyond their own noses? Or is the matter with me, always a poke-about, sticking my snout here and there, in other people's backyards and business, always in danger of freezing it off?

End of self-examination. I feel so flush, I might even catch a 'Hound to Jackson instead of hitchhiking across Antarctica. I hate to do it since that last lockout strike. Someday the drivers are really going to bite back. If labor even survives. Teamsters these days, they think Workers World is a theme park. Maybe that's why an old leftie like me can't get a job, or keep one . . . I'd rather scrabble for arrowheads in a frigid gale for a decent wage than sell my sore back to the man just to keep it warm a little longer.

Christmas Day. I had two options: spend Yule with the other derelicts in the mission at Pocatello, or drink beer with a Nez Percé/ Shoshone friend on the reservation. Since his ancestors were the source of my current largesse, I chose the latter. When I arrived with a turkey and a case of Rainier Ale, my intentions were misunderstood. A tribal official asked if I thought they wanted charity. "Not at all," I said. "Just looking for a place to spend Christmas out of the cold—I used to have some friends here." He'd never heard of my old pal.

"You'd better go to the mission in Pocatello with the other pale-face bums," he said. "They'd eat your turkey. In fact, so will we. You can't take beer there, so you'd best leave that here too. You can keep a couple for the road." I thanked him and split. Chief Joseph got a little of his own back this Christmas. I spent the winter feast in an all-night Denny's at a freeway interchange, where three people thought they were cute for asking if I was Santa Claus. The dishwasher said, "Hell no, he's Jerry Garcia!" which was better. His boss called me a shiftless hippie and invited me to depart into the bleak predawn ("On your way, longhair," were his actual words). Charged and convicted as a honky and a hippie on the same day—Merry Christmas!

December 26. Am I missing something? All I want for Christmas is a Magdalena. Oh, how I'd like to see my Maggie flying free and high, until I get hold of her. But I'm afraid she'll be a long time coming. Meanwhile, my heart hurts. This bus is all the home I've got, these bus people all the company I need, and a little extra. The mere thought of Magdalena seems surreal in this overheated winter canister. I guess I'll start the year in Jackson, and see what happens. Do mountain men still rendezvous there? Or mountain women? Can Magdalena be *that* far behind?

Mead closed the thick weather-beaten diary and rubbed his eyes. "He seems to have been some sort of a gypsy beachcomber," he said aloud, "or a fly-by-night scavenger, ever ready to turn his little finds into a buck or a burger—or a beer. I think we could get along." He shuffled his things and prepared to leave, but the reading was still on his mind. "Interesting guy, for sure. Thoughtful, too—maybe a tad cynical, though he seems to care about things. But that last bit"—he went back and reread the final entry—"about wanting a Magdalena—what the heck is *that* supposed to mean? What is a Magdalena? Maybe he was lonely or horny, and that's some sort of slang of his for a woman. Or a prostitute—wasn't Mary Magdalene supposed to be a harlot? Might make sense, after all the time he spent alone on the road. But why would he have to wait till spring to find a hooker?"

Mead liked having the amber spiders there because they were good listeners. He continued his exegesis of Carson's entries: "But then he also refers to '*his* Maggie, flying high and free'—that hardly sounds like a pickup. Maybe Magdalena is a particular woman—a lost love, a summertime sweetheart? Somehow, I don't think that's it either. I wonder . . ." But he didn't wonder much, as he nodded onto the laboratory table.

He roused himself and put the notebook away with his thoughts. "Well," he told the patient spiders, "it's too late to go home. Maybe I'll mount some butterflies." But before he had a chance to lift the lid of the relaxing jar, Mead's head dropped again onto the table and he fell into a deep sleep. All night he slept there as the wind off Long Island Sound pelted the museum tower with snowballs. In his strange, wintry dreams, jolly beachcombers and Hollywood Indians in full Plains regalia rubbed shoulders in a truck stop named Maggie's, where oysters and crabs held court with the walrus and the carpenter. The carpenter turned into the Cheshire cat, then a waitress in pink, serving little black biscuits like comic-book arrowheads to spiders in amber jars who morphed into hungry humans pawing at the windows and freezing to death outside.

When Mead awoke at seven, he was chilled, cramped, and agitated, and his neck felt like iron. He skipped class, spent the day wandering aimlessly around the snowy town and campus, and finally drifted home. "That journal is getting to me," he muttered as he unlocked the door, and then and there he resolved to ignore the rest of the diaries.

In his mailbox he found a letter from his mother. He wondered if it would be like the others, factual and antiseptic, about as personal as a Christmas newsletter. He took his time opening it. "Dear Son," he read.

We are well and hope you've avoided the flu they say is so rampant back there. Your brothers are both heavily into basketball and dating, but their grades are OK, so I suppose that's fine. They promised to write and send scores, but don't hold your breath. Lance is still over the moon about that game-winning basket he made against Raton. His head's about as big as the basketball, so I hope that doesn't set him up for a fall. Roger's spending a lot of time warming the varsity bench, but he's happy to be there. You know he's always been the more even of the two. I'm just glad that neither one seems to be interested in drugs.

Your dad is looking forward to his conference in Maui, his class load has been so heavy. He invited me to come, but I think I won't. Here are the boys' school pics. They still look nothing like you. Roger asked was it the milkman or the mailman? Very cute.

James laughed, and wondered if she had too when she wrote it. He didn't think he'd seen her really laugh since Molly had died. There was more family stuff, but almost nothing about her. And why in the world wouldn't she go to Maui with his father?

Then a scrawl, crossed out, and this: "James, some days I almost don't think I can make it. But I do. Will it get better? Dad says yes, but I don't know whether I believe him—what else is he going to say? Sorry. We're so proud of you. Write. Love, Your Mom."

James tried to write back right away. He felt vaguely excited, since this was the first sign of his mother's reaching out to him since the backpacking trip. But he gave up and talked himself to sleep instead. *I haven't a clue what to say to that: Will it get better? Does it get better? Ever? I wish I knew! Sounds like this Carson is none too* sure either, and I don't even know what's bugging *him*. Oh, hell. But *what* the hell is a Magdalena supposed to be? Maybe I need one, too. I need *something*. So, Mom? God, I don't know. He left his words unwritten and slept like a woodchuck in winter.

7

Snow tries to accumulate on the stony face of Magdalena Mountain, but Boreas scrapes it away with his rasping breath. As the storms grow in force and frequency into December, even the gale itself cannot remove its own white detritus. Then the peak changes color like the ptarmigan secreted on its slopes, from the gray-brown pelage of November to the pure white snow cone of January.

Marmots sleep their deep sleep that will last the mountain lion's share of a year, while pumas prowl hungry across the frozen hems of the boulder fields and retreat, finally, to the forests below. The pikas slumber less—and less deeply—than the marmots. They awaken later than their brief summer somnolence allowed, but awaken just the same each day to preen their lice away and to munch on the fragrant hay they've so busily laid by. Toward spring, both the sacked-out rock chucks and the catnapping conies will give birth and suckle their young in the crannies made cozy by their own body heat.

Now the ptarmigan and the varying hares make only tracks and shadows, not patches of brown, on the pallid winterscape. They forsake the wind-ravaged fellfields for the relative shelter of the forest fringe, twisted and clumped subalpine fir and Engelmann spruce almost bare on top but thick-skirted below the trimline of the wind.

The ptarmigan especially haunt the edges of the willow swales, feeding on their tight-packed buds. These snow ghosts are followed by hopeful coyotes, still brown and leaner than ever.

No one comes to Magdalena Mountain in the winter except a few foolhardy climbers and the helicopters sometimes sent to pluck them off. Cross-country skiers remain far below, and jets swerve north to avoid this conical object in their takeoff path as they gain altitude on their way from Denver to Salt Lake, Boise, Portland, or Seattle. Any climber reaching the summit has to clamber across hundreds of boulders, ice-rimed, slick, or cracking under winter's weight. Frost probes every cleft, then swells and splits the stones asunder. But no climber, sure to be quick or be dead, would hang around to watch the prying frost do its work, nor to listen for the slow heartbeat of marmot or the faster pulse of pika in the rockpile below.

With the summer sounds gone, the piping of the marmot stilled, the sentry-squeak of the pika silenced, Magdalena Mountain seems all but lifeless on the surface. But beneath the snow and the stones, life carries on, if not exactly teeming. Among the few creatures as happy now as ever are the grylloblattids. Wingless, primitive relatives of crickets, more resembling roaches, these ice crawlers (as they are called) cherish the cold and die if they become too warm. Glaciers, snowfields, and rockslides are their natural homes. In the dead of winter, a grylloblattid prowls the talus slope in search of any animal food it can find. With its slender antennae it probes here and there as its six legs carry it speedily over cold stone, solid ice, and rotting vegetation. A pale amber predator, the ice crawler works the frozen, uncrowded territory in its search for winter food.

Among the candidates are the winter-passage stages of arctic-alpine butterflies: eggs, caterpillars, and chrysalides, proof against the wind, carrying their fragile selves through hostilities so severe as to be found only in such high ranges of rock as these. For Erebia, winter is a time of passive repose, to be gotten through alive. Antifreeze in the tiny larva's blood keeps ice crystals from rupturing delicate tissues. His metabolism has dropped to near nil. Winter for the Magdalena alpine is a time when nothing happens at all other than bare, tenuous existence. This terrible season claims few lives among his brood. The flash freeze keeps most predators at bay while cold-storing the frost-free larvae for spring. Erebia, curled and still, guards a flicker of life inside his sliver of self, and that is all he has to do. Chances are, no one is going to interfere.

But the grylloblattid creeps into the hollow where Erebia and several of his siblings have gone to ground. It palps a beetle grub and consumes it in minutes before moving on to an egg mass of a rock spider, which it nibbles like popcorn. Two Magdalena larvettes, minor morsels that they are, fall prey to the grylloblattid before it swerves out of this particular declivity and moves on to a pika's den, looking for lice, and is fulfilled. This is winter's last close call for Erebia. He'll ride out the rest, secure in his alpine tent of silk and grass.

There comes a break in the weather. A hint of a promise of an imputation of the rumor of spring arrives on a warm Chinook wind. Grasses in the foothills show the first fleeting green, and along the streams, cottonwood buds swell toward bursting in balsamic waves of fragrance. Up on the mountain, a thaw too soon might start the growing season perilously early, and an unusually late blizzard could jeopardize the early birds.

But it isn't only temperature rising, or a warm wind. Too well honed by evolution to the irregular weather of the Rockies to be fooled, Erebia waits for the right combination of warmth and length of day before stirring. The alpine grasses he'll need are tuned to the same two signals. Both the intensity and the duration of the sun must agree before the key is turned.

Such conditions befall the face of Magdalena Mountain one day in late April. The sun strikes the easternmost of the mountain's twin summits twelve and a half hours before it sets behind the western peak. The temperature hits fifty-five Fahrenheit in the sunshine at noon. A pika pokes its gray face up into the sunshine, and a marmot rolls over in its dreams of green grass and glacier lilies.

Green creeps up a grass shoot cell by cell, and with it, a very small caterpillar. The worm turns, and Erebia begins to feed.

8

One day in late February, Mary Glanville looked into a mirror and recognized herself. Slender, tall, auburn-haired with a curl; high-cheeked, strong-nosed Mary, pretty in spite of recent extremis and winter's smoky pallor, yet as dull of eye and skin as olives left too long in a party dish. And there was a look to her mouth she didn't know at all. Her long, strong lips were forced back and down, their corners deep in her cheeks, making shadows beneath and creases to the side a little like a smile, but nothing like it really, for what it said was only this: *rue*. And though stretched at the corners, her lips pursed a little in the middle, pronouncing a sleek V below her well-formed philtrum. All these features were exaggerated by the cheap lipstick the home's beautician had applied after she washed Mary's curls. Rue, she thought. That's me.

So Mary hibernated, only eating, only sleeping, only expelling, seldom washing, and growing duller, running down, breathing roughly in the cigarette stench. In a more lucid moment she thought, Only a few months, and already resignation creeps over me. Soon I'll be like these others—I will steal clothes, grow filthy and scabby, leer at visitors, soil myself, turn crazy. And one day, far too far away from God knows where, I shall die.

After a sad parody of a Christmas party, someone mentioned that the days would be getting longer. "Why?" asked a resident.

"Well, honey, no season lasts forever," said the nurse. "The sun comes up and goes down, and the days go with it. Then, poof! One day it's spring, and the flowers bloom. You'll see."

"Season," Mary heard. Read the seasons, she thought. And then more thoughts. *To read*: the verb danced around and taunted her until she tried, but the first book she attempted seemed as belligerent and unwilling to make sense as half the people around her. She threw it down with disgust. The next time she tried, she picked up a battered black book of Bible stories. They made no more sense than the first one. But as she closed it in frustration, a title caught her eye and struck her through like a nurse's needle, but pricking that felt good. She couldn't read—*why?* It was maddening. She kept trying day after day, looking at pictures, fingering the pages, mouthing the syllables. After a month, Mary felt that she had the gist of the story. Excited, she tried to repeat it to a nurse, but her agitation only earned her an extra dose of meds.

Three days later, when again she was able to read, the book was gone from the little library. And this caused Mary to speak her first full sentence in six months: *"Where . . . is . . . that . . . book?"*

"Which book, dear?" asked a new aide who didn't know her.

"Bible stories . . . black." Mary struggled, but got it out.

"Hey, Agnes, Mary's talking!" shouted Nurse Dumfries, the administrator, who was passing through the floor when she heard the unfamiliar voice. Agnes and two other workers scooted over to hear for themselves.

"Mary, you're speaking—wonderful!" said Agnes, the nurse who had replaced Iris.

Mary grew more and more exercised. "WHERE IS IT?"

"She's missing some book of Bible stories," the aide explained.

"Oh, Mary, honey, that book isn't good for you. It got you overexcited, so we had to give you a shot. We discarded it. There are lots of other books."

Again Mary wanted to howl, but she didn't. It didn't matter. She knew the story by now, and although the book hadn't gotten all the details right, it had reminded her. And she knew something else. There would be no keeping her here now. Something had to happen, and if it didn't, she would kill herself, and that would bring it all around again, with a different outcome. She wandered off, oblivious to the nurses' pleas to "Talk more, Mary! Say something else!"

"Well, it's something. First time!" Agnes exclaimed.

"Yes," said Nurse Dumfries. "But I wish the mission would stop slipping those religious books and tracts in here. They make them crazier than they already are. Do you have any idea how many Jesus Christs we've got in here *this* week?"

"No, but Cyrus told me this morning that as the Messiah, he could damn well have French toast whenever he wanted," Agnes admitted. "And real maple syrup."

Mary spoke no more, but she thought. She remembered a time before the accident they said she'd had, even vaguely recalled where she was going at the time of the wreck, but not the ground squirrel that had loped beneath her wheel, nor the plummet itself. And, more important, she remembered before—a very long time before. Yes, one way or the other, things would change. They had to, now; they couldn't keep her there. As she lay and played herself to sleep, she took a little pleasure instead of mere relief from her sex. And why not? Spring was coming, as the nurse said. And with it, a real release, she felt sure, from the stinking, the sad, the unthinkable situation she'd endured for all these months.

It had to come. If not soon, by some agency, she would fashion her own escape. For to live on here among the lost, having found herself, would be intolerable. All right for some. A few adaptable and clever residents even managed to make some sort of satisfied accommodation. They ignored the worst of it, sleeping there but living lives largely outside the home thanks to shoe leather and the Denver Tramway Company pass. But that was not for Mary. There was nothing on the streets of Denver for her. As she became more and more sentient, she grew less and less capable of shutting out the despair around her. Her only conceivable solutions were departure, denial, or death; and denial was not going to work. Mary wrapped her pupal sheets around herself and slept the most peaceful sleep in what seemed like hundreds of years.

Then one day in March, the snow melted gray and ran brown down the gutters, and Denver entered its ugliest time. But a Chinook wind warmed that day, and a green thing precociously poked up into the vacant lot behind the center—a tumbleweed shoot. Mary saw it and recognized, with the sharpest sense since that first wail, a remnant of something that felt a little bit like hope.

9

"Spring!" announced Mead, alarming Francie Chan, his lab partner. That morning he'd seen something that looked like a swelling bud. He brought it into the lab, placed it in a beaker of water on his desk, and already it had unfurled into a small leaf smelling of balsam. "Spring," he said again more softly, carried back for the moment to a cottonwood-lined acequia outside Albuquerque. The word sounded almost foreign.

That igneous autumn in New Haven had passed quickly; then came in its place a kind of cold Mead had never known in New Mexico. Riding on particles of dampness, it penetrated his clothing and joints like frost fingers in a sidewalk. He was used to an arid chill, not this gelid breath between the ribs. Shifting between overheated buildings, the dank outside air, and his "all-season beach cottage" that wasn't really winterized for anyone but seals or penguins, he caught a bronchitis that clutched his thorax like a robber fly and wouldn't let go. He couldn't stop coughing without whiskey, and the hitchhike out to Branford became a slog in the freezing slush.

Christmas came cold. Mead spent Christmas Eve lonely in his lab and Christmas Day with the Winchesters, his only invitation. He decided after the break to move into New Haven. At first he had thought his fellowship enormous. He soon found that the high tuition and East Coast prices—no free coffee refills at Dunkin' Donuts, even—eroded his checking account like dust in a downpour. He couldn't afford the cheapest apartment. He was bewailing the fact one afternoon to Francie, who was finishing up that semester. "Maybe you should take my studio," she said. "I'll be moving out soon." Mead had heard that Francie used a room in the building as a printmaking studio. "Come on," she said, leading him down the hall and up a fold-down ladder, and gave him a tour. When his eyes adjusted, Mead beheld a tiny, high-ceilinged round room in one of the twin castellated towers of Osborn Lab. He moved in a week later. This was not strictly legal, but generations of ecology students had camped here or used it as Francie had, as an auxiliary space for their activities. The hexagonal stone walls were still hung with her wonderful silk-screened prints of Rocky Mountain wildflowers and scenes.

The tower seemed romantic, warmer than Mead's beach cottage, and convenient to both his lab and the museum. Plus, the price was right. By waiting late to scale the steep steel ladder to the turret, he could keep his occupancy discreet. And the move soon prompted an additional boon. Early in the new year, Winchester called Mead into his office. "James," he said, "are you still curious about the mild scent emanating from the room down the hall?" Mead didn't consider the stink mild, but he had grown accustomed to it. "Come along," Winchester continued, "and let me introduce you to some truly remarkable and amenable creatures. It's time to broaden your responsibilities, in any case. This little ceremony should be put off no longer."

Mead kept up with Winchester as well as he could as the professor ate the long hall with his stride, opened one outer door, then one inner one on which were posted dire warnings in his hand: DO NOT INTERFERE WITH THE LIGHTS IN THIS ROOM UNDER ANY CIRCUMSTANCES. As soon as they entered the lab, a great shuffling arose as the occupants of dozens of cages scattered in alarm or expectation. The odor was stronger here—not bad, just strong, sweet, feral. "What *are* they?" Mead asked.

"*Blaberus giganteus*, the giant cave roach. Surely you recognize them from anatomy lab? And a few other species of blattids." Then Winchester opened one of the cages and Mead beheld a score or so of the most massive roaches he had ever seen. True, he had dissected roaches nearly as large in an entomology lab, but he'd never seen one alive. His gaze must have betrayed his wonderment.

"We've worked on many aspects of these animals' biology," Winchester replied to Mead's unspoken question. "But their behavior is poorly known. They are relatively easy to keep and breed, and they offer an experimental animal that is both evolutionarily basal and ecologically sophisticated." Pleased to note that Mead appeared fascinated rather than revolted, always a toss-up with new students, he held up a grand roach that was nearly three inches long and asked, "How do you like them?"

"Very much," said Mead. "Their movement is a little creepy, but cockroaches have never bothered me the way they do most people."

"Well, these are not *cock*roaches. *Cockroach* refers to the Oriental, German, or American species: *Blatta orientalis*, *Blattella germanica*, or *Periplaneta americana*, all of which have become adept urban anthrophiles—or, as some would have it, pests. Anyway, the popular reaction to roaches—or rather, their unpopularity—has more to do with bad press than any actual threat they represent. The insecticides that people spray in their kitchens in an attempt to discourage them are far more dangerous than the insects themselves. Besides," he asked with mock incredulity, "how could anyone be repelled by such gentle and handsome animals?"

Mead, duly enchanted, simply nodded.

"Good. Then I'd like you to take over the feeding and basic monitoring of the colony for a term. You may then find some aspect of the roach program that interests you—if not for a thesis project, then perhaps for independent study. And your assistantship pay will increase a bit. At any rate, such an arrangement should quell Dr. Griffin's carping about you going into the lab. Here, let me show you the routine."

Mead adopted the roaches as if they were his own puppies (they did eat dog food), and their odor became all but imperceptible as he spent more and more time in their gentle, rustling presence.

The first committee meeting of the new year came and went. No problems attended the review of Mead's studies, except that Dr. Griffin demanded to know the usefulness of Runic Literature to a biologist. Mead extemporized: "The process of written language development is an evolutionary one. Runes can be thought of as occupying a linguistic position roughly analogous to life in the Paleozoic. From there, the phylogeny of language offers a useful logical paradigm for organic evolution." Phelps winked at Scotland, unseen by Griffin, who grunted and asked for no further elaboration. But when the discussion moved on to research, he let loose.

"Assuming your studies are adequate," he led, "what about your lab experience?"

"I've taken over management of the giant roach colony, Professor." Mead noticed how Griffin winced at that. "As you know, it has provided grist for several of Yale's best biochemical and physiological papers. I find I am particularly intrigued by their nocturnal behavior, which hasn't been much investigated, as it turns out."

"Behavior!" Griffin grunted again. "I allow that once they have been dispatched, ground, or sectioned and placed beneath the scope, those disgusting vermin have yielded some useful material. But I cannot begin to imagine that they exhibit any ethological traits worth wasting time or money on. Besides, what you suggest, Mr. Mead, sounds merely descriptive. Do you plan to try to make something of this cockroach caper for your thesis project? And if so, where are the experimental guts of it?"

Mead began to speak, but Winchester suggested that the question was a bit premature. Then Professor Phelps butted in to remind everyone of a departmental seminar about to begin. That got Mead off the hook, and he didn't object. Nor did Frank Griffin, eager to get off the subject of roaches.

"Good afternoon, gentlemen," George said as they all rose. "Six weeks, then? And Frank," he added, "they are not *cock*roaches, you know . . ." But Griffin was already out the door and down the hall, holding his nose as he passed the loathsome chamber. "Oh, well," Winchester continued. "He just doesn't know what he's missing."

The rest shared a laugh, and Scotland complimented Mead on his "masterful B.S." regarding the runes.

"But he meant every word!" replied Winchester on Mead's behalf, with a grave face and smiling eyes that James never did learn to interpret.

Later Mead asked the roaches, "Did he mean it or not?" but they wouldn't let on.

Living on campus meant two more hours per day in which to study, read, sleep, or socialize. In practice, Mead seemed to socialize mostly with the forgiving blattids. He began to conduct nocturnal vigils among the great insects to see how they spent their time. He would cook some sort of a dinner substitute over a Bunsen burner in his lab while fending off the small, feral relatives of his captive subjects; then he'd spend much of the night in the colony, noting their activity before turning in for a morning's sleep in his tower cell. This odd schedule suited him: he could rise, wash, and make a class in fifteen minutes flat. All in all, coming into town and the tower seemed a good move.

Mead had maintained his resolution to ignore October Carson's journals since he'd transferred his work from the museum to the roach room, but his curiosity remained. At last he decided to ask Winchester about Carson. As they were about to wrap up one of their regular weekly meetings, Mead said, "Professor, there's one other thing. Just who is, or was, October Carson? And why does the museum have his field journals?"

Winchester looked surprised, almost shocked. "Where?"

"What?"

"The journals—where are they?"

"I found them by accident in the Petrunkevitch Alcove, stacked on a deep shelf behind some works on amber spiders. I couldn't help looking them over." Then, afraid he might have trespassed where he ought not to have been, he said, "Gosh! I hope—"

"No. No, it's all right. They're no secret. I'm just relieved to know they are intact. I haven't seen them in a couple of years, and I was worried that they'd been discarded while I was on sabbatical at Oxford. My collections manager must have been short on space, tucked the journals back there, and promptly forgot about them. I've been unable to locate them, despite intensive searching. I'm delighted that you turned them up."

"Just a fluke," Mead said. "Who is he, and why are his journals important?"

"In the opposite order," Winchester replied. "The journals contain original field notes on many western butterflies by an excellent self-taught naturalist and very careful observer. Also, if I recall, they give something of an intimate look at a fascinating man."

"He seems to be," said Mead.

"Because of Carson's unusual habit of mixing field notes with personalia in his diaries, one cannot mine the former without eavesdropping on the latter."

"So I've noticed. Although some entries are more skeletal, others go on and on. I wonder when he slept! But then, I gather he often didn't sleep, stranded by the roadside and such. But who *is* this guy? And how did you get the books?"

Winchester leaned back in his swivel chair, his big hands behind his fuscous hair, and considered for a moment before replying. "I don't actually know very much about him." He became pensive, as if trying to recall the name of a boyhood pet. "I've never met him, and our correspondence was slender. But he supplied the museum with much good material, in superb condition, always meticulously labeled, and eventually he sent me his field books as well."

"So he was a professional collector?"

"Yes, among other things. What used to be called, in Alfred Russell Wallace's day, a 'flycatcher,' but much more curious than most and, in his way, more scientific too. And more than that . . . he was, I would say, sort of a quixotic searcher and scavenger. He moved about a great deal, never married, as far as I know."

"Footloose?"

"Very. He filled the niche of a kind of peripatetic forager of patchy habitats—like a high-class, curious tramp or rambler." He paused, looked thoughtful, and went on. "Maybe he sought to escape some past, some*body*? It seems as though he was always after something, anyway. Butterflies filled that need to a substantial extent in summer, and the market we provided gave him a modest grubstake. I could always weasel some funds from museum sources to buy his best material, just as I set aside a little fund for the purpose of scouring the amber markets in New York for spectacular specimens and new species. But beyond that, I know little of him."

"How about his name?" Mead asked, unwilling to let it lie.

"I asked him the origin of his interesting first name once in a letter. I think you'll find his reply in the files—let's look now!" At that sudden inspiration Winchester wheeled about and the two of them stalked over to the prof's rank of filing cabinets. "Carson, Hampton . . . great picture-winged fly man in Hawaii . . . Carson, Rachel" (ignoring Mead's incredulous "Golly, you knew *her*?") ". . . should be in between—yes, here it is." A thin sheaf of letters emerged from the gray filing cabinet in the great paw of George Winchester. "Here, you may as well read them all, since you're reading the journals. Please make a photocopy of each, charge it to my account, and put them with the journals. Then return these precisely here. I'd not like to lose the originals."

The letter in question began, "Dear George," and went on: "Since you ask, I'll tell you what I've been told about my name. My parents had five children, of which I was the last. The first four were named for their birth months—April, May, June, and August. Those were fairly ordinary names. So when I came along, the pattern stuck, and I was called October. Only sometimes I think it was an expression of the bleakness my mother felt as a recent widow during that lonely Depression autumn of 1932."

"And that," said George, "is all I know of October Carson's early life. And that he wandered the West for some ten years or more."

"And since? What's become of him?"

"I honestly don't know. The letters tell nothing, and the journals stop just over three years ago. That same fall, I received a large package containing the journals and a very extensive consignment of butterflies from all over the West. There was a brief note that I must not have saved, asking me to send payment to general delivery in Allenspark, Colorado . . . I'd never have remembered that, except that I used to frequent that part of the Front Range when I worked out of CU's Science Lodge above Ward."

"So that was it?"

"I sent the museum's check, it was cashed, and then I heard no more. I've never known whether he simply resumed his scavenging rambles, minus his butterfly net, or vanished somewhere, like Gauguin in the South Seas. I hadn't thought about Carson for many months, until you mentioned the journals just now." Winchester sighed and smiled high in one corner of his mouth. "So you see," he mused, "I'm just as curious as you are."

"I've just begun the journals. But with your permission," Mead said, forgetting his resolution, "I'd like to read the rest. Maybe I'll catch some clues."

"If you have time, feel free. Just don't let it become a detour from your important work. Do let me know what you discover. Well, I must get home, James. Jane and I have a rare date with the TV. Peter Freulich's going to appear on *The Tonight Show*, with yet another Carson, not yet represented in my files—and I want to see him. You know his important work on fritillaries and their population biology, but did you know we cofounded Natural Limits to Growth?"

"NLG—really!"

"Yes, and his famous book, *Nuking Ourselves*, has gained even more notoriety than his scholarly work and has had him on the talk shows ever since. He's a special favorite of Johnny Carson, who really seems to get the message. In any case, you'll be needing to see to our mutual friends down the hall."

For once, Mead didn't feel a bit like seeing to the noble roaches. He'd been learning some interesting things from their nighttime revels, but now, spurred on by Winchester's revelation and invitation, he was truly piqued by Carson and eager to learn more about him. So, after a perfunctory feeding and cleaning, he made a fresh path in the snow across to the museum, gathered up the journals, and returned to Osborn, his tracks already covered. As the snow swaddled the world outside, Mead took to his tower with the first volume of Carson's journal and a flask of hot tea from the Bunsen. He followed as Carson carried on across the pallid, frigid sagelands, eking food and shelter from his chancy pursuits through the coldest winter in almost forty years.

10

Mead's own winter passed too. His mental distance from New Mexico and his mother grew with the sum of the weeks. She wrote no more; his father sent short notes instead with family news of the light sort and the occasional check folded inside. The pain of his mother's frost became the kind of dull background ache that one mostly forgets, most of the time.

Something else troubled Mead when he thought about it, but in a very different way: that one young woman's smile, from his first visit to the department. He'd scarcely dated anyone in New Haven and was stewing in a stale winter's brew of his own testosterone. A remarkable face, he thought, the one he'd glimpsed flitting out of George Winchester's office that first day at Yale. He'd been right about her being part Asian—Hawaiian, in fact: some indigenous, some Japanese. Her smile infected him, made others smile; also made him want to kiss her mouth and lick her teeth. As he thought such thoughts, Mead realized he had been too long in the roach room at night, too long cooped in his monastic tower. When he next encountered Noni Blue, he asked her out, and she accepted.

After their first date, a movie and a drink, Mead walked home across the Old Campus. "I suppose that's grad school for you," he muttered, a touch of disgust in his voice. "I've thought about Noni all year, so here I am, on a rare night away from the roaches, facing her across our beers, and what do we talk about? Bloody committees!"

But that was natural. Few aspects of life affect the postgrad quite as much as the faculty committee. Your fortunes, fun, fury, and future rotate on the whim and judgments of this arbitrary posse of pedagogues. Given a sympathetic tribunal, life can be worth living. But let one or two be petulant prima donnas, and you may be screwed, regardless of scholarship. Mead had heard of committees that greased the skids, others that gummed up the works, but never one that failed to put up a few hoops to jump through. Along such runnels ran the conversation of James Mead and Noni Blue on their first date. *"Committees!"* Mead croaked again an hour later, trudging up the steps of the tower. "Couldn't I have thought of something more romantic?"

So the next time, he spoke of hissing roaches and their marvelous courtship rituals. That hadn't been quite right either.

On their third date, over coffee, Mead let out much more than he'd intended. They'd been getting to know each other, and Noni said, "Tell me about your family. And where you're from, besides just New Mexico."

"I was born in Las Cruces," Mead began. "Dad worked on rockets at White Sands—nothing nuclear, but they were getting ready. We moved to Albuquerque a few years ago when he got a job at the university. Mom's spent her whole life so far on me and my two brothers. Wants to paint, but never quite gets the brushes out, you know?"

"Or gets the lead out?" asked Noni. "My mom was like that— until she left."

"My mother would never do that."

"Any woman will, if she's had enough. Or maybe *not* enough."

"I don't think so. Anyway, she'd be an emotional cripple on her own."

"You sell her pretty short, don't you?"

"Never mind. Anyway, UNM waives tuition for faculty brats, so I stayed there. Then returned to Las Cruces for my master's."

Noni tried again. "So what do you mean about your mother? I don't mean to pry, but what you said was provocative. Why is she so emotionally dependent?"

"Well, nuts," he said, running his long fingers through his brown hair. "All right—you want to know? You might not like it."

She kept on nodding, if only just.

"Okay. My mother always wanted a girl; Dad too. They got us three boys—I'm the oldest, Lance and Roger are eighteen and fifteen. So eight years ago—Mom's fifty-four—she got pregnant again."

"Wow! And, yay for her—so she got her girl?"

"Don't cheer yet. They got their girl, all right. She was born with spina bifida."

"Oh, James, I'm sorry . . ."

"That's not the bad part," he continued. "The surgery was good, she was coming along, and we all loved her very much. But she took a lot of care." Mead was staring straight ahead, into his cooling cup. "It wore us out sometimes, but Molly got and gave all the love any kid could have." He paused, and Noni said nothing. "Then, two years ago, she died." Mead went pale. "And that's still not the worst of it," he said with a small, mirthless laugh. "Mom and Dad never got out anymore, what with the demands of Molly's care. One day I talked them into going hiking with us boys. For the first time, they consented to leave Molly with a respite worker from the county. Everything seemed fine. We all had a good time, almost like before, when we hiked all the time. Then we got home to find an ambulance in the driveway. The respite helper had fallen asleep, and Molly drowned in the bath."

Noni took his hand.

James snorted. "If only we hadn't gone hiking . . ." He let his head fall onto her shoulder, feeling way too close to blubbering. "I'm sorry," he said in a small voice. "I've never told anyone before."

Noni shoved him. "James, I *am* sorry, that's a horrible story. And my shoulder's yours if you want it. But you really carry guilt about this, don't you?"

"I know it's not my fault. And I can't say I saw a great future for Molly. But it's what it did to Mom. She's been very brittle ever since. Therapy doesn't work, and she'd never take pills."

"But James, tens of thousands of mothers have lost healthy sons, not to mention lovers and husbands and fathers, in Vietnam in these past few years. Like my aunt, when my cousin Charlie was killed in Khe Sanh. Most of them get on with it, as she does."

"You're right. And so does my mother, in her way. But . . ."

"But what?"

"Well, I almost think she blames *me*. The outing was my idea, after all, and I talked them into it. We were exceptionally close, always—great pals. But ever since Molly died, she's been stiff, even cold toward me. I guess that haunts me more than Molly's loss itself. That must sound incredibly selfish. Oh, shit."

Noni gave her shoulder back.

Later, as Noni spoke softly, trying to comfort him, James considered her face as well as her words. She flicked her long, dark brown hair, glinting red in some lights, black in others. Mead knew he was supposed to respond to what he thought she had said, but he let himself lose track in the flickers and sparks of her hair. That night it was hellishly hard to return to his lab, the roach room, and the lonely, chilly turret. Eventually he fell asleep, for once with more than randy roaches and western ramblers in his dreams.

More dates followed. When weekend weather permitted, they walked the trails of the traprock ridges outside of town. Or they caught a bus to some salt marsh village, dined on crab cakes and Schaefer beer in little beach bistros, and walked back on long-abandoned trolley lines that once served the university. When the snow closed in, they prowled weedy winter fields, stark with the heads of dried asters.

The day came at last when Mead kissed Noni's mouth and licked her teeth. And one night, sealed in her warm room by the bewitching glaze of a Connecticut ice storm off Long Island Sound, beside a little Christmas tree they'd fashioned from snapped-off boughs of pine, they became lovers. Afterward, Noni's almost negative weight buoyant across his belly beneath the sheets, Mead lay in a state of happy disbelief.

Lifting her hand to stroke his long side and his short brown beard, Noni said, "I was beginning to wonder whether we'd ever get here."

"I know," said Mead. "God, I've needed this."

"Need more?" she asked.

So the two of them, young and lithe and randier than the roaches from too much bookwork and too little life, wrapped themselves together again. Then, sweaty and laughing like mockingbirds, they slept into the morning. When Mead awoke, Noni's bedside candle burned low and bright as her grass-sweet breath lisped on in slumber.

Mead looked around him at Noni's books, records, prints, posters, family photos, and artifacts from a privileged and cosmopolitan upbringing. A field hockey stick angled across one corner while another supported a generous spiderweb unmolested. On a corner clothesline, a trio of pastel blouses danced with a pretty array of panties and bras. Mead worried that she was much more sophisticated than he in her background, and he mumbled something to himself. Just then she stirred, turned her warm front against his side, and asked, "What did you say?"

"You have a lot of books," he said, and then he crushed her petal lips, doing them no harm whatever.

One day about a week later Mead was working in the main museum collection, placing some butterflies of the brushfoot subfamily Satyrinae into unit trays. His eyes were arrested by the label on a tray of stunning black velvet butterflies: *Erebia magdalena,* read the label. "Eureka!" he erupted. The boss was on hand, working in another range of cabinets.

"The missing link?" Winchester asked.

Mead called him over. "Could be," he said, "or the missing Carson!" He explained.

"Yes, surely that is the Magdalena Carson referred to in his journal," Winchester confirmed. "Not only was it one of the man's most lucrative catches, when it could be had, but I believe he was also quite fond of the species."

Peering into the tray, Mead could see why that might be.

"If you'll look closely, you'll see that some of those specimens were collected by him." Indeed, the pin label on several read LEG. O. CARSON.

Mead beheld a series of large alpines. Unlike most members of the genus *Erebia*, these were devoid of eyespots or any other decoration. Magdalena spanned more than two inches across its spread wings, which were utterly unmarked. The long, rounded panes shone wholly black or darkest chocolate, or a weathered brown plush on older specimens. Aside from its immaculate ebony surfaces, it seemed an unremarkable insect, but then Mead knew nothing of its biology.

Winchester came alongside Mead again and set a case atop a low cabinet for viewing. "Look here, James," he said, pointing. "As you know, we have several specialty collections in the museum, such as species that have become extinct—I purchased several of these from the great insect bourses in London, Paris, and Hamburg after the war—as well as sexual gynanders and mosaics, mimicry pairs and rings, and so on." He indicated the "so on" with an all-inclusive sweep of his massive hands, which were capable of lofting Cornell insect drawers in a single grasp. Mead nodded; he had done some curating in several of these specialized groups.

"For example, look at these gynandromorphs," he said, pulling out a drawer of the oddest-looking butterflies Mead had ever seen. Most were bilateral—all male on one side, all female on the other—making for a particularly striking contrast in sexually dimorphic species. "Charlie Covell donated that superb bilateral of *Speyeria diana* from Kentucky," Winchester said, indicating an amazing half-and-half fritillary of jack-o'-lantern orange and black on one side, black and blue on the other. "The genetics of that are fairly straight-forward," he said. "But this one is much more rare, and complex." He pointed at a Queen Alexandra's sulphur that looked ordinary, until Mead noticed that it had one female wing to three male ones. "A young fellow named Michael Heap sent me that," Winchester said. "His mother collected it in Colorado."

"And Magdalena?" asked Mead, fascinated, but eager to get to the point.

"Well, this tray," said the prof, replacing the sexual oddities and returning to the drawer he'd pulled out earlier, "contains butterflies with bird-bill impressions on their wings. You see the sharply defined V or Vs on each specimen? What happens is that the bird strikes at the butterfly but changes its mind at the last moment and releases its grip before the wing tears. Whether the change of heart comes from being startled or from recognition that the captured prey is unpalatable, the act often leaves a crisp mark where the pressure of the bill removes the scales from the wing. The value of such specimens lies in what they can tell us of bird-butterfly interactions, distastefulness, and the evolution of predator-prey patterns. Yale Peabody probably has the best collection of such beak-marked butterflies anywhere."

Mead just listened. He'd found that he learned as much from GW's impromptu yet fully formed lecturettes as from his formal classes. After all, this was practically a tutorial with his own private don. He failed to catch the reason for the change of subject, but he did notice an obvious gap in the collection drawer. "That's my point," Winchester went on. "October Carson once saw a beak-marked *Erebia magdalena* in Colorado, but failed to capture it. He swore he would find another. I took him at his word and have kept that slot open ever since. I think some of his fascination with this species lies there, and in its alluring habitat, up among the arctic-alpine screes and scarps. Maybe also in its pure black wings, and its name. He alluded to all of these in his notes, often scribbled on packing slips, sadly not all saved. It seemed that for October Carson, *Erebia magdalena* represented something larger than itself—but I have no idea what.

"Anyway, almost time for that committee meeting; we'd better prepare for Professor G's onslaught. Whatever you do, don't tell him you're camping out in the tower and tracking down phantom nature tramps."

"Roger," said Mead.

"And since *phantom* is probably the operative word by now, perhaps you'd better just close up that gap in the bill-mark collection."

Mead hesitated, then said, "Um, Professor?"

"Mmmm?"

"Maybe, if you don't mind, we shouldn't be too hasty about that."

"As you please," said Winchester. "You're the curator."

11

Huddled by a kerosene lantern in his chilly battlement, Mead gained respect for his Anglo-Saxon ancestors who gutted out winters in northern European castles. And much as the learned among those cold-castle dwellers might have read ancient manuscripts by February firelight, Mead continued to pore over the journals of October Carson by the light of his high-intensity lamp. Night after solitary night, he tucked his roaches to bed and returned to the scribblings of the bearded itinerant. As he did so, James Mead followed Carson into spring.

The first volume saw the man working a construction job in California (brief, perfunctory jottings) and weekending in the near Sierra, trying to emulate John Muir in life and language (longer, lusher entries). Not until he left the job and the weekend frontcountry did he find his own voice, as he wandered from blank to blanker spot on the western map. Each volume told a year, and each roughly rhymed in route with the one that went before, as Carson circled back to favorite places and added new ones depending on transport and whim. Sometimes an intriguing name on a map would be enough to take him hundreds of miles out of his way. But then, as Mead learned, Carson really had no "way." The style became leaner, no longer mimicking Muir, as he passed through later seasons and lower places. His sense of destination, however, remained fuzzy, and he never betrayed a plan or a purpose.

So Mead found himself back where he'd first looked over Carson's shifting shoulder. He had dropped from Bear Lake down along the Great Salt Lake, taken a winter construction job in the city. It didn't sit well. He seemed to require an element of insecurity—searching, finding, losing, and searching again—and it was colder than hell on that job. So he collected his pay, took a Trailways bus to Jackson, and with the snow off early, began hunting for old bottles, insulators, and other bygones. He seemed to have eaten for a month or more off purple, green, and blue bottles he'd ferreted out of the sagebrush and aspen of old homesteads and cattle camps around Jackson Hole, while he went to ground in an abandoned cabin. He watched for sage thrashers, the big, sickle-billed brown birds erect on the blue-gray tips of the big basin sage. In such places more often than not he could find mauve medicine flasks, their manganese turned purple by long exposure to the sun, or old-time Coke bottles, and these he could flog to curio and bottle shops stocking up for the tourist season in Jackson. But soon he'd saturated the local market, and he needed something to get him through the rest of spring into summer. So he signed on as a boatman for one of the smaller Snake River rafting outfitters.

June 6. Nine p.m., exhausted. I love the river, but ye gods! These people work! Twelve to sixteen hours a day, six or seven days. They pay me well, but there is no time to walk the banks or ramble among the delectable spring-green salad bar of a countryside we pass through six or eight times a day. And I'm getting awfully tired of my voice, delivering the interpretive spiel. I find myself envying the passengers, who will be moving on down the highway after the float. Their families, station wagons, and most of their dogs, however, I do not covet.

June 12. Nor did I envy some people I took down the river yesterday. Our chat went something like this: "Where do you folks hail from?" I asked as we entered an eddy. A conversation always staggers to its feet at that calm point, as the boaters begin to sense my presence as something more than a pair of oars, and this was a safe start.

"Ottawa," came the clipped reply from the apparent patriarch.

"Cold up there last winter?"

"Ottawa, Kansas. Hotter'n hell right now."

"I guess," I offered. "Does your family generally come to Jackson to cool off?"

The porky Ottowan looked impatient, his tomato face crinkled at the corners in irritation, as if this was not exactly what he would have chosen to discuss. "Nah, usually Estes Park, or sometimes Glenwood Springs. They're cheaper'n this hole."

"Jackson Hole, you mean?" He didn't catch his own pale pun. "But always somewhere in the mountains?"

"Damn right," he said, "if I have anything to do with it." Carson guessed he did.

At that his wife broke in with a tentative plaint. "I'd love to stay in Kansas one summer and see the prairie flowers in the Flint Hills down around Cottonwood Falls, or go to the beach—any beach, even Lake Michigan would do fine." She sighed. "But as Elbert says, it's always the mountains."

"Now don'chu start, Ruth . . ."

Just what I didn't need on my boat, a family spat. I wished I'd kept my mouth shut.

"Elbert's family are Okies," Ruth continued. "And Okies reckon there's no vacation that IS a vacation unless it's in the Rockies. Texans are just as bad. If it isn't over a mile high, it doesn't count."

"We just <u>lahk</u> the mountains better . . . ain't that raght, kids?" Elbert said.

The Wheeldon children, inured to their parents' topographic dialectic and not about to get sucked in again, grunted as one and mumbled something about Disneyland. They knew they'd pay for taking sides, and they didn't really care where they went, as long as it was far away from school. The rushing river and the movements among the shore grasses were far more riveting than this ancient argument.

Ruth changed the subject. "And how about you, Mr. Carson? Are you a real mountain man?"

A taunt as much as a query?

I knew the trap. To describe my life only boils the husband's wanderlust, if it's still alive, and offends his wife's sense of security, or else confounds his propriety while piquing her curiosity. But I'd already managed to do all that, so I said, "Well, I'm not a trapper. My grandpa used to sum up Sunday dinner by saying that it was mighty fine, what there was of it, and plenty of it, such as it was. The Snake River is like that for me."

Elbert was fixing to ask me what the hell <u>that</u> was supposed to mean, when the current took the boat and swung us about. The hiss of the Snake in full spring runoff drowned out his further remarks. Slipped out of that one, you old codger.

An hour later, with our bow rope wrapped around a snag like a small python hungry for hardwood, I pulled the raft to shore. Beside a lime-green meadow where the tall white candles of corn lily screened the edge of the forest, I proposed lunch. I was hoarse from pointing out ospreys and moose over the river's voice and telling about the trappers' rendezvous that used to take place in Jackson Hole ("Now <u>those</u> were mountain men," Ruth had interjected, for Elbert's benefit or mine, I wasn't sure). So I grazed in silence, wishing I could slip off to search for morels beneath the chartreuse cottonwoods.

Ruth Wheeldon, wife to Elbert o' Mountains, stood and brushed the dust off her not unsightly bottom, walked over, and planted it on the grass beside me. Owner of a pretty face from a Penney's catalogue and a summer Sears sundress, she did not offend with her sunny Kansas presence. Elbert ignored us and snoozed some way off as the kids explored the shore, every now and then bringing back a bug or a snail to be admired and identified. I kept an eye on them, but they refused to fall in and take their dad with them.

"So what is it really about mountains for you, Mr. Carson? Your granddad's saying was charming, but a little obscure for a farm girl like me."

Not off the hook after all. I tried again, and said something like "Mountains soothe with horns and bones, make you rich with rocks. And they're the best place to spot a puma by far, except for some carnivals I've seen." Or perhaps I just said, "Maybe we should talk about rivers." I expected Ruth to be miffed at my seeming to take sides with Elbert and liberties with logic, and I was prepared to say that I loved oceans too, and prairies. But she surprised me.

"Not just the way I'd have thought to express it. But it sounds better than Elbert's my-way-or-the-highway reasoning. You know, I don't have anything against the mountains. This"—she waved a chapped but shapely hand around—"is lovely. It's just his damned bullheadedness about it. He's so <u>seffish</u> with our little bit of vacation time. John Deere only gives him two weeks off. He's got a right to enjoy them as he wishes. But <u>ah</u> work too . . . and I should have some say."

So here it comes, I thought; and it did. She asked if I worked (besides this), didn't I have a family to support, and . . . then stopped. "Sorry," she said, her slender neck pinker than before, "it's none of my business." And turned her sunflower face toward the river.

Elbert, disturbed by the deerflies, had risen from his nap and was struggling with a worm and a hook for an impatient daughter. He was paying us no attention.

"That's all right," I said. "I don't mind your asking. It's just hard to explain my way of life these days. I've been rafting only a little while, and it might not last much longer." Then a brown butterfly, one of the spring's first, caught my eye. "See that butterfly?" Ruth said she would not have noticed it, but she caught a glimpse as it nectared on an early arnica. It was a cocoa-colored, silver-threaded satyr called Hayden's ringlet. I told her a little, how its larvae nibble the fresh young grass and how its name came from the Hayden Geological Survey expeditions of 1871. We crept up on it.

"My, my!" said Ruth. She liked its blue, yellow-rimmed, silver-centered eyespots.

"Its relatives fly on the high mountain tundra," I said. "The river's rising means snowmelt upstairs, and the alpine butterflies can't be far behind. I'll be joining them down in Colorado."

"Why? Butterflies are beautiful, and very nice, but can you live on them?"

"That's another thing Grandpop used to say," I replied. "'Is there any money in butterflies?' I'd reply, 'I doubt it, Grandpop.' And I was mostly right. Actually, there is a little. I collect uncommon species and peddle them to museums. This is where I am sort of like those old mountain men—I just trade in butterflies instead of beaver pelts. I make enough in season to buy beer and ground beef, and it gives me an excuse to be up in the high country." I tried to tell her about the intoxicating fragrance of the tundra, the utter enchantment of the glacial peaks above timberline.

"And in winter?" she asked.

"I work the beaches for glass floats and other salable flotsam, as well as clams. My needs are few and easily met. It's mostly just to be there in the storms. So you see? I like beaches too! I'm not just a mountain guy. And certainly no Jim Bridger."

"No," said Ruth. "And maybe just as well." Then, something like this: "I sort of see. It does sound exciting, in a way, and certainly not boring. Scary at times, I'd think." Maybe I nodded. "But what do you do for insurance?" (She emphasized the <u>in</u>-.) "Or retirement, or next month's mortgage payment?"

"Well, I have none of those things," was all I could think to say.

"So you're one of those . . . you're <u>homeless</u>?" She said it with a slight but perceptible little shudder of fear or loathing, I couldn't tell.

"Can't take my shopping cart on the river," I said, "or up the trails." Trying for levity in case it was loathing. It worked; she laughed.

"Maybe all this traveling and poking about . . . maybe what you're looking for <u>is</u> a home, and a family . . . I assume you haven't got one of those, either?"

"Correct. Never reproduced, not presently married. And I don't want a home, Ruth, at least not right now. I've had one before and I may have one again, partner too. But for now, footloose seems to suit me better."

"Then maybe—forgive me—what you should be catching is a real job?"

I told Ruth she wasn't the first to say so, two wives among her antecedents. And that I worked construction sometimes. Then, maybe a little defensive, "I've worked hard at many different jobs, all colors of collars. But no job sticks for long these years."

"Do you <u>faght</u>? Drink? Gamble?" Ruth had dropped all pretense of reserve and manners. The river does that to clients sometimes. She seemed both repelled and fascinated. In any case, curious, to a degree she'd probably regret once we put to shore. But I didn't seem to mind.

"No," I said, "none of the above. I get along fine with my workmates, and I don't resent a good boss. I just always seem to walk away after a paycheck or two. The road and the country it crosses always call more strongly than the work whistle. It's just being in thrall—somebody else calling the shots, planning my day . . . my life. Abe Lincoln said, 'We must disenthrall ourselves, and then we shall save our country.' Or as Eric Clapton put it, I've got the keys to the highway, and I've just got to move." Only I probably didn't say it that well. What she said was, "We're driving to Estes Park from here. Would you like a <u>rahd</u>?"

I contemplated the Hayden's ringlets flip-flopping between the grass blades. Those saffron ovals brimming with silver scales that run out and rim the margins: beautiful. W. H. Edwards called it an <u>Erebia</u> back in the 1800s. He was mistaken in terms of taxonomy, but you can see why he made such an assignment. The real alpines will soon be out, up there in the Rockies: not only <u>Erebia magdalena</u>, but also <u>epipsodea</u>, <u>callias</u>, and <u>theano</u>. But especially <u>magdalena</u>. How could I resist the invitation even if I wanted to?

I'm not sure whether such reasoning or the promise of a little more time with Ruth made up my mind. Both, I suppose. So, notwithstanding the daunting prospect of hours cooped up with edgy Elbert, his sunburned spawn, and their pooch, I accepted. "Sure," I said at last. "If you think it will sit all right with your husband."

"Just don't pop too many of your grandpa's words of wisdom on him, and he'll be fine. He'll probably mutter a lot and I'll hear all about Charles Manson before we go to bed at night, but I don't think Elbert will veto the idea. And the kids will love the adventure of adopting a mountain man. Sometimes I do get my own way."

Swaying like prairie grass, Ruth rose and walked over to Elbert. He was drowsy after a six-pack all on his own. I guessed he would have left the cans if I hadn't been there, but I can't be sure. Ruth advised him of the change of plans. I saw him jerk, as if she had invited the aforementioned Manson to tea. I reckoned just then that Elbert could stay behind and be a boatman (or a raft) and Ruth and I could go to Colorado and sell the kids to Basque sheepherders, but no such luck. He decided to come along after all.

So that afternoon, after I'd docked the raft and drove us back in the bus, I handed in my oars. The river boss wasn't thrilled; he said I'd done a good job and he was hoping to keep me on through the summer, and maybe next year too. But river runners are notorious for being mercurial at best as employees. I collected my pay, cleared out of my cabin, and loaded my small pack of gear into the Toronado wagon between the kids and the coolers, the dog and the suitcases. We took off for Colorado, down past the Tetons, the Gros Ventre, the Wind Rivers, and the hot country east to Wamsutter and Laramie before cutting south on 287 through Virginia Dale. We made an unlikely crew, and Elbert's tomato face never did uncrinkle. But Ruth's sunflower smile often appeared in the rearview mirror.

12

Magdalena Mountain melts. At least its white carapace melts and slides away down avalanche chutes, sublimates into the alpine sky, or is sucked into stony rivulets by the thirsty warmth of spring. Blackened mosses along those rills regain their green as the running snowmelt fills their sponges and swells their thalli. The first of the flowers burst out—marsh marigolds in the wet edges, glacier lilies beneath the shrinking snowloads, pale mauve pasqueflowers down where the limber pines wrestle with the rocks in perpetual border dispute over timberline.

These early floral offerings are not without their croppers, for the diminishing cold grows too weak to hold pikas in their places. The gray harelets, a little less round than last autumn, pop out and eagerly see to the pruning of the early-spring vegetation. This is turning out to be a wet and lush year, with plenty of runoff and succulent regrowth, so no desperate pika or poor skinny coyote grazes the strawlike clump of grass at the edge of the rockslide where Erebia is coming back to life. About the size of an apostrophe, he shares that character's round black head, a feature that sets him apart from the young of the other three species of Colorado alpines. The rest of his body is colored pale flesh with purplish stripes. A greenish cast will overtake it as the grass's chlorophyll passes down the translucent tube of his hungry gut.

Activity accelerates on the scree, where so recently the only movement was white crystals falling or blocks of them breaking away. Now screaming flocks of silver-gray, black, and white birds—Clark's nutcrackers—swoop from one patch of pines to the next. Related ravens too pass upslope and over the rocks, kronking, their great black shapes foreshadowing the smaller ones that will mime their flight after another moon's circle. When the ravens cross overhead, pikas squeak *eek!* and dive for the safety of their crevices. When any big shadow could as well be a raptor as a corvid, why take chances?

Marmots at last shake off their somnolence and begin to bask on reflective slabs of granite. Soon their whistles will be heard, an academy of traffic cops shrilling contradictory commands from every major intersection on the mountain.

Erebia remains insensitive to all these goings-on. Only the rising, falling temperature rules his day, along with the intensity of the sunshine, such that he can seek the shelter of the grassroots when nightfall threatens late frosts. The duration, too, of the sun, for the gathering daylength quickens his hormones even as the rising sun thaws his muscles. Subject to desiccation at the drop of a dry grass blade, Erebia constantly seeks the dampest patch of turf, often resting on a spongy clump of moss or moss campion to maintain his water balance.

Now Erebia's sliver of a larva faces many dangers. Ground beetles, spiders, woodlice, ants, and many other creeping predators prowl the sparse vegetation, ready to catch and consume his tiny packet of protein. Parasitic wasps and flies probe his haunts. But the greatest threat comes from the presence or absence of moisture: too much means mold; too little, death by crisping. Any fool who has tried to rear mountain ringlets and graylings knows this. But Erebia finds his needs, is not himself found, and so he grazes and grows.

Then, not many days after spring breaks out on Magdalena

Mountain's southeast flank, at eleven thousand feet, Erebia reaches the point when his skin can stretch no more. Taut, sleek, and bulging, it splits, and along the new suture a softer, deeper green skin shows through. Like any dry seed erupting, cotyledon unfurling, atom splitting, the new form lunges into the come-what-may with vigor. This is Erebia's first molt of five—a shedding, a rebirthing that some of his siblings already experienced last fall, before their winter's diapause. Now, out comes a more supple and pliant caterpillar, bigger, the size of a shaved pencil point, his head still black but his tube suit gray-green and darker striped.

Erebia eats more, no longer restricted to the baby food of the softest blades, and so grows faster. He has it in him to go either way: if heavy weather or an early snowfall should cut short the season, he can reenter that state of winter grace and pass a second season of chill. After all, many alpines are routinely biennial, taking two full years to mature. But, for the robust black *Erebia magdalena*, just one year usually suffices. So this particular wee one feeds on, and feeds, and feeds some more.

As he grows, Erebia's range of potential predators only broadens. Rockslide rodents, passing bands of rosy finches, nesting pipits patrolling their territories, any of these and many more would readily snap up this black-tipped wormlet for an iota of their day's nutrition. Many of his brothers and sisters become such bites. But this one has the luck with him, and four more molts will follow in their time, each one delivering a larger, more succulent animal.

Nearing the summer solstice, Erebia slips into his final instar. Now he would be readily recognized for what he is—no tiny worm of indeterminate nature, but an actual caterpillar, precedent to butterfly or moth. A handsome animal he is as a mature larva, spring-green, lined and diagonally slashed with white. Now nearly an inch and a half long, he bends the grass blades over when he climbs them, like a child on a small aspen. His shape is that of a streamlined dirigible, tapering toward twin tails at the stern, thickening to that shiny, still-black head capsule: a black helmet to keep his brain ganglion warm, allowing longer feeding, greater alertness, faster development. That jet headpiece shines in the undeflected high-country sun.

Erebia's striped pattern and grassy coloration render him cryptic among the tussocks, confounding predators that by now would find him a more than worthwhile morsel. So refined is this crypsis that the majority of larvae reaching this stage (a small portion of those hatched last summer) will now survive to pupate. Because by now, color-sighted birds are the chief threat rather than creeping, tapping invertebrates. The new, mottled chicks of ptarmigan present a particular peril to Erebia and his like. Their parents eked their way through winter, white on white, stuffing themselves on willow buds before bundling under the snow for the night. But the new hatchlings need protein for rapid growth during the brief season when insects are available, so they work the greening sward like hens and chicks scratching their way across a barnyard. By chance and grace, no pecking ptarmigan or jabbing jay comes across Erebia.

So it is that in the last week of June, a final molt takes place. This time no larger, greener caterpillar comes out. First, Erebia goes walkabout for many yards—a risky, exposed procession, but one almost every caterpillar undertakes—negotiating sedge and stone, exposed and parching bare spots, and soaking mountain moss. Under and over the lichened rocks he wanders, across the pygmy savanna of alpine sedges and forget-me-nots. Finally he winds his way into a random wickerwork of last year's grasses, where he turns around, catlike, several times, and settles into the scrape. Then his skin splits one last time, he wriggles out of his old bodysuit and emerges as a grublike thing, dark viscous green, like a blob of crude oil in color and shine.

Even before the last used skin fell away, the body it held began to dissolve within. Now the prepupa quickly hardens on the outside into a black, sarcophagus-like case—but hardly that, since the insides are yet quick. These contents soften and fall apart, and their tissues break down almost entirely. A deer mouse biting into the fresh pupa would find no caterpillar, nor butterfly, but a portion of puslike soup devoid of apparent form. Nor does the pupal shell, embossed as it is with butterfly features, damasked with the shapes of wings, legs, tongue, antennae, and eyes, serve as a cast to mold the muddled substance within, to give it the form into which tissues may take shape, as the ancients concluded. No waxen die from some creator's hand, the chrysalis is a pod of change in which Pan works and plays. His tools are a set of imaginal disks, bundles of cells that direct the reassembly of materials into the adult hard and soft parts that make up a butterfly. Genes direct the scene, and enzymes and hormones carry it to completion.

Thus programmed, the new features come together from the inchoate brew and fill out into the waiting, shaped receptacle of the chrysalis shell. The engraved case then receives the form of the insect rather than tooling it from wet prepupal clay. And in this way, the finer details still obscure and of no moment whatever to Erebia, the black animal that is the Magdalena alpine comes into its improbable adult existence.

A day comes, just two weeks after pupation, when the finished butterfly presses to be released. His casket goes glassy black. Then it bursts open, dehiscing along the dotted lines of its seams, revealing that this was no coffin, but a birthing chamber. It is easy to see why the Arapaho of these summer peaks called the butterfly chrysalis an egg, for surely the pupa is to a butterfly what the egg is to a bird. The shell cracks and falls back, transparent. The blackness, which has deepened from soot to sable, belongs to the creature within rather than to its wrappers. That heavy pellet, the pupa, which seemed so solid as it lay ripening in the summer sun, now lies insubstantial as a November husk long since robbed of its kernel by mouse or maggot. Erebia steps out.

Crawling up a spike of grass, clinging to an overarching stone, Erebia hangs wet and rumpled and limp. But not for long. His swollen abdomen begins pumping. The wings expand slowly, erectile, as the sun-warmed hemolymph courses into their veins. They stiffen like the struts of a kite. Gradually the wings' oval shape comes clear as the body shrinks to normal proportions. For some hours the wings are as soft as silk and just as delicate. This is a dangerous time, for a fall or a scrape could crush them or prevent their proper expansion. But all goes well. Erebia shimmers with moisture for a few minutes before the droplets evaporate on the dry alpine air, and it continues to glisten with a violet-green sheen imparted by a layer of prismatic scales that will soon fall away.

And beneath the iridescence, *black*: a blackness so deep that it tells the entire tale of the long night of pupation at a glance, so thick that it hints, if you can see, at the depth of the void that provident evolution has filled with these wings and the body they will carry on high. Black-panther black, black-velvet black, far blacker than starlit-night black, but not as black as a hardrock hole because there is a luminosity to it also.

Such a blackness bears the Magdalena alpine.

This new-to-the-world *Erebia magdalena* creeps onto a patch of black lichen, warmer than the surrounding sugar-stone granite, and tilts his now-dry wings down against the surface, together. A constant cool breeze tries to chill all tissues, but the sun warms them faster. Soon his flight muscles reach the temperature necessary to work, to lift that black package off the rocks and set it sailing into thin air.

Erebia has passed the survival gauntlet of his profound metamorphosis. He has endured the long sentence of the ground-borne and the parole of the pupa. Now a butterfly, this creature flies free across the mountain's face for the first time.

13

The shaggy mat of yellow grass outside the nursing home, studded on warm days with forlorn people and cigarette butts, began to turn muddy green. Spring came fast to Denver, announcing itself with days that began blue, then turned brown by rush hour. Mary sat outside for as long as she was allowed, sometimes even walked to a nearby pocket park. Still she had no friends, no champion, no one who moved her to speak. The nurses had stopped trying, believing that her one lucid outburst had been an aberration.

Still the meds came each morning and night, leaving her too muddy-minded to read or to ponder. But each late afternoon, when the drugs began to wear off and the ozone air took on a mellow glow and a balmy feel, Mary came clear of mind. Then she would walk around to the vacant lot behind the squat white brick building. From there she could watch the little green things and see just a shoulder of Mount Evans between a distant shiny skyscraper and the redbrick Full Gospel Mount Pisgah Pentecostal Church. That glimpse of the Rockies sometimes made her soar, sometimes despair, always made her high, pale cheeks wet with tears of longing.

Mary felt sick every time the aide called her back in for dinner. To take food among all these unfortunates who drooled and looked through her, to face the evening ahead that would be filled with moans, shouts, and gurgled laughter against incessant radio and television babel and finally the lights-out of a forced pill and a flicked switch, it made her desperate, made her weep inside. As spring drew into summer, Mary knew that something had to happen soon or she would make it happen. Those clear times in the afternoon became her mental open space, where plans began to grow. She found whole scenarios forming themselves, but only during that hour of the day. More and more those thoughts inclined toward suicide.

The time came when the only obstacle seemed to be how to do it with as little chance of failing as possible. Mary knew nothing of killing. One day, another resident, who had been leering at Mary for weeks, rubbing himself and gesturing until the nurses had to remove him, jumped Mary in the laundry exchange. She was stronger, and help was nearby, so she escaped with bruises. The man was transferred, but the incident brought her despair to a head. By now she had reclaimed enough self-presence, yet not lost enough self-respect, to know that this existence was impossible; the injustice, intolerable. No matter the meds, acceptance would never, thank God, be hers.

So the next day when John Everson, the director, attempted to soothe and question her about the assault, she spoke.

"Are you okay, Mary?"

"Not hurt. But hardly okay. No business being here."

"No, but how good to hear you speak! Mary, where *do* you have business being?"

"Don't know. Yet. Just, not here. I'm not. Like them."

"No one is like anyone else here, Mary . . . except that all our clients need help."

Mary turned her face down and mumbled something.

"I beg your pardon?" asked Everson, a youngish man who'd been in VISTA before grad school and still clung to tatters of the ideals he'd gone in with.

"I said, that's so, but doesn't feel like help to me."

He could see that her intelligence was intact, and he considered calling the psychiatrist to ask whether he would agree to release Mary. But where to? First he asked, "Do you know who you are yet, beyond just 'Mary'?" And when she answered, his face clouded. "You'd better get to lunch, Mary," he said. "We'll talk again soon. I'm glad you weren't hurt. That poor fellow is in Fort Logan now, and he won't be bothering you anymore." As he paused outside the door, Mary heard him on the phone with the doctor.

"I almost thought she was better, Mitchell. That's right—speaking and cogent, bright, more or less logical. Well, then she blew it. She told me she was ... yes, that's right ... oh, you've already heard that from the nurse? Yes, I know she talked a bit a while back, before her seizure up in the mountains ... Well anyway, she seems as deluded as half the people here, staff excluded, by the way. Can you imagine how long she'd last out on the streets, believing what she does and telling people about it, pretty woman like her? No, not violent, and I don't think schizophrenic. Still, we'd better keep a watch on her ... right, and that was a close call. A rape or a suicide before the new facilities grant review is all we'd need. All right, goodbye, Mitchell."

Mary crumbled. They really think I'm mad, she thought. Here is best? God, *no*, can't be, can't stay here ... *can't!* Yet she knew the director might be right about her chances on the streets were she to run off. Everything was still too hazy: she had no idea where to seek real help, no idea of family, friends, place, or purpose, only a firm but filmy sense of identity, and that she must get to the mountains. Or (her train of thought always ran this way, like a toy locomotive on a slow track that comes around and around) failing that, she must end her life. After all, she thought before the evening pill took over, she'd died before. Maybe in order to get to the mountains, she'd have to go around again.

For several days Mary skipped her outing. She just lay on her bed, concentrating on nothingness, hoping that might help her achieve it. But she was too strong, and they made her eat; she'd live forever this way. Eventually her sloth made her stiff. She realized that to kill herself, she'd have to have strength, so she lumbered outside again. Feeling one hundred years old, she faced the fading day, paced the weedy yard a few times, then crumpled into the old dinette chair that someone had carried outside and no one had bothered to bring back in. All the others sat out front where they could watch the buses, the cars, and the pimps parading into the bar down the block. No one else sat out by the vacant lot, or even went there much, so she was startled when a voice tried on a hopeful, gentle "Hi."

Mary twirled to face the speaker and raised her hands, then dropped them. She recognized the tall, gangly young man named Howard. He was articulate, and she'd first wondered if he worked there, but the nurses' demeanor showed that he was another resident. Howard walked downtown early most days for coffee and came back after dinner, so she seldom saw him. She'd overheard that he liked to hang out at either a bar or a strip joint where the staff looked after him and gave him small jobs to do for a dollar or two. She wondered why he was here at all. "Hello," she returned, the first normal greeting she'd exchanged in nearly a year.

"Mind if I sit by you?" Howard asked, motioning at the alleyway beside her chair, overhung by pigweed.

"It's okay," she said. She noticed that his hand had a palsy, and when he sat, she saw a fearsome scar across his forehead.

"I'm Howard," he said.

"I'm Mary."

"I know." His voice held a deep quaver. "Well, hello, Mary!" He closed his nice, smiling lips over stained false teeth, adjusted his glasses, and lit a cigarette. Then he offered her one, which she declined with a shake of her ratty hair. "What are you in for?" he asked.

"They say I was in a car wreck up in the mountains. Hurt my head, supposedly."

"Oh, me too!" said Howard. "But up in Oregon. Benny fell asleep, and we hit a cattle truck head-on. Benny and Stan were killed. Well, so was I, but I came back. They call it frontal lobe damage."

"I'm sorry about your friends," said Mary.

"Maybe they were the lucky ones," said Howard.

Mary considered that and then went on, "I guess I've come back too, in a way."

After the way the director had responded, she paused before explaining. But Howard won't care, she thought, and she was right. When she told him who she was, he just crooned a long, low "Wooow," followed by a high staccato laugh without a shred of mockery. "Neat!" he summed.

Mary looked hard at Howard. He was skinny, and his features were small, almost childlike. He looked younger than his thirty-odd years, and his face, ringed by a downy, patchy beard, had a pleasant aspect in spite of its ravages.

"How long have you been here, Howard?"

"Uhhhhh . . . almost ten years, I guess."

Mary caught her breath and spurted, "Ten years! Why? You're okay, you're not confined . . . why don't you go somewhere else? How do you stand it?" Then she was afraid she had offended him, giving away her disgust for what was, after all, his home.

But he just said, "It's not so bad. True—nobody makes me stay, but there's nowhere else to go. I tried the streets, and that didn't work at all. I have my jobs and friends down on Colfax, and adequate meals and a bed here. My dad's Social Security pays for it, and they give me enough spending cash for smokes. I can panhandle if I need more. Not a bad deal, really."

"But, my God, it's so depressing!" She noticed that Howard

wore the same motley collection of clothes as all the rest. Anything of your own was soon stolen from the laundry. "Is it good enough for you?"

"My family used to ask me that," he replied after a thoughtful drag, "and make suggestions." He said that last word slowly, carefully: *Sug-gest-ions*. "Finally, they realized this *is* home for me, and they gave up. I feel safe here. And, Mary, I just don't notice the things I saw when I first came—I look right through the others. I get along with the nurses. I read, go out, watch TV—I like my soaps." He laughed.

Mary smiled.

"I used to want a girlfriend," he said. "In fact, I was married once . . . I think I was, anyway." He considered that, looked a little doubtful, and said, "But I guess the meds have shot my li-*bee*-do." He laughed his singular laugh that began as a crow's caw and ended in a starling's wheedle. To Mary's horrified look, he said, "You'll get used to it too."

"I *won't!*" she nearly shouted. "I mean, I'm sorry if this is your home and it suits you, then fine. I admire you for adapting." Mary failed to notice that her words were flowing almost as before. "But I *can't* stay, and I refuse to think I might get used to it. I'm not *supposed* to be here!"

Howard started to speak, his voice caught on phlegm, he cleared his throat and began again. "Excuse me, Mary—so who *is* 'supposed' to be here?" He raised one thin eyebrow as in mild reproof, and his hand shook as he took a smoke, keeping his gaze on her.

Mary said she was sorry for putting it like that.

"It's okay," Howard said. "I'm just saying there's worse places to be—like Fort Logan. I tried to kill myself there. In fact, I did—I jumped out of the window onto my head and died, but it just came back around again, like after the wreck. It always does . . ." He showed Mary the scars on his skinny, shaking wrists. "It always starts over again with my dream before the accident. So why go anywhere else?"

Mary began to understand: he was trapped in his own predicament as much as in this place, so maybe it wasn't so bad after all. Still, the thought of his suicide attempts quickened her pulse.

The next afternoon, Mary and Howard met again, and for several days after that. He repeated himself, especially when he tried to tell her about his dream before the wreck, in mythic terms, like an epic poem. He believed the dream foretold the outcome. When Mary reminded him that he'd already told her this story—she could repeat it back to him in its precise, stylized stanzas—he cawed and said, "See? Frontal lobe! My short-term memory is shot. Hah!"

"Howard—" Mary began.

He gave her his attention and his quizzical look.

"I'm thinking of taking my life, to get out of here. Will you help me, or at least tell me how?"

"NO!" Howard spurted. "No, *don't*, Mary. You're so pretty, and you're smart. Anyway, it doesn't work. Don't, don't, don't—please don't!"

"But it's the only way out I can see," Mary said, and began to cry softly.

Howard placed his hand on her shoulder, his tremor matching its soft convulsions. "It's no way at all. Why can't *you* go somewhere else?"

Mary gathered herself. She knew the nurse would come for her soon. "I *am* confined here, Howard. Besides, with the pills, I can't think . . . maybe I couldn't anyway. I don't know where I could go except that I've got to get up *there* someday"—she waved her hand toward Mount Evans—"that's where they found me, that's where I was going, I don't know why. I thought if I could die . . . see, I've died before, and—"

"You too, eh? Wow. But, Mary, you can't get to the mountains that way—except back to your wreck, and then you'd probably end up here again or, worse, in Fort Logan. It always goes back to the wreck. You know Tim, down the hall? Motorcycle. He says the same thing. And my brother says I can't get anywhere by suicide, and I guess he's right. Hey! If you want to go to the mountains, you oughta go with him. He's always going up there."

"Is he there now?" Mary asked.

"I don't know. He lives on the West Coast, shows up here most summers. I haven't heard from him yet this spring. At least I don't think I have. Hah! Like I said, my memory's not so hot."

"Doesn't sound as if I should hold my breath for him."

"Yeah, well. But, Mary, if you really want to go up there"—he gestured toward the Front Range, golden through the afternoon smog—"why not just go?"

"How?" Mary implored, frustrated.

"Take a bus to Idaho Springs, the ski train to Winter Park, hitchhike—*whatever*."

"But the meds . . ."

"Don't you know how to deal with them?" Howard asked. "I thought everyone did. You just dry out your mouth on your sleeve, fake a swallow, hide them under your tongue, and spit 'em out when no one's watching. The ones who don't like 'em trade 'em for cigarettes with the ones who do, or sell them on the street." This had never occurred to Mary. "On the other hand," Howard continued, forgetting the earlier thread of the conversation, "that's how Wendell killed himself last year: saved up a dozen double doses of Thorazine and took them all at once with a forty-ouncer of malt liquor . . ."

Mary's sudden interest brought him back.

"Oh, Mary!" he said. "I forgot . . . I shouldn't have told you that. *Don't* do what Wendell did, will you?"

She promised him she wouldn't, at least for now.

The scent of ozone and damp dust foretold the thunderstorm about to claim the day. Mary and Howard both felt its freshness and tried to stay outside for the skywash, but a nurse insisted that they come in and dry off for dinner. As they parted to head for their rooms, Howard said, "But I wish you'd stick around. You make this place nicer. Plus," he added, "you're mighty pretty."

"That's sweet. Thanks for getting me talking, Howard. You're nice too. But anyway, I thought your libido was shot." The thought of flirting in this repository made them both laugh, and almost cry. The warmth lasted, and though she clammed up again, Mary felt almost human through one meal and into sleep. But that night she dreamed of lovers in cribs with party hats on, and in the morning she felt sadder than ever, burdened with the new thought: Whatever do people who fall in love in a place like this *do*? Or in minds like these?

To love and not be able to do anything about it was her meditation that afternoon. But I know all about that from before, she told herself. There was no one else to tell. Howard hadn't come back from town. Perhaps he'd already forgotten their talks. More likely, she thought, he was reluctant to interfere with her clear-minded time and risk helping to drive her away. Or maybe he feared getting too close, feeling just as hopeless. This thought took her back to her theme—futility—and that made up her mind.

The next morning, after an oblivious and dreamless sleep, Mary began. She faked the swallowing of her pills, spitting them out each day and night thereafter and hoarding them in her bra. After a week she had more vitality and clarity, and she enjoyed her talks with Howard all the more. But her self-awareness also picked up, making her situation even less tolerable. By the twentieth day, she still hadn't decided which way to go, but she had stockpiled plenty of pills.

Then, on the twenty-first, ambition and anger reached a critical mass, and Mary simply walked away. One way or the other, she told herself over and over, I am leaving today. She taped a simple folded message to Howard's door. "Thank you," it read. "I'll always be grateful, and I'll watch for your brother up there. Good luck! M." Then she walked out into her alley, turned left, right past Mount Pisgah Pentecostal, and kept on going. But she took her pills with her, in case her escape should fail.

When the nurse went to fetch Mary for dinner, she was not to be found in her old chair by the vacant lot. A search party in the neighborhood failed to find her, or anyone who had noticed her. The sheriff and the Denver police drew blanks as well. When they closed out their brief effort that night—after all, there seemed to be no family to notify—Mary was sleeping in the back of a long-haul trucker's cab on the way up Loveland Pass. For the first few hairpins she slumbered, never minding the semi's labored passage through the gears. Then suddenly she started to the driver's voice. "Lady, wake up. I'm getting drowsy. I'll have to catch a night's sleep before heading on. Maybe you want to try for another ride."

Mary came awake, disbelieving, to an alpine scene—even in the dusk she could tell it was much like the last sight she'd seen before the walls of Denver General. "Oh!" she cried, then "Oh" and "Oh!" again. "Where . . . *mountains* . . . oh, God, am I *here?*" Mary's face found the space between laughing and weeping where they run together, making the driver nervous.

He was a skinny weed of a man with a goat's beard and a ball cap on a bald top, but she had barely registered him. "It's just Loveland Pass, ma'am. It'll be full dark soon, and you might wanna try to get a ride down the other side before then. Anyway, I'll need my bed. But you should take care. You're too good-looking to be up here on your own."

Mary gathered herself and mumbled her thanks. "Now, I'm a Christian man," the driver went on, "and if you're who you say you are—well, you're okay with me and you might be just fine anyway, but I wouldn't take it for granted. Why don't you try that family across the road in the rest area? Where was it you were trying to get to, anyway? You never really said."

Mary had caught the ride at a truck stop near the Mousetrap, a big concrete tangle where I-25 and I-70 mix it up in West Denver, having walked all the way there through rush-hour streets. She fell asleep so soon after stepping up into the Peterbilt, muttering in her exhaustion, that the driver had put her to bed in the back of the cab. He hadn't learned anything about her, only that she desperately wanted a ride westward. As they rolled, she spoke in her sleep.

Now she said, "Here."

"What?" said the driver.

"Thank you very much." Mary opened the cab door and stepped down onto the running board, then the roadside, then into the soft turf. She stood there, sucking the alpine air in gulps, as if doing so again and again could erase all those stale and wasted days. Then she walked on down the road. The driver, thinking she was headed for the Porta-Potty in the rest area, simply shrugged and took over the berth himself. But the cabin smelled of Mary, and he slept poorly, whether from concern or desire or both.

Having no idea where she was going, insensate to the rising damp of the high-country night, and hypnotized by the very presence of the peaks and the fragrance of the flowers, Mary continued along the edge of the old asphalt. Ecstatic with the boulders, the yellow woolly sunflowers, the spongy green tundra that stretched away into the dark fir forests below, she exulted. But fear of being found invaded her brain, marred the pleasure, and sent her off the road, across the trackless tundra.

Darkness took over the alpine, along with cold. It's all right, Mary thought. If I die here tonight, maybe I can go back, way back . . . Just to be *here* . . . Her mind, struggling for clarity in the limpid air, still made no sense, found no focus but the here and now. The scaling heights, the plunging glacial troughs. She trod on, her flimsy sneakers wicking the moist humors of the montane turf. This night held no terror for one released at last from a darker, colder night. Sweet breath of silky phacelia filled Mary's freshened head, its brush of florets deepest purple in the last of the alpine night, now going black.

14

Blue hyacinths began heavenly, turned cloying, then wilted around the borders of Sterling Library as the pale violet wisteria spread its heavy scents and vines over college courtyards. The brief New England spring hit Mead with the fresh savor of new love, but too soon, as infatuation often does, hinted at a coming sultry fatigue. The onrushing summer found Noni Blue still fresh in his fancy—no ennui there, and the prospect of parting after graduation gave no joy.

The hyacinths unsettled him, too, bringing to mind his mother and her beloved beds of spring bulbs. Nothing made her sparkle like the first burst of color from the crocuses and snowdrops, daffodils and scillas she nurtured, dividing and spreading their bulbs every few falls. Especially the hyacinths, her favorites. Nothing, that is, except Molly. Once Molly was gone, the flowerbeds might as well have been weedlots, which they soon became. Bulbs are persistent. They continued to spatter color among the pigweed and bindweed that tried to take over—a dwarf tulip here, a scraggly blue bunch of muscari over there. But these survivors were neither seen nor looked after. The coddled gardens of Yale reminded Mead of what his mother had once been like and was no more. He mulched his mind instead with Noni's rich and overriding presence, while it lasted.

Noni's finals were finished, and she had a little time for James before the scrum of graduation week. One night, they took a volume of Carson's field journal back to her room. Mead read it to her in bed, where they lay with tumblers of jug wine in their hands and the college cat on their laps. He wondered if it would be like this over the years, but made sure to keep the thought silent for a change. Out loud, he asked, "Isn't this a heck of a data book? By all rights, it should be nothing but dry observations, species lists, and invoices."

"Amazing," Noni agreed, as engrossed in Carson's progress as he was. "Does he make it to Estes with Ruth and Elbert? More to the point, does he make it with Ruth?"

"There's a problem or two. Elbert tries to ditch October at Little America, but Ruth and the kids make him go back. The kids adulate Carson, who takes them behind the motel to look for horny toads. He likes them too, but in measure. He resolves never to have either kids or dogs, at least not on the road, and to stay on the road."

"And? Get to the good bit."

"Well, they get to Estes Park in the end, and I like to think October and Ruth share a lovely tumble in the Wheeldons' rented log cabin while Elbert and the kids are off fishing. But he doesn't actually kiss and tell."

"Darn."

"I know. I was hoping for a little soft-core, too. Anyway, he was sorry to see Ruth go, and I know how he felt. When do you have to go, and have you decided where to?"

"Well, James, it seems your Mr. Carson isn't the only one going to Colorado."

Mead looked up from the book and waited.

"I heard today—thanks to Professor Winchester, I've been accepted to work with Dr. Freulich on butterfly ecology."

"At Stanford?"

"Eventually, maybe, but starting out at his summer lab at Gothic, in the Rockies."

Mead stared for a moment, then squeezed out a feeble "Fantastic." A heavy beat, then, "Butterflies, yet. Maybe you'll run into our man out there. Smile like a sunflower, and tell him hi for George and me."

"I'll visit my folks for a week or two, then fly to Denver. Dr. Freulich's assistant, Dave O'Leary, will meet me and take me up to the lab. I'm excited."

Mead smiled, more or less, and grunted.

"You sound a little less so," Noni said.

"Well . . . I am, I guess, for you. Great opportunity, beautiful place from what George says. And a fine teacher, so I hear, for all his fame." His eyes scraped the bedspread. "I'll miss you, Noni."

"Me too, you know." In a lame effort to salvage the mood, James crooned off-key a snatch of the old song: "'Will I see you, in Sep-te-em-ber, or lose you . . .'"

"Oh, stop! Don't be melodramatic."

Mead was taken aback by her quick-change act. Even as he realized he didn't know her very well, he saw new planes and hollows in her face. Beautiful, he thought, but the new Noni only filed his feelings rawer.

"Sorry," he said. "It's just sort of short notice. I mean . . . then what?" Both were embarrassed and short with each other.

"Who knows? This has been great, James, and it may be great later. But we were never going to worry about the hereafter, remember?"

So much for the cat, Mead thought as it leaped off the bed. "I know. But will you miss me?"

"I already *said* I would." Then, softer, "And long for you on cold Colorado nights, I do not doubt."

Mead softened a little at that and squeezed her shoulder. Of course they'd both been there before—the sweet young love, the rude interruption. Noni had started at Smith, transferred to Yale when it went coed. Mead knew all the jokes: Smith women were supposed to be both chilly and horny, brainy and dense. Noni was brainy and warm and eager, *horny* didn't do it justice. But she was much more besides.

"Anyway," he said, brighter, "we might yet have a chance to meet up at Gothic."

"Really?" Noni's magnetic eyes and lips flickered at the news.

"Well, it's a long shot, but maybe. Winchester himself goes there most years, you know; he and Jane have a cabin near the Freulichs'. He's said I might be able to come out too, if my project is well in hand and relates at all to the habitats out there. *And* if I have some grant support and the committee's blessing. Lots of ifs."

"Great, James! But what project could you do out there?"

"It's not in hand. But, relevantly, I have to go feed the roaches now. Want to come? You never have, you know."

"Um. Well, sure, why not? Lovely encore to a lovely evening."

"*Now* who's sarcastic? But, good! You'll love 'em, believe me."

Maples dangled their yellow tassels in the fresh spring air as the couple walked up Prospect Avenue, passed a walled cemetery of great age, and moved on toward the lab. Perhaps that May air enhanced the scent of Noni's Polynesian hair, but Mead was intoxicated by it. Yet as they arrived outside the roach room, its own odor reasserted itself, and Noni's wrinkled nose seconded the impression. She gritted her teeth as Mead opened and closed the heavy outer door. "It's so dark, James—can we have a light on?"

"No—whatever you do, don't touch the light switch! That would wreck the photoperiod and phototaxis experiments we have in progress, and I would be *very* unpopular. Here, we have to use this darkroom safety light for the roach work. I could have fed them by daylight, but as you know, I'm observing their nocturnal activity. Well, here they are. Noni, meet my friends. Roaches, this is Noni."

"Oh, James—I mean—God . . . I knew they were big, but . . ." Noni stepped back half a step. "They are vast!"

"Big bugs," Mead concurred. "Except that as George insists, they are not *bugs*, which are strictly only members of the order Heteroptera. They're big blattids." He pulled back the lid of one container, and a score of two-inch mega-roaches scuttled about the cage. "But finally," he said, "rather mouselike and kind of cute. Imagine the sheen of soft pelage instead of hard chitin, and you have a lovable little furry instead of a hateful brown bug. Nor are they cockroaches . . ."

"Oh, James, I know all that . . . don't forget, I've taken Winchester's entomology class too. I just managed to be absent for the roach room field trips."

"All the better that you're doing it now, then, with your own personal guide. So you probably also know that roaches do little actual harm, serve as powerful research subjects, have survived many millions of years of evolution virtually unchanged, and therefore may be regarded as some of earth's most successful creatures."

"You've learned that spiel well, James. Has the prof tested you on it?"

"Nah, just practicing for the dreaded Griffin. But you know, these animals have personalities all their own. I think the great size of *Blaberus giganteus* just makes it easier to relate to them one on one, you know?"

"Mmmm. I see what you mean . . . sorta. I think I could really warm up to these guys. It's just the combination of their *heft* and all those scratching tarsi and rustling wings against the plastic. That, and the smell. Does that get to you?"

"To paraphrase George, 'what smell?' No, I forget about it. But I finally figured out what it reminds me of."

"Do tell! For my part, I get notes of rotten apple and a tincture of burnt oatmeal."

"Not far off. When I was a boy, my folks used to take my brothers and me to Denver for the National Western Stock Show and Rodeo. I remember that when we got near the Denver Coliseum, there was a red-and-white-checked grain tower for the Ralston Purina Company. The malty, sort of molasses-and-sawdust smell that came out of there, mixing with the manure reek of the stockyards across the tracks, made a perfume not entirely unlike that of our friends here. Now, every time I get a whiff, I see that checkerboard dog food tower in my mind's eye."

"Nice. So evocative, smells." Mead nudged her hair with his nose. "So," she asked, "have you convinced His Nemesisness yet that roaches are peachy?"

"Heck, no. I'd love to lure him in here to see what I'm doing with them, and then leave and shut the door. But I'll never get him anywhere near."

"Cruel, but suitable. Nice to imagine, anyway."

"The experiments, actually, are going better than I expected. The roaches are very tractable and easily observed."

"Do you think there's a thesis in it? And are there big roaches in Colorado?"

"A double negatory on that, Good Buddy, as the truckers say. And another: no grant money in sight. Besides, I want to get out of the lab and into the habitat. I'm really a field man, you know."

"As a confirmed field woman, I surely see your point. In fact, it is my earnest hope that when we are both out, standing in our respective fields, we will be able to find a soft, flat meadow in between—with a few bushes for cover."

Mead yaffled and squirmed. "Ooh, such a thought," he said, and then, "but in the meantime, I'll make do trysting with my sweet nocturnal charges. However, a sad task looms."

"What's that?" Noni too wriggled at the imagery she had wrought, and she grew eager to trade the roach room for her bedroom in Branford College.

"See this cageful? They've gotta be liquidated, having been spoiled for other trials by my experiments. We need the room."

"Sad! That won't be easy for you, with the none-too-scientific attachment you've made. Can't they at least be pickled for dissection in 101?"

"Maybe, but there's quite an overstock already. I keep trying to think of a way to keep them from being killed to no purpose. I suppose I could send them home to Mom."

"Just to lighten the relationship—yes, that should help. Well, whatever you do, just don't bring them to bed, okay? A sexy itinerant is one thing, and roaches are fine in their place, which is here, but . . ."

"No worry there, love. I've no intention of sharing you with either the esteemed blattids *or* that randy rambler tonight. And, having raised the question yourself, and it being *late late late*, how about relieving the loneliness in my tower tonight? You've never yet graced my chilly chamber, so howzabout one more first?"

"Well . . . will you read me to sleep with your research notes?"

"No."

"All right, then."

15

Groans and sighs escaped from the bleak stairwell of Kline Tower as Mead ascended toward Frank Griffin's lair, skipping the elevator to delay the inevitable. All sides of all floors looked alike but for different cartoons, calligraphed nameplates, and taped-up graven images of idols affixed to brick walls and windows of TAs' doors in a vain attempt to humanize the place. Only the growth chambers, with their green shades, looked alive, and those were questionable, containing mostly tobacco plants. "Handy subjects for research," mumbled the investigators, cashing their grant checks from Philip Morris and R. J. Reynolds. Mead, no smoker, sneered, then remembered a weekend outing with Noni when he'd admired the handsome long barns up the Connecticut River valley. Upon learning that they existed for drying a premium local tobacco crop used for cigar wrappers, he'd put it down to one more of life's little paradoxes. Here was another: how architects designing a house for the study of life could come up with such a lifeless pile as this.

He reached 1107 and knocked. A fuzzy-headed, skinny technician of no obvious gender or social graces turned on its stool, asked, "Um?" then pointed to an inner chamber. James echoed "Um" and went in. Frank Griffin didn't rise. Reclined in a vinyl-covered swivel chair, he rotated several degrees toward the door in sole recognition of Mead's arrival. His round, sparsely haired brow, fiercely dilating nostrils, and fixed sneer (or was it a leer?) greeted the visitor as a pit bull might welcome a kitten.

Pointing with his cranial crest, the don indicated a hard seat for the young scholar. "Mead," he said; just "Mead." James felt apprehension, but he was no more intimidated than a bull by a rodeo clown, and in fact his opinion of the grants committee chairman dropped even lower, given his absence of common manners. Over the next few minutes that opinion rose to "clever fellow" and dropped to "conceited bigot," making several stops along the way as Griffin entered his soliloquy (you couldn't call it a conversation) into the afternoon's wilting archive.

"So you see, Mead, I haven't published all these papers and symposia, garnered my grants, and achieved my rank by playing nursemaid to nature boys and girls" (bloated ass, Mead thought). "I know you think I am on your case, but I assure you, I bear you no ill will. Believe me, Mead—if you want to act as chambermaid to those disgusting vermin for the rest of your academic career, such as it is, that's your concern. But I genuinely have your scientific future in mind, as well as the reputation of the Yale biology degree, when I say that you'd do well to fit into the program, stick to the mold, and toe the course" (malapropping twit). "Count on this: you'll thank me for it in the end."

"How do you mean, sir?"

"I mean this: stay in New Haven this summer. Demonstrate your idea of rigor. Do it with those foul cockroaches if you must—"

"Not *cock*roaches, Professor. They're—"

"Bloody bugs! But *do* it. If you succeed in modest measure, and *if* you pass your qualifying exams next fall, then maybe—*may-be*—we'll talk about funds for a turkey trot out to that putative 'laboratory,' that shabby set for a spaghetti western, that radicals' playpen, next summer. Or I might be able to find you a suitable, if minor, project in my laboratory" (that'll be the goddamned day that I die). "Of course, if I attain the chairmanship, I'll have to drop your committee" (or drop dead, I don't care, just get off).

"Thank you anyway, Professor" (all to hell). "But were you aware that twenty percent of the papers in the latest issue of *Evolution* stemmed from research performed at Rocky Mountain Biological Laboratory?"

"What, that nature lovers' tabloid? I am not impressed, Mr. Mead. Nor, when one of its chief contributors, who does so-called research on flutterbies at your beloved Rocky Mountain Biological Laboratory—a slander on the word!—appears on my television set and espouses doomsday, am I impressed. Some scientist! He hasn't even enough faith in science to trust it to solve his pet 'population problem'!"

"But have you actually read Professor Freulich's papers, or his book? And wasn't it Thomas Malthus's paper on population growth that inspired both Wallace and Darwin, independently, to come up with the mechanism of natural selection?"

"Enough! I have papers to write, a lecture to prepare, a grants committee meeting, and serious students to advise, who know a 'mechanism' when they see one and could run hoops around any ecologist over in Osborn when it comes to natural selection. You butterfly boys are all alike—pinko sentimentalists. You'd rather seize the headlines, scare the populace, wreck the economy, and play ringmaster to roaches than do any useful biology."

Mead detected a shudder at the word *roaches*.

"And I suggest that you, Mead, have larger lacunae in your scientific reading than I! Damned impertinent of you to suggest otherwise."

"But I didn't—"

"Insupportable! Even in these days of thugs and sluts in the colleges and declining standards of admission" (elitist conehead) "your presence here *amazes* me. Must've been some sort of regional recruitment quota. Oh, aren't you from the border country? Maybe your mother is a Mexican" (did he really say that?). "And let me tell you about affirmative action . . ."

Mead didn't want to hear it, and he was running out of epithets, let alone the patience for being looked through and not heard. "Excuse me, sir," (you scum-sucking toad—no, toads are cool—you scum-sucking scumbag) "I have a lecture at three. But I wish you would reconsider. I think a summer's hard work at Gothic would greatly enhance my studies."

"Out, Mead."

"At least I'd like to invite you to visit the roach colony one of these evenings and see for yourself what we're doing with them."

Griffin went pale.

"Could you come up this evening? At about seven the larger males are at their most active, the glossy females are feeding, and the soft white nymphs are prolific these days. In fact, Professor Winchester considers our insects to be at their aesthetic best at this season."

"OUT! Come see me in September with manuscript in hand, significant statistics, specimen slides and SEM images, and a realistic plan for adequate research that will not unduly stretch your meager gifts . . . or else you can return to Arizona, where I am sure Geronimo U. would welcome your insolence, indolence, and insects. I hear they eat grasshoppers out there."

"New Mexico," Mead muttered as he shut the door behind him, knowing it would leave Griffin's room, its air conditioner fritzed, even hotter than he'd found it. He rode the elevator down, walked out of the banklike lobby and onto the Science Hill lawn. For some distance he pounded the turf, imagining Griffin beneath his heels with every step. Then he walked up to a particularly derivative gargoyle on the physics hall and snorted into its astonished face: "Goddamned entomophobic dork!"

Mead headed over to the insect lab in search of Steve Manton, a forestry grad student from New Jersey who had fallen in love with insects. Mead knew that Steve would be wrapping up a lab practical exam. From halfway down the hall he heard Winchester's sonorous voice. As Mead entered the lab, the prof was remarking on Manton's mounting of a moth.

"I can see, Mr. Manton," he said, "that you have chosen to spread this noctuid in the ventral position. That is an interesting and unusual approach. I assume you've done so in order to more easily examine the tibial tufts of the tarsi?"

"Uhhhh . . ." said Manton. "Oh God . . . you mean I mounted this thing upside down?" He hadn't intended to set the specimen topsy-turvy, of that Mead was sure. Winchester knew it too, but there was none but the gentlest reproach in his quip. Manton heard only support. What a difference from Griffin, Mead thought as he stood in the doorway unobserved. It made him grateful all over again to be at Yale with Winchester.

"Well, that wraps it up, Steve. You pass. Extra points for originality. What are your plans for the summer?"

"Um, I don't know yet, Professor W." Manton spoke slowly, overenunciating. "I should help my dad. What? Oh, he's a distributor for Schaefer. You'd think I could get a deal on the beer for my buddies, but it never worked out that way. There's work for me if I want it, though."

"But?"

"Well, you've got me pretty turned on to bugs."

"Oh, you have a particular fondness for the Heteroptera?"

"*And* all the others. Anyway, too late, you already said I passed."

"I wish I could get you an assistant curatorship in the museum," Winchester mused, ever alert for a willing preparer. "So many specimens . . . But I've got funding for only one over the summer, and James has that nailed down."

"That's okay, Prof, thanks anyway. Jersey City's not so bad." Manton smiled wistfully at the thought, his broad, plastic mouth spreading so as to outstretch his sparse beginner's beard.

"Maybe I could take you on in the museum next fall," Winchester continued. "If, that is, you would be amenable to suppressing your experimental leanings and to set Lepidoptera in the conventional manner."

Mead gave himself away with a laugh.

"Eavesdropping, James? We have no secrets here, unless it's Mr. Manton's innovation."

"Hey, Jimbo, how ya doin'? Did you bring the beer?"

"Heck, no—that's supposed to be your department. Work on your dad, will you? But maybe I should have. It might help me forget a certain disagreeable figure whose name begins in *Grif* and ends in *fin* and goes nowhere nice in between."

"I'm sorry about that, James," Winchester said.

"What, the beer?"

"No, the bear. I feared he would turn you down for support. I really had hoped to have you at Gothic this summer. Next year, perhaps, if our NSF grant comes through. You'll enjoy it even more after a summer in balmy New Haven."

"Yeah, right."

"Remember, Charles Darwin was forced to remain in Plymouth harbor for months before the *Beagle* finally set sail on December 27, and even then it got stuck on a rock in the bay. His Griffin was the Irish Sea in winter. But he waited it out—and look what happened." Winchester's ginger-and-silver beard twitched at the great conclusion, and his blue eyes shone, as they did every time he spoke of Darwin.

"Great," James said. "But somehow 'Connecticut roaches' doesn't have the same ring as 'Galapagos finches.' *Are* there any roaches there, by the way?"

"Not as big as the tortoises. Yes, I suppose my little Darwinian allegory offers little solace for you, especially with Noni going to Gothic."

"I didn't know you knew we were dating," said Mead.

Manton snorted.

"Have you ever seen your face in her presence?" asked Winchester. "Or hers in yours? Lampyrids in your eyes."

Manton chuckled again at the reference to fireflies, then snatched it back when Mead failed to laugh.

"Darwin suffered heart palpitations when confined to port for so long," said George. "I hope that doesn't happen to you, James!" Winchester was in a witty mood; it must have been the belly-up miller moth. "And remember," he went on, his eyes wider, brighter, "even he had trouble living fully in the present toward the end of the *Beagle* junket. He couldn't keep his mind off Shropshire and his beloved cousin and fiancée."

Manton, who had recently read Irving Stone's *The Origin* at George's suggestion, piped up, "Oh, right—then she went and married some other dude while he was gone."

"Thanks, you guys," said Mead. "You're most helpful."

"But he did happily marry his other cousin, Emma Wedgwood, eventually."

"Super," said Mead. "Only, all my cousins are already married."

Winchester grew serious. "By the way, James, I really do appreciate your attention to the colony this summer. As you know, those insects are valuable, and I need to trust that they're in good hands in order to go away myself. You've come to be rather fond of them, haven't you? I thought so—no more odor, eh? And have you managed to dispose of that surplus colony yet? What, three or four dozen, are they?"

"About that many. No, not yet, but I will. Maybe one of the schools will take them ..."

"Yes. It would be a pity to kill them, or waste them. Fine animals indeed. Well, you do your best. I'm off home, gentlemen. A lift for anyone?"

"I think I'll troll the streets for a pizza and a pitcher," said Mead.

"Legend has it pizza was invented in New Haven—" began Winchester.

"Hamburgers too, right?" asked Manton.

"Actually, yes. You know 'the place where Louie dwells' in 'The Whiffenpoof Song'?"

"Whatever. Making me hungry. How about you, Jimbo?"

"Never more. Let's go."

Mead was hungry all right, and he wanted that beer in a bad way. But he was particularly ready to vent—and Manton was a good listener, especially when eating. In the end they walked all the way to the old Italian section of East Haven, which really was the putative birthplace of pizza. From a deep brick oven came a large prosciutto and tomato pie that the two of them would soon convert completely. By the third slice, Manton noticed that Mead was biting and chewing with a vengeance—just the right word, in the event. By the fourth, a plan began to form in the back of Mead's reptile brain, and by the bottom of the pitcher of Schaefer it had reached the front.

Manton noticed an actual smile creeping out of Mead's glower. "So what's up, Jimbo?"

"How'd you like to skip that beer truck in Jersey City this summer, Steve?"

16

Richard Phelps and Frank Griffin paced down Prospect Street toward their weekly tea. Their assignation always began with noncommittal small talk: university gossip or reports of weekend forays to antique shops in the Berkshires or resorts in the Thousand Islands or some such family outing. But this time Griffin only grunted at Phelps's pro forma entrée.

"So we thought we'd visit Mystic Seaport at last," Phelps was saying. "Elizabeth and the kids all like the seaside and sea lore, I've just reread *Moby-Dick*, and we've always meant to go there. It's that restored whaling village, you know, near Groton, where the submarines live."

"Hmm," muttered Griffin.

"But on the way, Sam spotted a sign for a steam train running up the valley. He's crazy about trains, and he couldn't be persuaded that it would wait for another time. You know how obdurate a teenager can be, and we're just thankful he's willing to do anything at all with the family anymore."

"Uh, right."

"So we rode the train upriver and took the riverboat back down. It made for a very satisfactory outing, with a good lunch at the midpoint landing. And after the inevitable recriminations about missing out on Mystic yet again and how it's been there since Ahab and will wait for us a little longer, there wasn't a cross word! Even Sherrie enjoyed it, though I really think what saved her from a sulk was a rather overly interested conductor-cum-deckhand. Given his attentions, she wouldn't have cared where she was. So a good time was had by all, as they say. We didn't hear the dread word *bor-ing* once. Good value, too—ten bucks each, up and down. Has your family ever done it? Frank?"

"Mm? Done what?" The upward lilt of his colleague's voice alerted Griffin to the fact that he'd been asked something, but truly, he'd barely registered a word before "ever done it?"

Dick's monologue had taken them past the colonial cemetery, past Woolsey Hall, with its war memorials to glorious fallen Yalies, dead for all that, past Architecture, to the Berkeley quad and, opposite that, the white clapboard house called the Elizabethan Club. Phelps held open the oaken front door of the "Lizzie" for an exiting couple, then blocked Griffin. "Oh, never mind," he said. "I was just blabbing on. But if you're going to be so abstracted, we might as well call it off this time. I've plenty to do, and I don't fancy conversation with a brick wall."

Frank apologized, an event rare enough to raise Phelps's eyebrows. "I'm sorry, Dick, I'll get off it." His slick dark hair, what there was of it, shone off his sweaty, bulbous brow as a grimace gave away his mood. "It's just that I've recently entertained that poseur, Mead, and he's tickled my hackles yet again."

"Ah," said Phelps. "I think you mean 'raised.' I would say that you two are less than simpatico."

"*That's* an understatement!"

"But really, Frank, don't you think you're a bit hard on the lad? He tries to be civil, and you gun him down every time. And why do you call him a poseur? I find him bright, accomplished, and sincere—promising, too." Phelps's blue agate eyes fired a beam of some intensity at his partner, giving him notice that a thoughtful reply was expected. He'd been intending to quiz Griffin on the matter anyway, though hardly cherishing the prospect. He stood aside, and the two of them entered the hall and doffed their coats.

The pair of professors, such a seeming mismatch—the one tweedy and giving off the essence of the typical untidy indoor forester, the other all business and white lab coat no matter what he wore; one trim, fit, and glowing from frequent field trips and squash matches, the other paunchy and pasty from a sedentary indoor existence; the first relaxed in his skin, the second carrying his as a hermit crab tugs at his shell to follow—stepped into the clubroom. Hardly boon companions at other times, they had scarcely missed a Tuesday tea in term time for years, not even when the rest of the campus was shut down by the student takeovers after Nixon and Kissinger's Cambodian massacre.

They took their seats—that is, as soon as a steward flushed out an unknowing young probationary member who had made the serious error of usurping one of their usual hardwood seats by a herringbone fireplace. Phelps, across a hammered copper table, awaited Griffin's reply.

"Tea!" Griffin ordered as the steward attended, "with milk. And lemon pound cake. Richard?" It was a formality. They always had the same thing. Griffin knew it, Phelps knew it, and the steward knew it too.

Phelps thought the ritual a bit silly after all these years, but he played his part. "The same, thank you." The aged steward turned away. "Now: Mead."

"Well, hell, Richard. The boy's a true provincial. He's got no sense of rigor, of real scholarship. He just wants to join our estimable colleague . . ."

"Careful, Frank, you're talking about my squash partner."

". . . our *estimable* colleague out there at his dude ranch excuse for a laboratory, come back with a merit badge in nature study, and get a doctorate of philosophy for it. I'll be double-damned if I'm going to grant my imprimatur, let alone departmental funds, for a Yale PhD based on a grammar school scam like that!"

"Frank, Frank . . . you harbor entirely the wrong idea about Gothic, about Winchester, about field studies in general, and especially about young Mr. Mead."

"I doubt it," grumbled Griffin. "You see, Dick, it's not just that I'm on the boy's back. Nor do I entirely disapprove of field studies . . . after all, we need to know *something* about our organisms in their brief state of life so that we might better comprehend their tissues, cells, and molecular constituents in the laboratory."

"I'd have thought it was the other way around," Phelps interjected.

Griffin ignored him. "Also, I recognize George's journeyman contribution to his little corner of biology, and to the institution . . ."

"Well, don't patronize him or anything, Frank. His 'little corner of biology' does happen to comprise the great majority of life on earth. You know very well that the collections he has so astutely assembled and curated are among the most respected anywhere."

"Fine, fine . . . I thought you wanted to talk about the Mead problem?"

"Okay, if you must characterize him that way. So what's the rub?" Phelps asked, taking his first sip of tea as he closed his assertive lips over the rim of the cup on *rub*.

The young assistant professor who had been ejected from his seat glanced over and announced, *"Hamlet*, Act Three, scene one, the so-called nunnery scene: 'Aye, there's the rub.'"

Griffin scowled at him and lowered his voice. "It's just that *I* had to work hard in under-equipped, badly funded labs for *my* degree. And I work hard now, you know I do. Science *is* work. Yet these eco-freaky excuses for students today, in their waffle stompers and sandals (if not bare feet!), seem to think that science should be *fun*." He spit out the word as if it were a bad grape. "Science is not supposed to be fun. Science is meant to *serve*! What's the matter with them, or their teachers, that they don't know that?"

"Well, *I* have fun out there," said Phelps, "and I pity you if you never do."

"I'm not saying it's never enjoyable. There are satisfactions. But these would-be Thoreaus and Lord Byrons have no more sense of service to society than they have work ethic or patriotism. Where will our institutions be after a generation or two of such so-called scholars?"

"Or the tobacco companies," Phelps said, tamping his pipe to make his point.

"What's that?"

"Oh, nothing," said Phelps. "Just an aside on some of your colleagues' sense of service to society. But do you really think things are as bad as all that?"

"Well, they're getting that way. Anyway," Griffin went on, his volume rising, "when the fun and games are over, after the dancing and showers, when we get down to ground zero, who's going to go into the lab prepared to crack the hard nuts of knowledge?"

Derisive laughter rose around them, interrupting the tirade. More than a couple of members had been listening in. The English lecturer, a philologist of minor but growing repute, busily scribbled that last remark into a pocket notebook and loosed another ripple of chortles for his unsolicited response: "The hard nuts of knowledge—brilliant!"

Griffin growled at the eavesdroppers, then continued just above a whisper. "What I mean to say is that this generation of postgraduates—especially after their treasonous behavior over the war—seems to think that their studies should be a lark and an unremitting pleasure. I don't believe that the point of scholarly research is to *enjoy* oneself, though one sometimes might, when applied labor yields the desired results. But a place like this, this—what is it, *Gothic*, for God's sake?—just encourages such a frivolous attitude."

As if it were the evil in question and he was rooting it out with his long, hard teeth, he attacked his lemon pound cake.

"But have you ever been there, Frank? Or to any other field station? The work they do there is often rock-solid, even cutting-edge. For that matter, have you ever been in the field, *period*?"

"Don't like bugs," Griffin muttered through his mouthful.

"Because fieldwork is fun, or can be, though it has its tedious times as well. Besides, it's essential if we're going to have a chance at arresting the global ecological crisis. Can you blame vigorous young students for aiming to take a little delight in learning about the world around them while trying to do their bit to save it?"

"And getting laid every ten minutes while they're at it, I don't doubt. *And* high. Global crisis, my white ass." He took another vicious bite. "Even if there *were* such a thing, their motto would be 'think globally, screw locally.'"

"Come on, Frank, even Nixon seems to believe in conservation. But never mind that. I do believe you are *jealous*! Or just plain envious. Don't you remember grad school? Who had time for hanky-panky every night? And you don't get many good data when you're stoned! You must not be getting enough at home, man. Is that it?"

Griffin swallowed, sucked his tea leaves, and said, "Never worry. Margaret is good to me. But I don't mind saying, I'd take graduate school again, at least that part. And speaking of vigorous young students doing their bit, haven't you seen Mead going gaga over that little Oriental bit? I'll bet he's *doing* it, all right."

Phelps just shook his head and smiled. "I knew you were a xenophobe, Frank, but a sexist one too? That's appalling language about a student." He'd long since given up trying to reform his colleague, and he did his best to ignore his worst warts.

"Hell, maybe you're at least partly right, Dick. Perhaps I am a little envious of the students. Aren't you, ever? No? Liar. Anyway, we shall be spared the resolution of all this, as Mead will *not* be going to Colorado—at least not this summer. Let him *attempt* to do some science, against all odds, in that wretched roach hole of Winchester's. Might as well be something out of Poe."

"Poe never wrote about roaches," said the philologist at the next table. "Cats, rats, and golden bugs, yes, but never cockroaches, I'm afraid. Maybe he should have . . ."

"Oh, stuff it," said Griffin. "We still have to vote on your membership, you know." He shuddered and spilled milk from the pitcher in his hand. Then, turning back to Phelps, "Let's change the subject before it puts me off my tea altogether." Not yet put off, he garfed another big bite of pound cake.

"I can see we'll get nowhere with it anyway," Phelps conceded. "But I predict you'll be surprised by the quality of Mead's work. I think you simply hold a grudge against GW and the whole ecological establishment, not to mention against youth in general, and most of the country, and you're taking it out on James. If you can't show a little fairness, Frank, someone's going to cry foul and remove you from his committee."

"His loss, Dick, I assure you. I'd be delighted to get shed of it. Except that I feel a certain responsibility—onus, even—to drum a little rigor into these prima donna Brownies and Cub Scouts we get these days. Anyway, Mr. Mead will, with any luck, get fed up with those horrid vermin in the heat of August, and he'll retreat to his cow college. *That* would be a favor to everyone involved." Emphatically, the last morsel went down.

"Nasty, Frank. I don't believe you mean it. At any rate, the roaches aren't so bad. Of course they aren't *birds*, but they're not bad. You should ask George or James to introduce you to them personally, show you their ins and outs. I tell you, those viviparous hissing roaches feel crazy when you let them walk all over your palm!"

At that, Griffin choked on his lemon pound cake, coughing so violently that Phelps rose and positioned himself behind his stricken, doubled-up colleague, ready to administer the Heimlich maneuver. Everyone else in the Lizzie, especially the probationary member, looked on expectantly. But Griffin recovered, expelling the soggy crumbs into the hearth. Crisis averted, the onlookers resumed their leather seats, crumpets, chess, and conversation, clearly disappointed by the anticlimactic outcome.

"And as for harboring a grudge," Griffin hacked when he was able, "you're wrong about that, though well I might. I should have been elected, you know. Disappointment never tastes good. Is it my fault I'm not the biggest fan of the Osborn contingent?"

Phelps struggled to think of an honest reply that would not ruin the afternoon. Before he found one, Griffin said, "Now, Richard, prepare to defend yourself, or else to wallow in your own growing grudge over your seemingly interminable losing streak."

"Why, you self-righteous, gloating, sad specimen of a biochemist— you *should* have choked! Just watch out, because one of these days you're going to lose, and lose bad—on or off the board."

Phelps opened the game board and placed the plastic pieces on the table before them. And as the firelight gleamed off the patina of First Folio Shakespeares in the burnished bookcase on their right, as discourse on all manner of recondite subjects hummed low around them, the two resumed the joint enterprise that had drawn them together against anyone's comprehension for some 403 Tuesday afternoons in term: Tiddlywinks.

17

The old panel truck made a noise like a louder version of its own heater as it lumbered up the high incline. Seated within, two cowled figures, one in green and one in brown, clung to their robes and their thoughts, receiving no warmth from the heater or from each other. At last the driver, the one in green, spoke up.

"Come on, Attalus. It was worth the attempt. We might have found recruits, and at least the lodging and food were good. Free, too. I admit it was a waste of time otherwise—except, never quite time wasted to be anywhere in these mountains."

"Oberon, Oberon . . . you've no judgment! I advised against this goose chase. How could such a place—a *resort*, mercantile philistinism run wild—bring anything of value to our order?"

"I said I agree. But I remembered Dillon before the dam, before the reservoir covered the old town, a fine little mountain village. When I saw that the request for our visit came from there, I never pictured the crap new town that's popped up in its place. Wildernest Road, Idlewylde Lane—you're right, Attalus, about the philistines. The barbarians aren't at the gates of the Rockies, they're well inside."

"All pretense and money and noise and smoke—of various kinds. And our so-called host, that plastic pantheist Holcomb, ensconced in his ersatz Rocky Mountain High of designer jeans, sequined women, liquor, and cocaine. He actually offered me a snort! Claimed it was a natural botanical, so why not? What in the world made you think anything could come of it?"

"Okay, Attalus. Lay off, already. I thought Holcomb's letter, asking guidance, sounded earnest. The guy is well intentioned, just has no idea of what the mountains really mean. In his own way, I think, he's looking for a way out of the modern mess he's gotten himself into. And, the gods know, we could use a chunk of his bankroll. Maybe if we'd stayed a little longer . . ."

"Oh, no, Oberon, now that *would* have angered me. Longer, in *that* rhinestone Sodom? And I think that term is no misnomer; there were *homosexuals* there! Nothing was to be gained. We should have turned around as soon as we got there. Or better yet, never left the Grove."

"Okay, okay. Anyway, Holcomb gave us a donation even after he realized we were a mismatch. He shows a little more of an ethic than most of the developers that infest both the Front Range and the Western Slope, and I was glad to have a chance to reinforce that. Besides, nobody *made* you come along. Next time I'll go it alone."

"You needed supervision . . . probably would have tried to recruit the lot of them. And I wanted to examine the lichens on that side of the Divide—only to find them all bulldozed away, paved, polluted, or inundated. The cryptogam crust everywhere shattered by knobby tires. I saw more lichens on that mansion's fireplace than anywhere outside! I tell you, the mountains are *going*, same as Gomorrah down there on the plain."

"A.k.a. Denver. On that we agree. But all the more reason for our principles to prevail. If anyone has a chance of bringing some sense into the land-use quagmire, it is those who think as we do. So much the better if some of them come from inside the belly of the beast, where Holcomb lives."

The one in brown simply grunted.

Oberon went on. "I think if we can influence the politics while keeping out of the fray, we . . . wait, what's that by the road?"

"Where?"

"Must be a deer—someone hit a deer," the bearded driver said as he swerved the truck to avoid hitting a lump stretched out onto the road from the tundra verge. "No, wait," he said, braking and backing up almost to the sprawled figure. "I think it's a person!"

"Go on, Oberon, it's a deer, as you said. Let's just get home."

"No, look, Attalus—it *is* a person . . . a woman!"

"That's worse! Go *on*, Oberon, it's no concern of ours. Leave it to the sheriff."

"Are you mad, Attalus? She might be hurt, or dead."

"Dead, it won't matter; injured, we aren't equipped. We can call an ambulance when we reach Idaho Springs."

Oberon set the hand brake and leaped out. He knelt beside the supine form. It was indeed a woman, unconscious. Feeling her wrist for a pulse and warmth, Oberon took in her fine features, wind-tangled dark hair, thin arms. He smelled human sweat and tundra musk. The sculpted lips moved but made no sound he could hear.

As he held her head and considered what to do, Oberon noticed his surroundings in the dim dawning. A tundra rill tumbled down through pungent willows above and into a mossy, stone-built culvert. Bistort, Indian paintbrush, elephant's head, and mountain harebells crowded the ditch, sending up a perfume that seemed to belong to the still-warm woman. They muffled the stream with their dense petals and foliage. A steep deer trail descended from the krummholz above the trickle. He reckoned the woman must have come down that trail, then stumbled onto the road. Her forehead was scarred, but long healed, and a blue bruise was flushing there too. Otherwise she seemed unhurt.

"Is she dead, Oberon? Can't we just leave her for the authorities to deal with?" Attalus's voice sounded way too much like hopeful.

"No such luck, Attalus. Sorry to disappoint you, but this woman is alive. Just passed out, or maybe knocked out from a fall. Probably been walking a long way. Maybe hypothermic, but I don't think so yet . . . she still feels warm. But it's cold on the pass, and the temp could still drop before sunup. Hurry and open the back, and I'll bring her inside and get a blanket around her."

Attalus complied, but with no joy. "Not a *woman*, Oberon. We get rid of her in Idaho Springs, and that's that."

"We'll see. She may be in need of our help. How could a young woman come to be lying on the edge of the tundra like this?"

"Abducted, raped, discarded. Happens all the time. Or so they say. She's lucky she didn't get her throat slit. And likely her own fault—probably a harlot from the city."

"That's unworthy of you, Attalus, and appalling! Can it now. You might be right that she was assaulted, but victims of rape are never at fault. Even you should know that. Where's your Christian compassion, man?"

Attalus shut up and retreated into the truculent husk he'd worn ever since Dillon, until they'd crested Loveland Pass and the truck began its nervous descent of the Eastern Slope. Then he said, "Why in the name of Asa Gray didn't you take the Eisenhower Tunnel as I suggested, Oberon?"

"As I told you: if the engine quit, as it very well might at any given point, I didn't want to be caught inside the tunnel with fumes of the night truck traffic—or with the trucks, for that matter. I don't relish getting rammed by a highballing semi at sixty-five in a hole in the ground. Anyway, I felt we *should* take the pass. Now it's clear why."

"You don't mean you think we were *meant* to find the woman?"

"Of course not. You know I'm no kind of fatalist. I revel in the come-what-may and the humble gifts of happenstance. But even in the indifferent universe that most of our brothers buy into, wonderful coincidences occur all the time, if our eyes are open."

"So?"

"Well, this poor person was in danger of death by exposure.

How fortunate that we saw her first, or before a gasoline tanker came along and crushed her there—you know they're barred from the tunnel."

"Might have been the merciful thing."

"I told you to drop such talk! You're doing yourself no credit, speaking like that. Anyway, she should be warm enough, wrapped in blankets. We'll take her to the Grove."

"Like *hell* we will! Oberon, don't speak madness. You know very well that I cannot abide any women there."

"And you know that must change, Attalus, if you are to remain. We've been over this time after time. Pan presides over a sexually mixed—and equal—realm. The refusal to recognize that fact has been one of the great failings of your former order. After all, Oberon was no superior to Titania. Astarte watched over wildness for the Phoenicians, Artemis for the Greeks, Diana the Romans. You know as well as I that Pan merely represents the male shadow of the great goddess. Your intolerance of women is not only despicable and out-worn but also unviable in our order. Attalus, you must adapt."

"And I also know," Attalus shot back, "that women tempt, defile, and destroy. Only the Virgin was free of stain. Women will ruin our hopes and our aspirations and undermine our comity. Only disso-nance can come from their entry to the Grove."

" 'No woman, no cry,' eh?"

"What?"

"Never mind. A reference outside your experience. Attalus, your ideas were obsolete even when they arose. If you still believe what you say—and in virgin birth, for Christ's sake—you should have gone down the mountain with the rest of the old order. Maybe it's not too late." Attalus said nothing, so Oberon pressed on. "How can you deny the essential feminine in Nature? Of Maia? Or Gaia? And you know full well that males are next to superfluous in most pop-ulations of plants and animals. Sperm and pollen are the height of redundancy, eggs and seeds essential."

"Nature is asexual, except at its basest level. Parthenogenesis and budding work best. Where females are a necessary evil, they must be subordinate, subordi*nated*. Kept within the bounds of secular function and service, out of the temple, and powerless to offend the affairs of men with their . . . their *sex*." A tiny sound, just this side of silence, was heard from the back, then nothing more.

"*Our* sex," said Oberon. "Now, no more of your ludicrous cant. She comes with us, and that's that. The ER in Idaho Springs might do her no good, and we'd be stuck there for hours, obliged to be interviewed, maybe even detained, by the police. Of course we'd be prime suspects for whatever happened to her. Do you really want to be questioned?"

Attalus only groaned.

"If she seems hurt or ill when Thomas examines her, he can request help from the hospital in Loveland, where we are known. Otherwise, she is welcome to our hospitality for as long as she needs or wants it. For now, she's sleeping soundly. With luck, she'll awaken in the safety of the monastery. Now deal with that the best you can, and keep your peace. If you persist in your bullshit dogma, I won't remonstrate with you again: I will simply invoke all possible powers of the community against you. That, I promise."

The faces of both men boiled with anger—one younger, sculpted of slabs of sandstone among copses of soft, mottled pelage; the other obdurate, older than its years, flaccid but for the tight thin lips drawn across audibly grinding teeth.

"And you might as well know," the driver carried on after calming down and considering whether to bring it up now, "that some of us are talking about a spiritual and physical union with the women's peace encampment at the Rocky Flats plutonium plant."

"WHAT?" Attalus roared.

"Keep it down. You'll wake her, and then you'll be in for it. She might tempt you right back there and pop your righteous cherry for you. You heard me correctly." Calm again, Oberon picked his words like peaches in a farmers' market. "Our methods, goals, and reverences are similar. We feel we would bring much to each other. We need their strength, commitment, vitality, and experience with direct action. They need shelter for the winter in sympathetic surroundings near the front. I spoke with some of their leaders when I attended the Earth and Peace Conference at Naropa in Boulder last month."

"Why haven't I been told of this?" Attalus fumed with a bitter croak, never ungritting his teeth. "As the only representative of the old order—"

"Exactly. And as the only misogynist among us. You were to be told at the upcoming Forest Meeting. Now be still and conjure on the good changes to come. Meditate on your own personal reformation. And yes, I do apologize for getting you out on this goose chase, except for the good we may be able to render this poor woman."

"I wish she had been dead, Oberon," Attalus muttered into his cowl.

"Where is the Christian in you?" Oberon gently taunted. "I refuse to believe that you mean it—you, who were once a caregiver. Now let's be quiet. We might wake up our passenger, and I suspect she needs her sleep."

Mary needed it, all right. She had walked, scrambled, finally crawled over the chill tundra and fellfields for several hours, eventually dropping through a shag of subalpine fir forest and meeting the road again. With no idea of the half circle she'd made or of any destination, caught between a vague sense of homing and a rising fear of being returned to the "home," she rambled on, a tundra creature herself. When the road appeared yet again, having snaked beneath her and back around into her random path, she collapsed in exhaustion at its side. Her last thought was to continue at dawn. But her head glanced off the stone culvert on the way down, putting her right out. Then, dreams: strange conversations about her, about women, about nature, and some names she seemed to recognize but could not quite recall, all in hushed, agitated voices.

A long time later Mary awoke in a small room. At first, when her head unfuzzed, she thought with a sick rush of despair that almost made her retch (she hadn't eaten in many hours) that she was back at the nursing home. Maybe she'd been captured; maybe she'd never really left. Then she opened her eyes wider. Followed the ceilings to their high, rough, whitewashed plaster heights, breathed in the scent of actual pine instead of pine freshener meant to cover the urine, tobacco, and other odors she didn't want to remember. Cool silence took the place of shouts, TV, and gobbledygook. Fear flushed away as a mountain stream of calm flowed in, and she felt washed all over in a kind of peace and rest she'd never known, or else had forgotten. For the first time since her crash, a spontaneous smile took over her unaccustomed lips. The creased brow of determination and frown of fear that had long molded her features now melted away. The smile lasted until a sour thought came: she might only be awaiting transportation back to Denver. Such was indeed the topic of a heated controversy downstairs, beyond her hearing.

"We've been through it already, Attalus, and it's nonnegotiable. Until we learn where she wants to be, the woman remains under our care and patronage. Brother Thomas here says she does not seem to be in need of further medical attention for now. She's had a bump on the head from a fall, but it appears to be minor. She is sleepy and confused, but that may have to do with exhaustion or the scar on her forehead. She has our full hospitality and protection." Oberon finished his recitation, and four of the five others present nodded.

"In other words, she's unbalanced," retorted Attalus. His thick-veined temples crowded down on the corners of his lipless scowl, and his nostrils twitched. "Crazy, and a wanton to boot. Probably a common streetwalker. You saw how provocatively she was dressed."

"Jacob, Jacob, Jacob . . . or Attalus, if you insist," said Thomas, the old medic. "Confusion and talking in one's sleep do not a madwoman make! And her dress is merely a simple cotton frock, a little torn from her ordeal. If you find her provocative, it is in your own mind."

"And the worst of it—" Attalus sputtered on. "You all heard her mutter who she claims she is! Dreams or not, no fantasy could be more damning than that. Or, if she's correct, surely you'll agree, disaster is within our doors."

"Rubbish," burst out a huge man from beneath his heaving cassock. "Quite the opposite would be true—you of all of us should see that. But clearly, confusion is the word. It has to do, surely, with the rigors she's been through and her arrival all unawares in this strange and intimidating place. She feels she has been here before, perhaps on the mountain, and her sense of the place must be mixed up with her personal identity in her dreams as she struggles to come out of a deep and troubled sleep." This was Abraxas.

Attalus made one last rant. "The woman is a whore and a witch. How else did she penetrate this place? She *must* leave! We would be within our rights to stone her, by the Old Book. But at least we must call the police, who will no doubt take her away."

"Attalus!" Oberon thundered. "Now I say it is *you* who are mad. Even if she were a prostitute, it wouldn't matter at all to us if she were in need of our aid and shelter. A witch, she well might be, and welcome. But if, at this fragile point in the germination of our experiment, you still regard women and witches in that archaic light—or *darkness*, rather—of stoning and locking away by men, then you don't belong among our number."

"That's right," broke in the fourth, a little man with a resolute mouth that he used little but well. "If you think such things, you must be gone from our midst. A love of nature is not enough. We're not the Audubon Society here. The fact that you are a respected lichenologist is not enough, either. Your renunciation of the Roman Catholic Church and coming over to the Grove is insufficient in itself. You seem to be against half of humankind, a misogynist worthy of the worst examples in the worst of times of your former faith, and that just won't wash here in this loving band of Pan."

"Well spoken, Xerxes," rumbled Abraxas, the large one.

"At the Forest Meeting," said Oberon, "I'll move for our learned brother's expulsion."

"Wait, Oberon," Xerxes said softly, taking his elbow. "You are forgetting—".

"Yes, he *is* forgetting," Attalus gritted, and glared.

"Attalus, as the representative of the previous order that occupied this monastery, was named trustee by the archdiocese," continued Thomas, "as a condition of deconsecration. We may all hold equal shares in the legal title to the place, but no major matters of policy can be decided without his concurrence for five full years."

Oberon sighed in frustration to be reminded of these facts. Grunts of grudging recognition rolled around the room and fell off the wooden walls onto the floor like rotten plums. "I suppose you're right, Xerxes," said Oberon. "At this point, I guess we can only censure him. But I fear that his malevolence toward this woman, and all women, will ruin our plans and, in the end, frustrate our movement altogether."

Attalus gloated. His lips smeared into a second's snicker before he turned grave. "Do not underestimate me. I left the old order and the church and joined with you because I embrace the anti-supernatural pantheism we all subscribe to. I have no desire to spoil the effort or wreck the communion. But as is written, woman is the vessel of the devil! If you attempt to populate the Grove with wantons, I will use all my powers to bring an early end to the experiment. Then the land and buildings will go to the second bidders— the Mormons—after all."

Oberon had been thinking, and now he spoke once more. "Hear me, Brother Attalus." Xerxes and Abraxas closed ranks behind him in support of whatever it was he intended to say, as Thomas made sure that his medical bag was still at the ready. "We recognize your expertise and your earnestness toward the elements, and we hope that we might still, somehow, reconcile you to the movement. But your views on half of humanity are both intolerant and intolerable. Since our kind of pantheism is in part humanistic, it embraces male *and* female human beings, along with all other species. Sexual differentiation is the great gift of the gods of evolution to us mortals, the very engine of natural selection, whether one chooses to use it or not."

No one else spoke, unsure of where he was going with this. "You will find in the Forest Meeting that you are a minority of one. Meanwhile, this woman, whatever her past or her mental state, is in our care for now. You will not go near her, nor will you seek her removal—she goes when she decides to go, and then only. Now, be off!"

Attalus went. Directly out of the monastery, off the grounds of the Grove, down the highway to the lodge below.

"Why, Brother Jacob!" said the woman at the desk. "We so seldom see you or your brother monks here anymore, since the new ones came." She smiled and took off her glasses. "How can I help you?"

"I want a telephone," he said.

18

June 23. Granby. Left Estes Park today, Ruth and family having headed back to Kansas. Hitched up Trail Ridge Road to assess the status of alpine fauna and flora. Snowmelt on schedule, wildflowers bursting out. Whole swatches of tundra already azure with alpine forget-me-not and skypilot, or molten gold with alpine arnica and woolly sunflower. Butterflies beginning to appear. Mead's sulphurs and Mead's alpines both on the wing as early, fresh-minted males. They make me think of their namesake, Theodore Mead, who explored these mountain heights for butterflies, traveling by stagecoach and foot a hundred years ago. I wonder if my path will cross the one he blazed. Will I swing my net in some of the same canyons and meadows where he collected these new species and so many others?

The sight of that first Erebia of the year—! So tempted to collect, but have no net as yet, and besides, the rangers would be on me like flies. Must find a good alpine expanse on the east side, outside the park, where I can collect unrestricted. Later, I'll return to the Western Slope.

June 27. Idaho Springs. Did the bearded prospector bit here for a couple of days. Rented a mule and pickax and gold pan, posed with kids and too rarely moms beside the old locomotive while Dad snapped photos at a buck apiece. My beard is long enough now to really pull 'em in. The littlest kids are afraid of it, or confuse me with the Christmas elf, but the older ones (and their mothers) love to stroke it. Just yesterday a lady from Colorado Springs latched onto it like a horse's tail and stroked away, saying "Nice beard, nice beard!" Funny how some kinds of secondary sexual characteristics are public property, whereas if one were to reciprocate, he'd be in the local hoosegow before he could say boo! Or, boob—as in "Nice." But I don't mind.

Earned enough to eat a little meat and beans, replace my rotting denim and chambray, and pick up supplies for a net: a long dowel, spring steel hoop, hose clamp, mesh, cotton duck, needles, and sturdy thread. For a while I thought I was going to have to use a lacy pink negligee (that had somehow ended up with me after Estes) for the net bag, until I found some grandma's mesh curtains at the Goodwill. Made the net, thus ensuring public notice from now on wherever I go, just in case the beard fails to do so.

A net can deter potential rides or snag them as certainly as a hapless dryad on a blossom, depending on the outlook of the driver. Get a guy who recalls his own golden boyhood days with netstick in hand, and you're in. In this instance, my net flagged a ride with three nubile dryads of my own species, northbound on the Peak to Peak Highway. I had a mind to get out at Ward and make my way into the Indian Peaks, where I've had good collecting up around Niwot Ridge, Lake Isabelle, and Mt. Audubon. But then I saw a mountain in the distance with rockslides so vast, tundra rolling down its shoulders so generously, that I had to try it out. None of us knew its name. Bidding the young women adieu before we came to Allenspark, I took off toward this fetching peak, cross-country.

June 30. At camp, below timberline on the same mountain. Two days ago I got up here, and I'm very glad that I came. The trail I eventually found picked its way up through pine forests. So did mountain chickadees, cadres of the little buggers. Black caps, white striped, they flicked from puff to heavy puff of green pine needles. Then there was no trail again, and I followed a watercourse—a vocal little brook, swelled with runoff, upslope through many more little pines, getting smaller as I rose, and emerald patches of aspens. At length I came to a kind of broad, very flat saddle between a rocky prominence on my left and the peak's great shoulder-ridge on my right. The saddle, a sandy micro-desert, supported sparse pines and very few flowers, and no butterflies save one vagrant Queen Alexandra's sulphur.

Ponderosas had given way to lodgepoles, and now they surrendered the crumbly pink granite gravel to gnarly limber pines. These twist as they grow, and fall over and still grow, so as to cast postcards and watercolor views on all sides. Where they take root in rock, it splits, giving them that much more broken stone to play with in place of more tractable soil. The fleshy granite spalls away, exfoliates they say, like thick onion skins, and sometimes leaves great cavernous hollows behind solid overhangs. It is beneath one of these great lintels that I now reside, safely out of the afternoon rain, with that pink gravel they call grus for my bed.

Yesterday I left the shelter of the limber pine wood to explore the open rocks of the ridgeline. The last scrabbly spruce and juniper clung to the steep, stony slope. Then only stones—stones and the herbaceous and grassy plants between them, and the palette of lichens that spattered the rocks themselves. What a study they would make here! I wonder if anyone ever has.

It was far too late in the day to climb the peak, which still stretched a couple thousand feet up the sharp and bony ridge above me. But I recognized Magdalena habitat when I saw it. There, perching pikalike on an orange boulder on the ridgeline, I surely saw it. In fact, never had I seen Magdalena habitat like it!

This peak rises to a pyramidal point, actually a double point, then drops back down the other side in another lengthy ridgeline with bumps. A snowy crease begins far down the face, where avalanches and feisty forests rush to meet each other at separate speeds. And, damn! <u>everything</u> in between—the entire front of the mountain, if east is forward—from ridge to ridge and tip-top to crotch, is one vast, uninterrupted, unbelievable talus slope of perfect aspect for <u>Erebia magdalena</u> and its rockslide cohort. The scree, from summit to snow pocket, roughly the avalanche lap and the sternum and plexus leading down to it, is nearly sheer. But trending away on both sides of the lethal slot, running up to my high ridge and the one opposite, lies talus of a feasible slope for a scramble. An old Magdalena hunter, I felt I had entered Valhalla.

I returned to my grotto like a child to its bed before the Christmas binge. The late sun set the russet pine trunks aglow as if they'd been burnished. I built a small fire from pinecones, needles, and twigs, then slept the sleep of one who expects much on the morrow. (The season is a smidge early yet, but give it one hot day, and Maggie will pop.)

<u>July 4</u>. The hot day came like fireworks, bringing insects out like living sparks. I spent a day or two working the willow bottoms for admirals, Scudder's sulphurs, and bolorians, but the mosquitoes drove me out. I reckoned it was time to go back up to the rocks anyhow. So I decided to celebrate Dependence Day (if only it were generally thought of that way!) by climbing this Roman candle of a mountain.

I reached the rocks by ten, then spent a couple of hours watching fresh, brilliant black Magdalenas coursing across the rockslides. But weirdly, unlike other years, I wasn't eager to begin catching them; almost reluctant. This surprised me. It was as if my imagination were rooted in the sooty sweep of wings described by the alpines as they quartered the scree. I made no attempt to catch them: just watched. And they rewarded me by sailing near and occasionally coming down to nectar on the cushion of campion right beside my battered boots.

I carried on, eager to see still more of the mountain. I'd lost my water bottle when its cap loop caught on a limber pine finger. Thirsty as could be by midday, I spied a snowbank with a rivulet springing from its foot, and I aimed straight toward it. Liquid heaven! Nothing smells or tastes like the boggy alpine sponge, fresh-squeezed. The icy stream ran through a deep green fissure of moss and across a lush meadow, one of the few spots with soil enough to support an alpine garden on the mountain's face. Between them, the water and the succulent vegetation slaked my thirst and spirit, Giardia be damned! I may pay later, but for now I was happy to be the mountain's very drunkard.

Finding myself just below the sharp south ridge of the mountain, I scrambled up to stand on the stony spine. A broad shoulder of fellfield and turf dropped away toward the southwest. This was seductive. I stepped off the ridge and onto the tundra, trying to travel rock to rock wherever I could so as not to trammel the plants. I hate to step on any alpine sedge or flower or even lichen, but it is impossible not to up here. I knelt to sniff a foreign fragrance or to peer at something minute and new to me—as if I'd never been on the Colorado tundra!—so often that my knees soon ached, the hours vanished, and I realized I faced a long hike down. But looking up, I saw the summit, not so far away or high above as I'd expected. And in a trice (a unit of time that effectively precludes either foresight or rational deliberation), I decided to try for it.

Back to the ridge. Boulder-claw and stone-clutch, rock-crawl and granite-scratch. Clamber and straddle, reach and grab, slip and catch. It was not technically difficult, it was merely a matter of scaling and storming a hundred broken-down castles at a 45-degree incline and 13,000 feet above sea level. Acclimated as I was, I still found oxygen wanting. But the promise of an incomparable view eased the scramble. A kind of euphoria lifted me skyward.

From time to time, black butterflies brushed my face or came almost that close. Meanwhile, a huge black caterpillar was crawling down the ridge to meet me halfway to the summit—a mafic outcrop against the white granite matrix. As I inclined upward, the distance closed between puny human and lava larva, making us seem to move in slow motion. At last we met face-to-face, and I made my way around its great black bulk with difficulty. But once I'd overtaken the dark dike, the final ascent came easy.

A golden eagle slid past a few yards away, causing all the marmots to whistle like hell and dive beneath their basking boulders. I settled onto the summit and opened my eyes to the west. A crowd of mountains pointed out the skyline forever, every one cradling cirques, embracing tarns, as a person might cup a tiny animal in hand while passing through a crowd. Steep, olive tundra slopes dropped away—flowerfields now, icefields geologic moments ago, fellfields seconds from now in terms of uplift time. Two thousand blues and purples might make the spectrum of the sky and mountains I could see, and as many greens and browns for the valleys and foothills below. As for the forms of the mountains themselves, the full dentition of oreodonts and theriodonts, titanotheres and T. rex would not these mountains make. Beyond, the Rockies carried on in an infinitude of passes and points. I felt I could disappear happily into their beckoning clefts and never come out again.

But one always emerges, after all.

Now I had to go back down. Sunset was near. Already it was too late to retrace my steps without taking the ankle-cracking rocks in the gloaming. Break an ankle up here, I might as well just jump, toboggan down that long, steep face without benefit of sled or snow, and die faster. So I decided to drop over the far side of the mountain into the next valley, where there ought to be a trail running down to the Peak to Peak. I started down the precipitous back side of the mountain, taking the slow plunge into the wild basin below.

A peak like an enormous, craggy egg loomed to the west,

screaming grandeur, drawing my eyes again and again when they ought to have been trained right before me. I dropped steadily down over tundra, fellfield, scree, and eventually into scattered trees on aching knees and tired ankles. On a grassy bench with a clear splashing pool I paused to rest and drink. A ghostly white water bug disturbed the glassy surface. A pallid reflection looked back. My compass would not fail me, but was my body still up to this?

At last the edge of the forest closed in around me. Through the firs, steeper yet, along elk trails, over logs, and down into gullies I tramped, losing the light and whatever cushion my used-up knees still had. Thousands more feet I dropped, straining to see the sharp branches and tripping rocks that lay in wait. So easy to put an eye out! Shatter a kneecap, crack a pelvis, split a skull. Come on, man— ease on down, nice and gentle.

Then the bottom, and it felt like stepping off some damn carnival ride in slow motion. Abruptly the boggy valley stretched out before me into the misty gray gullet of what sounded like a fast creek. I gasped in relief, then alarm as a twilit apparition arose before me and resolved into an immense cow elk facing me at twenty feet across the flat. The beast was just as startled. I thanked the goddess of wapiti that it wasn't a bull in rut. I'd probably chased her all the way down the maze of game trails. We confronted each other. One of us turned and bounded off as the other trudged into the mountain bog.

To find a major trail, I had only to cross the creek, then make my way over the wet meadow and across a piney knoll to a lake with a broad, sandy beach. But I knew none of this at the time. I did know I'd probably done the worst of it, but what lay ahead was a mystery. Then I had one of those stupid thoughts that kids taunt each other with, such as, what if you had to turn around tonight and go all the way back the way you've come or else the kidnappers will kill your mother? That's when I realized how bone-tired I really was. Such inane imponderables come to me only when I am ill or exhausted. Their joke is that they take even more energy to ignore. "Who thinks that's funny, anyway?" I asked aloud, but no one heard except the joker within, who, shamed or sleepy, shut up.

What I hadn't figured on was the fierceness and volume of a mountain creek in a summer of heavy snowmelt at the end of a sunny day. It couldn't be crossed, at least not by me, not safely, in the deep dusk. There must be a bridge, but where? Total darkness fell too soon to explore much farther. The skinny game trail on my side of the cascading creek fell away in little slides as I picked my way along it. To keep from a sheer drop into the narrowing canyon, I was obliged to climb up into the wild woods again. But these were steep, pitched about with sharp and brittle deadwood, and rocky to boot. Treacherous.

Then I fell down the back side of a downed log into a pit, scratching my side on a branch stub and knocking my wind out on hard earth. I stood, sucked air, and rubbed my bruises. Going on would have been plain stupid—I'd surely end up injured, and most likely bones for the coyotes. Besides, I was plum beat. So the simple day hike became an emergency bivouac. I worked my way slowly and carefully back down to the creek bank, which had gentled out below a falls that would turn out to be named Lyric. In the embrace of spruce roots, legs bent to conserve warmth and keep my feet out of the stream's spray, I curled up in the duff, listened to the lyrics, and slept straightaway.

Even summer nights grow cold at 10,000 feet, and I had no way to make a small fire à la John Muir. Bad habit: going out under-equipped. From time to time I got up to stretch, stomp around, and drink from the rushing stream. I knew the chances of giardiasis (so-called beaver fever, scapegoating the noble rodent just as bison get the rap for bovine TB) were greater up here than at the snowmelt rill, but dehydration could be worse, at least in the short term. Besides, it pisses me off that we have so fouled the mountains that we can't even drink their good waters . . . and then we blame it on the beavers! So I drank deeply. I had a light windbreaker to wrap around my legs, and one granola bar.

As I lay there through the longest hour, trying to sleep instead of shiver, I let the watervoices guide my random musings. Most folks, I guessed, would regard such an impromptu survival game as being "stuck," bringing on hysteria, or spoiling their taste for the out-of-doors and its surprises. But those types would never have been on the mountain in the first place. For my part, I didn't consider myself stuck so much as lucky. A twisted ankle could have been disastrous; no way to get help up here or to get down. No one to know where I was or to look for me. Hell, no one who even cared.

How easy to fall, get hurt, never get back to my cave. Be found next fall by an elk hunter, next summer by a hiker, a disarticulated pile of bleached bones . . . or maybe never. There could be a lot worse fates than nourishing coyote, raven, and deer mouse. But I had it in mind to live a little longer, at least until winter. If it was much like last winter, I wouldn't much mind checking out then. Or maybe joining the warblers in the tropics, catching agrias and morpho butterflies for collectors and little calistos and metalmarks for George. Or moving in with the pikas in their cozy haymows underneath the rocks. But here I was, alive if sore and chilly, and happy enough. I had risked my sorry ass for nothing, at least in monetary terms. Not a single dead butterfly graced my collecting bag. And that was fine too.

Again I slept. I imagined, dreamed, or maybe remembered that a puma padded up to my strange form, snuffled at it, batted it gently with a racquet-size paw, and walked on. That a great horned owl alighted above me to finish off a meal of snowshoe leveret. And of snuggling with a dipper and her downy young in a mossy cleft behind the lip of Lyric Falls. I didn't hear the saw-whet owl call to her mate over the very white noise of the cascades.

The next time I awoke, the thin, watery, four o'clock brand of dawn was trying to gain admission at the eastern portal of the forest. That was enough. I staggered up, worked my stiff limbs, threw water across my face, and took off. Now I could just see to probe my way safely. In a few minutes I came to the bridge I'd envisioned, and a major pack trail on the other side. It was broad, made of white sand ground down by glaciers and rivers from the mountains all around. I passed Sandbeach Lake, and by six, in sight of Wild Basin Lodge (I swear I made up the description above before I'd seen the sign), the trail was as bright as the Yellow Brick Road. Then I had merely to walk out to the highway, back to my starting point, and on up to my camp, maybe five more miles.

They gave me coffee at the lodge, along with a cinnamon roll. Twenty-seven hours, some twenty miles, and 8,000 feet gained and lost since I'd begun, I set my boots once more onto the macadam pad of the Peak to Peak Highway. When a well-broken-in F-150 pickup pulled up and the blonde driver offered me a lift ("such a fine sight to see," just as in Winslow, Arizona), I took it despite a little nag that I should finish the circuit on foot. She was tall, sturdy, and tanned, with long, straight sandy hair, bunched and held away from her face with an Indian beadwork clasp. She wore cowboy boots, clean jeans, and a brightly embroidered chambray shirt. Her smile brought to mind the arc of a nutcracker's flight. I wouldn't have called her a beauty, but she kept my eye just fine.

We spoke little but frankly on the way to my trailhead. When I told her about my unscheduled bivouac, she said I was slightly silly and damned lucky, but she admired how I had kept my head. "So you bagged the peak, huh?" she asked. I told her I didn't think of it that way . . . seemed more like the peak bagged me. She said I must be a man who loves mountains more than himself. "I get so tired of these rock jocks and cowboy climbers for whom the mountains are mere foils for their egos and escapades than companions," she said, pretty much like that. And that the mountains respected bravura above bravado, and maybe that's why I came out all right. I said I found the peak pretty overwhelming, and she said it will always be that way, or should be.

I showed her where to stop, and I got out. "Is that the one?" she asked, pointing off toward the rocky pyramid where I'd perched some twelve hours before. I nodded. "Well, it's not quite a four-teener," she said, "but almost." I was about to ask its name when she pulled out. I still don't know that mountain's name. Or hers.

19

Erebia skims the rocky face of Magdalena Mountain like a floater gliding across the surface of a big pale eye. His own eyes, paired black globes dominating each side of his head, survey a broad periphery for patches of pink that might mean nectar and for shapes of dark that could be females. Able to see the visible spectrum as well as ultraviolet, he can pick out many hues, though a flower we call yellow might fluoresce some other color to him and stand out even more. And while his compound eyes have thousands of lenses, Erebia sees no honeycomb image, but a single picture of fair clarity. Or so science believes, as butterflies decline to reveal their visions.

On his first flight, Erebia looks down and all around over the granite boulders that make up his rockslide. The stones lie as they fell when the mountains broke apart. Their colors are the pink and gray of feldspars, the white of quartz, the black and glass of micas, and the greens, yellows, oranges, and blacks of lichens. These rocks are home to Erebia and most of what he sees, aside from the sky. As for the sky, when it is blue, Erebia flies; when white or gray, he basks; and when purple, he creeps into the rocky cracks and holes. And when the sky turns his own color, it is time to take to the deeper shelter beneath the boulders until morning. Stone and sky make up most of his world.

There is more. Green grows now among the rocks, wisps of alpine grasses that give sustenance during Erebia's larval months. These blades will be sought by his future mates and all other female Magdalenas for egg-laying as they fly from stone to basking stone. Erebia is not unaware of these patches of grasses. Were his flight to graze the edge of the rocks or to reach the fellfield or the beginning of the tundra, Erebia would see much more green. Here, in July, if the snow melts, the whole of the arctic-alpine seed bank bursts its vaults, as if entire field guides spilled their flowered pages across the slopes in leaf and bloom. No one unfamiliar with the tundra, while surveying the winter mountain, could picture its summer profusion. No one having seen it once could but wish to behold it again. Magenta paintbrush daubs the variegated green canvas among a pointillist array of blue and white and gold and lavender. Insects hover and dart over all, nectaring and pollinating, mating and preying, laying eggs and eating leaves, feeding birds and one another as from the boggy turf rises a sweet stink of Ordovician richness.

But that rich turf is not this Erebia's realm. Other species of the genus fly there, such as the small chocolate and cinnamon Mead's alpine (*Erebia callias*), whose rabbit-gray underside blends so well with the lichened cobbles on which it basks. The still smaller Theano alpine (*E. theano*) haunts wet hollows, bogs, and swales among the tundra and subalpine forest and suns on the broad, round leaves of marsh marigolds. And the eye-spotted Butler's alpine (*E. epipsodea*), typical of its many relatives in the Alps, with dark brown wings and eyed russet bands, might be found as well on the tundra as in any other montane grassy habitat from ponderosa pines up to subalpine firs and beyond.

Of all the alpines, only Magdalena restricts itself to the rock realm. Anyone wishing to see it must take to the boulder fields as well. These dark dryads hold a special attraction for arcane cadres among lepidopterists who call themselves *Erebia* freaks. Most collectors prefer the cheaper charms of gaudy swallowtails and iridescent blue morphos to the understated hues of the dun, striated satyrs. Among those smitten by the subtle mystique of *Erebia* and its kin, *magdalena* stands out as a special favorite.

So, as Erebia surveys his rockdom, he perceives a butterfly collector: an anomaly in the landscape, an excrescence on the scene differing from any rock, which could be a tree, except that trees don't grow up here. With his bright clothing, his waving white net, and his erratic progress over the rocks, the human hardly blends into the scene. Generations of Magdalena hunters will testify that the black beast comes down the rocks directly toward them, only to swerve away at the last moment. Their futile sweep of the net results in the capture of nothing more than a black shadow on the breeze. Not a few such hunters take only air away as their trophy, and they blame not only the rocks, not only the altitude, not only the clouds that always seem to close in too soon, but also the sharp eyes and quick reactions of the butterflies themselves. Erebia is a dodger.

And so this July morning, as Erebia takes wing for the first time, he sees such a foreign object in his path. How can we know what goes on in his poppyseed brain, as, with a strong stroke of wing, he changes course? More predictable is the mental process of the English butterfly collector who leaps, sweeps, misses, swears, falls between two knee-abrading boulders, and curses the much-maligned, much-coveted animal who has sailed far beyond his reach across the scree. The hobbyist resolves to apply himself and do better at his next opportunity. The closest he has come to this experience was pursuing the mountain ringlet, *Erebia epiphron*, across the fells of Helvellyn in the Lake District, and the Scotch argus, *E. aethiops*, in the Cairngorms. Those places are fine and wild for Britain, but they're not like the Rockies; nor are those alpines the match of Magdalena when it comes to evasiveness. Now the hunter is eager to add this storied species to his cabinet.

Watching, watching. But there are other nets on the mountain, much more difficult to see. They cannot move about, yet they take a far greater toll on alpine insects than all the clumsy and adept collectors can manage together. These are the great webs of *Aculepeira carbonarioides*, the dark, granite-colored spiders that hunt the rock-slides for flying prey. Their three- or four-foot orbs anchor boulder to boulder by ten-foot guy-wires ballooned into place and not renewed daily with the rest of the web. These impressive nets are invisible when the angle of the sun is right. The collector is an expert, but *Aculepeira* is better.

Having missed another *magdalena* and once more fallen among the rocks, the Brit hauls himself up and steps face-first into one of these massive webs. A mild arachnophobe, he panics and flails wildly. Had he been less frantic to escape his own entrapment, he might have noticed near the center of the web, a few inches from his nose, a black mummy hanging lifeless. A brother of Erebia's who had survived until that morning, the hapless butterfly flew into the trap, and though he struggled with powerful wings and shed many a scale in the effort, he'd never had a chance. The female spider fell upon the insect and paralyzed him with a nip from her venomed fangs. Then she spun the fresh prey into a silken sandwich bag and sucked his hemolymph dry.

Now, alarmed by the collector's failed attempt, Erebia dodges, corrects too late, and he too strikes an orb weaver's web. But only by a tarsus on an outer, unsticky line. Lucky, he is away again unscathed before the spider can reach him.

Not every butterfly that lands in a spiderweb becomes a sacrifice to Arachne. Strong strugglers, many break the webs and get away. Others slip out with the loss of only scales. In fact, the scales of Lepi ("shingle")-dop-tera ("wing") may have evolved partly in response to selective pressure from spiders. To their owners, the survival advantage of such a slippery, deciduous coating can be great. Together with their other helpful properties, such as sexual communication, predator deception, solar collection, and rain deflection, the adaptive value of the scales as a spider escape kit could push along their evolution at a speedy pace, bringing on this major advance in insect upholstery. Collectors, too, have been known to help stuck butterflies escape from their rival netters either inadvertently, by striking the webs with their nets, or on purpose, torn three ways between seizing the specimen for themselves, letting nature take its course, or playing the god of mercy in expiation for their own lethal take.

Sailing, watching. Collectors and spiders are not the sole butterfly predators on the mountain. Erebia glides over a persistent snowbank. On the edge of the ice that still lids a small tarn, a flock of rosy finches forages. Their soft brown and blackish plumage contrasts with plummy highlights on cap, wing, and rump. They are pecking seeds and insects that have fallen into the snow and been immured there this season or last. It would not be beneath a rosy finch to turn flycatcher and go for an alpine, should one drift into nabbing range; even less so for a water pipit, that bobbing, straw-colored bird of the high meres, chiefly an insect eater. Nutcrackers will eat whatever they can, and the slow-gliding raven would not pass up a minor meal of its own dark shade.

None of these, but yet another black bird now stoops toward Erebia at great speed. Nine times out of ten, ravens, finches, even pipits might be too slow and clumsy to catch an active alpine on the wing, but now, in his third perilous encounter in as many hours of flight, Erebia is engaged by one of his few superiors in the air: a black swift. Covering vast areas of mountain sky in a day, the swift (her name is a great understatement) normally feeds at a higher level. But drawn down over the snowbank by the cloud of insects chilled in the updraft, the jet hunter swoops low over adjacent rocks, where she spots Erebia. In a flick of her sickle-shaped wings, the bird dives for the butterfly like a heat-seeking missile locked onto its target, like the black bullet her body resembles.

Had he swerved and dropped, as he did before the foreign white shape of the butterfly net, Erebia might have escaped. Instead, he actually changes course to fly directly at the predator. A male butterfly first locates his mate by sight; size and shape mean less than color, or even amplify the attraction. Any swarthy form passing near a male Magdalena is likely to elicit engagement on the wing. Now, in pursuit of a potential mate, Erebia flies in the face of danger.

No gentle lover, the swift opens her broad, froglike bill—a mousetrap triggered by sensitive vibrissae around the mouth—and clamps it shut on the insect. A friendly zephyr shifts Erebia's wings just enough to remove his body from that gaping maw, so that only the left forewing is caught. In another second the bird would have pulled Erebia into her gullet by tug of tongue and air and been off to another meal on the run, spitting bits of black wrapper into the wind. The catch takes place just over a large boulder, behind which the bruised and web-faced lepidopterist has been lying in wait for another alpine to course down the declivity. His move, from a concealed position this time, might have been successful—but the "bloody bird," as he calls it, beats him to it, sweeping the prize right out of the air above his head. Yet his net stroke has already been launched, and it nearly apprehends both black objects, *parva* and *magna*. It so alarms the swift that she shrieks, as swifts will in play, fear, or rage. Agape, she releases Erebia from her grip and speeds skyward, filled with a bird's version of frustration.

The butterfly flutters to earth, shaken but unhurt, and the entomologist falls upon him. The air rings with a metallic *clink* as he snaps his net over the grounded black Icarus. "At last!" he exults as he prepares to bottle his second-chance catch in a cyanide jar. But first he examines the specimen, held firmly and gently in his flat-bladed stamp tongs. "Bloody hell!" he curses. "Buggered up by that bloody bird!"

The fact that the collector is a true *Erebia* aficionado, intent upon bagging all the Rocky Mountain species on his brief holiday in the States, enflames his ire. Like many of his ilk, he desires only perfect specimens. Unless a "mint" individual were unobtainable, he would not place a "rag" among the ranks of meticulously spread, flawless butterflies in his cabinet. He fails to consider that his collection, which holds considerable scientific value and is willed to the British Museum of Natural History, would be still more worthwhile if it also documented the vagaries of butterfly life by including such damaged goods as he routinely rejects. But the collector fancies himself a conservationist, so he punctiliously releases his rejects unharmed so that they might still reproduce—just as he does when angling on the Thames or the Avon.

This fellow already has one satisfactory pair of *E. magdalena magdalena* from Alberta in his Satyrinae drawer, for which he swapped a series of Tasmanian beech satyrs (six males, six females) with a Canadian correspondent, who in turn had purchased them from an itinerant professional collector. So he has no need for a flawed male. Even for exchange, only A-one specimens will do. His desire now is to capture for himself a cabinet-quality, perfectly fresh and unfaded pair of the legendary black butterflies of the High Rockies. So, with further dark mutterings of bad luck, he replaces the cap on his killing bottle, stows it away in his collecting bag, gently sets Erebia upon a bright clump of moss campion, and quits the scene. But before he leaves the mountains later in the day, two perfect males (but no females) of *E. magdalena*, a pair of Melissa arctics, three rockslide checkerspots, and a pair of Snow's coppers will lie carefully stowed in his bag, bound for the setting boards in Rosebay Mount, his West Sussex semidetached cottage. Over a pint or two of King & Barnes bitter, he will show them to his admiring friends of a December evening in his study, far, far away from Magdalena Mountain.

Stunned by a whiff of cyanide, disoriented by the double jeopardy catches, Erebia perches on the clump. This, after all, is one of the objects of his search through all those repetitive flappings up, glidings down the rockslide: moss campion and other suitable nectar flowers to fuel his flights. He uncoils his watchspring proboscis, probes a pink floret, and sips the sweet substance, replenishing with sugars the energy expended in his first day as a butterfly—a day that the mountain's annals (were there any such kept) might fairly describe as "eventful." Then he crawls to a lump of granite, lays his folded black wings down against it, and basks, for a haze has come over the sun and cooled the mountain air. The haze darkens to a storm cloud, sending Erebia understone before the first cold drops fall. He will keep to the shelter of the boulders for the duration of the shower and all through to the next morning, when the sun will reassert itself.

And that might be just as well. Wasn't this enough to ask of a first day on the rocks? Erebia eluded the collector and the spider, only to fall prey to both the swift and the human, then escape them both through each other's agency. He has nectared several times, basked, and surveyed his stony domain as he carried out the age-old flight pattern of his kind: fly up to the ridge, float down to the bottom, investigate objects black, pink, and yellow, avoid all else. Then do it all over again, and again.

But so far, no female. Erebia and the collector looked in vain for females all day. It might be a week before any females even appear on the scene. As with many other butterfly species, the males eclose first, the female's emergence somewhat deferred. This way the females take fewer chances at losing their precious load to a late freeze, and the stronger, fitter males remain to mate and pass on their genes.

Will Erebia survive to do so? It's a toss-up at this point. At least a female of his species will not be put off by the flaw that caused the collector to reject him. As he basks one last time before roosting, that mark shines like a fresh brand on a black stallion: a bright, clear V, where the scales have been struck away and the thin membrane shows through—a permanent tattoo applied by the broad bill of the black swift.

20

Mead lay across his turret cot, Carson's journal on the floor beside him. He'd thought there might be solace in those pages, but they seemed a taunt instead. "If it weren't for that lackwit Griffin," he told a disinterested spider, "I could be following Carson's spoor! No matter how stale the trail, it'd be fresher than the air in here." He hoped a cola from the basement soda machine might quell his wormwood and cool his forehead. But leaping to his feet, he stumbled on the foot that was asleep and banged his knee against the iron railing of the trapdoor ladder.

"Shit!" chopped the stuffy air. Then, "Ah, shit!" again. Mead had heard his grandmother refer to a certain kind of mood as a brown study, and his Beat-era parents spoke of blue funks, but Mead's mood just now had no color, no character: it was just a shitty mood. He suffered them infrequently. Normally slung somewhere between reasonable cheer and mild melancholy, he was an implacably calm person with low blood pressure who seldom struck the ceiling or banged the bottom. No manic, Mead, unless it was "manic medium."

The only event over which he'd felt truly euphoric since coming to Yale was when Noni first took him to bed. The flipside of that high remained at bay until Noni left town that very afternoon.

Graduation had been the day before. Seats in the Old Campus were limited to family ticketholders, so Mead watched from the street outside as Noni processed with the others in the 267th commencement exercises of Eli Yale University. Like a great ruly flock of crows with many-colored ribbons around their necks, they came in their hundreds. At the head marched the faculty ravens, interspersed with blue jays and cardinals in their blue and scarlet robes from Oxford, Cambridge, and Harvard. President Coxley led, carrying a ceremonial mace. No possums were in evidence.

Afterward, Mead got Noni away from her parents long enough for a walk in the old burial ground, the most private place they could find. "James, you morbid man. Bringing me to a graveyard and then moping. We've got to live for the moment, and this is my moment— please don't spoil it. And you've got to enjoy your summer. Don't moon." Noni looked especially lovely in the greeny-gold light filtered through thirty kinds of leafing trees. Her smile was so unaffected by the pending split that James wondered whether she really felt it as he did. But her face carried in its corners such a joy for the moment that he couldn't doubt for long. Noni could dismiss her mopes at will, and could do so in James, most of the time, with a flick of her nutshell hair and a touch.

"You're right, Noni. It just gets me that if it weren't for you-know-who, I'd be able to go to Gothic too, and we could share it." They'd been through it all before, over and over.

Noni just looked down.

"Anyway, George says he can probably get me onto a new grant for next year. But he suggests that for now I try to content myself here in New Haven, caring for the great big blattids, and maybe get a publication or two out of them. I can swelter with a warm Schaefer while the rest of you are cooling with a Coors, and pray to Pan for Griffin's imminent demise, promotion, or transubstantiation."

There was nothing more to say. Noni had to meet her parents for a graduation dinner. They'd come to the brownstone portals of the cemetery. A golden moth the size of a turkey platter shone in the afternoon sun, mounted on the lintel of the Egyptian gateway. "Now there's a lep worthy of your roaches," said Noni. "Work on that."

"George says it's meant to symbolize resurrection, or— considering this lot of Puritans and Congregationalists—more likely decay. Anyway, congratulations, Noni dear. You've done well here. I'll get out too someday. I hope you have a fine time. I'll write." He held her hand, and she held his.

"Your summer will go fast, you'll see." Her mouth did a bright red yo-yo to his and back, her strong, slender arms pulled him quickly into their saffron curve; then she pushed him away and she was gone. Her lithe form slipped beneath the portal, down the road toward Woolsey, and into the crowd of flapping gowns. She hadn't looked back.

Now, in the middle of the night, James recalled that afternoon as he rubbed his shin in the dim light of Osborn's tower. Noni's absence and his latest contretemps with the surly Griffin ate at his gut like a roach gnawing on a stale biscuit. He clumped down the ladder from the tower to the fourth floor, down the stairwell to the third, second, and ground floors, and on to the basement. Focused purely on his funk, he failed to notice the stooped brown form in the cellar hallway until he collided with it. "Oh, I'm sorry!" he said. "Excuse me, I guess my eyes weren't adjusted."

The figure replied, "Not to worry, young man. No damage done. I'm just surprised to encounter anyone else down here at this time of night. Why . . . you're Mr. Mead, aren't you? George Winchester's student?"

"Yes," Mead said, surprised as well that the eminent professor emeritus recognized him. He knew the elder ecologist from his faithful appearance at departmental seminars, where he always stood to ask the crucial question of sweating speakers in a heavily accented British voice, sweet and creamy and mordant. "And you're Dr. Hutchinson."

"So I am. I see you are wondering what I am doing down here past the witching hour. Postgraduate students require no excuses for their nocturnal perambulations, which are often eccentric. But we of the pedantry are expected to behave, to keep regular office hours and routine home lives, watching television in the evenings and going round the shops on Saturdays. To come and go at respectable times and be found in predictable places—are we not?"

"Well, I don't know about that, sir. But since you ask—are you running some sort of experiment down here?" Mead had heard that the eminent professor was most resourceful, often conducting significant research in the near vicinity of the campus. Perhaps he was currently engaged in observing the mice and silverfish that skitted through the lower gut of the lab's corpus.

"No, I fear not!" The prof laughed. His height had never been the match of Mead's, and his elder stoop took him well below six feet. Shoulders once broad now sloped, but solidly. He wore a shiny old brown suit and butterscotch plaid necktie, the whole mounted on ancient oxblood oxfords a thousand times polished. A January shock of bleached straw thatched Hutchinson's crown, above a face of such kindness that Mead almost held his breath in its presence. Deep-set, clear blue eyes unaided by spectacles sat above several scoops of wrinkles around the weighty lids. An ample but chiseled nose perched between unsettled cheeks of a healthy rose. Strong jaws resisting the onset of jowls met in a delicate chin, and a tilde of a mouth completed the face.

Mead had noticed that mouth before. It seemed to have two basic, reversible expressions: a wistful, almost sad smile, and a down-turned daub of surprise or dismay. Variations provided by the eyes and their snowdrift brows, the rise and fall of the barely furrowed forehead, and the tilt of head and its keel, the nose, met all situations.

"You see, Mr. Mead, I've had to move out of my laboratory of many years into smaller quarters, and rightly so, in order to accommodate a fine new faculty appointment: a case of ecological succession, as it were. But in so doing, I was obliged to turf out some ancient office furniture, such as these old map cases." His liver-spotted but sure hand rested on a huge oaken cabinet. "One oughtn't be sentimental about such things. But I'm just down here bidding them goodbye, you know—they've served me well for decades—and making sure I've left nothing *in* them. My memory is not what it was at seventy."

Mead hoped his own memory would be as sharp at *thirty*. He was aware that Hutchinson was embarked on the fifth of a six-volume treatise on limnology: no task for an absent mind.

"Uh, oh—here, you see?" Hutchinson went on. "I *have* overlooked something!" He had opened a lower drawer and extracted a thin sheaf of papers. "Aha!" he said. "I've been wondering where these have been hiding! Most of my reprints are in good order, but *these* have been missing for ages."

Mead recalled his one earlier meeting with the man, at a departmental reception for the publication of his latest volume. The honoree had dismissed himself from a conversational knot and disappeared beneath the Galapagos tortoise that served as a lintel for his office. The matter under discussion had been a small, pied Eurasian species of merganser called the smew, one of which had fetched up on the shores of Long Island Sound. Mead thought Hutchinson might be consulting a field guide to acquaint himself with the species. Moments later he emerged, bearing an old paper of his on ancient illuminated manuscripts. "Was it rather like this?" he had asked, pointing to the margin of the paper, where stood an elegant fourteenth-century illumination of a smew. Winchester told him later that if there was anyone who might be expected to have published something on any given subject, it would be Evelyn Hutchinson.

Now, in the dusky cellar of Osborn Lab, James wondered what the missing reprints could possibly concern, and he asked as much.

"Oh, just a little aspection of the salt marshes around Indian Neck in Branford, which I conducted nearly forty years ago. Do you know the area?"

Indeed he did, though he didn't bother to mention that his view of Indian Neck had been largely through the bottom of a bottle of Schaefer.

Mead shook his head in wonder. "How is it, Professor, if I may ask, that you seem to have touched on almost every part of biology in your work? And a lot of other fields besides? I mean, how could one person do so much?"

"Well—" Hutchinson flushed a little at the run of questions but took it for sincere curiosity rather than flattery. "I'm not sure I've done quite so much as you seem to think I have. But remember, Mr. Mead, I am a year or two older than yourself. The studies—one's enthusiasms, their results—they do add up over the years, you know. At least that has been my experience."

"But when do you get the time to pursue them all?"

"*That*, Mr. Mead, is the one constant—it refuses to vary." He tipped his head and smiled with a sad, heavy-lidded nod. "It's merely a matter of how you use it. And, of course, I have had legions of helpful students."

"Is that all?" James sounded disappointed.

"Perhaps there is one other thing." Hutchinson sighed as he closed the drawer of the map case and shuffled the reprints. "Students seldom inquire about such matters anymore, and what I say may sound rather . . . archaic."

Mead shook his head no, go on.

"Or maybe I am speaking out of turn, as you are Professor Winchester's advisee?"

"No, please. George—Dr. Winchester—has often said that I should take advantage of any opportunity I might have to speak with you. I would truly welcome any advice."

"Well, it's not so strong a thing as *advice*, I daresay. Just this: I have found that above all, one must follow one's inclinations. The safe course seldom satisfies the mind in the long run. 'Taking risks,' I have noticed, is a popular phrase now among the young. But I suspect that few who utter it as a bromide know remotely what it means. In science and in letters, as in life itself, the rewarding course often proves to be the risky one, where the outcome is uncertain. With due intelligence and care, mind you—I'm not advocating foolhardiness or cavalier disregard for personal safety or responsibility."

Mead had to listen carefully to dredge each word from Hutchinson's clotted-cream speech, and he wasn't certain he'd caught every inflection or the full import. "Just how do you mean?" he asked.

"For example, when I put forth the concept of the ecological niche, as it is commonly known and misused today, it was not exactly the conservative thing to do. Actually, both Grinnell and Merriam had elucidated similar ideas early on, not to mention Darwin. But I expanded the concept and applied it theoretically into the n-dimensional hyperspace. It met a great deal of resistance before acceptance, general approbation, and finally co-option into the culture at large."

Mead nodded. Nowadays people spoke of their "niche" as blithely as they might say "lifestyle."

"Or," Hutchinson continued, "take a more recent case. I had a student, in fact my last, named Tim Lovelace—you've heard of him? I'm not surprised, he's one of the most famous conservation biologists around, right up there with Jacques Cousteau."

"Yes, I've heard of him in connection with tropical rainforests. What was his big risk?"

"Tim's family wanted him to follow the ancestral calling of stocks and securities. But his heart, conscience, mind, and professor all urged him toward the Amazon instead of Wall Street. He went there, all right—studied the amphibians with all the verve he might otherwise have squandered on debentures—and you see where it got him. He redefined how we look at the rapidly vanishing tropical forests, and how animals and plants respond to the fragmentation of those forests. His studies are now widely affecting policy. Few individuals have had as much influence on conservation or impact on the land. But, Mr. Mead, I fear I've kept you overlong. Will I see you at the departmental seminar tomorrow?"

"I expect so, Professor. If I can wake up by then. Thank you!"

"Yes, well, you'll be wanting to ascend to your battlement. Oh—I suppose I'm not meant to know about that. Well, good night!"

With that, the slumped brown shadow wheeled and receded down the dark hallway. Mead turned and punched the brass button that would summon the service elevator clunking down to his level. He was simply too tired to climb the stairs to his lair, and he still had a roach round to complete. At last he negotiated the ladder to the tower, and as he did, his head waggled like one of those doggies in the rear window of a '59 Buick. He'd forgotten all about the Coke. Entering his turret roundel, he sank onto his pallet in a hot, sweaty blanket of confusion.

"Well, that really helps," he complained to the tower's bats, the ones that arrived in May and came and went all summer. "Noni says to live in the present and make the most of my time here. Professor Hutchinson advises me to follow my whims, more or less. Great! Just like the average horoscope—something for everyone." As he tried to unscramble his brains, the bats squeaked and fanned his face with mothy wingbeats. That felt good, but their interpretation of the situation proved inscrutable. No help at all. He thought of Carson's late-night homilies, to the effect that the best way to deal with wanderlust is to follow it. "And Doc Hutchinson's counsel is pretty clear," he told the whirling bats. "Have the courage of your convictions."

With that, he dropped into a deep but troubled slumber. And when he awakened in the muggy cell, he ached all over. Carson's journeys in the wild mountains made his brain ache with desire to be there as well, to track him down, to see Magdalena for himself. His heart ached over Noni already; what would it be like in three months? And his mother was an ache in a place he couldn't name. As for Griffin, he was a specific pain in the ass. They all tugged, nagged, and smarted, and he wondered whether he'd be able to resist their collective westward push and pull.

He didn't think he could. He couldn't. Mead descended the ladder as soon as Tuesday morning pulled itself out of its sleeping bag of thick and woolly East Coast air. Then he walked downtown to the Greyhound depot and purchased a one-way ticket to Gunnison, Colorado.

That evening, when he'd finished his pastoral visit to the roach room, Mead went in search of Steve Manton and shanghaied him to Clark's Dairy for a malt. Entering the old campus hangout, they claimed a pair of curl-backed chairs on either side of an aluminum table. Mead rested his elbows on the worn, swirl-patterned Formica of the tabletop and waited for a menu. A robust waitress in a lime-green uniform emerged from behind the green faux marble counter and plopped menus, water glasses, napkins, and silverware before them. "What'll it be, bubs?"

"Hi, Stella," said Mead. Manton studied the menu as if he'd never seen it before. Mead, the menu committed to memory, studied the schmaltzy repro of a Swiss alpine oil on the wall beside them. Like everything else these days, it reminded him of Colorado.

"Uh, a double order of fries, please, and a root-beer soda." Steve ordered as if he were selecting the oysters Rockefeller and a suitable Semillon.

"Just a chocolate malt and a BLT for me, Stella," James added. "One bill, on me."

"You got it, bubs." Torturing her gum, the waitress scribbled the orders and padded back into the streamlined, key-lime and stainless steel world of the grill, toasters, malt makers, and glass racks behind the long U of the fountain bar. Her movements were as smooth, predictable, and anachronistic as the revolutions of the soda mixer itself. Mead had the sense that when these two finally wore out, they'd be making no more like them. Stella held the holders of endowed chairs in no greater awe than undergrads—in other words, none. Manton said she reminded him of his aunt, who'd waited tables to put his uncle through law school at Rutgers only to be dropped for a newer model somewhere between his bar exam and their son's bar mitzvah.

A plaque on the wall read THIS TABLE RESERVED FOR TWO OR MORE PERSONS, as grad students would settle in here, order a cup of coffee, and stay for the whole night, bogarting the table with books and papers. Manton cracked, "I used to think that sign had something to do with impromptu Gentile church services they held in here: 'wherever two or more are seated . . .'"

"God, you Jersey Jews can't even get the guy's lines right. It's 'wherever two or more are gathered in my name,' not 'gathered to scarf fries.'" On the way in, Mead had begun to feel fainthearted, wondering whether he really had the guts to go through with the mutiny. But the Swiss chocolate box scene recalled his purpose, the malt in his belly revived his strength, and the banter gave him heart. The vanilla walls and French vanilla ceiling (from ages of nicotine) gave the place a literal feel, old and mellow and milky wholesome. He said something to that effect.

"Yeah, all that's missing is the cows themselves," Manton said.

"Listen, Steve," said James, suddenly urgent. "Speaking of livestock . . ."

Three mornings later Mead awakened to a peeled peach of a moon setting over a thousand acres of sunflowers, and he was in Colorado. After a bleary-eyed cheeseburger at a downtown Denver lunch counter, he took the final 246 miles on a fresh bus to Gunnison. As the coach crossed South Park, crested Highway 287, and passed over Monarch Pass, Mead could not help looking out the window in the vain hope of spotting October Carson, net in hand and burro in tow, along the thoroughfare. But the wanderer was nearly four years and a dozen passes ahead of him. Those passes remained fresh in Mead's mind: Cottonwood, Weston, and Boreas, Hoosier, Independence, Mosquito, and the great Cumberland. Each one sounded like Mount Parnassus to Mead.

He had transcribed several pages of notes on *Erebia magdalena* from Carson's journal. Now, nearing the end of the line and nervous about what came next, he took them out to read. He found the part he liked best: "The butterflies are great. I'll never tire of Maggie. But she's got a rival in my mind: a face with no name. The brief encounters I've lived on for so long begin to seem wan, not to mention damned infrequent. I find myself longing for more than the occasional midnight mountain mating."

"Amen!" Mead exclaimed, and the Baptist across the aisle nodded his approval. Mead lay his head back, reclined the seat as far as it would go, and conjured midnight mountain matings to come.

PART TWO

21

For three days and nights Mary slept in her piney monastery cell, getting up only for a pee, a drink, or a bowl of soup. After she finally arose and bathed, she sat near an open window. The alpine air was redolent of willows and peaty mire. The sensation that she was really *here*, in the longed-for, wept-over mountains, almost whelmed her.

When her mind cleared, she wondered what kind of place this was. The robes of her hosts suggested some sort of a religious order, but the book on her bedside table gave her pause. At first she took it for a Bible, but the title on the spine, *Accepting the Universe: Essays in Naturalism*, said otherwise. It was by John Burroughs, and it lay open to an essay entitled "The Faith of a Naturalist." "I am persuaded that a man without religion falls short of the proper human ideal," it began.

"As I thought." Mary sighed and almost put it down both for the use of the word *man* and the word *religion*. "This is a religious house. Here comes the dogma." But she read on in spite of herself, and her reaction and her mind began to change.

"Religion," wrote Burroughs, "as I use the term, is a spiritual flowering, and the man who has it not is like a plant that never blooms. The mind that does not open and unfold its religious sensibilities in the sunshine of this infinite and spiritual universe is to be pitied. Men of science do well enough with no other religion than the love of truth, for this is indirectly a love of God."

"*Not* fundamentalists," Mary guessed. "But I wish he'd stop saying 'men.'" Then, checking the date of the essay's publication, 1920, she decided to cut it some slack.

> The astronomer, the geologist, the biologist, tracing the footsteps of the Creative Energy throughout the universe—what need has he of any formal, patent-right religion? Were not Darwin, Huxley, Tyndall and Lyell, and all other seekers and verifiers of natural truth among the most truly religious of men? Any of these men would have gone to hell for the truth—not the truth of creeds and rituals, but the truth as it exists in the councils of the Eternal and as it is written in the laws of matter and of life.

"Wow," she whispered. "Who *is* this guy?"

"The religion of a man that has no other aim than his own personal safety from some real or imaginary future calamity is of the selfish and ignoble kind."

Mary read faster.

> Amid the decay of creeds, love of nature has high religious value. This has saved many persons in this world—saved them from mammon-worship, and from frivolity and insincerity of the crowd. It has made their lives placid and sweet. It has given them an inexhaustible field for inquiry, for enjoyment, for the exercise of all their powers, and in the end has not left them soured and dissatisfied. It has made them contented and at home wherever they are in nature—in the house not made with hands.

"I'm *liking* this," Mary said, not beneath her breath.

"This house is their church," Burroughs went on,

and the rocks and the hills are the altars, and the creed is written in the leaves of the trees and in the flowers of the field and in the sands of the shore. A new creed every day and new preachers, and holy days all the week through. Every walk to the woods is a religious rite, every bath in the stream is a saving ordinance. Communion service is at all hours, and the bread and wine are from the heart and marrow of Mother Earth. There are no heretics in Nature's church; all are believers, all are communicants.

"Oh, yes!" Mary cried, reading with a fervor she had known only once in months and months: when she had found herself first able to read at all in the home and had come across an old story that seemed to matter deeply. She read on.

"The beauty of natural religion is that you have it all the time; you do not have to seek it afar off in myths and legends, in catacombs, in garbled texts, in miracles of dead saints . . ."

"Right on!"

". . . or wine-bibbing friars. It is of to-day; it is now and here; it is everywhere." Shivering with forgotten recognition, Mary began to read aloud:

"The crickets chirp it, the birds sing it, the breezes chant it, the thunder proclaims it, the streams murmur it, the unaffected man lives it. Its incense rises from the plowed fields, it is in the morning breeze, it is in the forest breath and in the spray of the wave. The frosts write it in exquisite characters, the dews impearl it, and the rainbow paints it on the cloud. It is not an insurance policy underwritten by a bishop or a priest; it is not even a faith; it is a love, an enthusiasm, a consecration to natural truth."

What kind of people *are* these robed mountain men, Mary wondered, who think like this? As they must, to put this here for me to see. Ravenous to finish, she hurried on. " 'The God of sunshine and of storms speaks a less equivocal language than the God of revelation.'"

Her voice rose:

"A man is not saved by the truth of the things he believes, but by the truth of his belief—its sincerity, its harmony with his character. The absurdities of the popular religions do not matter; what matters is the lukewarm belief, the empty forms, the shallow conceptions of life and duty. We are prone to think that if the creed is false, the religion is false. Religion is an emotion, an inspiration, a feeling of the Infinite, and may have its root in any creed or in no creed ... Any creed that ennobles character and opens a door or window upon the deeper meanings of this marvelous universe is good enough to live by, and good enough to die by."

"Amen!" Mary fairly shouted. And a chorus of "amens" mixed with gentle laughter rose outside her door, which was ajar. Mary started and turned to see a dozen friendly faces looking in. Drawn by her unself-conscious oration, they had come one by one to listen at the door. Mary stood and blushed, then smiled back and accepted a round of gentle, woolly hugs.

"So you see what we are about," said one.

"More or less," said Mary, "and I think I like it."

The next afternoon, when she seemed well rested, Oberon asked Mary if she was ready to take a walk. She paused, touched her chin, turned her head, and said, "Yes."

Oberon led her down a gravelly lane from the monastery to the state highway. She shielded her eyes from the high, bright sunlight, so much purer and sharper than she'd known it in the city. They passed a strange and pretty stone-built chapel, crossed the highway, and found a small trail on the other side. It led up a gentle grade through pink granite grus and twisted limber pines, above a series of beaver dams, to one of the round domes that pillow the Front Range here and there. Made of orange and gray feldspar, black and clear mica, and white and rose quartz, all bundled into granite by pressure, heat, and time and spattered pale green with lichens, these humps exfoliated slabs of themselves when the winter ice swelled and then melted in spring, like the layers of some tough kind of bulb. Their smooth tops make fine perches for ravens, watchers, and meditators. Oberon led Mary Glanville to one of these seats.

Mary's eyes, thirsty for fresh images, took in every nuance of the scene before her. It began at the double summit of Magdalena Mountain, sharp in the clear light, then followed the rocks and trees down the mountain's middle to the humpy forest, on the lip of which stood the monastery. Its five gable windows in the big shingled roof, twenty-two room windows below them, and twelve big windows on the ground level all shone in the afternoon sun like giant flakes of mica.

Her eyes continued farther down, across the willow bogs, to Cabin Creek and its culvert under the road between beaver ponds. Cerise fireweed, rose cranesbill, foamy white umbels and everlastings, lemony cinquefoils and goldenrods colored the marshy edges, and all around on the sandy floor the yellow and purple asters of the season filled in the colorless shell that Mary had become. Oberon kept his peace as Mary sucked in the view, growing drunk with relief and a swelling joy. Ravens echoed bass notes overhead, juncos and bushtits tinkled in the pines.

Mary fixed on the little stone chapel, a Byzantine confection more at home in Old Europe than Colorado. The south-end vestry was rounded like a boat's prow; the other end supported a cylindrical bell tower with a tiny circular window near the conical peak. Red sandstone Roman arches rounded the three tall windows of the gabled nave and smaller ones on either side. The whole sat seamlessly on the stone, as if it had grown out of the very bedrock, like a great fruiting body put forth by the lichens that covered its blocks. A massive white statue of Jesus stood on the outcrop just north of the chapel. "What is this place?" she asked. "Who *are* you all?"

"That mountain is called Magdalena," began Oberon. Gazing at the peak as he spoke, he missed the contented shade that crept across Mary's face. "The monastery borrowed its name, or vice versa, a long time ago, although we simply call it the Mountain Monastery now. And the little church, perched there above Cabin Creek, is the Chapel of St. Mary Magdalene."

"Of course it is," said Mary. "But which came first, the mountain or the chapel?"

"Why ... the *mountain*—"

"I mean, the *name*—which one was named first?"

"I have no idea. Although I suspect it was the mountain, since the chapel was not built until sometime after 1930. And here's another oddment for you: the settlement around the old lodge up the road is called Magdalena Park. It began in the twenties, I believe. So a tangled web indeed has been woven hereabouts, namewise."

"Don't you suppose there must be some connection?"

"Maybe so. But the world is full of marvelous coincidences, and all these Magdalenas may be just one more."

"I doubt it," Mary said. "It all fits. By the way, do you believe in coincidence?"

"Absolutely. Jung spoke of the physics of fate: so much is going on at any given time that if we pay attention, synchronicity is sure to pop up now and then." He paused. Then, as Mary said nothing, he went on. "It may seem so sometimes, but I don't accept that things are prearranged. Free will, flawed as it is by hubris and Murphy's Law, does exist. We can make it work, or we can screw it up. And at the moment, right here, it's a toss-up. If Attalus has his way—"

"Wait, wait. Slow down, back up," Mary pleaded. "Oberon, what *is* going on here? What is it you're trying to do, and why do you all have these funny names? And outfits? And you still haven't told me who you are—except Oberon, which I very much doubt was your given name. Oh, I've picked up bits, and the John Burroughs essay was wonderful. But I need to know more—especially since it seems that I'm the crux of your immediate problem. And because I *do* somehow feel that I am supposed to be here."

"Okay, fair enough. I know it all seems a bit strange. The monastery was built in 1925 to house a healing order of Catholic monks known as the Brothers of the Bleeding Bota. They took their name from an obscure and controversial 'miracle.' The order, never fully recognized by Rome but tolerated on account of the useful work they performed among the miners, many of whom were Italian, Irish, and Polish Catholics, was founded by Gunnison Whetstone."

"Who was?"

"A second-generation English immigrant rancher from the Western Slope. He took holy orders more to escape than to repent for a series of peccadilloes, or so the story goes. Following the putative miracle, and in a fit of belated contrition, he sold his ranches, built the monastery, gathered the brotherhood around him—mostly ex–World War One medics and defrocked country priests. Together, they set up the order."

"So what was the miracle?" Mary asked, her voice dripping with skepticism.

"On a hunting trip, Whetstone encountered a Basque padre ministering among the sheepherders from his homeland. He carried a leather bota of wine for Communion and other emergencies. The two men shared a campfire and company, and passed the bota. Whetstone, struck by the old man's sincere and simple faith, confessed to him, which took quite a while. In the morning the bota began dripping what the friar took for the blood of Christ. Doubtless having helped to consume the better portion of its contents, and feeling religious to boot, Whetstone found no grounds on which to disagree."

"And these two . . . 'wine-bibbing friars,' I think Burroughs called them . . . were believed?"

"Hardly. The priest submitted the vision and Whetstone's sworn witness to a Board of Miracles at the next papal review, or however they do that. But apparently the board regarded the bota as merely holey rather than holy, and the petitioners as earnest but deluded. Nonetheless, Whetstone was impressed—or maybe he just liked the symbolism. Some say he was never seen without a bota ever after, and that he presided personally over frequent bleedings of the icon."

"And you say this bemused sot ran a medical order?"

"Yes, and rather a good one, for both humans and other animals. He was a self-taught vet for cattle and horses and a cat lover. Several of the others had experience from the trenches and field hospitals in Europe. Over the years they recruited a talented band of disillusioned doctors, and eventually a small nursing sisterhood settled in across the road in an old log ranch house, since burnt down."

"Go on."

"Well," said Oberon, scanning the scene around him as he spoke, "between the two orders, they brought a modicum of care to a motley collection of patients along the Front Range: poor, uninsured, doctor-fearing, superstitious, itinerant, snowbound . . . they were a boon to the area for decades, even if Whetstone proved incorrigible."

"How so?"

"Well, he and the others often bartered for payment, of course. Some of the female clients, bearing cats and poodles for Gunnison's ministrations, were said to be recognizable from certain well-known houses in Central City and Blackhawk. This is mere hearsay, of course. Almost certainly apocryphal is the local legend that Whetstone built a tunnel between the monastery and the convent."

"A *tunnel*—in the rock?" Mary ran her soft hand over the unyielding granite.

"It was supposed to incorporate part of an old gold mine drift."

"So what became of them?"

Oberon combed his beard with his fingers, shook his head, and stretched. "Well, the nursing nuns aged and failed to attract recruits, given the shortage of nurses everywhere, and all of those going to Vietnam. The medical monks followed, whipped by a grand slam of malpractice suits by ingrates, insurance burdens, and harassment by the state licensing board. I'd guess a collective loss of faith finally did them in. The last of them, except for Attalus and the hermit Thomas, went down the mountain just last year."

"So then what? How did you all get here?"

"Xerxes, Sylvanus, Abraxas, and I were all bumming around the Peak to Peak or the park for one reason or another a few years ago, and we got to know each other. We were all naturalists. Sylvanus knew Attalus, a member of the old order, via botany. His name was Brother Jacob back then. Through Jacob, we found out that the whole place was going to be put on the block by the archdiocese. So we threw our bankrolls and grubstakes together, took out loans, and bought an option on it. Now we're trying to raise funds to buy the title outright from the Catholics."

"To continue the brotherhood?"

"In a manner of speaking. The original order was abolished by the court. The Vatican didn't give a hoot; neither the miracle nor the order was ever sanctioned. After suits were settled, the remaining assets went to the archdiocese, which had tolerated the brothers up to that point because they filled in a hole on the map. So we have no ties to the old regime, or to the church. We are now a new kind of brotherhood—soon, I hope, to be a sisterhood as well. But as you've seen, not much like the old outfit."

"Some kind of a New Age cult?" Mary asked, hoping it wasn't so.

"Hardly a cult—and definitely not new. We're a chapter, or Grove as it's called, of a more widespread federation called the Pan-Pacific League, inspired by the Old Religion, demystified. A band of pagans with a pantheistic bent, but not really theists for the most part, and with lowercase *p*'s, too. We try to live by consensus, have no leader as such, and share a set of core beliefs along the lines of that Burroughs piece you so enjoyed. What? Who was he? Oh—the best-known naturalist of the past century, friend of Muir, Whitman, and Teddy Roosevelt. One of the founders of conservation."

"Oh, is *that* all. So he's your prophet. What do you worship?"

"Nothing. But we venerate all the natural processes—including ourselves. We try not to recognize any real separation between humans and the rest of nature."

"'And no religion too'?" Mary asked, nodding toward Jesus as she quoted John Lennon.

"Well, we borrow some of the teachings of Christianity, yeah, as well as Judaism, Wicca, Buddhism, Islam, Shinto, Hinduism, Native American traditions, and other faiths, while rejecting the cant of any and all. But our fundament is nature itself. We revere the earth as a part of the universe, and our ultimate sympathies lie with the land. Hence the Burroughs creed, and of course Aldo Leopold's land ethic as a kind of doxology."

"I've heard of him, but what did he say? Remind me."

"'A thing is right when it tends to preserve the integrity, stability, and beauty of the biotic community. It is wrong when it tends otherwise.'"

"My, that's good! Says it all. Okay, no cult then."

"And certainly not New Age! We have no truck with the muddy-minded maundering that passes for thought under that heading. Crystals are lovely, but we prefer them in the ground or hanging from the rearview rather than casting spells or telling fortunes. To each his own, or hers, but we tend toward the hard head and the clear eye—or try to. So don't try to find anyone to push your horoscope or Tarot cards around here."

"Darn!"

"You could say the Pan-Pacific ideal is based on the real physical world, understanding it and keeping it alive and well and hospitable to humans and their neighbors as long as possible. We'd like to play a small role in that. But the outfit is young and pretty tentative at this point, with no bureaucracy, thank God—so to speak."

"And your, let's say, *unusual* names?"

"Well, some of the Groves are involved in direct actions of resistance, and they have sometimes found aliases useful in dealing with the law. But the names are also just for fun and, like our practical robes, a way to leave old lives behind. Monks know what they're doing, you know. Our names mostly come from the far past—rustic deities, mythic and classical figures, and so on, many of them in some way connected to fauna and flora. Our 'friend' Attalus, for example, chose his handle because at least two historical figures by that name were plant lovers."

"So you became Oberon—King of the Fairies in *A Midsummer Night's Dream?*"

"Yes. But long before Shakespeare got hold of him, the name appeared in an early-thirteenth-century epic poem by Huon de Bordeaux. He referred to Oberon as 'an elven man of the forest,' and I liked that. Plus, I just like his part in the play . . . that very clever bit with Bottom, for example. The fact that I am fond of donkeys might enter in."

"And is that your Puck?" Mary gestured to a striped imp, a golden-mantled ground squirrel that had been sniffing and jigging about the interlopers ever since they'd arrived on its stone. Observed, the rodent vanished as if embarrassed, then reappeared a few rocks off. They both laughed. A chipmunk chipped, scratched its cinnamon side, and flicked its russet tail as it held ground on an orange-sherbet rock. A ladybird beetle flew by like a saffron chip on the air. A handful of pink pellets Mary had collected from around her feet rattled down the boulder face as she let them go and spoke again. "But tell me: Might I have heard of your experiment here?"

"Sure. We've placed notices in the pagan press and in several ecological and peace journals: 'Magdalena Mountain, a new Grove of the Pan-Pacific League, seeks residents who place peace and nature above all,' et cetera, et cetera. Since then, a small but steady stream of applicants and inquiries have come in. Few are accepted. Druggies, nature voyeurs, and the ambitious we ferret out right away, as well as the would-be messiahs, narcissists, and metaphysical gamers—you know, those New Agers we were talking about who are all over the board and confuse oatmeal with ideas."

"So what kinds of people *have* you admitted?"

"Naturalists, field biologists, burned-out conservation radicals, a few abos . . ."

"Abos?"

"Not real aboriginals. Native Americans have shown no interest in us, possibly because we seem redundant or latecomers to their view of life. These are folks interested in a hunter-gatherer, nontechnological lifestyle. They call themselves abos—but most are too antisocial even for us. We get the odd intellectual interested in the human–nature nexus. We come from every walk of life, as they say. I, since you ask, have done many kinds of work in many different places. I was attracted by the chance to do something worthwhile, situated in one place for a change. So we're quite diverse, really. Though so far, no women have been admitted."

The mountain sky had clouded, and so did Mary's face. "For God's sake, *why?*" she nearly shouted, putting Puck in his place beneath the rocks for minutes to come.

"It bugs me as much as it does you, I promise," Oberon said. "We all deplore the fact—all except Attalus, whom you haven't yet met, in a wakeful state at least. For now, as the church's representative, he has veto power over major decisions."

"So what is his problem?"

"He's a classic misogynist, of the bad old school. He thinks women have a place, all right, and it's nowhere near him. He was furious that I insisted on bringing you here when we found you. He's after you, and he'll get rid of you if he can."

Mary bristled, and shuddered. "He'll have to put his back into it to dislodge me now, if the rest of you want me here."

"You know we do."

"But you haven't examined my application," Mary protested with a hint of a smile. "How do you know I'm not a narcissistic whatever?"

Oberon smiled. "You came to us by a kind of grace, and you're welcome to stay as long as you want. Attalus will have his way over several of our dead bodies." As they spoke, the sun swooped down onto the crown of Magdalena Mountain, then dropped below the edge. A beam shot through a gap on the western arête, falling onto the chapel. "Godbeams," he said, laughing.

"But no laughing matter, this Attalus character. Should I be afraid of him?"

"At least vigilant. He hates you, though he doesn't even know you, and he fears you more. He would have you put out, or down, without compunction. He actually wanted me to leave you in the road to die that night, and he cursed the fact that you were still alive!"

Mary shivered, whether from the rising cool, the enmity, or both.

"He imagines that you are a harlot and a sorceress, come to ruin us. Really *believes* it!"

"I've been *there* before," she murmured.

"I beg your pardon?"

"Well, it's nothing new, is it? But what should I do?"

"Just stay away from him for now, and be alone as little as possible. I'll be sleeping in the next cell, with an ear cocked. And I've asked a friend of mine, a woman named Annie, to share your room for a night or two, if you're willing."

"I am. Then what?"

"This is Sunday. Tuesday is our Forest Meeting, where we discuss whatever's on our minds and plates and attempt to reach consensus on any issues. After that, one of you will likely leave—and it won't be you, if I can help it."

Mary asked, "Is there a Queen of the Fairies?"

"Titania"—Oberon paused and cleared his throat—"has proven elusive."

Now it was cool dusk. A muskrat parted the surface of the beaver pond below with wavy-tailed ripples. Growing chilly yet reluctant to leave their stone aerie, Mary and Oberon watched its progress. A damp, musky-sweet breeze rose off the willow bog, bending the wispy stalks of grass over the edge of the rock against the dark conifers. Let this mad monk do his worst, Mary thought; I've known still worse. For blessed moments, dangers retreated before a rising mountain moon.

22

"Oberon!" The shout came from across the highway. "Come!"

"Who's that?" Mary whispered.

"It's Xerxes. We'd better do as he says—something must be wrong. Hurry down, but watch your step—that gravel is slippery." They retraced the path and hastened across the road to the chapel, where they encountered the panting monk.

"What is it, Xerxes?" Oberon demanded.

The big man struggled for his breath and his voice. His normally placid face was contorted and flushed in the last light, whether more from exertion or agitation it was hard to tell. "It's Attalus, Oberon. He telephoned the mental health authorities in Denver about Mary and summoned them."

Mary gasped.

"Now they've come for her, claiming she's a runaway from an institution of some kind, in need of care. They mean to take her away." Xerxes had a quaver in his voice, and he avoided Mary's eye.

"No!" Mary cried. "They can't take me back there. I'll die first! Oberon, Xerxes, help me. Don't let them!" She felt an old sick feeling climbing her stomach walls with crampons on.

"Come into the chapel." Oberon drew her inside, then guided

her up a narrow staircase into the tiny choir loft. "Now, here—you see, among the panels? This is a door. Behind it, a hidden compartment. It's a mock monk's hole, like the ones where the clergy used to hide from the various persecutions in Europe. Built just for fun, I'll bet, when this folly was erected. I found it while looking for someplace to stow the paraphernalia of the old order and other things. I doubt Attalus knows anything about it."

Looking into the black hidey-hole, Mary asked, "You want me to hide *there*?"

"Not now. Just wait up here until I come for you. But if you hear anyone else, duck inside. It's not bad; I cleaned it out and stashed some extra robes in there. You can wrap up in them. There's even some reading material—though I doubt it would interest you, and besides, it'll be pitch-black inside. Now, Xerxes, let's see about this invasion."

When they entered the monastery, they found two strangers seated in the hallway. They looked up. Attalus was nowhere to be seen.

"Can I help you, gentlemen?" Oberon offered, expressionless.

"Are you in charge around here?" one of them asked.

"As much as anyone. May I offer you something after your drive?"

"Never mind that," the same one shot back. "We understand you have a woman named Mary Glanville here."

"She has been," parried Oberon, "and may be again. What do you want with her?"

The second man spoke. "The young woman walked away from a care facility in Denver. We'd like to return her so that she may continue her treatment in safety."

Oberon shot back, "Apparently your 'treatment' amounted to drugging her silly. Since she has been with us, Ms. Glanville, if that's her name, has fully recovered her faculties." He paused, calmed himself, and continued. "Who are you, and who gives you the right to show up and take someone against her will?"

The paunchier of the two, dressed in a polyester suit beneath a zip-lined raincoat, replied, "I'm Sam Tonkin, State Department of Social Service." He nodded at his taller companion, who actually wore a white coat.

"And I'm Dr. Mitchell Ziegler, of the Denver Mental Health Corporation. We contract with the state of Colorado. I'm the state-appointed psychiatrist for the Mid-Continent Care Center, where the patient belongs. We've come to take her back there."

"She left for a reason," Oberon flicked back in his face. "Your 'home' was no kind of home for her. Why should we allow you to take her, even if she were still here?" Voices were rising, robed men assembling. The outer door opened, and a woman entered. She stood wide-eyed, exchanged brief looks with Oberon, and remained beside the door.

"Is that her?" Tonkin asked.

Ziegler said no, it was not; Mary was brunette.

"Look, mister," said Tonkin. "This woman is a charge of the state. She had a bad wreck and got brain damage. She has delusions, and she may represent a danger to herself or others. Now, you'd best cooperate with us."

"Mary got herself here," said Oberon. "She's capable, in control, and harmless. Since when does an accident make her subject to incarceration or suspension of her civil rights?"

"Mr. Oberon." The doctor stepped between Tonkin and Oberon. "In my professional opinion, this unfortunate woman—Mary—needs further care and confinement. It is our responsibility—"

"Further sedation, you mean. Did you ever examine her undrugged?"

"Well, I attempted to interview her upon admission," said Ziegler. "She couldn't, or wouldn't, speak. Later she managed a few words for the nurse and the center director, but her speech became hysterical and then degenerated into delusional nonsense."

"Now, Dr. Ziegler, she is articulate and cogent," said Xerxes.

"I'd be very happy to see that. Will you please bring her here?"

"Have you got a warrant? Or anything that empowers you to remove a person from a religious sanctuary?" asked Oberon. "Because if you haven't, you're wasting your time, and ours. Intimidation may work with your patients, but not here." Mutters of approval rose around them. "Or do you intend to abduct her by force?"

"We've got no warrant, mister," said Tonkin. "But it's our job, and we intend to finish it. We've had a complaint from one of your people, who says he is in charge and claims that the escapee is unwanted and disruptive and in need of medical attention."

"Attalus!" snorted Sylvanus and several others at once.

Now Xerxes spoke again. "Gentlemen, what you've heard is mistaken. One of our number, it is true, is dissatisfied in the matter. But he is at odds with the rest of us on several issues, essentially a malcontent. He has an ax to grind that has nothing to do directly with Ms. Glanville. Nor is he here to speak for himself." Silence for a moment, and then he continued. "Mary is welcome here. She has behaved rationally and has caused no trouble. She has been examined by a qualified physician and is pronounced healthy. Your informant is a minority of one, with no authority in this matter." Xerxes kept his cool better than Oberon would have.

"Just the same," retorted Tonkin, "we've come for her, and we intend to take her back."

"Well, you sure as hell won't have her," blurted Oberon. "I hate to deny our hospitality to anyone, but I hereby expel you from this monastery in the name of . . . hell, just get the fuck out!"

They hesitated. The woman by the door asked, "Oberon, shall I call the sheriff?"

Oberon looked the visitors in the eyes. "Gentlemen?"

Tonkin and Ziegler bought the bluff and turned. Annie held the door open and Xerxes ushered them out.

No one said goodbye, but as he stalked away, Tonkin growled, "They'll be sorry for this."

"Threats won't help," said Ziegler, and their voices trailed off as car doors slammed shut and the state motor pool Plymouth rolled down the drive. Once on the highway, Tonkin punched the accelerator and continued to fulminate. "Bunch of goddamned kooks, dressed in bathrobes and harboring mental deficients."

"Sam! She isn't deficient, she's injured—you've got to learn a new language if you're going to make it in this job. And you know we have no real authority here. Besides, if, as they say, Mary has improved, maybe she really is better off here."

"Stuff it, Doc! I knew this kind of crap would happen when I agreed to transfer from Corrections. There, you know where you stand. God, I miss my badge! I know where she'd be better off. And Ames will have my ass for breakfast for coming back empty-handed after the escape got in the *Post*. With the quarterly review coming up for the agency, for Christ's sake!"

"The timing is unfortunate," Ziegler agreed.

"Well, why the hell didn't you give me more backup in there? Anybody'd think you were on *their* side!"

"If what they say is so, maybe I am. It's the *patient's* side I'm supposed to be on, remember? You, too. But you're so damned concerned about your own hide that you forget entirely about our clients' well-being. Maybe it's that way in Corrections . . . maybe that's why the jails are overflowing. But I'd like to think we still care about the people in our . . . well, our *care*. There's no therapy like community, and she sure wasn't getting much of that at the center. Besides— we're way out of your jurisdiction here."

Throughout the encounter, Mary had clung to the railing in the choir, ready to dart into the monk's hole at the approach of footsteps in the gravel outside. The soft light of votive candles and an iron lamp dimly illuminated the chapel's interior. For the first time, Mary had a chance to examine the intimate space of the tiny church. She saw that the walls were stone within as well as without, pale granite flecked with black mica, daubed with lichens, banded by gray mortar. The vaulted wood ceiling ran to galleries at both ends, one of which Mary occupied. A polished red-granite altar stone stood upon a rough pink granite base and a maroon floor of Lyons flagstones. Varnished wainscoting echoed the dark shine of the pews.

Narrow niches held effigies of Jesus and his mother on either side of a rough-hewn crucifix, fresh mountain flowers in a brass vase at its base. In the arched windows, stained glass reflected the candles in yellow, green, and blue. Mary, from her own niche, could not see another window below her, nor would mere moonlight have lit up its vivid art nouveau portrait of Mary Magdalene, gowned in red, blue, and green. But she could see the graceful marble of the Holy Mother on a pedestal beside the stairs, jar of unguent in her hand. She seemed to be looking up at the living Mary, as if neither could take her eyes off the other. Mary's eyes shone with moonlight and fearful tears. She gathered a green cloak about her and prepared to do what thousands of clerics had done during the dissolution of the monasteries in England and other terrors over the centuries of persecution. She quivered in her waiting.

Then the spray of gravel on steel as her own persecutor tore out, punching the car onto Highway 7, pointing south. Soon, footsteps ended her vigil. Mary shrank into a shadow until Oberon called softly, "It's all right, Mary, it's me. They're gone."

He climbed the stairs, knelt beside Mary, and held her for some time as she trembled. When the shaking subsided, there among the soft green robes in the choir loft of the chapel, Mary took him to her.

23

<u>July 10</u>. Idaho Springs. Traditionally, I stop off at Loveland Pass to chase Magdalena alpines about this time. Most years, this is the peak of the flight period for fresh males, and the females have just begun to appear. So it was today. Conditions couldn't have been better for alpines or alpine hunters. And since I took none on that fine Front Range peak before getting stuck overnight, I worked doubly hard today.

My scruples retreated before the bright sunshine. I crisscrossed the easy-to-reach rockslide, tracking the black beast back and forth and up and down. What a day! I caught twelve good males, three fine females, and observed a courtship, a spider catch, and four nectaring episodes. Constantly, Milbert's tortoiseshells dashed at Magdalenas in apparent courtship approaches. The Maggies paid little attention. But whenever an alpine sailed near a perching tortoiseshell, the Milberts would blast off at it. The pairing of the fire-rimmed nymphalid and the ebony alpine in flight made a striking motion picture. Detailed observations follow, for George or whoever might find them of use.

<u>July 13</u>. Made my way on foot across Rollins Pass, an old and no doubt heart-stopping narrow-gauge railroad route. It still is, head-

ing down the other side—I hopped a D&RGW freight at Winter Park, jumped off here in Steamboat Springs. A railroad official spotted me, but didn't look twice. In this recession, it seems there are almost as many people riding the rails as there were in the Depression. The ones I met were Vietnam vets, now home and hurt and disillusioned, wondering what it was all for.

Now I'll begin my old circuit of the high passes and parklands, working south, hitching and walking. It'll be fine to be back in familiar country, to breathe nothing but the rarefied air of the Rockies, to find the good butterflies where I expect to find them—once I get past the gas fumes and glitz of all the once-pretty mountain towns gone to ski-burbs.

I plan to work the fritillary and checkerspot meadows of Rabbit Ears Pass, then head down to the high sage desert near Glenwood Springs to hunt Baird's and Minor's swallowtails and Nabokov's and Stretch's satyrs above those black and red canyons. If I don't decide to go west for Nokomis, I'll head up Grand Mesa for the Colorado hairstreak on the oaks (love that amethyst purple, silver, and orange!), then through Crystal and over Schofield Pass. Being footloose is exhilarating. But I do keep wondering what it would be like to have somewhere I felt I was supposed to be for a change.

July 19. Kebler Pass. Stopped into Gothic, hoping to meet George Winchester at last. Sadly, he was away in the field. I left him a note and a nice box o' butterflies. Didn't hang around, although there were plenty of butterfly types on hand. I did catch a lecture by Peter Freulich on population ecology of fritillaries and Homo sapiens, then crashed behind the old brothel. But I feel a little out of my element around all the academics, as if they wouldn't be interested in what a mere professional collector sans PhD has to say. Or maybe it's all the shiny students, making me feel my age and wonder about roads not taken. Not that I haven't taken a lot of roads. But what if

I'd taken theirs? Well, it doesn't matter now. No one bothered me, and I headed out in the morning.

I carried on down the East River meanders, stopping to crop the silver-bordered frits and Sonora skippers on the red clover they shared with the cattle, waving to flyfishers along the stream: to each his own. This is my own (though when no one was looking, I caught a couple of brookies in my net for supper). Rested over in Crested Butte for a day, acting the Old Prospector, but didn't do too well without a burro. Anyway, Crested has run toward the trendy since Mt. Crested Butte has been developed. It's no longer the crusty, dusty little coal town I knew years ago. They're even talking about paving Elk Avenue! I was glad to get back up into the hills. I've always loved this low little pass, covered in orange <u>Rudbeckia</u> sunflowers, and Charlotte's silverspots on the elk thistles down the other side toward Somerset.

<u>July 20</u>. Gunnison. From Kebler, a passing cowhand picked me up in his rattly jeep and took me eight bumpy miles down a pair of ruts to a remote line cabin he shares with his wife. Though there was cat shit in the bed, the view of Mount Marcellina over the meadows made up for it. This morning they fed me, gave me strong coffee, and drove me back up to the road.

<u>July 25</u>. Lake City. I made my way around to the Black Canyon, over the Blue Mesa, and up into the cool San Juans. Here, the proximity of the high tundra to the chic western towns allows me to play different roles for different urges and markets. Yesterday I collected 73 perfect Mead's sulphurs, without making a dent in their numbers, on Mesa Seco—the only huge, <u>flat</u> expanse of tundra I know where one can actually chase the brilliant burnt-orange critters without suffering cardiac arrest or broken ankles. (I love their dusky spring-green eyes and undersides, their rose-pink antennae and fringes. I can see why Japanese collectors will pay five dollars

a pair. I could make a lot more collecting strictly for them, but I prefer selling most of my catch to museums, where they at least have scientific value.) It's sort of like Trail Ridge Road in RMNP up there at Mesa Seco, without the road or the rangers. I caught some paint-numbered individuals and carefully released them; probably evidence of some Gothicite's research.

And the day before Mesa Seco, I'd posed as ye olde prospector for 27 families in stifling Durango, most of them waiting for the steam train. Rode the narrow-gauge myself to Silverton and got sixteen more. That bought me a good dinner, an estimable bottle, a soft bed and shower, and moleskin for my blisters, plus breakfast and lunchmeat.

Tomorrow I will cross the San Juans on foot. At my last campsite, I <u>thought</u> I saw a little real color in the stream, not just pyrite and mica, and tried panning with my Sierra Club cup. I had the good luck to pull in a small nugget, which I traded this afternoon for a sweet little burro named Betsy. Her company will improve the passage over Dallas Divide, distribute the load, and make the picture-pimping much easier in Ouray.

I don't really mind the posing, except for the time away from the habitat. In fact, back in Durango, a very attractive woman offered me a buck just to sit in my lap. She didn't even have a camera. I almost thought I'd found a camping companion, until <u>her</u> companion reclaimed her, with no smile. Well, Betsy's not quite as cute, but she's bound to carry more and cost less to feed.

I'll spend a couple of days around Ouray and its hot springs, then turn up to Telluride; I need to store up some more ready cash while I can. I'd like to try to find the old road above the town where Nabokov finally encountered the first female of <u>Lycaeides sublivens</u>, and where his Humbert realized the enormity of his crimes against Lolita. I want to listen for the voices of the children rising from the valley below, as he heard. Most likely these days, with the film festival on, all I'll hear is traffic. But hell, I might even blow some bucks for a livery, a room, and a movie ticket or two myself.

August 15. At last to Cumberland, pass of passes. How can one compare these Elysian lawns, these states of mind called passes, with one another? I've been to Hoosier, Boreas, Weston, Independence, and Mosquito, all in the past couple of weeks, and I love them all. But I love Cumberland best. You can walk in any direction onto the tundra, the rockslides, the fellfields, for miles and miles across endless ridges, across the Continental Divide itself and back, and not have to drop into civilization (or what passes for it), or into sagebrush, until the inclination strikes. And in so doing, you can find loads of the alpine butterflies "disporting in a paradise of floral profusion" as the old books say. It's the only place I know where Polyxenes, Melissa, white-veined, and chryxus arctics all fly together, along with all four Colorado alpines and the rest of their high-country company.

And that is just what I've done, sleeping for three nights in the rotting old cabin at the base of the talus, listening to the boulder bunnies and whistlepigs sort themselves out before bed and the pine grosbeaks piping down in the forest fringe, then (from this roofless ruin) watching the sky turn on as many stars as grains of mica in the rockslide.

Too bad I couldn't stay so high. What goes up, et cetera. Partly it's the damage wrought by jeeps and dirtbikes tearing up the tundra like a can opener on the inside of your wrist. They leave nothing but bare dirt and shredded plants, and when the rains come, another piece of Cumberland washes down into the trout stream far below.

On top of that, I'm growing sated with my carnage. I know it isn't a conservation matter: I could no more knock down the populations of these alpine insects with my net than I could rid our campsite of our fine companions, the mosquitoes—or Betsy's favorites, the horseflies—with a flyswatter. It's easy to make the argument that butterflies are a renewable resource, in the Forest Service's favorite phrase. And it's not like my specimens are going for trinkets. After all, the tedium of transcribing full data on every envelope ensures their scientific value and that my work is worth something. So much for the speech to self.

But to be confronted with so much living beauty only to still it—over and over, some three thousand times this summer alone—I am beginning to find it dulling and brutalizing. Not that I don't continue to take pleasure in a clean catch and in the preparation of specimens on the picnic table in the evening. But if this journal is more filled with behavioral observations of butterflies than earlier volumes, it is because I feel a greater and greater need to observe. So my catch is actually down from earlier seasons. Not that I'm becoming anti-collector. But I'd like to be involved in the serious study of these creatures, and conservation of their habitats, alongside their mere catching.

Trying to take a sum of my accounts, I find that I have regained great strength from the mountains and made enough to get me through the winter once I cash in the catch. But also that I need to train my energies elsewhere for a while. My reaction to the dirt-bikers disturbed me—I'd have lashed out if I'd seen them. I'd like to fight the tundra wreckers in some effective but nonviolent manner. Actually I'd like to blow them away—the jeeps, not the drivers—but maybe there's another way. I wonder what that might be, and where?

Besides, I feel autumn in the air. Cool air is moving in, there was frost on my sleeping bag last night. Forget the flyswatter— the mosquitoes are on their way out of their own accord. And the butterflies are beginning to grow tatty. Only the pine whites and Mead's wood nymphs remain to emerge afresh down in the ponderosa meadows. I'll look for them around Bailey, when I head down Turkey Creek in a few days.

And then I think I'll return to the Front Range for a while before heading back to the Coast. I love the early autumn there, the time of asters and gentians. And some of the little towns, like Raymond and Ward and Ferncliff and Allenspark, have been spared the mercantile ravages that are so mangling all the little ski towns nearer the Divide. Maybe I'll even hang around Boulder and Nederland a little, if they are bearable. But then there is Betsy. I hope I'll be able to keep her for a while longer. An old graybeard with a pretty good prospector shtick tried to buy her from me for fifty bucks back in Tincup. But she's become a good friend, worth more to me than the damn money. She'll limit my movements for winter if I stick around, but she might also keep me from freezing if I don't find a roof before the snow flies.

I will miss this high country, God knows I will. I almost put in an application to teach at Colorado Mountain College in Leadville. But it won't be long until snow blows deep over those old gray streets, and besides, an actual job seems a radical stretch. It's been so long since I left the classroom.

Anyway, maybe to do something for the mountains, you have to step back from them. Plus, I'm hungry for some company beyond tourists with dollars in their hands. I am not prepared to descend into the great wen on the prairie itself, as Dr. Johnson of London might have called Denver. But maybe there is a place for Betsy and me somewhere between here and there.

24

For five days Erebia courses up and down the craggy face of Magdalena Mountain. Nothing so serious befalls him as his first day offered time and again. Once, it is true, a young marmot nearly steps on Erebia as he basks chilly and sluggish on a cloudy afternoon. Another time a boulder slips in the night, jarred by a sonic boom, and Erebia has some difficulty the next morning finding his way out into the daylight. Otherwise, his second, third, fourth, and fifth days amount to a long series of investigative forays in fruitless search for a mate.

Even the weather is gentle, few scales lost to wind or rain. Except for his bill-mark tattoo, Erebia looks much as he did upon eclosure: dark chocolate, velvet, and whole, though the sparse overscaling of prismatic rainbow scales that made him iridesce at first have fallen away. Now the numbers of males are reduced, and the females are coming out. Testosterone flows in Erebia's hemolymph like meltwater in a mountain stream. More and more his behavior centers on the perception and interception of dark forms such as himself, and several times he rises a few feet toward the shadowy form of a raven overhead.

As he covers his route up and down the rocks, Erebia encounters the other members of the guild of rockslide butterflies that make this improbable habitat their home. Most often this means one-on-ones with Milbert's tortoiseshells. Nettle-feeders as larvae, these bark-brown, orange-and-yellow-edged nymphs fly in almost any habitat. They breed on the plains below but emigrate uphill in summer, and they love the rocks as much as the alpines do. Since they pass the winter as adult butterflies in a hollow tree or an old cabin, the fire-rims will glide back down before fall. These profligate wanderers can afford to dally all summer, having another spring to come before they must mate or go without. To Erebia, with his narrow window, they are merely gaudy distractions, flying up at every passing alpine and wasting everybody's energy. But by now Erebia has learned the look of *Nymphalis milberti*, and even at his most feverish, he seldom takes their decoy.

Nor do the little Snow's coppers, shimmering like red-hot ingots, or the larger rockslide checkerspots, brassy-orange like molten metal cooling, draw him from his course. The western whites, blowing over the boulders like stray bits of Kleenex; the waxy-white, ruby-spotted parnassians fluttering around patches of stonecrop where they breed and feed; and the tiny arctic and Shasta blues, sky-flecks scraped off by the mountain's high points—none of these seduce Erebia to investigate.

Only one high-country butterfly looks enough like his target to draw Erebia's attention: the Melissa arctic. *Oeneis melissa*, dusky gray-brown above and lichen-mottled below, blends into the rocks entirely. Almost colorless, like isinglass, on the wing it may look sooty against the sun. Collectors develop a search image to differen-tiate the several species of high-country satyrs. But to one another these butterflies are a little too similar to ignore. So when a female Melissa quits her favored fellfield swale for the talus slope, as her kind often do, Erebia is fooled for a flighty moment or two. But, passing near, her drab pallor gives her away for a bad bet.

Otherwise, not much intrudes on Erebia's morning. Marmots lope over the boulder field, bask like bear rugs before a fireplace, and pack away greens for their eight- or nine-month naps, soon to come. One old boar, portly, sleek, the size and color of a very large marmalade cat, scratches fleas and by that boisterous act disturbs the basking Erebia. All around, pikas like fat brown kittens play the rocks like acrobats, issuing their repertoire of buzzy *geek*s, *weet*s, and *eep*s. Near the tussock of Erebia's origin, a pika busies himself clear-cutting grasses and sedges, columbines and polemoniums, then dashes with a muzzle entirely too full to a haystack that lies curing in the sun. Lime-white patches and mounds of pellets give away the bounds of his territory. Fueled by his curing harvest, he and his family will prosper as the wind howls over the winter-rimed rocks above.

Winter seems a long way off to the basking marmots and reaping pikas. But with this afternoon comes a hint of what mountain weather can be. Following a week of almost undiluted sunshine, Erebia encounters his first thunderstorm. When the clouds come up, he takes to a lichened rock to bask, tilting his great solar panels toward the brightened part of the sky. Then, without warning, the rain breaks. Two or three raindrops strike his wings and are shed by the minuscule black shingles, washing a few of them away. Then a water bomb hits him on the head, parting over his palpi. No real damage done, though a facial palp could be broken off or an antenna injured by such a direct blow. There are no broad leaves about for umbrellas, such as the tortoiseshell might use for shelter in a nettle patch downslope. Erebia clambers into a dark, dry space between the rocks to avoid further drubbing, and that is the end of flight for another day.

Had bad weather settled in, he might have become too weak to take wing again and simply died among the cold stones without issue. But come morning following the shower, Erebia creeps up the damp walls of his nocturnal shelter, clinging to each granite grain with his tarsi, and emerges into a sunny morning. His receptors buzz to the warm and perfectly polarized light of a cloudless sky. Several minutes of basking on his side warm his flight muscles enough to work. As long as he lies there, his all-black wings are cryptic against the black heating pad of the lichen. Then, at the moment his body reaches the magic degree, he launches into flight and becomes anything but invisible against blue sky and white rock.

Erebia begins halfway up his favorite chute, which takes in a portion of the southeast-facing slope below the north ridge of Magdalena Mountain. He flies directly upslope, toward the zenith. Upon reaching the ridge, he is swept up on a morning updraft, and he almost drops over the arête to the other side, but it faces northwest and lies still in the clamp of cold shadow. The sunshine bids him back toward the east, whence it streams.

So he begins, for the first time today but perhaps the hundredth since emergence, his hang-gliding descent of the scree. Alert as always for a black shape other than his own, he falls, flaps once, glides, flaps again several times slowly, and glides again, up down across, up diagonal down, until he reaches the boundary of his proper habitat, signified by the greens of grass, prostrate juniper, and the first pines at the bottom of the slide: a ride of some three thousand vertical feet, but hardly direct, in twenty minutes. The ascent takes much longer and requires more energy. Erebia pauses twice to nectar and thrice to bask on the way back up.

During that first flight he encountered nothing but his own shadow, which diverted him briefly, as a kitten's tail will do when she has almost learned that it is attached. The next time, a randy tortoiseshell takes after him. Erebia circles once, perceives the bright borders of his wings, and gives him short shrift. On his third flight, curiosity over a water pipit nearly gets him into serious trouble, but the bird is sluggish from a recent meal of hellgrammites from a rivulet downslope. The fourth course brings interludes with two other Magdalena alpines, both male, and a Melissa arctic. With each one he does a do-si-do on the wing. But he's getting good, and none of these rendezvous give him a whiff of the scent that says female, no stimulus beyond the cheap trick of the initial visual cue, and Erebia proceeds on his aerial way.

It is good that in animals of poppyseed brains, hormones spring eternal. Never disillusioned, they simply try and try again. Or perhaps it is not so different with humans. Were it not for hope and hormones, in whatever mix, many of us would retire to the flowerfields too soon, disappointed, as Erebia surely would have done by now had something ineffable and undeniable not driven him back up those rocks once again to sail on down.

Biology doesn't mind a bachelor, for there tend to be too many males of most species; too many, that is, in view of the vast number of gametes that each one is capable of producing: "redundancy" hardly says it. But nature abhors a spinster. Her eggs are far too precious to go to waste in a dying, virgin body if survival is to keep apace of losses. Perhaps only our own kind stand outside that law, as surely we do, our great need being to limit our own numbers. But most creatures need all of their female kind mated, while the many superfluous males can mate or not, for all nature cares, as long as the fitter ones get their innings. Her motto might be, "Only the fit need apply." Which is why females of many butterflies emerge later than the males, waiting until the potential mates have thinned out, leaving the strongest alive. And then they mate rapidly: late encounters usually find females less than receptive, already gravid and uninterested in anything but nectar and host plants for their eggs. So without the omnipotent, ever-present urge on the part of the males, many of the fittest survivors might just give up too soon and never pass on their genes.

But there is such a force. So Erebia, showing now more than a hint of brown plush in the right light, flies once again to the knife-edge, where he finds an inflorescence of a yellow mustard whose nectar he has never before tasted. It suits him, and as he sucks the sweet liquor, his blood sugar rises and he prepares to fly. Carefully he withdraws his double drinking-straw proboscis from the nectary, preens it with his tiny brushlike forelegs, recoils its paired tubes, and tucks it between his furry labial palps. It is too valuable an implement to risk getting it stuck up with syrupy nectar or damaged. Thus nourished, groomed, and warm, Erebia takes off for his fifth descent of the day.

The sun slides past the meridian. If an alpine can discriminate between cumulus clouds and mountains, as it probably can, Erebia might feel a keener sense of urgency now. The clouds are busy rising in the west, and the day is doomed. Scarcely an hour's worth of courting time remains—and who knows how many more days?

Erebia scales a huge boulder and alights briefly on its top, surprising the pika in residence who says *Geek!* Then he sails off again as the mammal dives for cover. Near the bottom of the boulder a pink patch of moss campion draws him down to drink again. But a stronger impulse takes over as a dark smudge enters his broad, shortsighted field of view. He swerves to investigate.

The form rises to meet him, and they circle jerkily like paper dolls in a dust devil. It is another Magdalena—this time, a female. She glistens with the iridescence of a newly minted *Erebia*, shining amethyst and emerald like a violet-green swallow, and her blackness holds the depth of every night there ever was. She's come out of her chrysalis only this morning, and scarcely a scale is missing from her wings. His antennae find her perfume on the alpine air, and Erebia smells at last the fragrance he was born to find.

Now he senses something entirely new in his experience, as his counterpart's pheromones shiver his ganglia. With a fervor he's never felt in the false flights of earlier encounters, he charges his carbon copy. Unready before, she had already repelled two other courtiers today. Now, her wings dry and her own hormones flowing, she too feels a surge of urgency. The pair perform half a dozen pas de deux in an aerial ballet choreographed by centuries of selection, rising a dozen feet above the rocks. Close but not touching, exchanging aromas as intensity of purpose grows, the twin black shadows finally drop together among the stones.

Male and female circle each other in a dance of recognition. So important: don't mate with the wrong kind, don't waste your genes, don't blow your reason for living in this stony, bony land! Erebia palps the tip of his companion's body with his antennae and receives a strong dose of her special scent. She strokes his forewings with her own antennae, finding the thick patches of androconia, plush velvet pads of sex scales where male satyrs' pheromones arise. Now there is no doubt. Magdalena molecules, male and female, flow between them, released by their private dance. No arctic, no other sort of alpine could make this potion. There will be no mistake.

Like a series of locks and keys made smooth and slick with graphite, the partners' sexual rhythms flow together as they back end-to-end on a rock, everting their swollen genitalia. These exquisitely sensitive tissues rub together for a second or two before Erebia's handlike claspers gape wide and find their way around her endpoint. In a reversal of the common pattern, she enters his body before he can enter hers. Then he closes around her so that, should they be forced to fly in copula, she will be able to carry his passive form without losing hold.

Feeling only Pan knows what, Erebia probes his aedeagus into his mate's bursa copulatrix. Then slowly, smoothly, he passes his sperms to her, not in semen but parceled in a shining envelope. There the spermatophore will lodge, as each egg, passing down from her ovaries, receives the charge of life from Erebia's seed. The act completed, a kind of gentle subsidence overtakes the lovers—for may they not be called such? From first encounter through courtship to copulation, only a few minutes have passed. The giving of the spermatophore takes much longer. Even afterward, the mates cleave together.

Like each other's shadows, like an object and its reflection in a pool of ink, like a Rorschach test for a gentled mind, the two lie bonded. Like obsidian chips from an arrowhead's face, like paired punctuation marks inscribed on the tablet of the mountain's stone, like black valentines, they repose, Erebia's wings enfolded between those of the larger female, her tip embraced by his body's clasp. Such is butterfly love.

And so they remain throughout the long mountain night, for a storm arises and sends them understone for shelter, still paired.

25

The mated pair slid apart as day came and brought a stirring wakefulness. The spent male part shrunk from the female chamber, leaving it vacated but hardly empty, as her musky endpoint slipped from the grip of his claspers.

Oberon stretched his long, strong thighs, cramped from enclosing the rounded rump of Mary Glanville for hour after melded hour. "Mmmmm. Good morning."

Mary stretched too, her backside suddenly clammy from the loss of the other half of its shell, and turned over to kiss Oberon. Her breath carried the heavy scents of long kissing and night's breathing. Oberon inhaled it gratefully. "Hold my bottom?" she asked. "It's cold with you gone away."

"I'm here," he said, muffling her slender woman's buttocks in his rangy hands. Her firm frontage felt warm, and she *mmm*'d again. Their loving had evolved rapidly since that night in the chapel after Tonkin's incursion. It was still new, and they both felt a little silly and embarrassed by their naked pleasure.

Eventually Oberon had to get up to pee. "As long as I'm up, can I get you anything?"

"Would you mind getting me another of those like you got me before?"

"I can only try," he said. Oberon complied with his best attempt, a little doubtful. Since forty, he'd had slim pickings, and nothing at all like this. Seldom doubles, not since Estes Park a few summers ago, anyway. Another just might not work out. But it did. Cumulonimbi rose, billowed, and burst between the sheets in the Mountain Monastery: one a brief, violent prairie thunderstorm, heavy in output but no sooner spilt than spent; the other a gathering, prolonged mountain downpour, drawing into a moist, quiet close.

Oberon stroked Mary's pale, unbrushed hair, swept her cheek with it, Mary laughing and swatting him away. "Do you suppose we'll ever be the same?"

"As what, I guess is the question. But then we never are, one day to the next. Anyway, we seem to be fine—better than for some time, wouldn't you say? Anyway—I hate to say it, but we've got to be up and at 'em. I'm due at Rocky Flats in two hours."

Oberon departed in the old panel truck that had brought Mary to the mountain. He left her in the care of Sylvanus and Xerxes. An hour and fifty minutes after leaving their narrow bed, having rolled down the Middle St. Vrain to Lyons, then south along the Hogback to Boulder and beyond toward Golden, he arrived outside the gates of the Rocky Flats nuclear weapons plant. There he entered a chaos of marchers, police, hired goons, television crews, and bullhorns. The peaceful shield of calm left over from the morning began to unravel.

Established by the Atomic Energy Commission in 1952, Rocky Flats now supported fifty-six hundred jobs at a payroll of $280 million, becoming one of the most polluted places on earth—all devoted to the Flats' bumper crop of plutonium triggers for nuclear bombs. Contaminated workers, watershed, and air were the collateral damages—and finally, this jarring scene of conflict and change. Oberon parked the truck along the road, half a mile from the demo.

He looked down across the malign clutter of the plant, squatted up against Denver's dirty brown cloud. Oberon, who hadn't been downslope for months, wanted to hold his nostrils closed against the toxics of the plant and the noxious breath of the city, but he had to breathe. The air's ozone smell reminded him of snow melting in a parking lot somewhere in 1954, evocative and not unpleasant, but impure. A Euclid earthmover, chartreuse and immense, groped across a long barrow of earth that might never be safe to sift again. The white water tower stood on tiptoe like a Wellesian Martian over the scene of the crime. A creek ran from the foothills into the Flats' polluted precincts, a reminder that water will have its way, regardless.

A blue sign faced the demonstrators: U.S. DEPARTMENT OF ENERGY, ROCKY FLATS PLANT, OPERATED BY NORTH AMERICAN SPACE OPERATIONS, ROCKWELL INTERNATIONAL. Another with a star-studded shield advised all comers that this was U.S. GOVERNMENT PROPERTY and to ENTER ON OFFICIAL BUSINESS ONLY. Oberon felt as foreign here as it was possible to feel. Then he noticed a tiny garden at the base of a streetlight opposite the entrance. Petunias, marigolds, and snapdragons bloomed beside a hand-lettered little sign that read HELP WATER THE GREEN OF PEACE, reminding him of why he'd come.

Cacophony of dispute poured toward him as he approached on foot. Forces milled, putting off the face-to-face. Oberon tried to fix the abused land in his mind, to feel the rage it evoked. The great smear hung palpably on the eastern skyline, as if some Titan had browned his shorts and hung them out to air over Denver. Behind him, the painfully clear Front Range. And in between, plutonium pie. He wanted to flee back to the mountain and his bed with Mary.

"I'm sorry I had to leave before the action, Catherine."

"Before the head-banging began, and the arrests? I'm not. Thanks for getting me out of there when you did." Now there were two in the van, heading back north again.

"Well, it wouldn't have done for you to be arrested this time," he said from behind the wheel. "You couldn't have come back for the meeting."

"Which would have wasted your trip," Catherine Greenland said as the carryall rattled over the asphalt between Golden and Boulder. Blue yucca and purple gayfeather candled the grassland hems. A few overbright tracts of new houses intervened, but this stretch remained mostly pastoral, seeming far removed from the frenetic scene they'd left behind. "Anyway, there will be larger actions soon; this thing is really coming to a head. Though it might take another ten years and an election or two to shut it down at last. But when the Sierra Club and the Daniel Berrigan people are holding hands on the line, as they were back there, it must mean we're getting somewhere, doesn't it?"

"Let's hope," said Oberon as he shifted up to highway speed.

"As for this meeting," asked Catherine, "will I be the only woman there?"

"I hope Mary will be present, and our friend Annie Cloudcroft, too."

"Oberon, who is this Mary?"

"As we've recently learned, her full name is Mary Glanville. You've heard how she came to us. Since her injury, her recent past has become obscure to her. But she feels she has an older identity, that she was somehow drawn to the mountains by more than our ads alone."

"Oh God, she's not channeling Ramtha, is she?"

"No, nothing like that. She doesn't even summon Shirley MacLaine's grandma."

"Thank goodness. Can you tell me more?"

"I'll let her do that, if she wants to. She doesn't talk about herself much, so I haven't pushed it. Mostly she wants to learn about the mountains."

"Well, I should think you're the one to help her with that," Catherine said. "I know you've ranged all over them."

"Maybe I can help her with rocks and flowers and butterflies and such. But she could use someone like you to help her see inside, Catherine. Apparently she received no real counseling in the so-called home where those bozos lodged her—just drugs and more drugs."

"I'm a counselor, not a physician. But I'd be glad to talk with her. If our merger works out, maybe just having more women around will be good for her. It must be odd, living in an artificially all-male world."

"Odd for all of us," Oberon said. "I'd like to learn more about your group before the meeting, if I may." Green hills and red slopes of the Morrison Formation rolled by, shoved up against the metamorphics of the mountains. Boulder's trademark Flatirons showed the contact as the truck turned west to make the loop back via Boulder Canyon and the Peak to Peak. "For example," Oberon said, "how long will those arrested be kept, and what about their families?"

"If it's like last time," Catherine said, "they'll be booked under trespass, arraigned for a later trial date, then released. At most, they'll have to stay in jail just one night."

"How many of you are there?"

"Forty-three now, but sixteen have decided to remain with the camp over the winter. We have the resources for that, but no roof. We sixteen have arranged our lives, more or less, though some of our family members would dispute that, so that we can remain in the area all winter. We hope to set up a trailer and rotate in and out."

"I admire your conviction. I heard you were—"

"One tough bitch? I can say that, but no one else can. When I have to be. But our dedication pales beside the Greenham Common women's encampment in England. They are our inspiring angels. Housewives, single women, grandmothers, young girls, all living together to resist the cruise missiles and witness for peace."

"If you decided to join us on the mountain," said Oberon, "maybe you could help steer our bunch toward something worthwhile."

"In the meantime," said Catherine, "it sounds as if you have a misogyny problem."

"Just one of us," replied Oberon, "but he does create a roadblock for all of us. An otherwise smart man with a bone-built heart and a pretty twisted outlook on half of humanity."

"So why is this character part of your group, and how do you tolerate him?"

"One thorn at a time. He does have his good points. Attalus is a fine naturalist, one of the best lichenologists in the West. He published a monograph on the crustose lichens of the Rockies that stands today. And he was a good bonesetter from his days as pharmacist's mate in the Merchant Marine, and he kept our library beautifully. But he had a discharge and a conviction in his past, and now I wonder whether it was related to his hatred of women, which seems to have obscured everything else lately."

"And?"

"And we don't begin to tolerate him. He drives us nuts when he gets off on this. We've simply had no choice but to live with it—he's been the dealer, as the charterholder from the old order. But now Mary has forced the issue. It would have come up soon anyway, given the hopeful plans we share with you."

"So, what is the plan?"

"I'm making it up as we go. I'll emphasize the creative side of the union—with us providing winter shelter for the women, you bringing us your political strength and experience. Attalus should be able to understand the intrinsic value of diversity in a community, in ecological terms if nothing else." Oberon said it, but he didn't believe it.

They ricocheted through Boulder as quickly as they could and struck up Boulder Canyon toward Nederland, Ward, Allenspark, and finally Magdalena Mountain. They stopped for a stretch at Boulder Falls, where an odd boulder sat upon a plinth for public inspection. The action over the eons had carved it into a holey doughnut of stone. To Oberon, the rock looked like nothing so much as a vertebra from some great extinct beast. He was about to say so, but Catherine was already laughing her way through the middle like an otter in a waterfall pool. Fresh fir terps and piney essences swirled around her on the rushing stream's breath. The mood lifted and lasted a way up the canyon, until Catherine said, "Sounds charming. A drafty old ruin full of maladjusted monks and one lichen-loving psycho."

"Well," said Oberon, "if you'd prefer to freeze your buns off in your alfresco, glow-in-the-dark nunnery . . ."

"Maybe we'll take our chances with you after all. But tit for tat: I told you a little about us. Will you please fill me in a bit on your bunch?"

Oberon glanced at Catherine beside him. Maybe fifty-five or fifty-eight, possessed of short, neat cloud-colored hair, a riveting pair of hazel eyes in a narrow, high-cheeked face, and a runner's body, she had the brisk bearing of an AAUW chair or a city councilwoman. She looked more like a Realtor or a member of the bench than an earth mother activist willing to risk arrest to make a chink in the brick wall of war. "Okay," he said. "We come from many traditions. We have a Southern Baptist, and we have a Levi Samson, just as we have a Druid, a Zen Buddhist, and a Bacchus—even a Rastafarian."

"Sounds like a recipe for chaos!"

"On the contrary. We're not a religion, so we have no dogma; not a party, so no ideology. Nothing is compulsory except pacifism and a profound respect for the land."

"But how can a Baptist lie down with a Druid—or an evolutionary biologist?" They had slipped through Nederland and rolled past Caribou unnoticed by the locals.

"Because," Oberon went on as smoothly as the fresh-paved road, "we try to value each of our separate creation myths. Raven, Turtle, Jahweh, Darwin—they're all metaphors for something subtler than any of us know. Of course, evolution by natural selection is the central operating principle of biology, and each of us—even our Baptist—recognizes that. But we're inclusive—he can have his Genesis and eat it too, for all we care. After all, the myth of the Garden is just as useful as Darwin's version for bearing up hylozoism."

"Hylo . . ."

". . . zoism. It's the ancient and certainly correct view that there is no moral division between humans and the rest of life."

"Thanks. Like I need yet another *ism* to contend with. But it does sound more sensible than most. Do you have any Mormons or Witnesses among your fifty-seven varieties?"

"Only fallen ones. We admire the Latter-Days' sense of community, and the Witnesses' rejection of racism. And the Seventh-Days run some fine small hospitals. But none of them have found their way to us as yet. Of course, any flavor of fundamentalism, let alone proselytizing, would be incompatible with Pan-Pacific's essential approach."

"Actually, I subscribe to Genesis," said Catherine.

"Really," said Oberon, taken aback. "And I thought I knew you!"

"Sure. God created man; then she stood back and said, 'I'm sure I can do better than that!'" Her gag got a better laugh than it deserved. "So why Pan-Pacific?" she asked. "Do you have imperial plans to link the East and the West? What about Atlantis?"

"Nothing so grand; it's just a pun, really."

"Oh, I see . . . Pan, peace, the whole deal."

"Pretty much."

"So, if no dogma or doctrine, do you have any central . . . *idea*?"

"Just that nature is the whole show—body, spirit, and beyond—and should be treated accordingly. And that warfare is an unacceptable way to die, for anyone."

"But your names," Catherine persisted. "Ajax, from the Trojan wars, and Xerxes, wasn't he an old Persian warmonger?"

"The biggest. But even moldy old soldiers are educable. Each of our names is also associated with nature somehow. Xerxes defeated the Hebrews, but he also introduced land stewardship reforms that were way ahead of their time. Ajax, Polyxenes, and other names from Troy were given by Linnaeus to various swallowtails in his *Systemae Naturae* in 1758. War *has* been the way, and we know that our own primate lineage grew out of that. But we believe, as I know you do, or you wouldn't be camped at Rocky Flats, that peace must be the new way. Otherwise—oblivion for all."

Catherine asked, "And does Pan care about oblivion?"

"Touché. I assume not. He never comes to meetings, nor does his girlfriend, Gaia, though they have a standing invitation, so I haven't had a chance to ask. But nature bats last—it will survive all our insults. Nuclear wipeout or eco-collapse would be but a fly bite on Pan's ass, right? It might be the end of us, but he'd just set up shop elsewhere—some other planet or back home, without us."

"But, Oberon," Catherine objected, "I'm not entirely happy with that. I can't believe that Pan wouldn't bat an eyelash. Surely he'd shed more than one tear, and the Goddess would weep for the loss of beauty and life on earth. And anyway, do you really personify them like that?" A humanist, she was a little alarmed meeting a pagan in person.

"Some do, some don't," Oberon said. "Me, no. What is Pan? Our Great Old Horny God, Master of Ceremonies for Mother Earth, Puck and Robin Goodfellow, pansexual good-times elf, pipe-playing satyr of Grahame's willow island, bread, and Everything—all that, and more. One thing for sure: Pan is *us*, *we* are Mother Nature and Mother Earth. As Steinbeck and Ricketts put it in their *Log from the Sea of Cortez*, 'all things are one thing and one thing is all things.' Or in Robinson Jeffers's essential phrase, we are 'not man apart.'"

Catherine smiled at that.

Oberon went on. "I don't mean to preach to a captive choir,

but you asked. So when I say that Pan would relocate, I mean that nature will outlive the span of earth and its creatures whether we reach the end with the sun's big chill or hasten it by making things hot for ourselves. To think otherwise would be as arrogant as to set ourselves apart, and above, and to 'have dominion' over all the rest. So . . . tragedy in our extinction? Sure—but mostly for us. Existence will go on. If we're to persist, we need to worry less about Pan's sad face than our own thin ice."

The highway unrolled before them, past the hippie enclave of Ward down in its hollow, tucked among the Vs of old mining tailings. Oberon shifted down. Catherine said, "So we'd better be looking after nature if we want to save our own sweet asses."

"I think so. And looking after nature means getting to know our fellow creatures as much as getting along with our fellow humans."

Catherine said, "Heavens." Then, "I guess we humanists had better start reading our Roger Tory Peterson along with our Norman Vincent Peale, huh?"

"Can't hurt." Oberon laughed. "Aldo Leopold and Ed Abbey too, while you're at it. Anyway, now you'll have a little better idea of what we're all about, before we go into the meeting—which begins in twenty minutes, by the way."

The old truck sped past the mouth of Wild Basin, curled around the face of Magdalena Mountain, echoed off the log front of Magdalena Park Lodge, and came in sight of the stone Chapel of St. Mary Magdalene. "Why all the Magdalenes around here?" Catherine asked. "Was there once a nunnery here too, in the Shakespearean sense?"

"Some say that Gunnison Whetstone, the founder of the old order, ran something of the sort as a sideline," said Oberon. "But I have no real knowledge of it, in the biblical sense." Gravel scrunched as the tires turned off the long drive onto a sidetrack into the ponderosa woods, then came to a halt beside a big pink bubblegum of a boulder.

"From here it's on foot," Oberon announced, stepping out and stretching his road-bent frame. "But it's not far. Just back there where the grove grows thick. Where you can see a tall snag, that's the place. I've got to go—I've just got time. Come when you're ready."

"Speaking of having to go, it's been a long drive," said Catherine.

"We're blessed with bushes," said Oberon. "But, surprise—there is actually indoor plumbing in the monastery."

"Shall I roll up my sleeves?" asked Catherine. "It sounds like a rumble coming."

"I'll tell you this," said Oberon. "I won't live another night in this drafty bachelor's pad without change in sight. Think they've got any room in that jail cell?" He wheeled and crunched off across the granite Grape-Nuts that passed for soil in the Grove.

26

Mead slept against Noni's shoulder. When he awoke and tried to catch the dream, she was still there. He really was with Noni. She'd met his bus in Gunnison and driven him to Crested Butte for lunch. Now they were bouncing up the East River Road to Gothic. Noni braked hard for a herd of Herefords crossing the one-lane track, jolting him awake. Then he remembered what she'd told him and wished he were back on the bus. His first words, following their embrace, had been, "Noni, how about a midnight mountain mating in your cabin tonight?"

"I'd love to, James—but maybe not."

"No?" Mead's beard dropped as his mouth threw a pout.

"No. Look, your telegram was such a surprise! The thing is, O'Leary and I have been working together, and we've become pretty good friends."

"What?"

"Not *that* good, but I'd just as soon keep things cool with everybody right now."

"With *everybody*?"

"James, how was I to know you were going to show up on my doorstep?"

He groaned, remembering their last conversation before she left New Haven, trying not to remember the night before that. Noni gave him a one-armed hug as she jockeyed the lab's pickup with her other hand. The sun sank into the West Elks as they climbed the dusty washboard road. They reached Gothic in the twilight, where a small sign read WELCOME TO THE ROCKY MOUNTAIN BIOLOGI-CAL LABORATORY—FOUNDED IN 1928. Noni dropped him off at the tumbledown cabin she'd rustled up for him. "It's not much," she said, "but it has the advantage of being unoccupied. They weren't going to use it until it had a new roof. But it'll keep the mountain dew off your fevered brow. And don't miss breakfast, James—six to eight in the dining hall, over there. Bathhouse is the other way." Then, before she could change her mind, she kissed him as lightly as a butterfly tapping a leaf and said "Good night." Then she was gone as fast as she'd appeared at the station.

Alone, Mead sank into a funk. Now he wasn't sure that he shouldn't have stayed in New Haven with his illusions, and his roaches, who at least were faithful. "Damned *O'Leary!*" he cursed to any listening deer mice. Exhausted and grubby from the high-way caravan, crushed by Noni's news, troubled by Carson's vagrant shade, and bugged by the deer mice dancing across his mustache, Mead fell into a sort of sleep.

Even so, he awoke refreshed when the breakfast gong clanged at six. As he opened the door of East River Cabin, the panorama of the eastern sun illuminating Gothic Mountain erased the misgivings of the night before. Here stood a monolith to shame Kline Tower. Here were morning skies to make the hazed ones of the Eastern Seaboard fade into vague memory. Here were flowered mountain meadows to make even the long dog-ride all worth it.

At his feet, beyond a rickety board deck and across a ragged hem of willows and cow parsnip, flowed the East River. A dipper darted past, alighted on a slippery stone, bobbed in place, then dived for caddis larvae in their little pebble houses on the riverbed. Aspen groves rolled up the flanks of Gothic Mountain to shaggy meadows of yellow and light green interrupted by towers of corn lilies and green gentians, then into dark spruce swales. Then the rock began: a granite massif falling away upward for some thousands of feet into a craggy face and a long, bald crown. The front and flanks of the mountain, cut by early winters, tardy springs, and their diamond-bit frosts, stood out in ramparts of turrets, crags, castellations, and crocketed spires—hence "Gothic," recalling the towers of Kings College he knew so well in Cambridge.

Mead didn't fail to notice the rockslides tumbling down from every slope and snowfield. Not the most accessible, maybe, but surely here was habitat for the Magdalena alpine, "Granite Gobbler" and "black flag of the mountain domain," two of Carson's nicknames for it. He hoped there would soon be a chance to see it for himself.

He saw neither Noni nor O'Leary at breakfast, and he imagined the worst until he overheard someone mention that they were already in the field. Trying to get them out of his mind, Mead chowed down on pancakes and eggs with slabs of bacon, butter, and syrup. Then he strolled around the laboratory grounds to get the measure of the place.

He beheld a valley with mountains on four sides, bisected by the dusty road and trisected by the East River and Copper Creek, which met at the bottom of the townsite. These, along with an irregular warren of smaller drives, footpaths, and rills, tied together a willowy bottomland that rose gently into aspens, then conifers, and, finally, rocks and snow. Scattered about, a loose handful of wooden buildings. A few, including a ramshackle but handsome false-fronted former bordello, dated from the ghost town's silver-boom days of the 1880s. The rest, including more cabins, dorms, and labs, evidenced Gothic's resurrection as a twentieth-century biology boomtown. Their pleasing clutter seemed to have grown out of the thin mountain soil with the wildflowers that painted the valley. Delft larkspurs and grapy monkshoods lined the boardwalks among the pungent willow bogs. Many plants had red flags on wires stuck in the ground beside them to indicate "I'm an experiment: don't you *dare* tread on me!"

The hillsides all around were dappled with lavender and yellow daisies. Clumps of Colorado blue columbines decked the doorsteps of cabins and outhouses. A thunderstorm the previous afternoon had rained blue flax petals on the ground and damped down the dust of the road. It left the air so fresh it almost hurt Mead's lungs, though the lab's nine-thousand-foot elevation helped to take his breath away as well. He could see how one might become entranced by the place and return year after year, as Winchester, Freulich, and others did. Mead was not even there in his own right, but he *was* there. Fortunately for him, George was not, having flown to California for some research in the Channel Islands before settling into Gothic for the summer.

Mead's second enchantment came that afternoon. At someone's suggestion at breakfast he climbed the forest trail heading out of the townsite to the east. It led steeply past Judd Falls, with its rumors of love-struck suicide, farther up the long incline of Copper Creek, all the way to the turquoise bowl of Copper Lake in the arctic-alpine zone. From months in the Atlantic lowlands, Mead felt the altitude acutely, but his long, young body soon found its mountain legs and proper pace. Titania's fritillaries gave way to Freya's fritillaries as he stepped above treeline. A steep talus slope broke off to the southeast, hanging above the tarn. The trail continued in broken fashion across the rockslide, vanishing over boggy East Maroon Pass at the upper end of the lake, where it dived into the receding wilderness. "Imagine wagons taking silver and mail from Gothic to Aspen by this route!" Mead told the marmots, to whom it was all old hat. These days, the track across the talus was barely passable even on foot.

Mead cast his eyes over the stones below. At first he saw nothing but boulders. Then a black speck resolved, zigzagging up the rockslide toward him. "Magdalena!" he whispered. He knew it at once.

Exercising its sooty semaphore as it came nearer, the butterfly captured Mead's total devotion at first sight. He stood openmouthed, seduced, fully hooked by the black beauty of the rocks: a confirmed Erebia freak for life.

That night, footsore but happy, Mead found himself sitting with Noni awaiting a public lecture by Peter Freulich. The dining hall had metamorphosed from grubhouse to auditorium. Noni pointed out this and that well-known biologist, several of them working on butterflies, such as Freulich's Stanford colleagues Vern Volte and Carolyn Marsh. But in addition to the RMBL regulars, local ranchers, campers, and residents of Crested Butte, Paonia, and Gunnison had turned out too. Many of them had seen Freulich on Johnny Carson's show and were eager to hear this controversial public scold in person. Anticipation crackled like the air before a lightning storm over Mount Gothic. Mead intended to clear out of Gothic before he wore out his unmatriculated welcome, but he didn't want to miss a chance to hear George's famous friend.

Freulich always drew a good audience, whether he appeared on television coast-to-coast or in the Crested Butte town hall. With his wife and colleague, Amy, he had written major books on the human population crisis, the nuclear threat, and the importance of biodiversity, as well as popular textbooks on evolutionary biology. Taller even than Mead, lean, and salt-and-pepper pelted, Freulich wore the khaki field clothes that were the uniform of his generation of biologists. He commanded a deep and sonorous voice that drew in even naysayers. The most sought-after environmental speaker in the country, he came to Gothic every summer for a little peace and quiet and research among the butterflies and scholars. But he always contributed one talk to the summer lecture series, and tonight's was entitled "Fusion and the Megazoo."

As he warmed up, Freulich's now-confiding, now-sarcastic words penetrated the room like drive-in movie speakers hooked up to every seat. A constant wry smile hung on his thin, expressive mouth as he blasted those who, in their ignorance and cupidity, would shred the living fabric of the land to tatters. "Anyone with enough sense to count to twenty without using his toes," Freulich inveighed, "should be able to see that the death of the ecosystem means the death of ourselves." He was hot, and the audience—most of whom could presumably see that point—loved it. Mead only wished it were the toe counters who were hearing it, instead of a roomful of ecologists and ranchers, most of them already convinced.

As his students and colleagues knew he would, Freulich managed to bring in his research on his favorite butterflies, fritillaries, to illustrate his points. He was able to draw parables for all kinds of social comment from the biology of butterflies. "When any little thing goes wrong in a colony of these insects," he said, "they may flicker into extinction in a season. Then, if there is another population nearby to recolonize, fine. But if the intervening habitat is gone—the extinction sticks! Now what do you suppose we're doing to ensure *our* ability to bounce back from failure of *our* habitat base? Damn little!"

After cruising all the major global issues, he brought it all back home to Gothic before he finished. "Lest you think that all the threats to the megazoo lie outside this charmed valley," he said, "just look around you. Amax, not satisfied with decades of devastation over by Leadville, want to remove Mount Emmons for molybdenum. And for what? Money and munitions. Mount Crested Butte, meanwhile, plans to expand the ski area onto the very flanks of Mount Gothic, right below the lab. And those thirsty 'burbs on the Eastern Slope, Aurora, Colorado Springs, and their mother ship, Denver, have designs on the water in little old Copper Creek and the East River—they'll grab the rights, then divert them, if they get their way, to irrigate their own metastasis at the expense of these watersheds. To paraphrase Thomas Malthus: when there are too many toilets to flush for the available water, the world becomes a toilet—and a struggle for survival will ultimately follow. Darwin and Wallace both got the message. Why can't we see it now?"

A resort executive and a summer émigré or two from the megalopolis were squirming in their seats. But not content to leave anyone comfortable with his or her own complicity or complacency, Freulich went on to describe the way Gothicites were fouling their own nest with their growing numbers and effluents, endangering research, soil, and health. "Whether it's two hundred people here, two million in Denver's brown cloud, or twenty million gasping in the fecal snow of Mexico City, it's too damn many." He concluded with a crescendo of doomsday death rattle mixed with a hint of hope and an ain't-it-crazy chuckle that left his listeners buzzed and tingling, Mead as much as any other.

"I can see why you're excited to work with him, Noni," he said after the applause.

"Would you like to meet him?"

As Freulich was packing up his notes and signing a few books, most of his interrogators satisfied, Noni approached and introduced her friend.

"Sure—Mead," said Freulich. "George has mentioned you as a promising grad student. But I thought you weren't supposed to be out here until next year. Something about an unhelpful committee member . . ." Mead began to explain, lamely, but Freulich interrupted. "Never mind for now, I'm beat—I just flew my plane in after a killer semester, a couple of weeks in the field, and three days of speeches in Denver. Why not tell me about it on the way to Cumberland tomorrow?"

"Cumberland!" Mead echoed, his tingle rising all over again.

"Yes, Cumberland Pass. I'm leaving early to mark some *Boloria* populations up there. O'Leary and I would be glad to have another hand along. Are you any good with a butterfly net?"

"You bet!" Mead bubbled like a kid promised a picnic.

"Good! Be ready at six." Mead blinked, and Freulich was half-way up the aspen-lined trail to his cabin below Judd Falls. And then the full message settled like a black bomb in his belly: *O'Leary and I* . . . So his rival would be coming along too. And Noni? She'd excused herself after the introduction, so he couldn't ask her. But he'd had his first gander at Dave, who was on the short side, as was Noni, and good-looking, with a full blond mustache. "Well, hell," Mead mumbled to himself, "at least the guy's got good taste. Maybe I can nudge him over a cliff." Cold under a shotgun sky of stars, and lonesome but excited, he turned in.

At five thirty the next morning Mead left the cabin, dodging the territorial rockets of broad-tailed hummingbirds that pierced the cold and fragrant dawntime air. Mount Gothic loomed like a loaf of leaden bread until the sun topped Belleview Mountain and leavened it with light. Mead had scarcely thought of Noni last night, except in the cold depth of the dark when he couldn't sleep at all under the thin envelope of a sleeping bag he'd brought. Now, as he spent a chilly, hungry half hour waiting for O'Leary to appear from what he hoped would not be Noni's warm bed, Mead felt the wormwood rise. He spat it out and concentrated on the day to come.

At 5:55 Freulich pulled up and said, "Hop in. Turns out all my assistants and students have to work on their own projects, and Amy's hard at it on the next book. So it's just you and me. I'm glad you could come, otherwise I might have bagged it." Even better, James thought as he slung his daypack and his own lanky frame into the cab of the yellow Chevy Suburban with a Stanford U. logo on the door. A personal tutorial with Peter Freulich!

The East River meanders unwound far below as the truck followed a course as windy as the river's but considerably faster. They stopped at Tony's service station in Crested Butte for essentials—gas, coffee, coffee cake, lunchmeat, candy bars, and beer—and were away.

In the presence of Stanford University's Crosby Professor of Population Biology, Mead was at first speechless. His own monumental ignorance, as he saw it, seemed to well out of his brainpan. But this feeling didn't last. Freulich put him at his ease when he said, "You know, one of my first papers was on *Erebia epipsodea*. George says you share an enthusiasm for our little alpine friends." And they went from there. Mead learned a lot that day, about biology, human ecology, and the raw politics of conservation. But Freulich had a good pair of ears as well as a mouth, and for his part he learned about October Carson. Mead told him of Carson's love of *Erebia* and of Cumberland Pass, and about his disgust with the off-road vehicles he found there.

"I'm afraid we'll see the same," said Freulich. And sure enough, when they took a pee-and-coffee stop at Taylor Park, he pointed out a scream of dirt bikes sitting on their kickstands in front of a row of cabins. "There they are," he said, "the alpine hackers asleep in their lairs. If I were Beowulf . . ."

Mead cupped his hot mug and breathed in the vapors of coffee, sage, and dust.

From the ghost town of Tincup on up, they saw dirt bikes in growing numbers. The route rose fast and the landscape closed in steep around it. When they arrived at the summit of the pass, Mead turned his head, owl-like, around the full three-sixty. From the get-go he knew what Carson had meant on both counts: expansive alpine beauty, heavy ecological damage. The untidy lawn of the tundra seemed endless but blemished. Mead followed the lanky prof up a rutted trail toward a high ridge. When they reached it, two sea-level dwellers from opposite coasts, they paused to look, huff, and rest.

"Carson went on about both his pleasure and his pain up here," Mead said.

"Pain in the ass, is what it is," Freulich replied. "Most of them stay on the roads and designated trails, but the jerks who don't are

ruining some of the best high tundra in the Rockies. The Forest
Service stands by and watches—of course, they're used to permitting
cattle and sheep allotments in the high country, which can be just as
bad. Only time, and plenty of it, can repair the damage." He paused.
"But at least we can kick *those* bastards off the mountain!"

Mead followed Freulich's narrowed gaze toward a trio of bikers
climbing a trench in the tundra toward them. Six strides of his long
legs took Freulich into position above the bikers' path. At the last
moment he leaped into their path, startling them all to hell and making them brake, bunch, and fall about. He brandished his aluminum
butterfly net like Little John's staff holding back Robin Hood on the
bridge. He could see himself in their visors as the bikers regained
their balance. They flipped up the visors and glared as Freulich demanded, "Do you have any idea what you're doing to this landscape?"

"Who gives a flying fuck?" shot back the leader, who apparently
didn't. "And who the fuck are you to tell us what to do—some god-
damn *butterfly catcher*?"

But Freulich kept his enormous cool, and when one of the others
asked him to explain what he meant, he obliged. "Your tire marks in
the alpine turf will take decades to grow in, if they ever will. This is
fragile terrain, easy to scar and erode, but hard to heal."

The third rider said everyone else did it, so why shouldn't they,
to which Freulich replied, "Not quite, only the assholes who don't
give a damn about fish, wildlife, or the future of places such as this."

James thought it would be lost on them, but they huddled and
then vamoosed the way they came. The leader made a point of churn-
ing up some intact grasses and tiny flowers with his knobby tires,
flipping the bird on his way out. But the other two took it easy until
they reached the road. "They know not what they do," said Freulich,
shaking his head.

"But you made them think," said Mead. "Two out of three's
not bad."

The day improved with a sandwich, a beer, and a magical hike among arctics and alpines, shooting stars and dryas, into the fragrant bogs of *Boloria frigga*. The two able netmen caught the small fritillaries, looking for marked individuals, recording then releasing them. Freulich said, "It might be this very species that Nabokov wrote of in *Speak, Memory*, when he went into the bogs by the Oredezh as a boy in pursuit of a dusky little fritillary bearing the name of a Norse goddess. He called it 'the highest enjoyment of timelessness—when I stand among rare butterflies and their food plants.'"

"I know the piece," Mead said, suddenly not so ignorant. "'This is ecstasy . . . a momentary vacuum into which rushes all that I love . . .'"

Freulich's voice joined his, and they finished it together: "'a sense of oneness with sun and stone.'" Then they laughed. Freulich marked a fresh fritillary, gently released it, and smiled. They both knew that ecstasy, that sense of sun, stone, plants, and butterflies. It would take more than a few dirt bikes to spoil it.

27

Steam curled around the cinnamon nipples of Noni Blue as she reclined against the smooth stone wall. Her pubescence like black moss tickled an alpine zephyr at the surface of the hot spring pool. "James, what a marvelous idea to come up here together. You were sweet to invite me, after the beast I've been to you."

"No beast, Noni. No holds, remember? Just a strong hearttug. Anyway, I'm glad you like this place—how could anyone help it?" He stretched his long body across the granite basin, meeting her toes with his own.

"I'm sorry anyway, James. But it's just as well that Professor Freulich sent O'Leary back to their Nevada research site. True, I was feeling my heart (or something) tugged two ways. But he was getting heavier than I wanted, for sure, and I would have really regretted if we hadn't any time together after you took the gutsy risk to come west."

Mead hadn't even thought of it that way, but hearing her say it, he guessed he had taken a bit of a risk. He said, "Can't say I'm sorry the guy left. What if he'd stayed?"

"Who knows? What-ifs are never worth much, are they? Never mind, he didn't, and that's fine. But do you really have to go so soon,

James?" Noni rubbed her dusty rose thighs across James's knees, floated them up onto his lap.

"I do, Noni. It's not fair to the lab for me to squat here much longer without paying for tuition or a meal ticket, let alone for the cabin, basic as it is. Anyway, without George here, I can't really get started on a project."

"Or are you just afraid to be here when he arrives?"

"No, no. Well . . . maybe a little bit. Maybe a lot. Anyway, I'm going to try to see Magdalena in some other habitats and see if I can't winkle October Carson out of the hills—or at least find some fresher tracks." He was not unaware of her sweet weight. "So, yes, as much as I'd like to stay on, I really must go. But you make it hard."

"So I see." Noni chuckled, wriggling into his arms. "We'll have to do something about that. But I'd say you're becoming obsessed with the butterfly *and* the bloke. Still, if my charms can't keep you here, so be it. Guess I deserve it."

"That's not quite fair to either of us, Noni. It has nothing to do with deserving or charming, and I'm not leaving to spite you for being interested in O'Leary. Nor do I think I'm obsessed. You go out daily to work on your project hour after hour, rain and flies be damned. Is that obsession or dedication? Well, it's the same with me and my 'research'; it's just unofficial—and unfunded."

"No funds, no form, no function—you're obsessed, all right. But maybe that's just disappointment talking."

"Well, now, *that's* something I could tell you about. Okay, call it obsession . . . but my ideas aren't strictly formless. I happen to think that Carson would have a lot to teach us, if he could be found. And as for function, I want to work out Magdalena's ecology—find out how it lives so well in such a harsh, high habitat. I realized that when I finally saw it alive up at Copper Lake a couple of days ago. I don't think that's any less valuable than most of what folks up here are doing. But first I've got to figure out some questions that might lend themselves to experimentation. Pure description won't hack it anymore—certainly not with a Yale committee, Griffin or no."

Noni looked up at the stone walls around the canyon. "It *is* a rather intimidating environment," she said. "Except in here."

"Anyway, my fixation isn't only with Magdalena and Carson. And your charms haven't lost their power, never mind my leaving. But, Noni, don't you think we've been boiling our bods long enough?"

"Yes, for sure. We're turning into maraschino prunes. To the tent, then!"

They stepped from the steamy pool and dried off as a group from Aspen arrived, disrobed, and climbed in to many a footsore "oooh!" and "aaah!" The alpine colors faded as the sun dropped below Castle Peak, casting purple shadow smears on the Maroon Bells' back sides. A quick chill arose with the mosquitoes. James and Noni dispensed with dinner in favor of a longer night together, likely their last for many weeks, as well as their first for what seemed like years.

Mead had already planned to leave Gothic via the Maroon Bells–Snowmass Wilderness, past Conundrum Hot Springs to Aspen and points east. All he had with him fit in his backpack, and the hike—especially with the hot springs rest stop in the middle—sounded far preferable to a repeat of his bus ride from Gunnison to Denver. Cheaper, too, which suited his anemic wallet. When Noni ended up with a couple of days free from her research, he asked her to accompany him as far as the springs, and she readily agreed.

They left Gothic early, trekking the steep old mining road past Judd Falls. Soon they entered the wilderness area, took a junction to the right off the Copper Creek Trail toward White Rock Mountain, and climbed a basin directly opposite Mount Gothic. This brought them across a broad talus to Triangle Pass, at nearly thirteen thousand feet. Mead had to concentrate on the rugged trail instead of watching for Magdalena. On top, Castle Peak sprawled and spired off to their right, more Gothic than Gothic itself. The Maroon Bells sawed the air to the north, their striated red faces no less wonderful for their familiarity from a thousand postcards and calendars.

A long valley dropped away toward where Aspen was rumored to lie. Many switchbacks led through the lushest of alpine meadows. Speckled with magenta paintbrush, cream marsh marigolds, and buttery arnicas, purpled with patches of asters and elephant heads, all against a panoply of greens, the meadows soaked up afternoon rains and turned them into this spectrum. The peaty softness swaddled both the minds and the feet of the stone-weary hikers. But the greater reward lay two thousand feet below, where natural hot springs bubbled out of the mountainside and flowed through a series of stone basins before joining the cold stream. This was Conundrum, the celebrated hot springs of the Maroon Bells–Snowmass. Noni went first, and Mead had difficulty keeping his eyes on the trail and off her shorts, which she would soon lose.

Noni and James arrived to find the place deserted. Quickly out of their backpacks, boots, shirts, shorts, and undies, they lay their sweaty, achy bodies in the whirlpool of the hills. They soaked, splashed, and played for the rest of that day. Only a handful of hikers stripped to take the waters in all these hours, and most of those were Gothic folks or bronzed, slim skiers and hikers. Thanks to the designated wilderness area that surrounded the site, no party of gawky flatlanders appeared, not a single jeeper hoisting a beer in one hand, binoculars in the other.

Running at about 97 degrees, situated at eleven thousand feet above sea level, the springs were not too hot for a long sit, especially when soaks were interspersed with brief rambles into nearby meadows and chilly snowplay in the algae-stained red snowbank at the foot of the north-facing valley walls. "Hey, I've never been naked in the snow before," Mead shouted over Noni's laughter. She lobbed another snowball that caught him smack on his not-very-hairy chest. "But I'm freezing my butt off, aren't you?"

"I love it!" she protested, throwing another, hitting him in the alleged frigid butt. "Uh-oh, I'm getting a little close to the vitals," she said. "That could work against my own interests."

James dumped Noni and hennaed her shining hair with the algal-red snow. He finally had to carry her back to the spring, she loved the snow so, but she didn't resist. Her small body made scarcely a load for Mead's long arms.

"You've got a blue butt, too," he observed, patting it with the carrying hand and almost dropping her. "We could call you Noni Bluebottom!" Noni yelped and squirmed until he set her gently into the steaming basin and slushed in beside her. They shivered with the decadent delight of it all. "A great way to leave Gothic, my first time." He sighed.

Noni shivered, but said nothing.

Later, they lay on their ripstop nylon cloud in Mead's tiny tent, a quarter mile from the springs. The Forest Service wisely imposed this no-camping perimeter around Conundrum Hot Springs to prevent trampling of the fragile site. They made love in the early dusk. Passion strong enough to keep the mosquitoes at mind's bay glued their bodies together with the tangy mucilage of love. No thoughts of butterflies or tramps interloped; no sense of falling temperature or rising dew intervened between their fitted, flushy seam. James came first, and at that moment some late arrivals at the hot pool thought they heard a coyote howl down in the forest fringe. When Noni followed through, they guessed they heard an owl.

Afterward, the reunited lovers felt the temperature drop, the dew rise, and the mosquitoes suck, so they pulled their bags up around their shoulders, cocoonlike. They lay on their surfeited bellies, sharing a Sierra Club cupful of red wine drawn from a battered bota borrowed from one of Noni's new friends at the lab. Faces lifted toward a moon-through-spruce, they issued soft sounds that no one heard but themselves. Reaching one arm back over Noni's supine curve, James stroked the cleft apple of her ass. "Not so cold now," he said. "Not so blue."

"But *I* am," Noni argued. "I don't want to be apart."

"Won't be for long. I fact, I have a rising feeling . . ."

"Already?" Noni asked, wide-eyed.

". . . feeling that we'll see one another again this summer."

"Hmmm." Noni considered that. Then asked, changing the subject, "James, do you suppose everyone who comes here looks for a conundrum in his or her life?"

"Maybe so. At least those who have an inkling of what it means."

"It's a riddle, isn't it?"

"Right, but one with no easy answer. An imponderable. So what kinds of conundrums do you suppose people pose here?"

"Oh—like, whether or not to take all their clothes off in front of strangers . . ."

"Or how could there be such heavenly hot water right beside the ice-cold creek?"

"Sure, though that's got a right answer, if we knew the facts. How about this one: Why do people leave the aforementioned heaven to jump around in a snowbank?"

"Yeah. Or, for those who come here on a weekend, why the hell did I do *that?*"

They both laughed, glad they hadn't. Then Noni said, "James, here's mine."

"Shoot. I'll try to play your oracle and answer the unanswerable." Truth to tell, he had no idea what was coming and was a little nervous as to what it might be.

"Good luck. Okay. How can you—or I, or anyone—travel around, do interesting things in interesting places, and meet pretty people without falling for someone now and then? And if you do, how can you ever honestly bond with one person?"

"Damned if I know," Mead said. He'd often asked himself the same thing.

"Some oracle!"

"So, how about this? No possession, no jealousy. Sure, loneliness and disappointment from time to time, as with me when I got to Gothic. Too bad, so sad. But no end of the world. We're young, for Christ's sake; maybe we have no business bonding at this point in our lives anyway." This was easier to say now than it was a few days ago.

"That just sounds like the hippies and their free love, doesn't it?"

"Like, 'love the one you're with'? I guess so. But they're just re-cycling the Beats on the subject, as they did the Bohemians before them . . . Rimbaud, Verlaine . . ."

"Or Bo Diddley: 'Who do you love?' Well, maybe it makes sense for now. But when does one switch? And then, how does one become instantly monogamous?"

"I'm not even going to try that one. Look at those stars! The Milky Way looks like the sandy bed of Conundrum Creek."

"Nice dodge, Mr. Delphi. Well, it should be a fine day for your trek out tomorrow. I'll miss you, James Mead. You'll probably meet some Nordic blonde ski-bunny chick getting out of the springs after breakfast, take up company with her on the way to Aspen, and move in together, and that'll be the last we hear of you." In the pale glim-mer Noni's face looked luminous. Streaks of risen dew on her brown cheeks might have been taken for tears.

"That's just silly," he said. "Nordics aren't even my type. I'll be there with open arms when you get back to New Haven."

Hot springs ran down Noni's face as she said, "About that, James." She paused. Then, "I won't be coming back to New Haven this fall. I've been offered a fellowship in Cambridge."

"Well—" James felt just as dumbstruck as when Noni had met him in Crested Butte with the news of her new friend, but he recov-ered well. "Oh, congratulations, Noni! Anyway, Harvard isn't *that* far up the line from Yale—just a few hours."

"Not *that* Cambridge, James."

"Oh. Shit." After a silence of a few bat-beats in the night, Mead hobbled out on a broken voice, "Well, it's a super place. Remember to ask me for some contacts and the names of a few good pubs, like the Free Press . . ." His voice trailed off into the gurgling of the stream beyond their thin, thin wall.

Nothing more to be said. James drew Noni down into the bag and pulled the tent fly tight. In their down nest, Noni's body felt even warmer than the hot springs. Her softness beside him all but blotted out the sense of the rocks beneath their bed. He would long for the nearness later, just as he had during the previous days when he thought someone else was enjoying it. But he was damned if he wasn't going to feel it fully now. He'd learned that much. He nestled his head between Noni's breasts and went to sleep.

For once, his dreams contained hints of neither Carson nor Magdalena, but just a long, rowdy snowball fight among naked people, including almost everyone he knew. "That's crazy," he mumbled in his half sleep. "How can you see someone naked in a dream when you never have in real life?"

Noni muttered, "Conundrum," and turned her warm bottom into the bowl of his belly. Then she dove back into her own dreams. They featured a troupe of Nordic blonds and blondes, nude, disporting together in a huge outdoor Jacuzzi. To her satisfaction, James was not among them. But she was.

28

After mating, Erebia seeks shelter from a brief shower beneath a handy parasol, the leaf of a Parry's primrose. Its rose-pink petals glisten with raindrops as Erebia sits snug and dry, his wings folded tight. The urge to fly and seek a partner assuaged for now, he rests as his next spermatophore recharges the costly nutrient package it will bear along with sperms. When the rain lets up, he creeps down a fissure for the night. In the morning he will resume his up and down flights over the rocks, seeking to mate as many times as he can during his lifetime. If he manages to couple with a female already mated, his spermatophore will displace the other, so his genes will be the ones passed on. So there's no giving up just because he has succeeded once.

Of course, the same fate could befall his own germ cells, left with his first mate. Not for now, however. Since their parting on the morning after their union, she has been unreceptive to further courtship, raising her abdomen high and spreading her wings low whenever approached, until the frustrated males give up. Instead, she hops, flutters, and crawls from tuft of grass to sedge tussock to lump of stone. From time to time she taps a grass blade with her antennae, dips her body's tip, and deposits a single egg on one surface or another, cementing it into place. More often than not, the chosen substrate is an overhang of rock, where the egg is inconspicuous but never very far from a succulent supply of grass.

Large for a satyr's egg, more the size of a swallowtail's, the ovum resembles an oblong vase for a petit point flower. Ribbed and creamy white when laid, it turns tan and purplish brown and in a few hours ripens to silver-gray with a Prussian blue band around the dimple on top. Finally, before hatching, it goes putty-gray against the grayer granite and fading grass. About ten days after the egg is deposited, a thrip-size larva will eat its way out, consume the eggshell, and switch to tender grass. How many times Erebia's offspring will molt before diving into the grassroots will depend upon how many days remain before the alpine herbage dries out between summer's last breath and autumn's first frost.

Of all this, Erebia knows nothing. He has resumed his patrols, sometimes top to bottom and back, other times back and forth in a drunken glide path to the edges of the willow thickets and *Boloria* bogs below. A Clark's nutcracker makes a halfhearted pass at the butterfly. Distracted by a checkerspot, it loses both in a classic fox-and-grapes act of indecision. The corvid settles for a fat rock spider instead, thus getting the distilled goodness of ten scree moths, two Magdalenas, four checkerspots, and a tortoiseshell, as well as various flies, caddis flies, and lacewings harvested over the orb weaver's lifetime.

Erebia hasn't quite the same vigor as before. Shiny chitin is beginning to show through the sparser scales on the veins of his wings, especially the big, swollen vein at the base of the forewing that sets the satyrs apart from other lineages of butterflies. Still, but for the beak brand applied by the black swift, his wings are entire. Few shrubs grow on the rockslides to tear butterflies' wings, and nights spent safe among the lockbox of the rocks mean no scratches or tears from branches blowing on the nighttime breeze.

The most obvious sign of Erebia's aging shows in his coloring;

no longer truly black, but a rich coffee-bean brown, he has faded in
the harsh ultraviolet rays of the alpine sky. Built and colored for the
purpose of gathering sunbeams, those sable vanes nonetheless lose
their luster in the performance of that very function.

So Erebia is a little past his prime when he meets a fresh misfortune. During a late passage, he is taken by a sudden gust and
carried over the ridge to the steep snowfield that gathers, then melts
annually in the lap of the mountain's other side—a mere ghost of the
glacier that carved out this cirque. Only once before has he ventured
here, all the way down the north-facing slope to the protalus ram-
part at its base, but that was a warm day, and he sailed right back up
and over to his accustomed home range. Now, as he blows over the
snow-bowl, the cold-blooded insect feels its chill. A stiff, sharp shaft
of upwelling air clutches him, sucking him down onto the surface of
the firn. There his body temperature rapidly drops toward the danger
point.

A watcher at the snowfield would notice the surface speckled
and spotted with the bodies and wings of grasshoppers, butterflies,
and other insects thus entrapped. This strange fallout proves a boon
to foraging birds and entomologists. Rosy finches and water pipits
alight in the middle of these refrigerated larders for the cold cuts
they contain. Ptarmigan, leaving off their accustomed willow buds
for the high-protein opportunity, work the edges. Birds draw other
birds to the bonanza. Helpless when the temperature of their flight
muscles drops below a critical point, most insects become easy prey
when so chilled—or simply freeze to death and become immured
in the snowpack. Sometimes entire strata of this snow plankton
have been preserved in glaciers, and famous among scientists are the
places, such as Grasshopper Glacier in Montana, where the melting
feet of these ice sheets give forth their insect lodes. The lesser museum of Magdalena Mountain is about to gain one more specimen.

Instinctively, just before numbness sets in for good, Erebia lays
his closed wings flat against the reflective surface of the snow. At just

this time of day the sun shines directly onto the mountain's far face, blinding birds, pikas, and passersby unless they shield their eyes. For a time, Erebia's temperature flirts with the point of total shutdown. Then a calorie or two convects from that spread black beam catcher to his body and into his muscle fibers, the nodes of nerves. Heat gain begins to overcome loss by an immeasurable margin, but not too small for Erebia to feel and respond to. Slowly, slowly, he reclaims precious degrees. The snowfield struggled its best to drain the BTUs from his blood, but those elegantly evolved solar panels, the wings of an alpine, suck back at the sunbeams for all they are worth.

Finally, just able, Erebia rights himself and begins to crawl. In a few labored minutes he reaches the edge of the snow, struggles onto warm granite, continues to a hot black patch of lichen, and lies flat again. In seconds his flight muscles reach the takeoff temperature, well above the ambient high for the day—and he takes flight. The first patch of campion he passes over draws him like a butterfly collector to beer, and he quaffs the sugar-rich nectar for minutes.

Renewed, as the sun sinks to the ridgetop, Erebia follows another time-grooved pattern and flies to a shadowed cleft in the rockslide. Alighting on the rim of the rock, he fairly dives into the void that promises safety for the high montane night. He'll never know how close he came to frozen death that day, but if he knows anything, it is how to pass a high-country sunset. He crawls down the fluted side of a rock chimney. At last, warm against the stone-walled haystack of a providential pika, Erebia sleeps his Stygian sleep, a black butterfly down a black hole in a black night. Thus ends the twelfth day of adult existence for one alpine resident of Magdalena Mountain.

29

Mary stepped from the dark, cool hollow of the monastery into the bright light of day. A pineborne breeze carried a conifer whiff and the sound of women's voices. A raven call away, Oberon stepped into the Grove. Six or eight ponderosa pines, half as many lodgepoles, Douglas firs, and a couple of aspens circled a pink sand clearing, in the center of which stood a tall boulder, a megalith beside a single blue spruce.

The others were already present, except for Attalus. Xerxes, Sylvanus, Abraxas the Baptist, Levi Samson, Ajax, Bacchus, Polyxenes, and a dozen others stood about talking quietly or perched on stones, each wearing the soft green robe that was the one visible sign of their order, worn only on certain occasions. Several had their robes hitched up above their knees or open at the chest to reveal T-shirts variously emblazoned.

"Abraxas," called Ajax, an ardent atheist, "I have noticed that Jesus has a lightning rod." He nodded toward the tall statue jutting from a high rock. "Doesn't this show a singular lack of faith on the part of the Catholics?"

"Well said, Ajax. We Baptists would have felt no need for such a precaution. You, on the other hand, might be advised to get one yourself!" Laughter rolled around the group like a cat's ball with a bell inside.

"Gentlemen, lovers of nature and peacefulness," Oberon began in the prescribed lingo. He presided as founder of the Grove. "Sylvanus, will you please give us a poem?" It was customary to begin the Forest Meeting with verse that spoke reverence for trees.

"I think that I shall never see" having grown a little thin in the foliage, Sylvanus (reflecting his assumed name) had taken it upon himself to enlarge the Grove's library of dendrophilic verse. Dickinson, Frost, Jeffers, Merwin, Snyder, all were read here.

"Here is a poem," he said, "you will not have heard. A friend found it on a plaque hanging on a tree in Agra, India, and sent it to me on a postcard. I would move to adopt it as our standard opening, but then it would become as common as Joyce Kilmer's verse. Anyway . . ." Sylvanus's introductions often went on longer than the poems themselves. This suited Oberon today, as he needed time to stall; just so it didn't go on *too* long. He stroked his mica-flecked beard, thinking fast on his feet as Sylvanus spoke. ". . . So here it is: 'The Prayer of the Tree': 'Man, I am the warmth of your home in cold winter night . . .'"

After the poem, a grunt of approval escaped the Grove like an audible puff. It seemed that a general discussion of Indian and Nepalese de- and afforestation was about to break out, when Oberon spoke again.

"Brothers, excuse me, I need to speak with some urgency. And I want to stop addressing you as 'brothers' or 'gentlemen.' I ask your consensus for the admission of women to the Forest Meeting today."

This came as no surprise. Xerxes said, "Oberon, you know we're all in accord with that proposal. We've never wanted to exclude women."

"Except Attalus!" came two or three voices.

"I second that," said Sylvanus, short, stout, in his robe very much the Friar Tuck figure. "Bring them on, I say!"

"Now, quickly—do we have a consensus to admit women to this assembly and, in principle, to our order?" No discussion was necessary, no "nays" were recorded. Mary, Annie, and Catherine stepped into the Grove.

After happy words of welcome, Mary asked Oberon on the QT, "But what kept Attalus from destroying the consensus?"

Just then the monastery carillon rang two. "Why, I think Attalus will be with us directly," Oberon answered. "He was absent when I announced that the Forest Meeting would be moved up half an hour due to the shortening of the days. Too bad."

"Oberon! And you say you have no power here!" Annie whispered.

"A mere parliamentary maneuver," he hushed back.

Annie smirked, and a few monks chortled, feeling a little too clever. Oberon knew the main battle lay ahead, but at least Mary and Catherine could now speak for themselves.

Just then Attalus appeared, a chilly shadow falling out of the forest into the sunlit glade. "Oberon!" he raged. "What are these *women* doing here?" He uttered the word as some would say *snakes* or *cockroaches.*

"They are our guests, Attalus. You were late, and we agreed to admit them."

"Late! It's just past two sharp, how was there time—"

"The time was moved up, with the sun. You were absent for the announcement."

"You've tricked me!"

"Then call it quid pro quo for your betrayal of Mary."

"Never mind that. They cannot remain. You know I have to approve—"

"Then be still for now. You'll have a chance to have your say and to exercise your veto if you so decide. But you'll have to wait your turn. There are other items on the agenda first, and these sisters are here and will remain for now." Not a few of those present were half hoping Attalus's apoplexy might translate into something more serious. He sputtered, flapped like a big brown bat, and eventually settled in the shade.

"We have three items of business to discuss," Oberon continued. "In the following order. First, the presence of Jesus Christ on our 'property,' if you will excuse that term. Second, our proper response to the mountain pine beetles here. And third, whether we shall invite the women's encampment at Rocky Flats to winter under our over-large roof and, if that works out, perhaps to merge with our order." A sound such as suffocating toads might make issued from Attalus's shadow. Oberon hoped that if he handled the other tedious matters first, Attalus might be worn down by the time they got to the women.

"As to the statue of Jesus—" Oberon turned and swept his hand in its direction, for there was nowhere in the precincts of the Grove from which it could not be seen. "The church included it in the deed, therefore it is ours, like it or not. Do we want to keep an image from one particular religion, and such a prominent one as this, on land devoted to pantheistic ecumenism? Maybe the chief proponent and opponent among us will be good enough to state their cases. Ajax first, please."

"As you say, Oberon, the Grove is the habitat of Pan and all the rest. To permit a monumental symbol of one cult to dominate the place is tantamount to promoting the worship of Jehovah and Jesus Christ. I say remove the effigy, lightning rod and all, and leave it on the doorstep of the Lutherans down the road. Or better yet, trade it for beetle-killed cordwood." Murmurs of "Right on!" and "Blasphemy!" rumbled around the wood.

"Oh, boy," muttered Oberon, "this'll be fun." Then, "Now Abraxas, please."

"Thank you, Oberon. As he is an avowed atheist, Brother Ajax's position is of course biased. But consider that Jesus spoke to all men as the Prince of Peace—surely apt for all of us, especially in these times. It's not his fault that wars have been fought—"

"*Are* being fought," said someone.

"—in his name. Let us keep his benign presence as a clear sign that we are on his side, in that way if not in an ecclesiastical context. You don't have to accept him as your personal savior to admire his teachings."

Ajax was listening.

"Besides, the statue has diplomatic value in a largely Christian neighborhood. We rely on the goodwill of our neighbors to be able to function. As you know, some of the fundamentalists around here already confound our Pan with the Beast (the oldest frame-up in the book), and we'd best not reinforce the rumor that we're Satanists. Animists are bad enough in their minds. We might as well hang a big 666 on our mailbox as pull down that statue, which would surely be seen as thumbing our noses at local churches."

"A good point, Abraxas," put in Levi Samson.

Ajax asked for a consensus, but only a few voices responded. This is where rule by consensus sucks, thought Oberon, and then he announced that perhaps the issue should be tabled for the time being. "You may take comfort in the statue quo, Abraxas."

"So it seems. But I wish we could agree on a warm welcome instead."

"Oberon, may I speak?" It was Mary's voice, nervous but firm.

"Of course, Mary."

Anticipation buzzed like the deerflies that sought to get up their robes. "Jesus, it is true, became the man-god of one large group of sects," Mary began. "But he was also a pacifist and a pantheist—a Jew by birth, a healer by grace, Messiah by conscription—but a man for all that, in sympathy with all life. A true lover of nature."

At that, a dull roar of surprise rose up to greet the songs of juncos and tanagers above. "A pantheist? Christ?" "Who—*Jesus* Christ?" "What about dominion of nature?" "I know some Baptist birders—but I never thought of Jesus as a naturalist."

Oberon banged his stick for order.

Now Polyxenes spoke up. "Oberon, I may be able to cast some light on this topic. I brought another poem today, which I found in a neo-pagan rag out of Glastonbury."

Oberon nodded for him to continue.

"It's called 'Pan's Dance,' and it includes these lines: 'Dearest Pan, brother of Christ, / we lay claim to the crown of summer— / together.' Apparently Mary is not alone in holding such thoughts."

"Is Mary a biblical scholar?" Abraxas whispered to Oberon.

"Of a sort," he replied. "Maybe self-taught."

"Thank you, Polyxenes. Furthermore," Mary went on, "of all the male characters in the New Testament, Jesus was the least bigoted toward women. You could almost call him a feminist, in the context of the times—in contrast to his apostles, especially Paul, and many later leaders in his name. Abraxas, you said that Jesus spoke to all men of peace—but he spoke to the women as well, and loved them as much."

"Lying witch!" Attalus hissed. "Heretic!"

Oberon spoke with controlled rage. "I'll accept that as opinion, Attalus, if ungenerous." He pinioned Attalus with his iron eyes. "Now, that's it. Leave, and abide by our decisions, or *shut up*—unless you have something temperate to say. Any more acid like that and we'll next see you in court."

Attalus began to rise, thought better of it, and ground back into the grus.

"Please go on, Mary," said Oberon.

"You are partly right, Attalus. I am a witch—of the old kind. One of the matrons of the Old Religion—the peaceful handmaidens to Diana and Demeter, the knowers of knowledge, the keepers of the green and the herbs. Too bad you and I can't compare notes on lichens as medicinals and dyestuffs. But no witch of Satan, there being no Satan. The twisting of the horned one into the devil, the switching of witches into black-magic bitches, was accomplished by the same bureaucrats of the early church who edited the biblical canon to leave out some of the best bits—including certain passages that confirm what I have to say. Jesus knew that all life was intimately related and must be respected as such. Why do you think he went to the wilderness for revelation? It seems to me that he belongs here, right among Pan and the rest of his retinue."

Consensus came quickly after that. Ajax laughed, shaking his head. "Well spoken, Mary—so he stays. Does the lightning rod remain as well?"

"Damn right it does," a hitherto quiet brother named Homerus supplied. "Gaia plays no favorites, and Thor is an equal opportunity slinger of thunderbolts. But let's hear your story, Mary. How did you come by your knowledge?"

"Not now," Oberon insisted. "We've got to finish our business so Catherine can get back to Golden when her sisters are released from jail." Attalus began to mutter about that being where they belonged, but an eye-arrow from Oberon hushed him cold. Then he said, "I am humbled, Mary. Now, on to an even pricklier point. How should we respond to the pine bark beetle and spruce budworm infestations that are killing many conifers in Colorado? Some say that left alone, they'll turn the mountains brown and gray. They might threaten this very Grove. So what shall it be? Spray, or let them be?"

They all looked around them; dead red branches or rusty crowns signaled trees that would sooner or later perish before their time. "Oberon, what are our options?" asked Menelaus, a thickly bearded, thick-bodied beetle of a man, a former farrier.

"Well, aerial spraying has been attempted for both organisms, especially the budworm. They even tried DDT in Oregon until a bunch of students showed that it did more harm than good, shutting them down. The spraying has had little effect on the target insects, which are cyclical in any case, but it's killed many other life-forms and sold a lot of chemicals. Sometimes individual trees can be successfully treated, but it's expensive."

"Does the National Park Service spray?" Menelaus asked.

"No. Essentially, they treat it as a natural phenomenon, although public pressure is rising to 'do something' up in certain scenic areas such as Forest Canyon in RMNP."

"How about the Forest Service?"

"They're equivocal, and in a tizzy about it. Lately, for the budworm, they've been blanketing whole forests with a bacterium that kills the larvae. Problem is, it kills butterflies and beneficial moths as well as the budworm."

"Nukes 'em all, eh?"

"More than intended, anyway, as usual."

"And what do private foresters do?" Menelaus concluded.

"Oh, they recommend clear-cutting forests at risk in order to halt the beetles' spread. Which it does—at the loss of the forest. Clearly a case of the cure being worse, et cetera."

And so it went, the nature monks debating questions of natural succession, the role of fire, insect population fluctuation and control, and whether it was appropriate to use biocides in a Pan-Pacific Grove. Oberon suggested that between cost, growing resistance, and the great acreage involved, eradication was impossible even if it were desirable. "The sooner we let things adjust to their own regime, the better. The so-called pests will crash, and the forest eventually regenerate. We've got to look at nature holistically, over the long term, and realize that death is not always a bad thing."

"But brothers and sisters," rebutted Sylvanus, who affected his idea of old-time monk's talk, "I chose my name because I venerate trees. What will befall us, or avail us, if the Grove itself dies? Haven't we a duty to these trees at least?"

"We all cherish trees, Sylvanus," replied Xerxes. "But what do you love more? The trees or the forest? The nozzleheads believe in a chemical fix for everything, and the loggers can't see the forest for the fees. But we wouldn't think of paying off our mortgage with timber money." He let this sink in. "Of course it's sad when a beloved tree dies. Spray, you might save it; cut, you might save its neighbor. If these trees die, woodpeckers and nuthatches will join our meetings. And in time, aspens will take their place."

"Oberon, let me speak." Every eye looked toward Attalus.

"Go ahead," said Oberon, thinking it had damned well better be on topic.

"I would only add," he began, "that a forest with dead and dying trees supports a much more interesting and diverse flora of lichens and greater ecological complexity. Some foresters refer to such a dynamic forest as 'overmature,' in support of their clear-cutting agenda. It is folly to manage forests solely for profit. They'll have their way at the forests' peril. We must protect the trees from people more than from beetles."

Shocked silence filled the Grove. His speech reminded them all of this brother's worth, and why he was among them in the first place, and made them wish that he could somehow be reconciled to their common cause. Consensus followed for a watchful but tolerant stance toward the insects in question.

The air in the pine grove took on a new flavor and feel as the sun passed below the highest needles. A coolness arose, so that some members who had doffed their robes in favor of T-shirts and shorts now gathered the heavier garments around them again. Mary Glanville, in a long, plain cotton dress that Annie had lent her, pulled a shawl around her shoulders and drew in her sandaled feet. Catherine brought out a woolen sweater from her daypack. Annie felt a shiver beneath her chambray, more than the sweat of the earlier afternoon wicking off. The three women squeezed one another's hands.

"Finally," said Oberon, "we come to that matter of our joining households and peaceful forces with the Rocky Flats women's encampment. We have already agreed in principle. Now, the actual union will take some doing, but I have no doubt it can happen if we decide that is the right end to pursue. Catherine, will you please say a word?" Then, "This is our guest, Catherine Greenland. She'll tell us about the camp, and what she and her sisters hope to gain, and bring, by coming here to join us this winter—and perhaps beyond."

Catherine's sneakers crunched on the mix of gravel and pine needles underfoot. "Hello, everyone, good afternoon. I'm impressed by how you arrive at decisions, without the bitter factionalism that frustrates so many well-intended movements. I hope that will continue after you hear what I have to say." She went on to tell the story of her band of women resisters. "And so we aim to advertise daily," she summarized, "by our own presence, arrest, and commitment, that both preparation for nuclear holocaust and plutonium poisoning are going on in Colorado right now."

"Catherine," asked Bacchus, who'd so far been silent, "we admire your dedication to people. But what are your attitudes toward the rest of nature?"

"Most of us are unsophisticated in natural history, but we care about the countryside, the air, and the water; a lot of us feed and watch birds, and we garden. You can teach us a lot, and I hope we'll have something to teach in return."

"I have no doubt of that. But what conflicts do you foresee?" asked Levi Samson, a fair and slender autumn aspen of a man.

"None, if you will respect our privacy and our equality in all matters, and if we can manage the same. There may be, of course, some personality differences. But in a place where ego is kept in check and civility is respected"—she paused for a moment—"there should be no big problems."

"Are all the members much like you?" asked Ajax.

"Not at all. We number among us radical feminists, lesbians, even two marginal misanthropes who have both been abused by men, but also mothers such as myself, a grown daughter or two, nurses, teachers, and clergy. If any among us can't handle your lot, they need not come along, as a small presence will remain in Golden all winter."

"And I daresay," inserted Abraxas, "some of us will join you on the demonstration line if we are welcome."

"You are most welcome," Catherine replied. "But I know that at least one among you opposes this whole thing. Oberon, may we hear from the one who bears us ill will?"

"I bear no man ill will!" thundered Attalus. "Oberon! *May I speak?*"

"Carry on, Attalus. But be mindful of Catherine's word: be civil!"

"It is difficult, when the Grove of Peace is invaded by evil in the flesh. I repeat: I bear no man ill will. And I include women, as long as they keep their own peace, apart from men of faith who would carry out their business—*our* business—away from sin and temptation. I may have rejected Rome in favor of an older Roman pantheon, but the early church got it right about women, as exemplified by Eve and Mary Magdalene. They carry the stain of sin and the capacity to corrupt good men. The Virgin alone—if only a metaphor, biologically speaking—was free of it. My brothers—you must see this! If we allow women in here, our fraternal comity will corrode, we will be tempted, we will fight, and the harridans will prevail. Why else do you think they want to intrude?"

"Attalus, I believe the invitation came from here, not from Golden. Anyway, aren't you simply admitting the weakness of your own flesh, and your fear of it?"

"Miss Greenland. I respect you and your friends' convictions. But you are wrong to leave your homes to confront men. If you win, it will be through corruption of those you oppose. These are matters for men to work out."

"You think we're trying to lay the boys from Rockwell?" she asked, astonished.

"This is plain nuts!" howled Xerxes.

"You too be civil, Xerxes," said Oberon. "We must at least hear the man out."

"Listen to yourselves," Attalus implored. "You're all bewitched already, or besotted with the prospects of the flesh."

Menelaus turned to Ajax: "It's worse than I thought; he's completely mad."

"Stark, raving," agreed Ajax.

"That is *fucked up*," came from the rear, and similar opinions flicked around the glade.

Contempt crackled like ozone before a storm, and a storm was indeed arising. Mary, Annie, and Catherine silently quaked in anger, too abashed to speak. Oberon was dying to quash Attalus, but resolved to let him cook his own goose a little longer.

"If you persist in this gambit," Attalus continued, "then the order will fall. But you cannot do it without my approval; nor will you be able to achieve the necessary consensus, since I will never agree . . . and I daresay I may have won two or three adherents to my view." He looked around, but found no takers.

"Attalus," Sylvanus said with exquisite restraint, "we all love you as a brother of peace and Pan. We respect your knowledge, experience, and oratory, a lost art. But listen to yourself: you are severely misguided in the way of female human beings, not to mention wildly out of date. Don't you know that that such notions have long been repudiated in all but the most benighted quarters?"

"But—"

"Besides," Mary intervened, "are you equally deaf to Gaia and Mother Nature herself? Don't you realize the essential femininity of the Old Ways? The preeminence of the female organism in biology? In evolution itself? No pistil, no stamen."

"And many of the best botanists have been women," Annie added.

"These women botanists of whom you speak," Atallus answered, "they're all right as amateurs, but they should confine their field of interest to the dooryard and the kitchen garden. As for those female earth deities, they are metaphors, nothing more, mythically expressing the fecundity and profligacy of the earth. Even you, Oberon, are a metaphor—you're no unbiased founder. You're a fanatical feminist, bent on shoving Titania down our throats."

"Not the most felicitous way to put it," said Oberon. "Look, Attalus, metaphor though I may be, I beg you to exercise the same sound judgment you displayed in the matter of the pine beetles. If for no other reason, consider the Grove! You said we must protect it. Well, if we fail, the Mormons are just waiting to pick up the mortgage and develop the place as a resort and conference center. Remember how you hated the new Dillon, the night we found Mary? This could be worse. Would you willingly sacrifice the Mountain Monastery as the thin edge of the wedge for the whole Peak to Peak under asphalt, plastic, and profit? All in the name of your narrow prejudices?"

Attalus stood dumb, like a stone.

"So. I call for a consensus on merger with the women's encampment. If you dissent, you may walk the razor and fall on either side. Abide, or leave us!"

"But my veto . . ." whined Attalus through tears of rage. "The trusteeship . . ."

"Damn the trusteeship! If it holds up in court, which I doubt, there are plenty of other places we can go. The YMCA camp at Estes Park is going broke, we could get it for a song. The Lutherans are looking for an out from Twin Sisters Ranch. Since the Boy Scouts' legal suit went against them, Camp Tahosa has been on the block. Any of these would do for us. You exercise your veto, and we will not only expel *you* from Magdalena Mountain, we too will likely leave. Then, if it's developed, the fault will all be yours."

Oberon was bluffing his socks off, but he knew the ruse was necessary as his only tool against the veto. No one wanted to leave this place, least of all him.

"And then, Attalus, you'll be out of the only home you've known for forty years; out of the brotherhood; out of the habitats you know and love; out of your lichen lab, library, and collections. *And* out of favor with the archbishop for blowing the deal. If they let you back in, you'll be lucky to find yourself frying with the Franciscans down in Alamosa, where, by the way, I hear they have loose nuns as well. We would prefer to have you with us—*if* you can swallow your pride, your venom, and your ludicrous misconceptions about our sisters. Now chew on that, my friend, and make up your mind. I call for consensus."

Lips tight like oysters all around, all hands went up but one. "And one abstention. Now"—Oberon could scarcely be heard—"will the trustee exercise his veto?" A single ponderosa needle fell onto Mary's lap, and everyone heard it land.

Attalus, his fallen face smeared, rose and withdrew into the forest. And as the pines closed around the dark, departing form, Mary just watched.

30

In the morning, pulling apart was harder for James and Noni than splitting a geode with a rubber mallet. But knowing they had to, after one more sweet merger, they disconnected. Not risking another leisured soak in the hot springs, they washed the sex and sweat from their sore parts and limbs, dressed, kissed, and set out in separate directions. Each had a heck of a hike ahead, though Noni's was mostly uphill before she could drop again to Gothic, while Mead's was almost all downhill for fifteen miles. "Some Gothic people do the whole thing in a day," Noni had told him. "Gothic to Conundrum to Aspen."

"Now that would be a day hike and a half," Mead told the aspens as he brachiated downslope between them. The scent of Noni hadn't all washed off, especially on his mustache; every little while he curled his upper lip to his nostrils and smiled.

He didn't reach Aspen until early evening—too late to hitchhike out—and wondered where he would spend the night. Old masonry, brick, and wooden buildings lined the leafy streets, tucked between slopes of grass, sage, and the eponymous white-barked poplars. But from the looks of the place, there weren't likely to be any cheap digs, and certainly no place to throw down his sleeping bag. He was dying to get his pack frame off his shoulders. He thought of Professor Winchester, the massive bookcase behind his desk, and felt he was carrying the whole of it on his back right now.

Just then a Ford Fairlane rolled by, and a voice called, "Is that a butterfly net?" Mead had borrowed one from Freulich for the duration of the summer. He gritted his teeth and girded his loins for derision, but it never came. The driver parked, got out, and extended his hand. He had been a collector as a kid, until the taunts got to him. He was as pleased as punch, he said, to meet someone who had "made it through the gauntlet" and would even walk the posh streets of Aspen with his net on full display. Before he knew it, Mead had a warm dinner and good wine in his belly and a soft condominium pillow under his head. It wouldn't be the last time that net would help him land on his feet this summer. The next, in fact, was only hours away.

Glitzy Aspen was Babylon to Gothic's simplicity and the unadorned hills. Seductive playthings and delectables crowded the shop windows the next morning. Skinny hippie climbers in denim and tie-dye threaded their way among paunchy polyester flatlanders on the crowded sidewalks while the sleek and the chic trolled expensive boutiques. Out of place, Mead suspected that Carson would have felt the same. Then, in a small square, he spotted a prospector and his burro. His heart raced as he approached the hoary gold hunter and saw the short line of tourists waiting to have their pictures taken with him.

"Good God!" he screeched. "Could it be . . ." Several in the queue turned to see what he was on about, and one smart-ass Texan said, "No, he's not Santa Claus, son. Just a bum who's about to jigger me out of five bucks!"

Mead remembered that Carson's journal had mentioned rival entrepreneurs. When his turn came, trying to sound casual, he asked, "Been doing this gig for long?"

"Too damn long, kid. What's it to ya?"

"Well, I used to, uh, know someone who did this around here. Did you ever have a colleague named October Carson?" There, he'd spilled it, for what it was worth.

"Have a *what*? You mean a partner? Never had one at all. Never even knew nobody named *October*—what kind of a weird name is that, anyhow? Wait a minute ... *Carson*, you say? That mighta been the handle of the bugger I bought my gear off. He made it sound more, how'd he say it—*LOO-cru-tiv*—than it's turned out ta be. He wouldn't sell me his dunkey, talked me inta buyin' Ginny here from a herd over ta Leadville. That bum never told me how much she ate er how short a ways she'd go between feedbags!"

"Yes, that's him!" Mead said. "What did he look like?"

"Thought he was your friend? Hell, I don't rightly remember. This was a couple-three summers ago. What's it matter?" Mead's eyes told him it did. "Well, hell. Big fella, not in the belly like me, but taller. Beard kinda like mine, but not as gray or as long. Real *distant* sort—anxious to get the hell outta there, like maybe the gold pan was hot or he was on the run. Hey, are you the law after him? I don't wanna stool on my *colleague*!"

"Do I look like the Man?" Mead asked. "Don't worry, sir, he's just a long-lost friend. I'd like to run into him is all ... again, that is. Any idea where he was headed?"

"Not a damn notion. But like I say, it's been a while. Guy could be over in that café or halfway ta China, fer all I know."

"Well, thanks anyway," Mead said, and handed him a scarce five-dollar bill. "Good prospecting!"

"I ain't no beggar, buddy—doncha wantcher pitcher taken?"

"I don't even have a camera," Mead replied. "But that fiver is no insult. I really appreciate your time, and the word—I've been looking for him for a long time. Have a coffee and a doughnut on Carson and me, and buy Ginny some oats." He patted the burro on her soft brown muzzle. Though she wasn't Betsy, she was the closest he'd come to Carson yet. The Kodak crowd was gathering again, so Mead turned on down the street. He'd gotten all he could—a line to Carson—enough to tell him he wasn't just plain nuts.

Feeling he ought to enjoy Aspen while he was there, Mead loitered in a bookstore for an hour. A novel and a field guide asked to go along, so he paid for them and fitted them into the side pockets of his backpack. Halfway down the block, entering a coffee shop, he noticed an unusual buzz among the patrons. Then he heard a few *Hooray*s, *All RIGHT*s, and *Fucking A*s from the street. "What's up?" he asked the waitress.

"Richard Nixon has just resigned!" she said. On that high note, the best news he'd heard since . . . when? . . . he inhaled a turkey and avocado croissant with three glasses of milk. "Well, here's to Gerald Ford," he said to no one in particular as he raised the last glass, and then he bought three rolls for the road. From there he walked to the edge of town, put out his thumb, and settled in for the wait.

Mead had been hitchhiking for no more than twenty minutes and eaten only one of the rolls when a battered bright green Toyota station wagon pulled over onto the grass verge beside him. It was a hot day, and he would have taken any ride. He ran to the window, lugging his pack awkwardly, and confronted a giant of a man crammed into the driver's seat. A broad baby face, crowned with wavy yellow hair and crossed by a generous smile, looked back at him. "Hop in, entomologist! Where are you headed?"

"Uh"—Mead had not quite asked himself that question nor answered it—"over to the Front Range . . . Boulder, Estes Park," he said, mouthing names he remembered from the journals. "Eventually, maybe, a place called Allenspark."

"What's happenin' in old Allenspark?"

"I don't know—maybe nothing."

"Well, we can take you to Loveland Pass, anyway." Once Mead was installed, the driver said, "We're entomologists too. You can tell by our outfits."

Mead looked back at a trio of young women in the back seat (one had leaped out of the front, leaving it for him). And behind them, he beheld a bouquet of insect nets stacked atop coolers and packs.

"Are you a collector?" the driver asked.

"Butterfly researcher—to be—I hope," Mead answered. "What about you all?"

The man's musical voice rose an octave with interest. "Well, I'll be! You picked the right ride, young man. Welcome to Bagdonitz's Flying Circus!"

Mead settled into the passenger seat of the Nordic Green Aphid, official lead car of the itinerant field team of which his current patron, Carolinus Bagdonitz, was leader. Mead scarcely noticed the broken suspension as the story of the BFC unfolded: Bagdonitz taught at Jim Bridger University in Wyoming, where he'd landed after a boyhood catching butterflies and frogs in Colorado, graduate school in Fort Collins, a postdoc in Uppsala, and a teaching job on Long Island. He taught all sorts of biology courses, but his heart was really in the field, with the Lepidoptera and the students he called "the kids." Ten years earlier he'd first brought students out west to study Rocky Mountain butterflies and moths. Now his field teams were a regular summer institution, staging out of research houses he rented in Lyons and Dubois. "And why the BFC?" asked Mead, who could barely believe his luck.

"That's because of our crazy schedule," Bagdonitz explained, "running all over the Rockies all summer long in motley vehicles and on foot, investigating everything from miller moths to grizzly bears, but mostly butterflies. We hit as many habitats as we can, mostly high country and wilderness areas. We also caravan to annual meetings of the Lepidopterists' Society to give papers on our projects. One year, someone there called us Bagdonitz's Flying Circus, and it stuck." Bagdonitz cruised around a tight curve.

"Do you have any trouble filling your research teams?" Mead asked. This seemed a lovely alternative to the roach room, especially if he got kicked out for abandoning it, and more especially if the BFC always included the likes of his traveling companions in the back seat. One in particular caught his eye, and he hers, when he'd climbed in.

"Hell, no!" said the prof. "Everyone in the department wants to come, and a few outside. Positions on the field team are so sought after, even with the modest wages . . ."

Hoots rose from the back: *"Modest?* Try *slave!"*

". . . that I have to conduct auditions with a butterfly net each spring."

"Or a spatula," came from behind. "Or a church key!"

On cue, CB, as he was called to save syllables for everyone, handed Mead a Hamm's. "We operate on an incredibly tight budget, so we get the cheapest beer, the cheapest gas, and the cheapest women." He winked into the rearview and got a kick in return. "Everyone gets his or her choice of camp jobs—cooking, washing up, or cleaning fish."

"That's *if* we pin specimens until three a.m. every night! Otherwise we lose those privileges," came a voice from the back. But the grousing passengers were clearly on top of the situation, each of them a grad student further along on her thesis than Mead was. With his own project embryonic, joining this Foreign Legion of Lepidoptera sounded even more attractive. He steered the talk away from his studies, but they were all impressed that he was a student of the legendary George Winchester, cofounder of the Lepidopterists' Society, and that he knew Freulich.

"The living gods of Lepidoptera," said CB. "You keep good company."

"Until now," came a chorus of three.

The route took the Flying Circus up the Roaring Fork to Independence Pass, one lane and spectacular in places, with a broad tundra lawn on top; down Lake Creek past the south shoulder of Mount Elbert, Colorado's tallest mountain at 14,323 feet; then north to Leadville before turning off on an old mining road toward the east.

"'Road Unsuitable for Passenger Vehicles,'" Mead read aloud from a weathered sign.

"Signs like that mean nothing to us," CB replied gravely. "This will save us many miles." The backseat gallery let out a collective groan.

A rugged and bumpy ride took the travelers over the Mosquito Range via Weston Pass, "a butterfly paradise," according to Bagdonitz. He spotted a stunning burnt-orange-and-green beauty beside the road and said, "A nice male Mead's sulphur!" Then, to James, "You do know about T. L. Mead, right?"

"George told me a little of his exploits out here."

"For a while, during that productive summer of his in 1871, he was based just southwest of here in Twin Lakes. He—" Just then CB hit a deep puddle at speed, flooded the distributor, and brought about an hour's wait while he dried it out. The time out gave Mead and the other students a chance to stretch their legs in the blessed alpine and to sample three bog fritillaries on which Freulich had recently tutored him. Each bore the name of a Norse goddess and might as well have been named for his new companions. "God, that seems like a month ago," Mead said aloud, thinking of the day on Cumberland with Freulich and the bikers.

"Oh, we get stranded for much longer than this sometimes," said Emily.

Near dark, the Nordic Green Aphid rolled into the night's camp, well below Loveland Pass. This was always an occasion for relief and celebration, for (as Mead learned) anywhere from a quarter to half the time, it didn't make it without repairs. A venerable gent awaited them, the hands on his hips missing a fingertip or two, just a few teeth showing in his broad troll's smile. "So you made it," he said. CB's father, Tiny, a retired immigrant coal miner who wasn't even small, often preceded the rest in an advance car. He had camp set up and many fish ready to fry by the time anyone else arrived. The fact that all the other students were female (another carful had arrived from the north) struck Mead as odd but agreeable. Was Jim Bridger a girls' school? he wondered. But he asked no questions aloud.

Food rolled out, and the camp meal got under way. Mead was included so naturally that he didn't even question it, other than to quip that he had fallen out of the hills into heaven. "Or out of the hot springs into the frying pan," CB came back as he flipped a burger. Mead had mentioned the sojourn at Conundrum, as much as was decent, and CB had guessed the rest.

"The field team spent a few days in the Maroon-Snowmass last summer, and we always seemed to find our way back to Conundrum," Lisa said. "Ah, such a paradise that place is."

"Yes," said Kate, "but don't forget that the Big Man made us leap out of the water every time a moth came to our black light!"

"Do you suppose CB is short for Humbert Humbert?" asked Emily.

"Come on, you guys," said CB. "Remember what we're up here for." A ritual chorus went up, "For *biology*!" and Hamms were raised all around. In spite of himself, Mead had to admit that the idea of all those present disporting *au naturel* around Conundrum might quite rightly be described as paradisiacal.

About that time another van rolled in. A knot of gangly young men unfolded from it and pushed toward the cooler. Until then Mead had thought the sex ratio of the BFC to be excellent. But it had to be too good to last, he thought. "Hey, Sterling, what kept you guys? And how'd you do?" CB was obviously relieved to see them arrive safely, never mind the bluff banter.

"Not bad, Boss," replied a compact, fair youth, gritty with the dust of many miles of mountain trails and roads. "We got maybe three hundred moths at the lights, including a few arctiids I didn't recognize. I think one or two might be that relict tiger species you've been after. And some nice series of sulphurs and coppers and stuff like that."

"All right!" CB tossed Sterling some praise wrapped around a can of beer. Then he turned to Mead. "These guys have just returned from Mount Zirkel Wilderness, north of Rabbit Ears. They had to drive all day to make this rendezvous, after hiking out. Now we're complete again, in terms of the Colorado contingent. About the same number of kids are up in the Wind Rivers and Absarokas. We'll all gather in Dubois later to compare notes, take care of the bugs and data before we close up shop and head back to campus."

Carolinus Bagdonitz presided over the picnic table in the rustic campground. With the stream gurgling in the background and the evening warm, thirsts rose. The ringmaster, trail boss, and barkeep shifted from beer to his specialty, an occasional treat granted the crew in moderation after a long, hard day in the field, like a sailor's dram of grog. This concoction, called a "tall cooler," consisted of equal parts, more or less, depending on age and body weight (3:2:1 for CB, 1:2:3 for little Lisa), of lab alcohol, lemonade, and creek water. "A lot cheaper than gin," said CB, "and it looks better on the requisition. Have one?" His meaty pink arm stretched out of his sleeveless striped T-shirt toward the bemused Mead. "Don't worry, the water's been boiled, then recooled. I much prefer to use it right out of the river, but the giardia is too bad nowadays. That's all we need, for the whole crew to come down with that! We'd be out of business for weeks, and there's only one head in the research house."

"And then the prof'd be even more full of shit than usual," came a voice from the dark edge of the site.

Mead was still considering the drink offer. What could he say? Don't offend the natives. To his surprise, the cooler was not only refreshing but also delicious. He made a note to locate the lab alcohol stores at Osborn, though he suspected the pure Rocky Mountain spring water, as Coors called it, had something to do with it.

Over the campfire, rainbow trout caught by Tiny fried in their heavenly scent as bears and beavers sang "The Land of Sky Blue Waters" from the famous Hamm's ad over the reflections in the mountain stream. "You're awfully lucky to have such a great dad, CB—provider, camp retainer, and field companion, all rolled into one," Mead said. Tiny heard that and grumped. But Mead meant it. He thought of his own father's preoccupation, which made him too often distant, if not actually absent. And he thought of the one time they had all gone to the mountains together. It hadn't worked out so well. His mind changed the subject.

"Darn tootin'," CB said. "Dad's wonderful. The girls all love him, too. That keeps the rest of us in line." Emphasizing "in line," he popped a bottle top off a Hamm's. "Plus, he teaches the boys to fish, the girls too if they want. But we seldom have time for it, so he limits daily for us."

"That must stretch the food budget."

"You bet! And he provides our field vials for free." CB gestured to the little jars on the table, each bright with specimens.

Looking closely, Mead saw that they were salmon egg jars— dozens of them. "So you don't use cyanide bottles?"

"For moths we do. But for butterflies we pinch the thorax while they're still in the net, then transfer them with tweezers to these jars."

Carson did much the same, Mead knew, only he used triangular envelopes instead of jars. But that was for shipping dry—Mead had moistened, relaxed, and mounted many of his specimens—while the protocol here called for pinning the specimens directly from the jar. Looking around the table, he saw several members field pinning so the harvest could be transported safely in boxes and properly spread later. Others were making labels or transcribing field notes, all by the light of a Coleman lantern. Still others were cleaning up after supper while a couple of students played soft harmonica and guitar by the fireside.

"So what will you be doing here?" Mead asked.

"We're meeting a friend, Michael Heap, so the kids can see his field experiment."

"I heard Heap mentioned by Professor Freulich; apparently he's a conservationist. Does he teach, or what?"

"Not full-time. He got a PhD in butterfly ecology, but he's never had a university job. He teaches some, summer institutes and such. Mostly he tries to write. He lives in some rain-sodden backwater up in Oregon, but he has family in Colorado. He still does some work with butterflies, and he has a neat little project here at Loveland Pass."

"What's it about?"

"Has to do with *Erebia magdalena*."

Mead's heart leaped and sank at the same time. Did somersaults. Stopped and started again. "Gee," he said. "That's the species I'm interested in."

"Well, well—you'll be glad to meet Mike, then. He's crazy about Magdalena—calls it Maggie May, after the Rod Stewart song a couple years back."

"You can never tell when you'll see ol' Michael," Tiny chimed in.

"That's for darned sure," said Sterling, and "I *guess*," said Kate. Then she added, "But he usually shows up at the field house in Wyoming before he heads back home. Why don't you do the same, and you might run into him?" She smiled. She was the one from the car.

Mead's ego was just big enough, and Noni's riddle just fresh enough, that he imagined he was being invited in his own right. Then he wondered just how much Tiny really kept them in line, and how the sexual dynamics of a coed butterfly circus, thick with lusty and attractive young men and women, could possibly work, and how they ever got any fieldwork done at all. He didn't ask these things, but he smiled back.

Mead yawned. He laid out his sleeping bag, hoping for clear skies overnight or, failing that, a beckoning from Kate's tent. Then he reformed and let thoughts of Noni carry him off to sleep. He'd landed with a Nordic blond all right, just as she'd imagined. But it was no long-tressed Swedish centerfold. Instead, a middle-aged Polish Adonis with a harem—not exactly the threat Noni had conjured from the mists of Conundrum. Carolinus bid them all sweet dreams, popped another beer, and continued his curatorial tasks beside the cinnabar coals of the campfire.

No rain fell, and when the tang of coffee, trout, and bacon hit Mead's nostrils at six, he crept out like a bagworm, bloated with Hamm's he'd forgotten to recycle the night before and crowned with a light hangover from the tall cooler on top of the cheap beer.

Bagdonitz hurled him a bright "Good morning" from beside the fire as Mead passed by on a mission to a bush. Whether CB ever slept, or simply swapped his beer for a coffee cup at dawn, James never knew.

31

As the Nordic Green Aphid panted toward the summit of Loveland Pass the next morning, Mead beheld something extraordinary. A parking area and a small tarn lay beside the road, and beyond them, a big rockslide tumbled down. At the base of the rocks stood a man holding what appeared to be a jumbo butterfly net and a large black object. "Holy cow!" he said. "What *is* that?"

He was riding in back between Kate and Lisa. "That's Michael," said CB, "and Maggie."

By the time they had parked beside the lake and walked to the base of the rocks, the figure was still in sight, but now he was high up the talus slope. Mead watched with his binoculars and saw the man hold the black thing over his head and give it a toss. Down it came, almost directly at Mead. He could see that it was not free-flying, but gliding down a monofilament line that shone like a rock spider's web in the sun. "What's the deal?" Mead asked, but only a frightened pika replied: *Weet!* Then Mead made it out: the object was a giant Magdalena alpine, hang gliding down the rocks after the fashion of the real thing. "Holy cow," he said again as the model butterfly reached the end of its tether and alighted—a bit roughly—among the rocks.

Michael Heap climbed down the slide. He reached his model about the same time as the field team, Mead in tow, reached him. "Mike, you ol' son!" crooned Carolinus, and the two big men embraced.

"CB! I thought you'd never get here, or the clouds would come first!" In turn, Heap hugged each of the Circus members on hand. Then he was introduced to Mead.

"I saw your mega-Magdalena fly," said Mead. "Do you always do this here?"

"Well, usually—it's the easiest place. Not much of a hike, and when you have to go up and down the rocks as much as I do, that counts. Plus, not too many rubberneckers, thanks to the I-70 tunnel under the pass. So—you figured out what this baby represents?"

"Sure! I have a big interest in *Erebia magdalena* myself."

"Aha!" Heap exclaimed. "The two magic words!"

"So, Michael," Carolinus butted in. "I didn't bring these boys and girls all the way up here in order to get rained on, which we will pretty soon. Why don't you show the kids what you're up to with that big hunk of black cardboard."

"Sure," Heap agreed. "If you all want to watch and maybe help out a little, I'll run a couple more trials."

"So what's the point of the experiment, Mike?" asked Sterling.

"Well, you've all read about Niko Tinbergen's experiments with the European grayling butterfly?"

"They'd *better* say yes," said CB, laughing, as most of their heads nodded.

It's closely related to the arctics up here, which aren't far from the alpines. Tinbergen found that super-female models elicit more intense courtship responses from the males than normal-size and colored females."

"So what's new?" came a male voice, bringing a female's "Boar!"

"Be nice, kids. Well, back in those unenlightened days, this was called the Raquel Welch effect."

Lisa: "Not the Bagdonitz principle?" Kate: "It's good to know he's not the only one."

"I'm sorry about these guys, Michael. Cheap labor, you know," said CB.

"It beats no labor, CB. I used to have an assistant, David Shawmutt from Cornell. But he got tired of the climb up and down the rockpile and went into premed. Wants to be a doctor—a real one, not a butterfly doctor, like us."

"Smart lad," said CB. "He'd never get rich in this game."

Young heads nodded.

"Don't I know it," said Heap. "Still, I'll take Maggie over myocardial infarction any day—she's good medicine for what ails you, right? Well, anyway, I'm just trying to see if I can replicate Tinbergen's result in black-and-white instead of gray. When it works, the males go bananas over Maggie May here. Now why don't you all spread out up and down the rockslide and watch for responses. I'll carry Maggie up, release her, and watch with binoculars. CB, maybe you could try to catch her down here so she doesn't get so beat up on these sharp rocks."

As Mead climbed the rocks behind Michael, he wondered if all lepidopterists were big. Heap was of average height, but bore his large head on broad shoulders over a deep chest. His short legs could have been hewn from the same Colorado cottonwood as his big net was. He was a man who fought the paunch, now more on top of the paunch than the other way around. Mead guessed the balance swung in wintertime, when he came in from the field, especially if he drank beer, as most of his kind seemed to.

Heap wore an old Panama with sweat-stained brim bent low over his high red forehead. Long, light hair hung behind in waves. His truly notable feature was his beard: sternum-length, full, and many hued, leaving little of the face showing but his high cheeks, harebell eyes, and sunburned nose over a long mustache and permanent smile. His pelt of many colors, hinting at a white future, reputedly waxed and waned, giving him a metamorphic nature not unlike that of the insects he studied. Right now he seemed to be between molting stages, beard just brushing his belly.

Michael Heap was not graceful as he lumbered up the boulders like a silverback marmot, but he knew his way around a rockslide and had good wind, climbing the scree faster than students half his age. More than once he tottered on a loose rock, but then he would leap to a sounder stepping-stone or balance himself with his net pole as a logroller might use his pike. A livid purple scar across one massive calf testified to a rockslide mishap of yore, when a companion loosed a sharp slate right above him. But Heap seldom if ever fell. Mead, naturally coordinated, nonetheless beat his knees to a pulp the first few times he tried to navigate the talus.

Mead positioned himself halfway up. As he awaited takeoff, he watched the pikas arrayed along the ridgeline every fifty feet or so. They shouted their opinions of the invaders' impertinence with shrill *geek*s and stern little peace-sign faces. One, skinny as pikas go, lifted its right paw each time it squeaked, like an action doll. Another, a plump one with its head up, was a mere fluffball against the Rockies themselves—just a pellet with little rabbity ears no longer than the wind would allow.

Heap reached the anchored top of the fishline and held Maggie May aloft. She consisted of a matte-black silhouette cut from thick photographic board, two feet in wingspan, affixed to a pinewood body. A brass ferrule on her thorax channeled the heavy-test leader that kept her from gravity's grasp. Heap drew Maggie May behind his head with both hands, counted down, and made the launch. The Flying Circus cheered as one, sending all the marmots scurrying.

Two pikas dove for cover with extra sharp *geek*s as the shadow of the dusky flier passed overhead. The last fifty feet of its glide drew four real Magdalenas who shot up at Maggie with terrific zeal. Mead watched openmouthed as the optimistic male Erebias made none-too-subtle advances toward the impressive sex symbol. Just before

Maggie reached the bottom of her flight path, her line snapped, and the heavier-than-air kite crashed onto the rocks, out of CB's frantic grasp. That signaled the end of the day's trials. Heap rescued Maggie, not badly damaged, while Mead reeled in the line. Everyone met at tarnside to compare notes while Heap entered the data. "Not bad for the butterflies," said Randy, "but it *really* works for pikas!"

"Maybe they thought it was a raven," suggested Lisa, "or a golden eagle."

"The boy butterflies worked out too," said Sterling. "She sure does something for them. I wonder if it cuts both ways?"

"Well, try this," said Michael. He drew an envelope from his collecting bag, a little leather pouch with a willowware pattern toffee tin in it to protect the butterflies, and removed a live alpine with his forceps. This he gently placed on a surprised Randy's nose, where it remained, basking for some minutes. "See if that does anything for your popularity," said Heap. Apparently it worked, as the girls all gathered around him.

Heap stored away the tableau as a vision not to be squandered; Mead memorized the technique for future reference; even CB was stilled. There stood Randy, hard young chest held high in his white tee, chin back, beatific smile curling his sculpted mouth, his strong arched nose, as yet unmarred by alcohol or hard knocks, graced by the pure black oval of an alpine the same color as his curls. And all about him, a roundel of bewitched young women: Alice, forehead shining in the alpine sun, her smile one of unaffected bliss, her hand on the shoulder of Lisa, who held her hand over her heart as if in a swoon; Nancy, on the other side, simply rapt. Kate, harder, less readily beguiled, and already distracted by Mead's nearness, still cracked a down-curved grin that drew her ample dimples, as well as Mead's eye, down toward her low-cut halter, making dark declivities that an alpine at evening or an imprudent graduate student might drop into, forever.

Then the sun hit it full on, and the butterfly on Randy's nose flew off. Randy, handsome lad though he was, became just one more dude on the field team, and the tableau dissolved. "I think he's got something there," said Sterling to CB, sotto voce.

"No shit," said CB. "That'll be on the test."

Just then an uncommon bog fritillary appeared in their midst and weaved its way between their legs. Four or five nets swung at once, like jousting janitors, and about as effective. "*Boloria eunomia*," said Mead. "Dr. Freulich says it's the rarest one up here." Sterling zigzagged after the butterfly, took a wild swing, and fell into the willow bog.

"Sterling bricked it," Carolinus observed to Mead. "They've gotta do better than that, or no tall coolers tonight."

Mead wondered whether it wasn't last night's tall coolers at fault here, but he held his tongue.

The BFC made its farewells, thanked Michael Heap for the demonstration, and headed up the far slope for a little collecting before the clouds closed in. "Come on, you guys," rang CB's injunction. "Let's go see some *biology*!"

Mead stuck around Loveland Pass for a while with Heap, hoping to romance one more Magdalena out of the shattered granite for another look. But when the early-afternoon clouds rose over the rim of the pass like sinister blimps fixing to drop water bombs on their heads, they retreated to the shelter of Heap's old maroon VW bus. "Where to?" he asked.

"Your call," said Mead. "I'm in your hands and at your mercy."

"Right. To the Red Ram, then!" And so the two fellow sufferers of their particular infatuation repaired to the Red Ram saloon in Georgetown, down canyon from the pass. Over a malt whiskey at the massive mahogany bar, Mead's first ever, Heap's first for the day, the younger one picked the other's brain about the black glider of the stonefields as a gray mountain storm pounded the tin roofs of the old mining town. "You know, don't you," Michael asked, "that George-town was named as the type locality of *Erebia magdalena*?"

"No!" James choked on his Scotch. *"Here?"*

"Of course it's a couple thousand feet too low. But in those days it was common to generalize localities. Collectors often used the name of the nearest rail or stage stop for their specimen data. You were lucky to get more than 'Rocky Mountains' on a pin label! Any-way, Herman Strecker described the species in 1880 from material sent him by a Professor Owen of Wisconsin who labeled the locality 'Georgetown.' I strongly suspect that the type specimens actually came from Loveland Pass—a classic Magdalena locale on an early stage route—where we've just been."

"So that one on Randy's nose could be a topotype?"

"Right—if it had a pin in it, which Randy might resent. I reckon that first collector drove down to the Red Ram, just as we've done, except by horseback or stagecoach, and wrote 'Georgetown' on his labels as the nearest depot—maybe at this very bar!"

Mead drank to that, bought a round, and drank to it again. Then, while still able, they went in search of food. Mead, elevated somewhat by the malt, felt a twinge of envy for the early collectors, traveling by stage and steam, discovering fabulous new species, but he suspected that they fared worse when it came to dining. They entered a small trattoria where the several inches, difference in their height and girth melted as they pulled up to a red-checked table-cloth. Awaiting their order, Mead said, "Look, Mike. I know Mag-gie's your bug ..."

"Mine! Last I heard, nobody was patenting insects. Remember, butterflies are free, as the saying goes—nobody owns them, or the research rights to them."

"I mean, you're working on it."

"I guess you caught me black-handed on that."

"Well, I've noticed that biologists can be a little proprietary about their chosen topics. I really don't want to trespass on your turf, so if you feel there's no room for both of us in this here town, just tell me, and I'll retreat to my roaches."

"Heck, no! Forget that, James! Several folks are looking at Maggie already, such as Gerald Hilchie in Alberta, Charles Slater right down the road in Central City, Ken Philip in Alaska for *mackinleyensis*, and Piotr Rombostislov in Siberia, for starters. This butterfly is a big black tent—no one has a corner on it. She presents so many fascinating questions that no one worker could answer them all—just as with Peter Freulich and his frits or Vern Volte with his sulphurs. Why do you think they have grad students doing so many projects on them? It takes all hands to the wheel to get a three-D picture of these complex beasts."

Mead sat back and sipped his Chianti, digesting that, as their food came.

"I couldn't begin to do justice to all of Maggie's charms by myself," Heap went on, twirling his spaghetti. "Besides, I'm an amateur now. I dabble at it endlessly, but I don't publish much. Maybe you can get something really useful done."

By now Mead felt easy with Heap, so he brought up the subject of October Carson. Heap had never heard of him, though he knew George, having done his own doctorate with Winchester's first grad student, Abe Brewer, at UConn. Mead took the first bite of his lasagna, then told Heap about Carson's procession across the West and his own flirtation with *Erebia magdalena*. "So what do you know about Maggie's name?"

"Well," Michael garbled through his pasta, "I've often wondered. Obviously it has to do with Mary Magdalene. Turns out her Saint's Day is July twenty-ninth. Since that date falls well within Maggie's flight period, maybe Owen caught the first one on that day and Strecker named the species in her honor. I don't know whether he was Catholic or not. Anyway, that's my only hypothesis on the question. You might want to ask Brownie about it."

"Brownie?"

"F. Martin Brown, author of *Colorado Butterflies*, my New Testament. Holland's *Butterfly Book* and Klots's *Peterson Field Guide* were my Genesis and Revelations."

"I loved those books too; being from New Mexico, I ought to know Brown's."

"It didn't get around enough—sold mostly at the Denver Museum of Natural History, my childhood haunt when I couldn't be outdoors. Hell of a book. Check this out." Michael cleared his throat and recited from memory: "'This large and uniformly black alpine is a real prize. It cannot be confused with any other Colorado butterfly. Its dark wings, free from markings, make it easy to recognize . . . The Magdalena Alpine haunts the rockslides at timber line' . . . Let's see . . . yes, that's it: 'It is very difficult to capture because of the treacherous footing afforded by the tumbled rocks . . . Once in a while conditions have been such that a large brood of the species is produced. Then if a collector is around he has a field day.' Page twenty-nine, *Colorado Butterflies*."

"Bravo! Chapter and verse, yet. A real devout."

"You should see my copy of the book," said Michael. "*Dog-eared* is hardly the word. The dust jacket, with the beautiful purple Colorado hairstreak, is in tatters, and the red buckram binding is pretty soft at the corners."

"And Brownie's still around?"

"You bet. These days he studies fossil butterflies at Florissant, along with the itineraries of the early Colorado butterfly explorers, among other things."

"Sounds like a real Renaissance man."

"Or polymath. He's taught almost everything at Fountain Valley School in the Springs. He could tell you about your namesake, Theodore L. Mead, of Mead's sulphur and Mead's wood nymph fame. He's studied Mead's itinerary in the West. Do you know about him?"

"Of course I've noticed the butterflies with his name. CB started to tell me about his travels in Colorado back on Weston Pass yesterday, but we were . . . interrupted. Another stagecoach butterfly hunter, wasn't he?"

"Among other things. In the summer of 1871, Teddy Mead and his brother Sam came out collecting for W. H. Edwards of West Virginia, the great butterfly man of his day. Mead covered a lot of territory, reaching lots of remote places by horseback, rail, and stage. He even came right here to Georgetown. His letters home were full of tales of Arapaho after scalps, Utes running them back to their reservation, and marauding bears, bandits, and bedbugs. Those guys were tough, don't you think? To come into a gold rush saloon like the Red Ram with butterfly nets?"

"No kidding. I wouldn't even do it these days."

"He also had his priorities right. In one of his letters home he compared a visit to Europe with his western adventures: 'what profiteth a man that he sees twenty miles of pictured saints and "Holy Families" and loseth the sight of the Rocky Mountains?'"

"I'll drink to that," James said, raising his glass. "So what did it profiteth him coming here, other than having some beautiful butterflies bear his name forevermore?"

"Well, I'll let you be the judge. Mead was one of several entomological suitors of Edwards's daughter, Edith. He named Edith's copper after her. And yes, he eventually won out over his rivals. The couple were wed and lived pretty happily for a long time after, raising oranges and orchids in Florida. But not till he fulfilled his quest out west and brought back a dowry of new butterflies—twenty-eight new kinds!—did Edith's dad give her hand to Mead."

"Nice story. Florida, eh? So he got the girl and the best of both worlds."

"Florida might look pretty good pretty soon if an early autumn is riding in on that storm out there. Anyway, I'll bet you're related to ol' T. L."

"I wonder. Can you inherit scientific patronyms, like titles? I'll take Mead's alpine! Well, I'll be sure to get in touch with Brownie if I do dive into Magdalena."

"Okay, and while you're at it, here's a nice mystery for you. One of the best Magdalena habitats I know is a mountain on the edge of Rocky Mountain National Park, in the Front Range. It's got the most extensive rockslides for miles around."

"Oh?" Mead's ears pricked. "So what's the mystery?"

"The peak is called Magdalena Mountain, and the place at its foot is known as Magdalena Park. And there's an old log hotel there called Magdalena Park Lodge."

"Too much! So what's the connection with the butterflies?"

"Beats me," said Heap. "I've admired the mountain and the lodge for years, but I've always been too lazy or busy to look into it. If you should discover the reason for the many Magdalenas, if there is one, please be sure to let me know!"

"For sure. So where is this Magdalena Mountain, exactly?"

"It's on the Peak to Peak Highway, between Allenspark and Estes Park. Let's see, it's not too far from . . . What's the matter, James? Is the lasagna bad?"

Mead, a little too much wine in his belly, slept while Heap, with more body mass to absorb it, drove down Highway 40 and then north out of Clear Creek Canyon. He awoke only when the hand-brake squeaked. "Where are we?" he asked, rubbing his eyes.

"Central City," said Heap. "Someone I think you ought to know lives here."

Mead followed Heap up to an old cabin. Its clapboards as black as the unlit night around them, the cabin perched near the very rim of a deep ice-cream scoop out of the ground. "The Glory Hole," said Heap. "They used to mine gold this way here. Richest Square Mile on Earth, they called it. That money went down to Denver, except for what stayed in the opera house and gingerbread Victorians here in town." He gestured with a thrust of his shoulder. "It won't last, but for now, life is still cheap enough up here on the tailings for a destitute lepidopterist to hole up."

Heap's knock was answered by a thin man with a thin brown beard and a look of constant surprise. Sure, he was surprised by a knock at the cabin door way up here late at night, but the look never left, through smile or frown. Mead came to understand that this was the look of infatuation with the world and all its working parts.

Heap introduced him to Charles Slater and his wife, Ellie. "If you think I have a claim on Maggie," Heap whispered, "just talk with Charles for a spell." And so James Mead, for the third time in three days, settled into the company of someone who put his own knowledge of his chosen subject to shame. Slater, the softest-spoken of men, not only had a close acquaintance with all the Colorado species of *Erebia* and *Oeneis* in the field, he also kept various life stages of each of them in his makeshift cabin "lab." So came James to see his first immature *magdalena*—a pale green tube with reddish lines and a black head—as well as those of several other arctics and alpines. And by the time they left, he held under his arm a copy of a sheaf of notes headed "**magdalena**: Loveland I. elev. 3680 m." His to keep! So much for proprietary egos in natural history. Mead didn't know how to thank him, so he simply said, "I'll try to do them justice."

The next day, he found himself on his own, sitting on the asphalt of the Peak to Peak, reading Slater's Maggie notes. Heap had spent the night in his bus in a campground near Rollinsville while Mead laid out his sleeping bag beside the VW. In the morning they shared a breakfast of granola with wild currants and raspberries, just coming ripe, and boiled coffee. "I hate to leave the hills for what lies below," said Heap, "but I've got a brother down there expecting me today—if he even remembers that I'm coming." They made their goodbyes, and Michael left Mead happy to hitch north. But it was a Monday morning with precious little traffic, so Mead finally gave in, recoiled his thumb, and sat. It gave him a chance to get into the precious notes, which he was eager to do.

Slater must have been a soulbrother of Carson's, each approaching the world as both poet and scientist. The eight xeroxed pages mixed typed third-person notations of careful observation and data with handwritten flights of lyrical first-person appreciation: a complex graph of daily flight patterns next to a judgment of July 19, 1973, as "a day of haunting beauty so intense as to remain in memory for life." Slater gave away his conservationist bent, lamenting truck traffic excluded from the tunnel and forced to drive over the pass. "Despite heavy jet and car traffic," he wrote, "magdalena, damoetus, and cupreus survive, classic alpine glacial relicts sequestered by drifting snow in their last refugia, indicators of intolerable environmental change."

This was followed by pages of rearing notes—the first successful rearing of this species ever, as Edwards had got only to first instar with an egg sent him by T. L. Mead, and no one had tried since, until Slater. Charles had been enjoying scrambled eggs and puffballs fried in butter

when a fresh female Magdalena Alpine flew by as if to flirt with possible capture. Right at that moment, I was thinking how observation sometimes reveals clues to the secrets of nature and how it works. There was lightning in the dark cloud to the south of the divide and thunder rolled far down into the valleys with a slow grumbling. In a burst of sun from behind the cloud I dropped the net on the ground as if hypnotized and followed the female magdalena up the steep slope of the rockslide. She flew to a place where bedrock outcropped. Below the outcrop was a little hollow, and in the hollow, a mound, and on the mound some grass and flowers. And on a rock below and to the left of this mound, she found a cleft which will be in shadow, except for about two hours a day. And in this small cleft on the rock, she laid an egg by backing up to it and reaching over the edge with her abdomen. It seemed to be placed very carefully, on lichen.

This was the first oviposition by a Magdalena alpine ever reported from the wild.

Mead read all this as if he were buried in a novel that he couldn't put down. A dozen cars went by without him so much as lifting a thumb. He could see why Slater would probably never get this material published in a journal, and also why Heap had told him that it was a rich lode, mined by a fine naturalist. The experiments realized and imagined, the observations, the experience—all there, offered to him for his use.

And when again Mead stood, brushed off his butt, and ran for a jeep that slowed for him, he knew something that he had only hoped before. He knew there was help for him in his deepening desire to know this creature intimately—help all around, everywhere he looked and didn't look. He knew he could do it and that it was right for him to be here.

32

A cloudy afternoon in early August found James Mead in a piney place in Allenspark called the Meadow Mountain Café. A weathered red-and-yellow sign nailed onto the faded yellow-and-red porch of upright logs read COFFEE 25¢. That drew him in, and he also ordered a well-upholstered vegetarian sandwich and a blueberry-peach smoothie, in spite of its designation as "booberry" on the menu.

The man at the next table was bantering with the waitress. "Children say amazing things, Nina. This morning some tourist's daughter asked me whether I believed in God." Oh god, even here, Mead thought, thinking back to the Greyhound evangelists.

"So what did you tell her?"

"I said no. She seemed a little crestfallen to hear it." He smiled at Mead as he said it.

Mead noticed, as the other guy shifted in his seat, a necklace that fell out of his half-open purple shirt. The pendant was a crucifix, crafted from heavy-gauge silver nails.

"Then, if I may ask," said Mead, "why do you wear that cross?"

"Keeps the amateur preachers off my back," he said. "These hills are full of 'em, from Anabaptists to Zionists, as thick as Amway reps. Besides, it's my livelihood, such as it is. I make these things and sell them. I do really well peddling my crown-of-thorns virginity pins to all the waitresses in the resorts around here—for all the good it does them."

I could like this guy, thought Mead. And then a thought struck him in the midsection like a booberry smoothie in the face: What if this is Carson? He could be. He looked about the right age—mid-forties or so, body features carved of driftwood by the adze of experience, long teeth mostly straight. In addition to the cross of nails he wore a big silver ring on a massive hand that would be equally comfortable gripping a netstick, a splitting maul, or a fountain pen. Yes, this could be Carson—he wrote that he was going to Allenspark. Mead was pretty sure it was. His search over so soon, so coincidentally, it was almost anticlimactic.

"Name's Tony Lee," the silversmith said. "What's yours?"

"Not October Carson?"

"How should I know?"

"No, you—I mean, I'm James Mead, but *you're* not actually October Carson?"

"I told you, I'm Tony Lee." A shade passed over Lee's face that told Mead he was in danger of dismissal, just as he'd written off the various loons of the road.

"Sorry," he said. "It's just that I thought you might be someone I've been looking for. Have you ever heard that name around here?"

"Can't say as I have, and I've been here for years, all seasons, unlike most of 'em. Ever since I got back from Da Nang, mostly in one piece. *Hey*—is that *great* about Nixon, or what? What a parcel of poop. Did you see his insane smile as he was waving from the helicopter before he split the White House for the last time? None of those poor bastards scrambling for a lift off the roof of the embassy in Saigon were smiling like that. Felt bad for Pat, though. Nice woman, your basic martyr to a Messiah complex. Anyway, back to your dude. Hey, Nina?"

The waitress, in an embroidered blue peasant dress, changed

course as her pixie cut flipped about. "More java, Tony? You'll float out of here on a caffeine cloud!"

"At least that's still legal. No thanks, Nina, I've had enough, believe it or else. Gotta get back to the shop and get into my afternoon downers from Golden now that I've been sucking down your good cheap uppers all morning."

"How can you drink that trout piss, anyway?"

"Well, it's cheap too. But not too much Coors today—I need to keep a level head. That little girl's father is coming by tomorrow to pick up crucifixes for all his deacons."

"He doesn't mind buying them from a confessed infidel?" Mead asked.

"Hell, no. My price is right, and he prayed for me."

"You need it," said Nina. "So what'll it be? You've already paid your quarter, and I've got paying customers waiting for me over here."

"Don't forget the nickel for you, Nina. If you can help my friend James here, he might do you even better. He wants to know if we've ever heard of some cat named November Wilson."

"October Carson," said Mead.

"Nooo . . . no. Doesn't ring a bell. Let me ask Jake." Nina took an order, then disappeared into the kitchen to confer with the cook, a Jesus-bearded hippie.

The cook appeared, tugging at the stringy brown tuft on his chin. "Howdy, Tony," he said, nodding at Mead. "Hmmmm. You know, it seems to me that I *have* heard that name. A couple-three summers ago, right? Yeah . . . seems some dude come in here by that name several times for about a week running, always had the booberry, then disappeared. Yeah, that's right. He liked our cinnamon rolls too, and now that I think of it, he asked me for a large juice jar so he could get some water from Silver Spring up the road across from the Fawn Brook."

"I told you," said Nina. "Jake remembers everything and every*body*."

"Now, why didn't I see him?" Lee asked, slightly piqued. "I see most folks who stick around here at all, and I remember most of them too, whether they come into the shop or not. Wait . . . three summers ago, you say? Okay—I was living down in Ward for a while with Cindy . . . that Cindy! Coulda missed him then. And Nina wasn't here yet."

"No, that's right—I started that fall, after I escaped Reno, so I wouldn'ta seen him."

"There you go," said Jake with a quiet note of triumph at finding no contrary witnesses. He spoke with the sort of bogus Oklahoma drawl that many Front Rangers had taken on in a curious blend of hippie looks and redneck lingo. They got it from Dylan, who got it from Woody, who got it by rights. "Yeah, this Carson cat, he come in here several times. Booberry and a cinnamon roll. Tried one yet?"

Mead finally got a word in. "No."

"But I don't know what become of 'im—I sure ain't seen 'im since," said Jake. "Can't tell you much more. But, besides the fact that he had a donkey tied up outside, I do remember one thing. Prob'ly why I recollect him at all—that and his strange name."

"Yes?" Mead asked, his anxiousness dripping off his sleeve. "What is it?" He could see that the stores of information here were lean, but he was starved for any crumb.

"Well," continued the cook, enjoying his reprieve from the kitchen and his central role here, "it's kinda hard to define. He wasn't really . . . *nervous*, in fact he was stone calm, I'd say. And I don't think he was stoned—seemed totally straight. But he had this look in his eye . . . what the Stones called a 'faraway look'—that's it. Now you're looking for something too, but you know what it is—it's this cat. But he seemed like he didn't know *what* it was he was looking for."

"Sounds like my man. He had a burro, all right. Anything else?"

"Just that he had no patience for small talk. He wanted to hear about the area, the hills around here, the trails, and so on. When he left—one morning he just didn't come in no more—I wondered if he wasn't a prospector onto a possible strike."

"You might say that," said Mead.

Nina asked him outright why he was trailing the guy, like, did he owe him money or something?

Mead just said, "We've got a girlfriend in common. I'd like to buy him a smoothie and compare notes." And they let it drop.

"Me, I came here searching for fresh air, man," said Tony, "and quiet. After Agent Orange and Denver smog, bombs and traffic." He lit up the Woodbine he'd been rolling, and stepped outside.

"People around here," Nina said, "do not aspire toward making a whole hell of a lot of sense. They have many fine qualities, consistency not necessarily one of them."

"I see," said Mead. "Real individuals."

"They like to think so. Then there's this macho thing. Camels, trucks, and big dogs, and yet they eat Jake's quiche. Individuals. But then from the little you've said, it sounds like this fellow you're tailing is another one."

"Oh, yeah. I don't know a lot about him. But I know he has good taste. If the cinnamon rolls were good enough for October Carson, I'd better try one."

"All *right*," said Jake, ducking back into the kitchen.

"And one for the road."

On his way out to the porch, a cloying scent overwhelmed even the scent of the cinnamon rolls. Planters of petunias rimmed his vision in Popsicle pink, magenta, deep purple, violet-and-white stripes, and red in pinwheels and barber poles. He leaned over and smelled the perfume, recalling unbidden his mother's garden borders of petunias and four o'clocks, and how they were haunted by big sphinx moths, like gray and pink hummingbirds coming for their nectar in the summer's dusk. He tried to pull back to Carson, but it was too late: damned petunias.

He hadn't heard from his mother since he'd fled New Haven, and he hadn't yet informed his family of his change of plans—they were just a couple of hundred miles to the south, and they had no idea. New thoughts and experiences had kept them mostly at bay, which was part of his plan. If he couldn't be close to his mother, if past misfortunes had to interfere forever, if he had to be blamed for them, maybe it just wasn't worth it. Before he knew it, Mead was fully mired in bitter reverie over his family, what it once had been and what it had become: something, nothing. The cinnamon roll vanished unnoticed; so did Nina when she came out to refill his mug. She assumed it was memories of that old girlfriend that had him so abstracted, and she said nothing.

The scent of those flowers! Would he ever be able to smell petunias again without reliving Molly's drowning, the getaway-turned-nightmare, the family's arrival home to the porch of petunias illuminated by the ambulance's spinning red pinwheel? Would the gray ghosting of a sphinx moth always bear the unbearable knowledge of catastrophe? He couldn't get off this mental track until he'd made a decision. Time was ticking. He'd spent weeks on the bus, at Gothic, roaming the hills with Noni, the BFC, Heap, and on his own. Now he felt he was finally closing in on something, and the summer was into its shorter side. "Okay, I *will* come to New Mexico," he said. "Now leave me alone!" Nina looked startled and veered away, but Mead snagged her back and said, "No, not you. By the way, can you tell me the way to Magdalena Park?"

"It's just up the highway," she said, "but I thought you were going to New Mexico to see that girl?"

Mead set off through Allenspark and its twin hamlet, Ferncliff, which had been spared the glitter and gold of Aspen or Telluride and the taffy-and-tack raunch of Estes Park. Wildflowers punctuated the ponderosa pine forest, and gaillardia's red-and-yellow spoked wheels colored the verge. Fuzzy mullein stalks lined the roadway, the tallest pointing with a longer yellow finger toward the COFFEE 25¢ sign, a

Colorado blue spruce poking the hot day's blue sky. He watched a big Weidemeyer's admiral butterfly as it settled at damp gravel to sip salts, fanning its brilliant black-and-white wings. Come winter, everyone said, it was hard to beat the cold in these thin-walled cabins, hard to make a living when the tourists went home, hard to take the cabin fever. These things would not concern Mead, back among the crocketed, cosseted towers of Yale. That is, if George would have him back after this Colorado caper. He quaffed fresh, sweet water from Silver Spring, rejoined the highway, and continued north.

Soon he came in view of a great peak standing largely on its own on the very eastern edge of the high range. A truly *mountain-like* mountain, it rose in three sharp ridges to a double summit. The knees of the ridges ran down into the pines, but everything above was stone—massive granite outcrops and vast rockslides rising thousands of feet into the azure air. A green sign beside the highway read MAGDALENA MOUNTAIN: 13,311 FEET.

So taken was Mead with this mountain that he almost failed to notice the old log lodge across the road. He liked its look: logs weathered almost black, green composition roof, not a garish sign in sight. Along the roofline of the westward-pointing ell, above an open second-story porch, ran a dark brown wooden sign with white block letters: MAGDALENA PARK LODGE. On a whim, he walked in and asked about a room. Laura, the welcoming blonde woman at the desk, gave him a key, and he climbed the rustic wooden staircase. Its gnarled banister, polished smooth by hundreds of human hands, received his own ready paw like a warm handshake.

After taking his gear to room 14, he settled into a pine-slab rocker on the upstairs balcony to watch the mountain as the late sun brought it alive. Afternoon clouds had gathered, spit out a quick cloudburst, then dispersed into virga to the north. Now the western sky contained the summit and the sun, nothing else. Each ridge, tooth, furrow, chute, and suture stood out, every stone. Instead of the olive-pink smear that described the mountain's face in many lights,

Mead beheld a mountain whose pocks and wrinkles, warts and fine features displayed themselves sharply and without vain reticence. He remained on the balcony until the mountain swallowed the sun.

The next morning, after a peaceful night in a warm trundle bed under knotty pine, James came downstairs for breakfast. Afterward, on the back porch, he met the proprietors. Up for hours already, they were taking a well-deserved coffee break in the morning sun. "Pull up a chair," said the man. Keith and Marion Dever were handsome, robust, both ruddy of hair and cheek, in their fifties. They wore the glow of people devoted to what they do and the furrows of constant obligation and hard labor.

"I love this place!" Mead said. "How long has it been here?"

"Well," said Keith, "my dad and mom, Danny and Crete Dever, bought the place in 1922. They renovated the homestead, put up some rental cabins and the store. Then—was it 1929, Marion?—they began the lodge."

"He built it mostly with fire-killed logs," said Marion. "But it took years to finish, because Danny would never take a loan."

"Right," said Keith. "Opened the lodge in about 1933. Danny and Crete ran it for many years while their partners, the Nowels, ran a furniture company on Longmont and built all the rustic pine furniture."

"Crete is a power to reckon with," said Marion of her mother-in-law. "Danny died just last year, and we've run been running it ever since, with our daughters. But Crete is still with us. She'll probably live to a hundred."

Mead took it all in, then showed his cards. "Marion, where did the name Magdalena come from? It's sprinkled all around this area like powdered sugar on that good French toast Keith made me."

"Yes, it is, isn't it? Well, the lodge is named for the 'park'—never a town, but a sort of little village that Danny began. You know, in Colorado, *park* just means a sort of clearing in the pines—like Estes Park, Winter Park, South Park, and so on."

"And Magdalena Park came from the mountain, I guess," said Keith. "Then there's the Chapel of St. Mary Magdalene up the road—have you seen that yet?"

"No!" Mead said. "That's a new one on me. How do they all relate?"

"It all gets a little fuzzy back then," said Keith. "Crete tells a story about a priest who was camping up here around 1916. Buzzoli, was it, Marion?"

"Bosetti, I think. Joseph. Crete would know."

"Anyway, this priest saw a meteor overhead. Looking for a crater, he found that rock outcrop on Cabin Creek, where he vowed he would one day build a chapel."

"That's right," said Marion. "He was Italian, all right, but he had a Scottish friend named William McPhee. I've heard Crete tell this so often, it feels like my own story. McPhee put up some money and also bought the spot."

"Just in time, too," Keith chimed in. "The highway department was going to blow up the rock to get rid of that curve back when they were carving Highway 7 out of the old stage road."

"Lucky," said James.

"They don't care about the beauty," Marion said. "A few years back, they widened the road right here and took out some beautiful big pines in front of the lodge. You'll see them on the older postcards in the store."

"And the name?" Mead prodded.

"Well, McPhee built only a little wooden chapel. The Chapel on the Rock as we know it came later. But everything since then is a blur of bedsheets and broken pipes. So I don't know if it's always had the same name."

"I keep intending to look into the history more," said Keith, "and write it all up someday. But we keep so busy here in the summer, and then we usually recover in Mexico over the winter." As if on cue, Keith mounted his golf cart and buzzed off to see about some delinquent plumbing. Mead followed Marion into the big kitchen and accepted another cup of strong coffee.

"So whether Magdalena came in with the mountain or the chapel is a toss-up," she said. "This mountain, like most of them, has had different names over the years. I'm not sure when they settled on this one." She shifted her weight, put her hand on her womanly hip, and bit her upper lip in concentration. "Or, for the life of me, why. But it's a pretty name, don't you think?"

Mead, leaning against the huge double-door fridge from the 1940s, took a sip of his coffee and said, "It certainly is. Well, I have one remote possibility."

"Oh, what's that? Leave it to strangers to teach you about your own backyard! We used to have time to explore such things . . ." Her wistfulness was as thick as the lingering scent of the breakfast bacon. Mead cut through it by telling her about *Erebia magdalena.* "But I have no idea whether there is any connection."

"Well, that's very interesting. Come to Annie's nature talk tonight. Maybe she knows something about it."

So he did. After wandering the local hills, he returned to the lodge's great room and settled into a log-slab armchair. The entire room was furnished with varnished rustic-work—tables and chairs, rockers, desks for writing postcards or novels, bookcases, a broad table with a topographic map of the area under glass—all built of native lodgepole pine. Two enormous elk heads hung out from log-and-batten walls, their racks far too heavy for any animal to actually carry, or so it seemed to Mead. The thick neck pelage of one shagged into his own lengthening hair when he sat beneath it. The mane of the other hid the old black-and-white television, which suited him fine. A grand stone hearth shared pride of place with an upright piano. Sofas faced the fire, sturdy in spite of heavy use by heavy people for many years. Skinned log beams spanned the ceiling, and down the middle of the room ran a crossways beam supported by gnarled, barkless tree trunks. Garlands of aspen leaves hung from the rafters, from faux candlestick lights, from antlers of the elks, and all around the rustic frames of old mountain scene prints. The dry leaves, copper after seasoning for a year or ten, imparted an autumnal smell and a papery rustle as a breeze from the front door played with them each time a guest entered the lodge.

The room began to fill up. Mead chatted amicably, without purpose, with this retired teacher from Omaha, that minister from Wichita. He noticed a tall blonde woman, western-dressed, enter from the rear and begin to set up a projector and screen. This was to be an intimate fireside chat. When she was ready, Marion introduced the speaker to the assembled guests and neighbors and some folks in off the road.

"Ladies and gentlemen, I'd like you to meet Annie Cloudcroft—or Mountain Annie, as everyone around here calls her. Annie lives in Allenspark, and she has done just about everything up here in the Front Range, from waiting tables to fighting fires. She came to Magdalena Park from Wisconsin with her folks when she was a little girl, and she worked for us at the lodge as a teenager. Annie graduated from C.U., then went to work for the Forest Service as a ranger—is that right, Annie?—oh, the *Park* Service, that's right, in the summertime, up in Rocky Mountain. Now she is what you call a freelance naturalist: She works for the school districts to get the kids *outside*—that's *so* important!—and writes booklets on the plants and animals of the area. You'll find them in our gift shop, and Annie will be happy to sign them for you. Well, like I say, Annie's done about everything—just so's it's in the *mountains*. We're so lucky to have her here tonight to tell us about the summer wildflowers around here. Annie?"

"Thanks, Marion," the woman began after polite applause. "That's right, just so it's out in the hills, among the wildlife. Of course it's thanks to you Devers that I came here to begin with, and that I finally came to stay." The lights went down, and the first slide came on. Half an hour later, a blue gentian on the screen, she concluded, "In the mellow autumn, the blue and fringed gentians line the high meadows just before the aspens turn. I invite you all to open your eyes to the small wonders around you as well as the big ones." At this she gestured to the looming elk beneath which Mead was seated, and their eyes met.

Refreshments were served beside the rocky mountain mantelpiece. Soon the cluster of questioners had gone back to their picture puzzles or magazines, leaving James and Annie to talk together. "I was pleased to see you include local butterflies," he said after introducing himself. "Most naturalists seem to ignore them, let alone regular folk."

"Well, they're pollinators for my wildflowers," said Annie. "And perhaps that's because most folks just don't see them at all."

"I think you're right. Did you take that super shot of Weidemeyer's admiral?"

"Yes, thanks; down the Middle St. Vrain, in the willows. But you're right. Butterflies do seem to receive short shrift in national park interpretation, and it makes no sense, since everyone adores them in the abstract. The truth is, I think, most people just ignore insects altogether, except when they're trying to get rid of them."

"Wasn't it Nabokov," James asked, "who said 'It is astounding how little the ordinary person notices butterflies'?"

"It was. In *Speak, Memory,* I think."

"So how come you do?"

"What, know that quotation? I love Nabokov."

"No, notice butterflies."

"Well, I try to notice everything out there. It's my job but also my passion. Besides, I have a friend who teaches butterfly classes sometimes up at the Y camp out of Estes, and he's helped me to see them better. He often uses that quotation in his classes. Now

I always notice butterflies, even at the expense of flowers and birds sometimes."

"This mentor wouldn't be Michael Heap, would it?"

"It would. Do you know him too?"

"I've just spent a couple of days with him up at Loveland Pass. He's the one who steered me here, as a matter of fact."

"No, really?"

"Yeah—you see, we share a common interest in the Magdalena alpine. Do you know that great black butterfly of the arctic-alpine?"

"*Do* I! I take groups up to see it sometimes at Rock Cut on Trail Ridge Road. That's the only place I know where you can see it so easily, without a hike. Of course it was Michael who taught me about it. Where did you meet him? Is he around now?" The two went on to speak in the cool of the porch outside, as the fireplace was a little warm and Keith was holding forth with stories beside it. They watched a crescent moon sit on the summit of Magdalena Mountain before setting somewhere on the western slope.

Mead mentioned the prolific use of the name Magdalena in the area. "Maybe I'm going to have to become a biblical scholar to figure it out," he said.

"James," said Annie, "if you're interested in Magdalena around here, I can give you a couple of tips. Follow me back inside." Back in the great room, Annie strode to the bookshelf in the back. It should be here ... right." She pulled down a black book. "I told you I loved Nabokov. This is his newest novel. I just finished it and left it here for others to read. Take it back to your room tonight. I think you'd better have a look inside."

"Gladly. And? You said you had a couple of tips."

"You really should see the chapel, it's lovely. And while you're at it ..." She paused, uncertain as to whether she should go on. But if he was a friend of Michael's ...

"Yes?"

"Well, if you really want to learn about Mary Magdalene, you could do worse than to visit the old monastery near the chapel."

"Oh?" said Mead, thinking she must mean its library. "And why is that?"

"Because ... she lives there."

33

Annie had packed up and gone, and James was settled in by the fire to examine the book she'd instructed him to read, when a guest burst through the front door. He was clearly distressed. "What's the matter?" asked Keith, rising from his chair, fearing a fire.

"It's bad," said the man in a quavery voice. "We've got a *bat*!" The problem was a bat in the cabin, and the man and his wife were terrified. Keith shrugged and asked him if he'd tried to sweep it out. "Won't sit still," said the agitated guest. "Won't fly out. What will we do?"

Someone suggested sending him back with a can of Raid, which is when James offered to deal with it. He fetched his butterfly net, followed them back to their cabin, caught the bat, and released it into the alpine air. It was a tiny *Myotis* to cause such a fuss, happy as a gnat to be free. Everyone was happy. James thought, if this butterfly deal doesn't work out, maybe I'll have a future in extermination. But that wasn't funny: several of his entomology major friends from State had ended up doing just that. He also thought, no wonder people don't notice butterflies.

The Devers retired, leaving James to douse the lights and the fire. He took his place again after tossing on another log. Now, the book. It was Vladimir Nabokov's newest novel, *Look at the Har-lequins!*, just published—Annie had bought it hot off the press. Mead wondered if it would flesh out Nabokov's visit here with Winchester, which George had told him about. George had been working out of C.U.'s Science Lodge before he adopted RMBL for his summer field base. He was completing his PhD at Harvard, where Nabokov was curating the Lepidoptera while teaching Russian at Wellesley, and they became friends. Nabokov traveled in the West each summer, his wife, Véra, driving, him collecting on sunny days and writing on cloudy ones. Winchester invited the author to go afield with him in Colorado, and on July 13, 1947, they did so. GW collected VN at his cabin at Columbine Lodge and took him to Tolland Bog, near the Moffat Tunnel on the D&RGW railroad line, in search of *Boloria selene tollandensis* and other treasures. James knew all this from his prof. But what had this new book to do with it, or with anything?

He began on page 1, always a good place: "I met the first of my three or four successive wives in somewhat odd circumstances," he read, then told the elk head beside him, "Uh-oh, maybe this isn't what I need to read right now—sounds like romantic vertigo to me." But he persevered, and well before breakfast, he came to familiar territory:

> I spent what remained of the summer exploring the incredibly lyr-ical Rocky Mountain states, getting drunk on whiffs of Oriental Russia in the sagebrush zone and on the North Russian fragrances so faithfully reproduced above timberline by certain small bogs along trickles of sky between the snowbank and the orchid. And yet—was that all? What form of mysterious pursuit caused me to get my feet wet like a child, to pant up a talus, to stare every dandelion in the face, to start at every colored mote passing just beyond my field of vision? What was the dream sensation of hav-ing come empty-handed—without what? A gun? A wand?

Mead knew just what he meant about the talus, the dandelions, and the motes, and he knew exactly what it was his hand was missing in the dream. Elsewhere, Nabokov himself had written of a sunlit saunter that "the cold of the metal netstick in my right hand magnifies the pleasure to almost intolerable bliss." That feeling too, Mead knew. So the narrator, Vadim, was a collector, or had been. "Amazing," he muttered to the elk.

He was even more amazed a little further on when Vadim and his daughter Bel, traveling in what he called "the paradise part of Colorado," come to stay in Lupine Lodge—surely Columbine Lodge where V. and V. Nabokov stayed in that summer of 1947. "We spent a whole month walking a path margined with blue flowers [that] led through aspen groves." And then he found it. On a walk near Longs Peak, "sharing a picnic lunch, somewhere between those great rocks and the beginning of The Cable," Bel scribbled a poem that she later copied on the back of a photograph in violet ink:

> Longs' Peacock Lake:
> the Hut and its Old Marmot;
> Boulderfield and its Black Butterfly;
> And the intelligent trail.

Mead read it several times. To his ear, it sounded more like a koan written by Gary Snyder than like Nabokov's lush cadences. And precocious, certainly, for eleven-year-old Bel. But all that aside, it showed him that someone had been aware of Magdalena the butterfly here for many years—and not just anyone, but *Vladimir Nabokov*! Mead wasn't the first to make the connection.

Nor was Nabokov the first to make it, as Mead learned the next morning. In spite of his late night, he struggled up for pancakes at eight, intending to spend another day on the mountain. There he found a message from Annie beside his place. "James," it read. "Nice to meet you. While you're at it, there's something else you should see. If you're willing, I'll take you—I have to drive up toward Estes anyway. I'll check in around nine and see if you'd like to go with me. Annie C."

Mead was ready on the porch when Annie rolled up in her truck, and he climbed in. "Look," she said, "I may have been out of line when I told you about Mary. Some people have been harassing her, but you seemed harmless."

He wasn't sure it was a compliment, but Mead said, "You can trust me," not even clear on what he was implying.

"Your only interest is in the butterfly, right?"

"Right—that and the history of its name." He figured Carson could come later, after he waded through all these new revelations.

"Then I guess it's okay. Well, I'll take you up to the monastery, but first I have a little surprise. It's a few miles farther along the road. Did you have a chance to check out that novel last night?"

"Did I ever! I only skimmed the story, of course, but I found the good parts."

"By that I assume you don't mean the sexy bits."

"No, they were too many, by the looks of it. I mean the drunken whiffs of timberline and talus. And Bel's amazing poem . . . what a find! Who would've known?"

"Nice, eh?"

"More than you know." Mead filled her in on Nabokov and Winchester's field trip to Tolland in 1947, and then said, " 'Boulderfield and its Black Butterfly'—that's just marvelous! Only it sounded sort of Gary Snyderesque to me, especially that last bit about 'the intelligent trail'—the part Vadim likes so much."

"I see what you mean. Well, maybe Nabokov has read Snyder, who knows? Anyway, if you liked that, wait till you see the next thing I have to show you."

As the two cruised north on the Peak to Peak, Annie pointed out the chapel and the monastery. "How *cute*," said Mead when the chapel came into view. "And to think the highway almost took the rock it's sitting on—no, growing out of!" he added, craning his neck as they passed.

"We'll be back soon," said Mary. Then, a few miles on, "Now look to your left. Those cabins up there? That's Columbine Lodge—Lupine Lodge in the book, according to you. As you can see, Vladimir/Vadim could walk right out his back door and up onto the boulder field of Magdalena Mountain."

"Meaning he probably netted his first one right here," said Mead. "That would have given him a kick, if I've gotten any sense from Dr. Winchester of the man and his love of wordplay. While the actual type locality of the species is Georgetown, this is its namesake. You could call a specimen from here a 'nominotype.'"

"If you say so—you're getting beyond my ken. Now, over there, just beyond—that's the Longs Peak Inn, at least a modern version thereof. Have you heard of Enos Mills?"

"Sounds familiar, but do tell."

"Father of RMNP, as John Muir was of Yosemite—a friend of Muir's, and of John Burroughs as well. In fact, the three of them formed a kind of trinity of conservationist-naturalists on either side of the turn of the century. Mills never was as well known as the other two, but he wrote a bunch of books set here in the Rockies, very popular in their day."

"One of them is about grizzlies, right?"

"Yes, that's right. *The Story of a Thousand Year Pine* was his bestseller. But he also initiated the practice of what he called 'nature guiding,' which anticipated the Park Service's ranger-naturalists, of which I was one. Plus, he was a great mountaineer, and he built and ran Longs Peak Lodge. Later he fell afoul of the parks and the heavy hand of government, he died too young, and his rustic buildings sadly burned. But there—other side of the road—see that? It's the sole survivor from those days—the Enos Mills Cabin!" The truck slowed to pull into the long dirt driveway to a little log structure back up among the pines.

"Is anyone home?" asked Mead.

"I hope so." They parked, got out, and walked up to the door, where Annie knocked. "Hello, Enda!" she said warmly, hugging the middle-aged woman who appeared at the door. "Enda Mills, James Mead. Enda is Enos's daughter, James, and she runs the cabin as a museum." Enda Mills was sturdy, as tough as the winters she had weathered, and protective of a legacy that had not received the rec-ognition it deserved, in her judgment. But she was also warm and welcoming to any pilgrim who came there out of a genuine respect for nature, and that clearly included Annie and anyone who was her friend.

For the next half hour Annie and James talked with Enda and pored over Millsian artifacts, photographs, a letter from Muir and another from an ancient Burroughs, and shelves upon shelves of books. James bought a postcard with Enos's photo of the bark-on, elfin little post office he'd built in the lodge. Then Annie asked, "Enda, may I show James your dad's correction copy of *Wild Life on the Rockies*?"

"No, you go right ahead," said Enda. "But don't walk off with it. Nothing is rarer here, unless it's that copy of *Romance of Geology* he inscribed to Bob Marshall."

Annie lifted a green buckram-bound volume from a special shelf and opened it to the back pages. "Check this out," she told James, crooking her long, graceful index finger. As James peered at the open book, he saw that a page had been pasted in. There in a fine hand script lay lines of words in black ink. "Read it aloud, James, why don't you. I found it by accident. You might be amused . . . or amazed."

"'FOR NEXT EDITION,'" read Mead,

"must include some of our friends, the insects, as well as the large-scale wildlife I have recorded here. The cicadas in the juni-pers, the mole-crickets and yellow jackets, the bumblebees in the high meadows. But most especially, write about Strecker's butterfly, <u>Erebia magdalena</u>. Seldom, if ever, have I trod the rocks above here—whether on Mills Moraine (as they insist on calling it) or Battle Mountain, Ship's Prow or Boulder Field, The Loft, The Trough, the Keyhole, or Keyboard of the Winds, in summer on a sunny day, that I have failed to see the living shadow of the Black Butterfly. For me, it is the signature creature of these rocky redoubts, every bit as much as the pika and the marmot, as it drifts along the bases of the minarets, touching the stones with the gentleness of a lover's hand. I cannot imagine how it makes a living up there, never coming down (as even I do eventually for the comfort of the fire, the succor of the table). Nor can I imagine how I have failed, all these years and all these books, to so much as mention it before. Oh, I like the brightly colored butterflies well enough, as old John o' Birds loves his orioles; but more, I think, do I love these dun beauties of the stony places, even as John o' Mountains cherishes his soft-hued thrushes. So that settles it—I shall write about Magdalena—perhaps even a book! E.M. 1921.

"P.S. Must get Cockerell from the Denver Museum up here to teach me about it."

"Good God!" said Mead. "But he didn't, did he?"

"No," said Enda. "He showed me the black butterflies many times, and I suspect he really would have done it. But life had grown complicated, and the next year, Daddy died." She seemed as sad as if she were speaking of events that had occurred yesterday. "Now—some tea?"

Annie hugged her and said, "Thank you, Enda. You are so kind. But we must love you and leave you. James is collecting clues rather than butterflies, and he has one more important witness to visit."

James shrugged, smiled, and made his goodbye as well.

"Come back," said Enda, closing the door behind them as a campervan with Nebraska plates drove up and an excited young couple climbed out.

"So what do you think?" asked Annie.

"I think I want to read Mills's books. Especially the one he never wrote."

34

James, already whacked by the one-two punch of Nabokov and Mills, had no idea what to expect at the monastery. Annie dropped him off at the foot of the massive rock atop which the big white Jesus presided. "You're not coming with me?" he asked, like a child being left by his mother on his first day of kindergarten.

"No. I have a program to give at Allenspark Lodge on squirrels and raccoons. I'll check with you later at the lodge—it's just a short walk back from here. Ask for Mary Glanville," she added, shutting the door. "And tell them Mountain Annie sent you."

At the far end of a willow bog braided by Cabin Creek, a big wooden building sat dwarfed by Magdalena Mountain's northern face. Before walking up the drive, Mead peeked into the chapel in case Mary might be at her own devotions, but all he found was a sad-faced icon of the saint. Outside, Cabin Creek poured from the willows into a pool, willow leaves swirling on its surface before diving into the culvert beneath the road. Mead gazed into the brown water, seeking his questions.

On the way up the sandy path to the monastery, two or three men in work clothes nodded serenely, and one in a brown robe walked by fast and scowling. A knot of women in ordinary clothing who were seated in a circle on a pine needle floor mostly ignored him. Mead wondered whether Mary might be among them, but decided he'd rather inquire at the monastery than invade the female conclave. The feeling brought back elementary school again, where boys and girls dotted the playground in mutually impregnable knots.

Mead entered the Great Hall of the Mountain Monastery through an open door. A figure taller than himself stood beside a desk in an adjoining room. "Excuse me," Mead said as he entered, rapping on the doorjamb. "My name is James Mead."

"Mine is Oberon," the other said, extending his hand. "How can I help you?"

"I'm looking for a woman named Mary . . . Mary Glanville."

Oberon stiffened visibly in shoulder and jaw. "What's your business with her?" he snapped. "Are you from the state?"

"N-no, not at all," Mead stammered. "I'm just a graduate student."

"Say more."

"I have a purely academic interest in Magdalena Mountain and its name," said Mead. He said nothing about butterflies so as not to complicate things. "I understand Ms. Glanville may know something about it."

"And who told you about Mary?" asked a calmer Oberon.

"Oh, right . . . I was supposed to mention that Mountain Annie sent me."

Oberon relaxed more, but he was still unsure.

Then a voice behind him said, "It's all right, Oberon. I'll see him. Alone is okay."

"Okay, Mary, if you say so. Call me if you need me."

Moments later, Mead faced Mary in the library. "Do you know me?" she asked.

"No, I don't. I've been told that you might know about this place and its name."

"What is your interest?" she asked with a faint hint of a smile.

James told her, including the butterfly. "So I thought you might be able to help."

Mary looked down, pursed her fine ash-bow lips, stood with her left hand between her right collarbone and her breast. She was silent for more than a minute. Then, "You have heard correctly." Another pause. "I am Mary Glanville, according to those who found me after an accident. Of uncertain origins and unknown connections, in this life. But the trauma I suffered"—the hand swept up and across her forehead, where auburn curls cascaded—"let me see a prior existence. I feel as if I am—or at least I was—Mary of Magdala, known as Saint Mary Magdalene."

Never having met a saint before, unless it was Marion Dever, nor anyone who claimed to be reincarnated, except on the Greyhound and that didn't count, Mead wasn't sure of the protocol. He stood speechless. She seemed sane enough on the surface: sound, and somehow full of grace.

"I do not advertise the fact widely, for reasons that will be clear to you if you have ever been incarcerated."

He had not, though school sometimes felt like it when spring stretched out on the wrong side of the window. Eloquently he said, "Wow. Uhhhh—you see, umm. Geez!"

She was clearer. Echoing Oberon, she asked, "How can I help you?"

The cat gave back his tongue, and James explained further. "If it turns out that the butterfly, the chapel, and the mountain all have a historical connection, I'd love to know more about their common inspiration. I am not schooled in classical theology . . ."

"Not that that would help you much in this case," Mary said.

"Well, can you tell me a little about Mary . . . about yourself?"

"If you wish," Mary said, flicking back her hair, which was almost as it used to be before the windshield, the scalpel, and the nursing home shears got at it. A few strands and coils refined copper out of the afternoon light. Mead was beguiled even before, and now bewitched outright. So much for objectivity. "How much do you know?" she asked.

"Not much. Only that you were supposed to have been . . ."

". . . a whore?"

". . . and were . . ."

"Forgiven?"

"Something like that."

"Well, if that's all you've got, we have a long way to go. But you're not alone." She settled back, and Mead did the same. "Mary Magdalene is not who you think she is—certainly not the un-named sinner in Luke. Pope Gregory the so-called Great, on a Sunday in the year 591, having lumped several Marys together for convenience, proclaimed the Magdalene a prostitute redeemed by grace. You see, the early church needed a symbol of a fallen, for-given woman who gave up her power over men by prostrating her shamed self at the feet of a blameless man. Jesus's mother was unbe-smirched, so she wouldn't do; a racier role model was needed. Mary Magdalene-as-prostitute evolved to fill the bill."

"That's *weird*."

"But true," said Mary. "Not that it's such an insult—Leonard Cohen calls prostitutes sisters of mercy, after all—just incorrect. I was just another disciple, not a 'comfort woman' for Pontius Pilate's shock troops."

"So—you . . . knew . . . Jesus? Not as in 'come be saved,' but ac-tually *knew* him?"

"Jesus paid me more attention than the others. Which was part of the problem."

"You're said to have washed and anointed his feet, and there's the bit about his saving you from being stoned, glass houses, and so on, and healing you—'ridding you of seven devils,' didn't they put it that way?"

"There was a lot of footwashing going on in those days; it was a common courtesy, an act of humility. It had nothing to do with worship, let alone abasement."

James was all ears. "And the stoning?" He flinched as he said it.

"Both Mark and Luke chalked up that episode with varying degrees of license. It is quite true that I was about to be stoned to death and that Jesus interceded on my behalf, challenging the one who was blameless to toss the first rock. That image was very strong, and it stuck, though the bit about glass houses came in somewhat later."

"So what were those 'devils'?" he asked, hoping he wasn't out of line. He could not believe himself. After fending off the missionaries on the bus, here he was lapping up Bible stories from a self-proclaimed saint! He thought he might be just as keen if she were selling Amway products.

"Jesus quelled my fears and hurts with what has been called his *grace*. So in a way you could say that he cast devilments from me, in much the same way as these naturalist brothers have done for me here. Devilments like depression, loneliness, alienation, bitterness, fear, despair—how many's that, six? Okay, and how about vindictiveness? There's seven of the worst for you."

James considered that, and Mary continued. "But many people, including someone here who should know better, have taken 'devils' literally, as if they were pesty little imps with horns. Horny little devils, in fact—for of course they were supposed to be devils of lust and carnal weakness above all, so as to bolster the oh-so-sorry hooker scenario."

"So," said James. "Who were you really?"

"To put it simply: Mary of Magdala was a witch. So if I was that chick, so was I."

"A *what*?" Did she say that?

Mary giggled. "That's right, a witch. Oh, not a Halloween type with a pointy black hat and a broom, but a witch in the sense of Wicca, the Old Way—women who had special knowledge of herbs and healing, animals, and the countryside." At that Mary's head lifted, the dimples below her lips became crescents, and she gave him a calm smile.

"But I thought you were a Jew—and later a Christian," James spluttered.

"I visited Jerusalem, where travelers came bringing tales and lore from far away. I learned of certain women in Syria who followed a goatlike god and the great Earth Goddess and practiced healing arts and gentle ways. So I begged to visit an uncle who had crossed the Sea of Galilee to Syria, and I persuaded my father to send me there on one of his fishing boats. Simon, a mellower man back then, rowed me over. I set off to learn more about these women who brought Pan from Greece, Demeter from Rome, Astarte from Phoenicia, Gaia from everywhere—all secretly, of course—and I took it all in: the teachings and practices were down-to-earth and came from wise women of many lands."

"Secretly?"

"Out of necessity. Already, Pan was being twisted into the devil by big men who feared women and couldn't handle such a powerful pagan god as the wee piper. Neither could witches—uppity women in their eyes—be tolerated by uptight men. In Canaan, if a woman made love outside marriage, the Levite priests condemned her to death, branding her a harlot. Which brings us back to the stones, and Jesus's good timing, showing up when he did to call off the stoners. You don't need to know all the details leading up to it, or what followed. But can you imagine what it felt like when that calm man intervened, placed his hand on my brow, and spoke those words? Like cool water from a flower-scented spring pouring over my head, my overheated heart, my bruises. Like love."

"Golly," said James, and that seemed about adequate. His head was spinning like a spider, fashioning intricate new patterns out of old cobwebs.

They each looked away, a little embarrassed. Mary's hand went back to her fine clavicle. After a few breaths James asked, "And Jesus? How'd he take to witches?"

"He respected women, including lovers and Goddess followers. Much of the Old Way was based on sensitivity to all life. And as I told the brothers here the other day, Jesus was a nature lover."

"Really?" James sat upright.

"It's right here," she said, picking up a fat, sprung paperback and turning to a page she'd marked. "I found this in the library here, and it sounded familiar. It's from the *Gnostic Gospels*, or Nag Hammadi scrolls. This part is from a scroll called 'The Gospel of Mary Magdalene,' how about that? Mary asks Jesus, 'Will matter then be destroyed or not?' And Jesus says, 'All natures, all formations, all creatures exist in and with one another, and they will be resolved again into their own roots. For the nature of matter is resolved into the roots of its nature alone.'"

"Jesus!" said Mead. "That sounds like something John Muir would have said."

"Or John Burroughs; he practically did, in *The Faith of a Naturalist*."

"Or Enos Mills, who lived just down the road. Or Aldo Leopold, or Ed Abbey!"

"Rachel Carson," said Mary.

"Right, Saint Rachel of the Silent Spring. But *not* the JC that I'm used to." So Jehu was no yahoo, thought Mead, but fortunately didn't say it. His mind flipped back to Cumberland Pass, where he'd wished that he (or Freulich) had the jawbone of an ass to smite those cycle jerks up alongside the head. Now he wondered whether a New Testament approach might work better.

Returning to the here and now, he asked, "So, were you—"

"Lovers? Of course. That's what we women did, and we loved our love."

"Did you—"

"Have children? That's another story. Someone will write all about it one day."

"And how shall I think of you?"

Mary looked straight ahead. Mead was glad for that, for her dark eyes were incinerating; he couldn't take them for long. "I don't know . . . I can't seem to remember anything about myself from the time I last saw Jesus to the morning I awoke in Denver."

"Wow, that's—"

"Yeah, I know, a long time . . . almost two thousand years. Well, hell . . . saint, schmaint. Goddess? Maybe. Witch for sure, of the Wiccan kind. Keeper of nature's true wisdom from ancient Syria to this modern mountain. And consort and lover of Christ in every sense of the word. At least of the Jesus I knew—or seem to have known—as opposed to the whitewashed version there on the rock. Hooker? Not that I recall. But really? I don't have a clue.

"I'm supposed to have had a life as Mary G., but she's as lost to me as Mary M. One of us really did go to France, as legend says, and rusticated among the flowered Alps. Maybe that's why I was so drawn by these mountains . . . why I dream of them."

Mead merely listened, the spider spinning.

"So who the heck *am* I?" asked Mary. "In *Paradiso*, Dante wrote that I was 'a sunbeam in clear water.' I think I'll settle for that."

Mead said, "That's lovely. Reminds me of what Enda Mills told me that Thomas Hardy wrote upon hearing of her father's death: 'It is as if a mountain peak had sunk below the horizon.'"

The sun passed over the ridge of the building and the ridge of Magdalena Mountain that it mimicked. James and Mary faced each other in the diminished light. "I guess all this doesn't have much to do with your butterfly," she said.

"*Yours*, if anyone's. Mary, have you seen the butterfly that bears your name?"

"No. Annie has promised to show me. Is it very beautiful?"

"Like a sunbeam in black water," he said. "But you'd better hurry—its flight period won't last much longer."

"I'll go as soon as Annie is free to take me."

"Look, I have to go to New Mexico for a quick visit home. But when I get back, if you haven't seen your namesake by then, we'll go find her. Likely be a female, this late."

"I'd like that. Maybe I can learn something from her, too."

Having safely escaped Mary's eyes and crescent dimples without actually disgracing himself, Mead walked back along the Peak to Peak to the lodge. Lost as he was in Mary's face and story, it came as a shock to read the postcard that awaited him. The return address in Colorado Springs showed it was from Dr. Brown, the author of *Colorado Butterflies*. He hadn't expected an answer so soon. He read it on the balcony:

> Dear James: Your card in the morning mail. Mike Heap's theory about Mary Magdalene's feast day (which is fast upon us) won't wash. Strecker was irreligious!
>
> He gave the name Jehovah to a very dull sort of moth just to antagonize his best friend, a parson. As a matter of fact he antagonized everyone with his blasphemous comments. If in any way it could be construed as derogatory to a biblical character, he used <u>magdalena</u> in that fashion. You would not be wrong in assigning the name to commemorate Mary Magdalene, but not to honor her: more likely to rub his parson pal's face in her besmirched reputation. Let me know your thoughts on <u>E. magdalena</u> when you have a chance. Good luck to you, Brownie.

Mead felt shell-shocked. Mary's blow to the solar perplexus, Brownie's uppercut about Strecker . . . and the great F. Martin Brown asking for *his* thoughts on *magdalena*? By now he'd certainly had a lot of them, and heard of a number of others' views, but he wished he'd been able to query Carson on the matter. Carson! He remembered

Mary's reference to Saint Rachel Carson, and he flashed on George Winchester pulling out his file drawers: *Carson, Hampton . . . Carson, Rachel . . . should be in between—yes, here it is.* "Damn!" he said. "I completely forgot to ask Mary about October Carson, my other main object in this weird scavenger hunt. Oh well, next time."

That night, with a moist breeze sifting the lace curtain of his window across his face, Mead fell into deep sleep. His dreams—wild, crazy, sacrilegious, yet sweet, with soft, swirling crescents, long, lithe limbs, and sunstruck water all through them, could never be told.

35

On a cloudless August morning, Erebia, now slower, browner, reticulated with small scratches but still robust, sets off for his first sortie very near the top of the north ridge. As the sun sinks lower to the south and also sinks behind the mountain earlier each day, his activity centers farther upslope. The nights are not yet cold enough to militate against a bivouac at thirteen thousand feet. Nor do his sallies extend as far downslope before he turns back. There is not always a handy updraft to rise upon, and gaining altitude under his own power is becoming harder each day.

At the same hour, Mary Glanville leaves the monastery on foot. Oberon, occupied with the business of the merger, does not see her go. Annie too, busy with the Boy Scouts at Camp Tahosa, begged off the field trip ("I've got to gather the bacon bits now," she told Mary, "because there won't be many gigs come winter"). But she pointed out where Mary must go to see the alpines. So Mary sets out, reluctant to wait for Mead's return in case the weather should change and the alpines finish their flight without her. Grown strong again since coming to the mountains, Mary assays the steep pinestone slope behind the monastery and reckons she can do it. An hour or two of agreeable climbing should take her to the rockslide.

A Steller's jay perched on the ridgeline of the monastery notices a figure in blue, like his own but softer, with a saffron cape, leaving the building and entering the forest. A few minutes later a gray jay sees a second person take the same route. This other one wears gray too. Even jays, with their sharp color vision, would have a hard time following this dun animal once it reached the rocks. And that is its intention: to remain unseen. The gray jay scrawls an alarm call across the sky, but no one who matters hears.

When Mary reaches the rockslide, she chooses a boulder and sits to watch. James had told her that the best way to see the alpines is simply to take up a perch where they are likely to fly by and to be watchful and patient. While she waits for the sun to come out from behind a small cloud, she amuses herself by watching pikas. Apparently she has planted herself on the edge of several territories, because four or five buck pikas begin calling at her irately with their absurd little voices. Mary can't help laughing at their utter indignation and answering back: "Peent!" she squeaks.

Then a dark fleck crosses the rods of her eyes and the back of her brain. Swinging her head to point up the scree, Mary catches full sight of the Magdalena alpine as it drops over the boulders toward her place. She freezes, knowing from Annie that any rapid movement of hers might startle the insect away. So she becomes part of the late-summer landscape, an immobile piece of alpine furniture, watching and waiting.

Mary wears a bright pink bandanna as a scarf. Taking it for a patch of moss campion, Erebia directs his flight straight toward her face. Or is it the flick of her dark, iridescent hair that draws him down to her? Anyway, down he comes, to within inches of her eyes, settling for a second or two on her bandanna and again on her hair. Receiving no scent, no taste worth sticking around for, he flutters there in place for a second and takes off again to her right. Mary cannot see, but she somehow knows that she was touched by the butterfly.

But the cloudlet chases the sun again and the Magdalena drops onto the rocks. Though he becomes invisible against the black lichen on the granite, Mary spots another a few yards away. She approaches carefully, closely, and for several minutes she is allowed to watch the creature bask. This one is a new female, one of the last to emerge. Erebia had followed her down the defile, the only reason he was low enough to encounter Mary. Without the distraction she provided, he might have reached the female of his own kind; he might yet. For now, drawing still nearer, Mary places her forefinger before the bright black butterfly, who, sensing the warmth, crawls onto her hand. For just a moment she holds the butterfly that bears her name.

Why a *black* butterfly? she wonders. Is my reputation really that bad? To be stoned and sainted and still stigmatized seems a sour joke. But why should black be an insult in any case? After all, Mary thinks, is this not a glorious creature with which to share a name? Forgetting herself in all this, she is lost in the beauty of the butterfly as it shimmers in the sunshine. Only hours old, she is still fresh, ebony, iridescent, unlike her prospective mate, who lingers in the rocks nearby, waiting for the interloper to leave.

If Mead were here, he would have told her that few persons have been so well honored. His possible kinsman, Theodore Mead, did very well with patronyms such as Mead's sulphur and Mead's wood nymph, while his sweetheart Edith lives on in her copper. An otherwise largely forgotten monarch won a kind of immortality in Queen Alexandra's sulphur, a butter-yellow and lime-green Colorado beauty, and Queen Alexandra's birdwing of New Guinea, which has the wingspan of a robin. But no one else could claim the matronym of this splendid black animal. It carries the name of Mary Magdalene, and none other. Forget the reason. That fact alone is sufficient unto its purpose.

But Mead is not here on the rockslide, nor is Oberon, nor anyone to warn Mary of the danger hulking nearby. Once or twice, out of the corner of her eye, she thinks she sees a gray object moving from rock to rock, but she takes it for a pika or a marmot or a hawk dropping behind a boulder.

Mary contemplates "her" butterfly, deciding that she likes it very much. Thus intent, she remains still, and all is silence on the mountain for several moments. Then a shrill whistle pierces the thin air from a few yards above her as a marmot calls its ancient alarum. As every other marmot in the vicinity ducks, Mary looks up barely in time to see a missile shooting toward her. Quick reaction yanks her aside just enough to miss it. As rock splits rock hard beside her, feldspar splinters sting her hand.

Mary shrieks and recovers her balance enough to glance upward at the hurler. Her butterfly flies off, as does the waiting Erebia, and if Mary could, she would be with them. But alas, groundborne, she is left behind to face her assailant.

At first she does not recognize him, as he is dressed in gray work clothes instead of a brown habit. But his mad voice cannot be mistaken as he screams, "Woman! Harlot! Temptress! I said you should never come here, but you came. I warned Oberon, I warned them all—I warned *you*. Now see what you have done? I must destroy you, so the others will stay away. I *will* take the mountain and the monastery back." Then he lifts another great stone and heaves it in Mary's direction, roaring "Die, Jezebel!" But it's too heavy, his aim is bad, and Mary dodges it easily.

"Attalus!" Mary implores. *"Why?"*

"You know why, witch!"

"But you cannot kill me—I'll come back, as I have this time. And my sisters will come to the mountain regardless."

"Then stand and be stoned," Attalus snarls. "I *can* kill you—as it is written—and I shall. You are not who you say you are, you're just a madwoman, a common whore, come to destroy the brotherhood. Mary Magdalene admitted her carnal sins, repented, and was forgiven. There is no repentance in you. Even if you *were* the Magda-

lene, you deserved stoning then and you deserve it now. Saint—*bah!*"
And he hurls another rock.

So far, both have been rooted in the here and now. But seeing
that he has every intention of killing her, Mary finds her feet. She
runs—as well as anyone can run over a rockslide at twelve thousand
feet. Attalus follows, spitting obscenities, cursing, and throwing
rocks at intervals. Mary, much the younger and fitter of the two,
gains distance for a while. But each time she stumbles in her horror,
tearing the blue dress and abrading her knees, knuckles, and arms,
he comes nearer. Attalus moves deliberately, with the experience of a
longtime rock crawler, across the habitat of his beloved lichens.

There ensues a time more terrible than any Mary has ever known,
in this or any life. For hours the grisly chase continues, sometimes in
slow motion, sometimes in bursts, both hunter and hunted stopping
for breath in sight of the other when they can go no farther without
rest. Although the monk's projectiles fail to find their mark, Mary
bleeds from tumbles on the unforgiving stones. The sun drops over
the far ridge, and the clarity of the day begins to thicken. If only I
could go *down*, she thinks. But Attalus has worked his way into a position below her, so he can cut off any route she attempts. She angles
up, to the north, to try to get around him.

Now it is Attalus who falls and cries out, so that Mary looks
back and sees him disappear behind a cabin-size boulder. She sees
a chance and takes it. The chase has taken them to the top of the
northern ridge, halfway across the mountain from the trough she
originally ascended. Over the ridge, a vast talus of huge boulders
rolls down toward the Roaring Fork and Peacock Pool. Each of the
rocks could hide an elephant, and here and there crevices between
them make cavelike fissures. As the light begins to fade in earnest,
Mary chooses one of these and dives for it. By the time Attalus,
more crazed than ever in his pain, baldpate bleeding, appears on
the ridgeline, Mary lies concealed in a close cocoon of silky gray
granite.

Attalus searches and curses all around her, coming within a few feet several times and once, as she holds her breath, peering into her very holt without seeing her. Then he moves off over the ridge again and Mary breathes easier for the first time, for she can see his dusky retreat. She thinks about making a run for it toward the Longs Peak Trail far below, where there would be hikers and help. But she's seen it only on a map, doesn't really know the way, and besides, every part of her aches, and bruises stiffen her limbs. Exhausted from labor on the hard rockpile, drained by fear, and desperately thirsty, seeking any way out of the nightmare, Mary sleeps.

Deep in the night, the temperature hovering around forty-five in her hidey-hole, Mary awakens shivering and almost screams coming back into her terror. At first she doesn't recognize her impossible surroundings, and for a moment she wonders if she is back in the home, finally driven mad. But the reality is still worse. She remembers, and despairs. If she doesn't freeze (and now the cold hurts as much as her wounds, but how to separate them?), what will the daylight bring? Another day's chase across the bony incline, a game of tag where "you're it" means "you're dead"? Or cat and mouse, with rocks for claws? Mary pulls her woolen cape around her—thank God for that affectation, of a color she always loved, found in a monastery closet, worn in the spirit of the place, and almost gone without for what she expected to be a short hike on a warm afternoon—and wonders where her persecutor is now.

Crawling as far into the cleft as she can and reaching still farther, she feels a vein of ancient ice. She manages to break off a piece and sucks it to assuage her fierce thirst. It helps. Her throat soothed, dulled by drudge and dread, lulled by cold, Mary Glanville or Magdalene sleeps again. Mercifully, she does not dream at all. Nor is she aware that two mating alpines, twelve pikas, and a brood of marmots and their mother all share this labyrinthine system of cavities with her. That knowledge might have been some cold comfort in the night.

Attalus never sleeps. Suffering greatly from cold and contusions, he huddles against a slab of eroded schist on the ridgeline. The rock blocks the wind, but every degree that drops off the scale falls right into the frigid pit of his gut. It doesn't matter. He could take much worse without giving up. And it never even occurs to him that he might be mistaken.

The monk drools from hunger and hate. But the only hunger that matters is the kind that blood alone can quell. His plan is to remain in sight of both mountain faces, northwest and southeast, so that Mary cannot escape his scrutiny. He knows she had not gotten off the rocks before night fell, nor could she in the black, clouded night. If she tries, and dies in the attempt, so much the better; it would solve his problem neatly.

But no. That would give the mountain the satisfaction of dispatching the witch, the sweet vengeance against this impostor who assumes its holy name. Only the dark engine of enmity, fueled by animus, warms the knotted heart of Attalus and keeps it from becoming one more stone in the cold mountain night.

No, you couldn't call it sleep. But in the depth of the darkness, the brain of Attalus falls into a state of self-recognition that he fends off successfully almost every waking hour. His grizzled gray and pink cheeks rise and fall almost as in slumber. His cramped fat legs jerk, as before a shallow dream. And then certain images thrust their way into his semiconsciousness against his every particle of will. His fingers, pressed against the long slope of his brown-spotted forehead and the thin, colorless hair that runs back from it, begin to tremble. The tears that find their way out almost freeze to his lashless eyes. Some might call the sound that issues from him a moan, heavy, rising to a sob; to the pine marten working the ridge for ground squirrels in their dens, it becomes a howl from a species of animal beyond her ken. But what follows is clear to every ear on the mountain except Mary's: the wailing of one name: "Anna . . . Anna . . . *Annnnaaaa!*"

Mary shivers piteously. Then, sometime before dawn, her shivering ceases.

James Mead slumbers warmly at the lodge. Oberon paces the monastery, uneasy. Somewhere on Magdalena Mountain a torpid brown butterfly lies among the rocks, unaware of anything at all.

36

"So what did it prove?" The dash lights glowed but failed to reply, and the radio just talked back.

Rolling uphill from Lyons in his Rent-a-Wreck Mercury, on his way back to Magdalena Mountain, Mead ran over the trip home in his mind for the twenty-third time. Nothing was revealed. But the images came back as sharp as the oncoming headlights or the sunset outlines of the Indian Peaks.

Laura Dever had given him a lift to Loveland, where he'd picked up the car. From there it was a straight shot south on I-25 all the way to Raton Pass, then west. He could reach his parents' house from Magdalena Park by taking about three turns, but he wasn't sure he was all that eager to get there. He'd skirted Denver's inchoate smudge with all possible speed, but its smog still stung his eyes as he neared Colorado Springs. When he pulled into a rest area that had mosaic pumas and pinecones on the side of the john and got out for a stretch, the scent of hot sun on soil damp from last night's rain among Gambel oaks hit his nostrils hard. An aroma of his youth, it tingled in his memory. His preoccupations had helped keep the family barbs sheathed inside him, but they were near the surface, ever ready to cut through the fragile integument of his conscience. That scent of wet dirt and tannin did it. He was going home, for better or for worse.

But first there was a quick visit with F. M. Brown out in Fountain Valley, southeast of the Springs. More of a pilgrimage than a proper visit. Brown, longtime teacher and butterfly author, greeted Mead with a powerful handshake, a bouquet of scientific reprints, and questions about his genealogy. He really wanted him to be related to Theodore Mead, several papers about whom were among the sheaf. "Couldn't have a better name for a butterfly man," he said, biting his pipe between his Colonel Sanders goatee and mustache. They discussed lepidopterists they knew, and when the name of Nabokov came up, Brown surprised Mead as much as he had with his postcard about the name Magdalena.

"Ol' Nabokov loved the satyrs almost as much as the blues," he said. "His student and driver once kicked up a new species for him in the Grand Canyon, which he named *Neonympha dorothea* for her. So I'm sure he was delighted to find *magdalena*. At least it's got no spots! He and I got into quite a tiff over the spots on ochre ringlets one time. George Winchester, as editor of the *Lep. News*, egged us on. I didn't think much of Nabokov's statistics, and he reckoned I couldn't see the butterfly for its eyespots! We resolved it in a friendly fashion and became great pals." Winchester had told Mead the same story, but it hadn't sounded quite so chummy.

"So, Dr. Brown—"

"Call me Brownie."

"... Brownie, I appreciated your postcard. Is there anything else you can tell me about the Black Butterfly of the Boulderfield, as Nabokov called it?"

"Funny you should come by and ask. Something has been scratching at the back of my mind like a cricket in a tin can. I haven't put my finger on it yet, but I have some ideas where to find it. If I do, may I still write you care of Magdalena Park Lodge?"

"Yes, sir . . . Brownie. I'll be back there in a few days at most, and I'd be grateful."

On his way out, Brownie told him to stick with it; he might be as successful as his namesake. "But I'm afraid the lovely Edith Edwards is already taken," he quipped. Mead thought, Thank Christ! What I *don't* need is one more cute chick! Brownie had pointed out that W. H. Edwards, T. L. Mead's father-in-law, had named numerous butterflies after unknown females, such as the Sara, Flora, Stella, and Julia orangetips. Maybe he had suffered romantic vertigo too, thought Mead, or else had a lot of daughters or nieces. He was pretty sure there were not enough new butterflies in Colorado to name after all the pretty women he'd fallen for this summer.

But all that was just diversion. Colorado Springs to Albuquerque was normally an eight-hour drive, but Mead's agitation fueled his foot with such octane that he took it most of the way in six. It was late, so he spent the rags of the night in the car in a corner of the Sandias that he remembered well. When he had taken his family camping in the mountains, that bad time, they were not far from here.

He pulled into the driveway at breakfast time, expecting in the manner of all who travel lost in their own thoughts that the world would be awaiting them. But no clamor of welcome greeted his arrival. Then he remembered. His brothers both had jobs in Santa Fe, helping an uncle with his business during the annual summer-long Fiesta. At least he'd expected to find his parents breakfasting together, smiling their surprised if abstracted greeting. But through the broad window of the sunroom, no faces showed. He entered through the garage, saw that his dad's VW was missing. His mother's Falcon stood alone. The door was unlocked. He knocked anyway, then went in.

"Mom?" He listened, heard nothing, and decided everyone must be gone. But wandering the hallway toward the bedrooms, he heard a muffled mewing and pursued it from room to room. As he neared the master bedroom, the mews resolved into soft sobs. He found his mother weeping on her bed.

Helga Mead, fifty, slender, and fair, was the daughter of Norwegian immigrants. She grew up in a stern, not unloving, but not too touchy household, where crying was seen as weakness letting itself out for all to see. Helga's life had been little lubricated by tears. When Mead found her that way, he was surprised and frightened.

Watching from the doorway, afraid to step in and shock her, he recalled that she'd barely wept even after Molly's death. She was inconsolable but stoic. Her mirth had fled, but she seldom openly shed tears. At the funeral, when her sobs never came, some had thought her cold behind her statue's face, like those white granite figures that shine with winter's frost in Oslo. But no one had seen her—no one—a few days later when she disappeared for forty-eight hours. She came home after, said nothing. Only her eyes, cast from red sandstone, gave away her private grief.

Mead entered the room, sat on the bed, put his hand on her shoulder. She didn't start, but her shoulder shook like an aspen leaf in the breeze. She did not put her hand on his. "Mom."

Helga shook in silence. Finally she said, "I knew your voice."

"Where's Dad?"

"Fishing. He's always fishing. I can't blame him."

They were quiet for a long time. Then Mead asked, "Mother? Do you hate me?"

"No. Though I can see why you think so."

"Then, do you love me?"

"I don't know ... if I love."

"Do you blame me?"

Helga made a kind of sobbing moan, which said less yet far more than any word. Mead, half as Nordic as his mother, the other half English, was not a speedy weeper either. But he cried then, softly. The fact is, they cried themselves to sleep, side by side but not touching.

In the afternoon, James got up, left Helga sleeping, showered, and made a bite to eat. He'd often cooked for her in high school, when she was attending classes or therapy with Molly. She smelled the cooking odors, and though they nauseated her at first, she rose, washed, and came out to the kitchen. "Thank you, James."

"Okay, Mom."

"I'm sorry I didn't have breakfast for you when you got here."

"Well, I hardly announced my ETA, did I?"

"We expected you sometime. Dad will be sorry to have missed you. He's deep in the Sandias, won't be back till Tuesday. I don't suppose you can stay?"

"No—I've got to head back north tomorrow. Maybe I'll be able to come back for a week or so in September."

"What's the rush?" asked Helga between bites of omelet. "I thought your research was on hold and you were just visiting out here."

"Well—I'm on to something else, sort of. More of a whim than bona fide research. But it could be important, may lead to a worthwhile thesis project."

"So what's wrong with whims? At least we tried to raise you boys to be aware of the possibilities that present themselves."

"That's true, and I'm thankful for it . . . I guess that's what I'm doing."

"After all, your dad's coming here from White Sands was a

whim, and it got him out of that atomic mess. So was your Fulbright, wouldn't you say?"

"Yes, well, I guess it was, really. Maybe not as whimsical as this."

"So tell me. Is Yale okay with this whim? And your professor?"

"Umm, they don't . . . actually . . . know about it yet. Sorry, it's too complicated and weird. Maybe I'll be able to share it better in September. It has to do with a big black butterfly named Magdalena. Anyway, time is short, and I wanted—"

"James, please—I can't."

"Can't talk about it?"

"No!" She snapped her fork down on the table.

"You can't cry your life away either, Mother. And you're not going to brush me off that easily." They went silent again and resumed eating.

"I don't cry, very much," Helga said. "Just now and then . . . when I *think* I'm alone."

"Well, excuuuuuse me! I'm sorry I disturbed your solitude."

"No . . . no, James, I didn't mean that. I'm glad you came, I really am. Just—I don't seem to be able to *share* what I feel. Poor Ed's going crazy with me."

"Have you tried counseling?"

"Of course! We're not *that* backward here, you know. But it hasn't helped. Religious ones are no good; you have to *have* faith to be reached by faith."

Mead's eyes went up at that; he'd always thought she did have faith.

"And the secular is just bleak. Plus, the private costs so much. Ed's insurance won't cover 'mental.' Besides, they all try to appeal to my love of myself and you all. But I'm not feeling much of that. And they're big on there being no victims, taking responsibility for your grief, and such hogwash. Or else they prescribe pills—and you know how I hate pharmaceuticals."

"You're young, Mom. And healthy, right?"

"Disgustingly so. But drawing down. And starting to drink. Oh, don't look like that, it's just a little. I can't hold enough to help, or to hurt, for that matter. Oh, James—if only *I* could have a whim! But I haven't even known what whimsy tastes like for years."

"A whim . . . like what?"

"Oh, *I* don't know . . . some sort of grand enthusiasm . . . some kind of mental *involvement* I could care about, just to get my mind off Molly. Some travel, maybe, I don't know. But it seems so pointless. James, to follow a passion, you need a dream. I don't think I have any more dreams."

James sighed, his head in his hands, wishing he could lend her a few of his own. Then he looked up. "Do you remember that letter you wrote me at Yale? The one where you asked if I thought things could get better?"

"Yes, I guess so. You didn't tell me the answer."

"I replied to the letter, I just didn't know the answer. But I've seen some things—some people—lately who make me think that even quite desperate situations can get better. I don't mean to belittle your pain . . . *our* pain, we share it too, you know . . . but don't you think that people with even deeper cuts have healed?" He went on, though he knew it was probably a mistake. "I mean, I stopped to rest in a little pioneer cemetery out of Raton. Every other stone was for a child of one day, six weeks, six or eight or ten years old, sometimes two or three of them in the same family. Or the mother died too, in childbirth. And 1918! So many, with the flu. Not to even mention World War One . . ."

"So you think it's me—" Helga looked at her plate.

"I didn't say that. I just think you've got to get out of your tailspin. Other people seem to, and I believe you can too."

"I'm glad someone thinks so. Tailspin, it is. I really am afraid that I'll just dig myself deeper and deeper into despair, until Ed gets fed up and leaves . . . and then what? I'd be lost without him." Her voice came tremulous with that, and she looked pale, bleak . . . beat.

"Mom, you don't—"

"Contemplate suicide?" Mrs. Mead's narrow nose spread slightly, and she reared her head, flared her nostrils, and took a deep breath. As she did, she saw beyond James to the plates arrayed in the Welsh dresser beyond him. Blue willowware, Fiesta, Carnival. Whenever she looked over those plates, she felt the warm weight of history, like an extra blanket on a winter night. Some of them came from her side, some from Ed's. A few were acquired during their own marriage, and a baby plate for each of the children. Each, except Molly. Somehow, with Molly, there was never time to do things like choose a baby plate. Remembering that her daughter had never had a baby plate, had never even had her handprint bronzed (the boys' golden patty-cakes were there in the dresser too), almost made her cry out.

James waited, chewing on his mustache, breathing slowly.

"Of course. Daily."

"Mom!"

"But would I do it? No, I don't suppose so." She gazed over the plates again. "If only because I know how you would all feel. It's a pretty damned selfish thing to do."

James wanted to ask, And you don't think *this* is pretty damned selfish? Instead he said, "Sometimes I wonder if you *want* us to feel bad, or at least me."

"James! No! Do I?"

"You've got to blame me some, Mom. I know you do. Or else, what's happened to us?" He was shaky in his throat, tripping on thin ice. "You don't know anything about me now . . . my studies, my girl-friend, my plans . . . my dreams. You've just let me go by the wayside. You don't really care; you can't."

Helga shook her head slowly from side to side, opened her mouth as if in a broad smile, but bent her brow in a way no laugh ever knew. Then she started to quake. She raised her hands beside her head, held it, let it go, made fists, slammed them down on the table. Lifted her head and sucked in her breath in a loud, wailing croak. "Oooohh, James. Do you think that?" Her voice foundered on sucked-in sobs, and she had to draw out each word as if it were hooked inside, just like a little girl with her feelings hurt beyond repair.

James held her and told her yes, he couldn't help it. She shoved him away, stood, and shouted, "Well, all right then— damn you, you *did* take us away! If we hadn't gone with you, Molly would still . . ." Her wretched sobs swallowed the rest of the accusation.

James didn't cry this time. He'd faced his own guilt, not easily or well, but as best he could. Hers seemed implacable. He wanted so badly to cast these devils from his mother's heart. But he was no Jesus, and he didn't know how. So he decided to get the hell out instead, and pronto.

When Helga subsided, he rose to get his things.

"You're leaving tonight?" she asked from far away when he returned.

"No point in staying, is there? I seem to be lost on you, and you're lost to everyone—yourself included. I don't know what I could possibly do."

He carried his backpack out to the Mercury. When he came back in to say goodbye, his mother faced him, as pale and old as she'd ever looked. Her face had corroded even since he'd arrived. Her dress seemed hung on a rack. Her hands were motionless beside her thighs. "Jimmy," she quavered.

He held her lightly and said. "I'll be back in a few weeks, Mom. Try to be here."

"James—I know it isn't you. It's just . . . *Molly* . . . she never had a chance. Not a damn *chance!*"

"That's true—poor, sweet girl. But let her go, Ma. *I'm* still here, and I love you. How about giving *me* a chance?"

He jumped in the car and pulled hard out of the drive.

37

One day later, Mead arrived at the monastery to find it nearly deserted. The brothers had almost all gone to Rocky Flats to join the
women's camp in another demonstration. Sylvanus had fallen and
suffered a broken ankle while checking on a northern three-toed
woodpecker's nest in a beetle tree. He sat on the porch nursing his
fresh cast as Oberon paced the flagstones.

"Mead!" Oberon called out upon seeing him. "Have you seen
Mary?"

"No, I haven't. I'd hoped to meet her again today."

"We can't find her. She never leaves . . . where could she be?"
Oberon's long face looked drawn, his eyes afraid.

Mead remembered Mary's plan. "When I talked with her, she
said she hoped to go up on the mountain with Annie or you to see
the Magdalena alpine butterfly."

"Up on the mountain! So that's what she was talking about. I
was too busy, thought she only wanted to go for a walk. She must
have gone by herself, as Annie's come and gone. But that was yesterday—good gods, I hope she's all right!"

"What worries me," Sylvanus put in, "is that Attalus has not
been seen, either."

"Oh, hell." Oberon clenched his fists and looked about in a fever of worry. "Mead, will you help me look for her?"

"Of course!"

"Sylvanus, you're stuck here anyway, so please watch the place and stay near the telephone. We may be required to post bail in Golden if anyone's arrested today."

The two tall, bearded men, one graying, the other not, set off for Magdalena Mountain immediately. Oberon took just enough time to trade his robe for jeans and a flannel shirt and to squeeze into his boots and grab some water, raisins, and a first-aid kit. Mead already wore his boots, and he had some apples from home. Clouds were rising behind the distant summit. Sylvanus wished the pair godspeed as they took off up Cabin Creek for the mountain face.

Oberon said nothing as he led the way. The searchers burned up the creek trail, through the willows, past the pines, and into the subalpine firs. They entered the avalanche trough where it drops from the subalpine, weeping the water for Cabin Creek from its snowfield like some deep tear gland. Mead thought of the annual contest at the lodge, to guess the date when the snow's all gone. Once they reached the rotten snow, a decision had to be made on which way to go. To split up now would be dangerous. Oberon decided they should work uphill in parallel, along the right-hand side of the tear-track cleft, toward the ridge on the north. They would stay in sight of each other, one working his way across the slope a hundred feet or so above the other's traverse.

Magdalena Mountain is a very big peak, and Oberon began to regret that they hadn't called in Park and Front Range search and rescue teams instead of trying to find Mary by themselves. But in his fervor to prove her safe and to keep their order beneath the notice of officialdom as much as possible, poor judgment ruled.

The lay of the land brought the two men together again partway across the great central stone face of the peak, rockpits like pores making every step a gamble. "Watch for orange," Oberon said, "and blue. She was probably wearing a sort of saffron cape over a long blue dress. That's what she's had on lately."

"Right," was all that James could reply, trying to maintain his balance as well as his hopes against the odds of Mary's survival through the night up here so clad. He wondered about the simultaneous absence of Attalus and Mary, but he didn't ask.

Just that filled Oberon's mind. He'd thought that Attalus might have reconciled himself to the women, albeit with great reluctance. How naive! He should have expelled him, even at the cost of unhousing the brotherhood. And he should have listened more carefully to what Mary had proposed, and he should have taken time to come up here with her. Should, should, should— what good are "should haves" when in fact you didn't? And what chance could Mary have up here alone with a psychopath, probably intent on her destruction, on a cold mountain where destruction means nothing?

Thus darkly musing as he watched his every step and the near and far distance too, Oberon almost failed to notice the brown flicker in the foreground—almost, but not quite. Mead saw it too. In the partial sunshine, one of them had kicked up a Magdalena alpine, which settled now between them to resume basking. Its flight was fairly weak, the wings old and faded, but the butterfly was whole and still viable, and for a moment it drew the attention of both distracted men. Mead looked closely, for something about it had struck him. Then he saw what it was: this *Erebia* bore a crisp, shiny brand on its left forewing, the sort of broad imprint, Mead thought, that a bird such as a nighthawk might leave. His mind shot back two thousand miles and two months, to George Winchester's drawer of bill-marked butterflies and the conspicuous gap in the cabinet.

Mead noticed that Oberon was studying the butterfly too, but he felt the grave circumstances scarcely called for small talk about tattooed butterflies, so he left it unremarked. Oberon simply said, "Mary's butterfly. I thought it might be finished by now," and strode off across the talus. His movement put Erebia to flight. Mead took one more look as it disappeared into the horizon of the north ridge, and he muttered, "Damn, I wish I had my net!" Then he felt ashamed, and suffered an insight having to do with loyalty.

That summer, Mead was learning rapidly a truth that few people know, though millions forget it every day: that the heart is a fickle beast, subject to the charms of the moment, prone to forget yesterday's thrall for tomorrow's, under the influence of the novel and the fresh. Whether circus women or saints, cowboy collectors or beak-marked butterflies, someone or something is always lying in wait to grab your attention. Wasn't he ready to die for Mary the other day? And now, with Mary in real danger of dying, he forgets her momentarily in favor of some bird-marked bug. In a strange way, he supposed that was what Noni had been talking about in the hot springs—her conundrum. There was nowhere more to go with that, and an endless expanse of rock to range across in search of Mary. How would they ever find her? Just let her be safe!

As they bought space dearly across the stingy stones, the men cast their eyes in every direction for a stain of saffron, a swatch of blue, a soft form among the hard edges of the rockworld. In his own way, Mead was as anxious as Oberon, as eager to find Mary. He wanted her to know that he didn't think she was mad. Mary Glanville, Mary Magdalene, whoever—just be there! Where the hell *are* you? He just wanted her gentle self to be safe. Oberon's thoughts ran through similar channels, over and over. And neither of them could see how she really *could* be safe.

Roaming the phantasmagorical boulderfall, Mead was haunted
by visions almost like waking dreams, brought on by fatigue, hunger, and worry. The raisins and apples were long gone. Visions of Erebia, Carson, and Annie, of the absent Noni and the missing Mary,
not to mention Molly and, behind them all, his tortured mother,
all these and more trundled through his field of vision as he tried
to place his feet. "This is not fun," he muttered as he lost his balance again and skinned his last fresh knee. What was going on in
Oberon's mind, he could only guess, and scarcely even wanted to
know.

As the sun rises, igniting Magdalena Mountain to a cool yellow,
Mary stirs in her granitic hideout. She has survived the night, and
somehow she doesn't feel cold upon awakening. The fresh scent
of hay fills her nostrils, and she finds that she has pillowed her
head on a pika's stack. She sucks more ice, slaking her thirst and
damping her hunger. Though she longs to stand and stretch her
legs (there is no side to lie on that isn't bruised or sore), she scarcely
dares even to poke her head out. For a tortured hour she lies there,
too petrified to leave her safe haven. Then, at last, she gathers confidence that Attalus might be gone. With the greatest care, she
peers out and around. The sight of a vigilant gray lump on the
ridge turns her stomach sour with fresh fear, and she says, "Oh!"
What if I scream and scream? she thinks. But who would hear,
except him?

Mary can't help sobbing, just skirting resignation. But before her
sobs can gather into a defeated curse and a dead giveaway, she sees
Attalus rise and resolutely cross the ridge to the other side. Clearly,
this is the time to act. She creeps out of her cleft, pika hay in her
hair, and slowly, quietly begins to make her way down the back side

of Magdalena Mountain toward the busy Longs Peak Trail, toward safety in numbers.

There is no sign of her hunter. Her pace quickens as her muscles wake up, but she cannot move swiftly, as stiff and bruised as she is, trying hard not to fall any more. Mary has almost begun to believe she will be safe when a cobble meets her square between the shoulder blades, sending her sprawling onto the rocks below with a thud and a cry. She lies crumpled in the talus like an overheavy marmot dropped by a golden eagle from far above. A pair of circling ravens, disturbed by the spectacle, wheel and whinny away.

Stunned but sentient, groaning, Mary turns over just in time to see the form of Attalus outlined above her, a great leaden cloud eclipsing the silver sky behind him as he raises his right forearm to sling another pellet. Mary hears thunder and feels rain pelt her cheeks just before the stone strikes her left temple, leaving her senseless.

Attalus crows, spittle flecking his jowls, his eyes and forehead red but his slit-thin mouth white. "Now, woman, I shall end all fleshly temptations, as they should have ended before they began!" Straining, he lifts a boulder as big as a basketball to his waist. An old hernia cries out, but he ignores it. "God was *wrong* to drive Eve from the garden. He should have left her there with the serpent and given the rest to Adam!" He fumbles with the boulder as he struggles to raise it high enough to hurl.

Mary's shape lies fluid across the sacrificial slab, still and limp, yet fundamentally female. Attalus looks his victim over in spite of himself, and he drops the rock. The rain comes on now. Her blue dress wetted, Mary's strong thighs and brown areolae show through, and the material gathers darkly at her Y. The monk steps down to the lifeless form. He kneels, running one hand over her breast, another along her thigh. But instead of stiffening, he weeps. Again he gutters, "Anna . . . Anna."

Then he rips his hands away as if they'd been fondling molten ingots. He straightens, raises his swollen face to the gathering weather, and cries, "You see? It's she, SHE . . . WOMAN . . . and it *is* SHE! I didn't do it, didn't, God, oh God. Why did she?" and he crumples, whimpering, in his misery. For a time, he weeps and mumbles confused prayers, imprecations, and babble. Then he struggles up, grunting, to finish what he has begun. He takes up the boulder again in his wet, trembling hands. The rain and cloud and sun dance over the mountain in a confusion of light and darkness.

In a guttural whisper, Attalus speaks: "Scripture says, 'Thou shalt not suffer a witch to live . . . nor an adulteress' . . . and suffer her I have not, and shall not!" He wrests the rock higher, against his belly and then his chest. Panting, he raves: "Jezebel was eaten by dogs for her sins. Many were burned. But you—when you were found out, and the people tried to stone you as instructed, you escaped! Jesus stopped them."

Attalus's words are lost on the rising wind, but there is no one to hear them anyway. "He said, 'Let ye who have not sinned, cast the first stone,' and they dropped their rocks. Fools! Jesus too was bewitched by the temptress. All flesh is weak when you are near . . . even mine, incorrupt, even mine! But you shall corrupt us no longer," he croaks. "I'll make up for Christ's mistake, and He'll thank me for it." His crazed voice rises with the gathering howl on the air. "*I* will finish the job that they abandoned!"

Pressing the stone over his head at last, he shouts, "Sorceress! Whore! WOMAN—DIE!"

Oberon and Mead had reached a spot below the south ridge when the rain began. "We'd better find shelter, Oberon," called Mead. "It can be Electricity City up here!"

"NO! Got to find Mary. She wouldn't have crossed the ridge. Let's work back toward the trough, higher up."

Mead knew they would be prime lightning targets, but Oberon would not be deterred, and they were far from safe shelter in any case. Soaked and slipping on wet rocks, they clambered back across the face. Weirdly, every now and then the sun broke through. There was a sundog over the peak, and once, they saw orange, but it was only a rockslide checkerspot they spooked during one of these sun-breaks. Then the cloud and rain returned, and the thunderstorm broke.

Cold mountain breath howled around them, the rocks became grease beneath their feet, and Mead was afraid. His hair really did stand on end, and Oberon had a ghostly glow about him. They could actually smell the ozone. Mead felt like a sparkplug awaiting ignition.

"Keep looking!" Oberon yelled above the thunder. How stupid, Mead thought, to end my summer cooked on a mountain—even if it is Magdalena Mountain.

His own concern for Mary battled with images of being snug between the sheets at the lodge, safe in Noni's bosom, or someone's. Then a great flash blotted out those thoughts and all others as both men were dashed to the ground. The rocks sang as electrons danced their crazy steps all along the wet circuits of the stone. Fried grass and burning ozone stank in their noses. Blinded for a moment but unhurt, Oberon called, "You all right, Mead?"

"Scared shitless! Get me offa here!"

When they could see again, Oberon signaled toward the trough. "If we get down in there, we won't be as exposed." That sounded good to Mead. They scrambled toward the middle of the mountain. But reaching it, they found the great tear-track running brimful. As one, they both thought to slip down the waterslide of the chute as a quicker way to the shelter of the forest. It was no smooth ride, more like a freefall over Niagara than an otterslide. But it worked, and they were not far from the pines when another pyrotechnic went off in their faces. They went down again, and this time stayed down. The lightning bit stone a hundred yards away. It was the ground flash that got them.

And that's where Annie Cloudcroft found them an hour later.

38

Since completing their twelve-pass circuit, the BFC team had returned to the research house in Lyons, where the hogback meets the mountains and the Morrison Formation gives forth the town's famous red flagstones. Days of spreading specimens and recording data drove the field team close to revolt, so Carolinus Bagdonitz promised them a return to Rocky Mountain National Park, their original hunting grounds. Their collecting permits were good for another month. The members were working on an annotated checklist of the butterflies and moths of the park, and Bagdonitz hoped a quick trip might help fill in some gaps as well as soothe their cabin fever. Like their boss, not to mention Michael Heap, James Mead, and F. M. Brown himself, these kids had grown up on the loose. They'd joined the field team because it promised summers out-of-doors while their peers were working between walls in town.

"We've never light-trapped the high-country moths this late in the summer," CB said. "Sterling, you take half the team into the Never Summers for three days. I'll take the rest of the kids up to the base of Longs Peak. We leave tomorrow at four. Load up. And don't forget the beer, like last time!"

Though the Hamm's would remain in the cars at the trail-head, their packs were heavy with supplies as CB's team trudged up the Longs Peak Trail. Spirits rose with the elevation as the Flying Circus clowned its way up into the alpine. When other hikers challenged their nets, CB said with a straight face that they were sampling killer wasps for the Department of Defense. After their interrogators hurried on, he said to Lisa, "Funny, isn't it? We're cool with the rangers, who dig what we're doing. But these self-appointed game wardens think we're catching all the butterflies, and they want to turn us in."

"Yeah," she said, "as they slap mosquitoes—as if leps weren't insects too. Last time on Hoosier Pass, Nancy and I told one pain-in-the-butt person we were conducting a pollination survey—true enough, in a way—and that satisfied her."

"Good thinking," said the boss. "And after all, back at camp, we do nectar studies." They made camp at Jim's Grove and ranged out for sampling at Mills Moraine, Peacock Pool, Chasm Lake, around Mount Lady Washington, over to the Boulder Field below Storm Peak, and back via Granite Pass. At the first campfire, after a bottle of gentian schnapps made the rounds, CB surprised the team by whipping out Bel's poem and reading it to them:

"Longs' Peacock Lake:
the Hut and its Old Marmot;
Boulderfield and its Black Butterfly;
And the intelligent trail."

One of his colleagues, a professor of Russian literature, had brought it to his attention, and he shared it, and its context, with the team. "I knew you were related to Humbert," joshed Kate. But a genuine thrill ran around the fire ring as they realized they were in the very place where Vladimir Nabokov had commemorated Magdalena in his latest novel.

From every point, they shared the presence and the view of that great, improbably carved chunk, Longs Peak, with its flat top and flat face and every other feature anything but flat. It was named after Colonel Stephen H. Long, who sighted the mountain from the Poudre River in 1819 but never set foot upon it. Perhaps a better nominee would have been John Wesley Powell, the one-armed conservationist who first climbed it in 1868. Instead, he got Lake Powell, the abomination that inundated Glen Canyon and inspired Abbey's fictional insurrection in *The Monkey Wrench Gang*.

Or call it Tahosa, the local Indian name for "dwellers of the mountaintops." The mountain was scaled hundreds of times by Enos Mills and those he guided, by thousands more since, and was admired by millions. The next day, one or two hardy truants from the BFC became the latest to reach the summit by way of the Keyhole, a steep and stony route. The others worked its flanks. At night they all pupated in thick down against the deepening cold, as strange, hardy moths that generate their own body heat circled in toward their black lights.

The catch for three nights numbered only 203 moths, but among them could be counted several rarities, moths new to the state and park lists, a postglacial relict tiger moth with sharply striped primaries and hindwings of delicate rose that had been found no nearer than Montana, and a species of owlet moth possibly new to science. The cracks flew as to whether it should be dubbed *Icyassus bagdonitzii* or *Longspikus marmota*. Randy suggested *Humberta lolita*, since the moth had a slender, golden-haired thorax, and it had been collected by the youngest female member of the BFC, Elise, a new recruit to CB's tutelage.

"Very funny," said the prof. "You are *not* walking the intelligent trail he talks about. But there actually is a connection to Nabokov here. Professor Strelnikov told me that when Nabokov was a boy in Russia, he proposed a new species of *Plusia* to the experts, only to learn that he had been gazumped by a German named Kretschmar. Out of revenge, Nabokov gave that name to a blind man in one of his stories. And this moth appears to be a plusiine; we could redeem things by naming it *Plusia nabokovii*—though there's already a Nabokov's blue and a Nabokov's satyr."

"I know what Tiny would call it," said Lisa.

"What's that?"

"Bait!"

The third morning out, ice on their sleeping bags, food depleted, schnapps extinct, beer back at the cars, and diminishing returns setting in on the traplines, CB and crew decided to head down. Their planned route out, not exactly direct—as no one was eager to trade the high country for the parched plain below—would take them under Columbine Falls, below Ship's Prow and the north summit of Magdalena Mountain, down that peak's north ridge to the Roaring Fork, and thence back to the main trail again, with a fair bit of bushwhacking along the way. Sterling's band would meet them at the Longs Peak campground, having driven back across Trail Ridge Road from the Never Summer Range. If they got there on schedule, there might be some beer left.

Late afternoon found the trekkers taking a break in the lee of Magdalena Mountain. The weather began to close in, and they all looked up and around. The wind got up, and a few clouds rose. Kate said to Lisa, "Magdalena Mountain! What a name."

"Yes, it is. So Bel saw the Black Butterfly at Peacock Pool, but I wonder if anyone's collected *E. magdalena* up there on the mountain itself."

"Should be perfect habitat—rocks, rocks, and more rocks. We really ought to have a voucher specimen from here."

"It's too late in the season, too late in the day, and too cold, isn't it?" This from Andy, the most promising ecologist in the group.

"Maybe," said CB. "But that's never stopped us before. Anyway, Mike Heap would never forgive us if we didn't try. Shall we take a look?" That was all the challenge the BFC needed to delay their descent a little longer. No one was quite ready to abandon the field for the classroom, least of all the boss.

No sooner had they taken to the rocks than the clouds grouped overhead like a rugby scrum and a light rain began. They donned their army surplus ponchos, stinking as old rubber does, but serviceable. Then the rain slackened, and the sun came back out for an encore, as it sometimes will in the arctic-alpine zone, just long enough to put butterflies to flight and make a rubberized poncho a sweaty thing.

The butterfly in question was a chimera, a swirling sliver off the black cloud. So fresh was its image in his mind's eye, it took CB a second to realize that he was actually seeing a Magdalena in real life. He hadn't given it any odds at all, in spite of his pep talk. But always the enthusiast, he was never one to dampen the plan for fun or adventure. He figured that if he was able to get these kids excited about anything out here, long odds or not, he was doing his job. Who knew? Maybe the day would come when young people would no longer go outside to get their thrills. But not for now, not if he could help it. And there it was—or was it? "Look!" he called to the others, who were debating turning back downhill. "There's Maggie after all!"

For Erebia's part, he shouldn't have been here at all. But his recent proclivity for the upper slopes, two alarming encounters with large moving objects, and his subsequent pursuit of a fresh female had brought him to the lip of the arête. And when the wind arose, he found himself lifted over to the north slope for the second time in his life. But unlike the other time, when he landed on the snow-field and nearly died there, he was now much lower, and most of the snow had melted. Now he was in new territory, and the weather was unsettled: one moment wholly threatening, the next alluring for a last forage before what could be his final night, if he only knew. But he did not. He merely followed the mercurial cues of the fugitive sun, as always.

"This late, it's probably a female," said CB. "Maybe we can get some eggs to rear them."

Bagdonitz, fit but you couldn't say lean, puffed after the insect, raised by a shaft of sun but about to take to its sepulcher before the rain came in earnest. "You come up from below, Lisa—we'll double-team her." Between the two experienced netters, Erebia fluttered, fell, and basked to suck the last warmth from the late beam. "Hold on—nah, it's a rag—an old brown one, probably a spent male." Then, "Aw, heck—let's go for it anyway, for the voucher. The NPS folks will want it for the database. Old guy's done his job." Several members spread out in a circular gauntlet around the late-season Magdalena.

Deviating eastward toward the high ridge, they tracked the insect from perch to perch. Rain and sunshine and even a spit of sleet kept trading places, putting the butterfly up and down like an ebony yo-yo, and still they followed. One or two snapped a net down, but each time the elusive animal squeezed out through the rocks like oil. It was as if they each knew that their idyll was over, and only this hunt could prolong it. All Erebia knew was that something beyond his experience kept disturbing his perch as his old muscles grew colder and weaker.

"I think he went behind that boulder up there, Boss," Kevin called as he went on point. "Maybe we can find it in the rockpile."

CB looked, spooked it again, then followed the alpine down into a hidden depression at the base of a broad scree that assumed the angle of repose below the ridgeline. Having lost sight of the creature again, he scanned the rocks around him. At last he saw it, attempting to bask on a wet bare stone of little warmth. "What that butterfly is," he huffed, "is *tough*." He was of half a mind to let it go for its valor.

The butterfly hunkered. Bagdonitz approached, raised his net, and paused, savoring that moment of suspense just before the strike, that nanosecond of indecision that often costs collectors their quarry at the very last moment. About to clap his net over the brown butterfly, he heard a strange, gargling noise on the wind. It sounded almost human. He looked up, and the butterfly flew. "Damn!" he said, and took up the pursuit again around a massive boulder and across the open rockslide. On the last of the day's sunbeams, Erebia fluttered feebly over the ridge, back to home territory, escaping onto the infinite and kindly face of Magdalena Mountain. Then clouds closed for good and the rain came hard, as if someone had pulled a plug in the sky.

Bagdonitz abandoned the chase and wished the butterfly godspeed. Then he heard the strange noise again, and it sounded even more like a human voice raised in anger, though he couldn't make it out. He turned in the direction it seemed to come from, covered some ground, and rounded another great screening rock. And there, straight ahead, he beheld a monstrous spectacle: thirty feet beyond, a man was lofting a boulder overhead, looking for all the world as if he was about to drop it on a woman lying still at his feet. The man screamed, "Sorceress! Whore! WOMAN—DIE!"

"Hold it!" Bagdonitz shouted. "What the *hell* do you think you're doing?" He lunged toward the crazy scene. Some of the others followed on his flying heels. None could fathom what seemed to be happening. Scrambling up the rocks toward the gruesome tableau, they gave out shrieks, squeals, the flight honks of wildebeests on the run from lions, the roars of the lions in pursuit, all the noises a circus should make when busted loose in chaos.

Attalus wheeled to see what this commotion was that rose over the wind and his own wails. His foot slipped on the rain-licked granite. Slowly but irrevocably, he tipped, and as gravity took over, he lost his hard-won grip on the hundredweight stone. The jealous mountain sucked its own back down to earth. Attalus struck ore with his bare head one second before the boulder went to ground in the same place. His brain burst from his smashed skull, returning its only true knowledge to the lichens whence it came, and freeing its madness to the palpable ozone of the sane, sane sky.

"Oh, God!" cried Bagdonitz, struggling to believe what his eyes told him.

"Oh, Christ!" said Lisa, turning aside to vomit behind a rock.

All the others, for once dumbstruck, were thinking, Oh, gross!

Carolinus hastened to the woman. She was alive, but this storm was gathering force, and she lay wet and cold as well as bleeding. "We've got to get her to shelter," CB cried above the whining wind. He knew that caution would dictate making her warm and leaving her inert and still against possible back injury, then sending for experienced rescue help. But given the danger of lightning and exposure, there wasn't time for that. He ripped open his pack for the first-aid kit, applied a couple of bandages, and wrapped Mary in his parka.

"We'd better head straight for the trailhead and the ranger station," CB said. Handing Randy his net, he adjusted his pack and collected Mary in his arms. She hung limp, her bloodied head resting against his big shoulder. Blood cemented her dark hair to his face as he carried her down the rockslide one stone at a time.

"Can you handle her alone, CB?"

"I am a giant of a man," he said. "I can manage." But they knew their leader, and behind his confidence they heard fear for this woman, so hurt, so terrorized, and, for all they knew, so near death.

39

Sylvanus sat alone in a corner of the Great Hall of the Mountain Monastery, his leg propped up, trying to read without success. His ankle throbbed, and his anxiety grew as the sky over Magdalena Mountain darkened from lapis through steel to graphite, then slate. The wind gathered; it whispered down the great stone chimney that Sylvanus had better build a fire, for if Oberon and James ever did return, with or without Mary, they'd need it. He hobbled to the grate and wrestled a big beetle-mined log into place behind the andirons. Then he laid kindling of ponderosa pine needles, beetle-bark, and old Catholic tracts underneath, and applied a long wooden match to the pyre.

Soon a fire blew back at the wind, driving the chilly howl from the chimney. Warmth began to flow from the reddening wood and reflect from the black stone fireback. Sylvanus pulled his chair close. Tending the blaze, he murmured into it, as much to drive off loneliness and apprehension as to romance the licking flames.

"A fireplace: perfect altar to Pan. Here we give wood back to ash and air, taking warmth and cheer for our part. No tree that grows escapes the cycle, though it may be petrified for the ages. Here we hasten the process, making warmth, not war, with trees, leaving the better part of the forest to grow and die and rot and grow again so that our Grove too might prosper. In the benevolent shade of the ambered aspen, in the beneficent glow of the embered pine, all things thrive and nothing diminishes."

Sylvanus extemporized. He enjoyed making up reverential homilies to express his idea of the Pan-Pacific principle. But he did so mostly alone, in company of firelight, sunshine, or moonglow, and he always found it a soporific practice. Now his fringed chin tumbled onto his trunky chest and he dozed before the fire, comfortable yet troubled in his dreams of dark figures playing a deadly hide-and-seek among the rocks above.

Outside, aspens trembled more than usual as the wind stiffened. Daylight diminished and firelight flickered, casting between them a strange warm glow. If crickets watch rooms, as they seem to do, those posted in the cracks about the hearth—that classic cricket habitat—would have seen in that glow a chamber a hundred leaps long and fifty across, bottomed with old, scratched, once-polished pine and topped with rough beams so high that only by crawling up the scroll-carved wainscoting might they gauge the loft of the ceiling; long walls window-lined; others, once hung with portraits of saints and abbots, now lined with a neo-"Belgian" Taiwanese tapestries of *The Peaceable Kingdom*, only vaguely suggestive of the originals in Bruges.

Yet a warm hearth nonetheless, nocturnal lodgings for hundreds of generations of their ancestors, where the gryllids would note the flagstone floor, the terra-cotta sunrays set into the chimneybreast built of massive, lichen-painted blocks of granite; ornamented iron screens at the sides, cast in a fancy fish-and-seaweed motif; the oval mouth opening into a gaping fireplace with deep inglenooks on either side intended for rising bread, dripping roast on a spit, or bone-chilled grandparents; the heavy andirons and grate containing just now a live fire; and, before the blaze, a dozing Druid in a rocking chair.

But the blaze shrank to a flicker, the wind in the chimney (its fingers fiddling at the battens) gained the advantage, and the warmth of the scene threatened to flee before the glowering cloud of the late afternoon. One of the crickets chirruped louder than usual, waking up the watchman who then rallied the fire back into life.

Sylvanus checked the old carriage clock on the rock-and-pine mantelpiece. Annie had instructed him to call NPS and request a full-scale search for four or five persons missing on the mountain if she failed to return by six o'clock. They both knew that that was foolishly late, but the order tried to keep as low a profile as possible with the Park, existing as it did at the superintendent's pleasure. The order owned the buildings, but much of the land was occupied under a special-use permit that was vaguely grandfathered in place. Piss off the Park Service, and they could be out. The carriage clock read 5:48. Sylvanus jerked alert and began to prepare his speech to the ranger, who would not be remotely amused at anything he had to say.

Then the fire guttered as the wind blew in from a new direction. Mountain Annie stood in the open doorway. "I've got them," she said in a cryptic whisper, and disappeared again without. Sylvanus let out a deep sigh of relief that changed into one of worry when he realized that she could be bearing corpses. He clumbered to the tall, heavy door and pulled the hasp, opening it inward in time to see Annie tugging the second of two limp, Indian-blanketed forms from a travois hitched behind her big gray. They looked like corpses, after all. But Annie said, "Help me if you can, get them to the fireplace."

Between them, the two sentient ones in the room hauled the two who were still to woven mats before the hearth. The crickets gave up their places to those in greater need, who breathed, barely. Slowly, blue lips purpled, waxen cheeks were massaged to milky pink. "Their pulses seem okay, if not strong, but they could have arrhythmia. Please hurry and call 911."

Sylvanus reached for the telephone to summon an ambulance.

"Annie, the phone is dead. It must be the storm. And there are no cars here. We'd better forget about getting an ambulance. But Thomas is up in his hut, behind a big pointed boulder, a hundred yards northwest of the Forest Grove. He set my leg—he should be there." He kept on warming the storm's first victims while Annie ran for Thomas. Though not one of the new brotherhood, the old relic of the previous order of healers had remained on the premises, sometimes ministering to the members, as he had to Mary.

Annie returned in fifteen minutes with Thomas in his ragged brown robe and Gore-Tex poncho and carrying an old-fashioned black doctor's bag. Shyness and worry vied over the little man's face. Weathered yet smooth, ageless but growing old, his skin glistened with rain and perspiration after the dash through the pines in Annie's tow. She took him by surprise, the first woman to visit his hermitage since the nursing nuns, decades ago. But he came without question.

Annie wrung her wet, chilled hands before the fire, wondering whether to try to get out through the storm on her horse. "I left my truck and trailer in Allenspark," she said. "If I ride there on Grimalkin, I could drive to the hospital in Lyons . . ."

"No need, no need," Thomas called from the hearth. He was administering shots of epinephrine to the men's bared arms. "Their heartbeats are steady and regular, vital signs all stabilizing, from what I can tell. They're cold, but in the nineties—not dangerously hypothermic. You got there in time, thank God."

"What do you think happened to them?"

"I'd say a little ground flash from lightning. Light case, no obvious burns or cardiac arrest. I've seen much worse. But it's good that you got to them when you did, Miss Cloudcroft, and with blankets. Those are the good ones Charlie Eagle Plume sells, aren't they? Every now and then I slip out to barter some dried venison for one." Sylvanus raised an eyebrow. All these years, he'd never known that Thomas ever hunted, or left the place. "And your fire, Sylvanus. They couldn't have lasted long without that."

"But they're okay?" Annie begged for confirmation.

"I think so. Please prepare some hot broth, for when they are able to take it."

Already, they were stirring. Sylvanus eventually produced a spiced bouillon, and in another twenty minutes all five were sipping it as steam rose from tea in cups, from wet clothing on racks beside the hearth, and from their hair.

Swathed in a warm robe, Oberon spoke with a catch in his weak voice. "Mary?"

"We haven't found her, Oberon. Don't give up hope—she's probably safe somewhere. Just drink the broth. At least you two idiots are safe."

"You must have rescued us, Annie. Were we hit?"

"Thomas reckons ground flash. The entire slick surface of that mountain must have been conductive. But you two were darned lucky—only knocked you out, apparently. I've been on rescues where people were badly burned or killed by ground shock or direct hits. And I was lucky too—lucky to have brought Grimalkin today, lucky to have the travois along, lucky you'd made it nearly to the trail—hell, lucky to have spotted you at all."

"Lucky with the travois, or prescient?" Oberon asked.

"Were you expecting bodies?" Mead asked, his first words since "Oh, shit!" on the rocks.

"Well, I almost got 'em, by the looks of you. Or maybe a broken leg? Anyway, I knew I couldn't carry anyone down by myself. Actually, I had the travois out for a demonstration at the lodge. I came by here afterward so Grimalkin could visit Betsy, and Sylvanus told me you two were missing. Faster to sling the travois and set out from here than load, ride home, and drive."

"Well, thank the gods," said Oberon, "and thank *you*, Annie. I didn't use the best judgment up there. I should have called the Park. Sorry, James, for getting you into it."

"It's okay, we're down. Is there a search on for Mary?"

"Telephone's out; no way to reach them," said Sylvanus. "Maybe in the morning, if we haven't heard anything, someone can walk out to the rangers."

"But that will be two nights!" Oberon erupted feebly. "She'd never survive the storm, even if she has lived this long . . . if Attalus hasn't found her."

"Do you really think Attalus would harm Mary?" Annie asked.

"Well, he has threatened her. *Where is he?*"

"Maybe, feeling threatened, she just left," said Annie, "and will contact us later."

"Or maybe Attalus kidnapped her," offered Sylvanus, "just to take her far away and drop her, as the Park Service does with bad bears."

Oberon did not appreciate their ideas. "I was too damn busy to go with her," he said.

"Me, too," said Annie. "She asked me to take her up."

"And I was away," said Mead.

Lightning flared outside, and its recent victims jumped. Thunder percussed. The power went out, dowsing the few small lights that had been lit and casting the room into an even deeper gloom. Mead felt a prick of guilt. Hadn't he urged Mary to go see the butterfly? The others nursed their own guilt as moroseness overcame the little cluster huddled around the fireplace, shoving out the relief of their own rescue. Then the flames sputtered as the door flew open and Carolinus Bagdonitz took its place. "We have a woman," he said, "and she is hurt."

Annie rushed to the knot of people at the door. "It's Mary!" she cried, "and"—she checked to be sure—"she's alive!"

Mead made the sound a child makes when its parent banishes a nightmare. "Thank God," he uttered at the same moment Oberon choked out "Thank Pan!"

"Thank CB while you're at it," said a young voice from the doorway behind Bagdonitz, but the teacher hushed him with a knuckle in the ribs.

They laid Mary down on the mat in the warm shadows of one of the inglenooks, gently pillowing her battered head. The old hermit, paramedic of the mountain, drew near. With Annie's assistance, and for the second time, he tenderly and adroitly examined an unconscious Mary Glanville.

"May we come in and get dry, please?" Bagdonitz asked.

"Oh, yes, all of you. I'm sorry! Come in here, get near the fire," Sylvanus insisted, promising more hospitality than the already crowded fireside could readily deliver. He threw on more wood. As the dripping contingent of the BFC pressed close to the hearth, the steam from so many sopping bodies—not to mention the smoky, sweaty pong of the unwashed trampers—rose into the beams as if the clouds themselves had breached the sanctum.

By now dusk was indiscriminable from tempest, and little light came through the eastern windows. The wind howled like wildebeests wounded in pride. "Carolinus," Mead called out above it, struggling to be heard. "Sterling, Kate. Hello, everybody."

"Why, it's young James!" CB recognized the third recumbent form, if not his partner. As for Mary, he still had her blood on his cheek. "What happened to you, son?"

"A light touch of lightning," Mead replied.

Kate was beside him in a cricket's breath, and his head was suddenly in a better place.

"Wow," said Brian. "Guys got hit by lightning and they aren't even dead."

As soon as Oberon saw that Mary was in Thomas's hands, and Annie's, and there was nothing he could do for now, he turned and said, "Thank you with all our hearts for bringing Mary to us, sir. Will you please tell us what happened to her?"

"You're very welcome. We did nothing but show up by luck, and then nothing more than anyone else would have done."

"Not that they could have," said Randy.

"Go on."

"Well, I don't know how she got to be where she was, but when we came upon your friend up above Peacock Lake, a maniac was about to drop a big rock on her."

"Attalus!" cried Oberon. "He really meant to kill her after all!"

Annie and Mead looked on, appalled, as Sylvanus shook his head sadly.

Carolinus went on. "I guess we disturbed him, and he dropped the rock."

"So where is the bastard? Did he get away?"

"Well, not hardly . . ."

"He slipped, and the rock fell on his head," said Lisa, "and his brains just busted out." Saying it, she almost repeated her previous performance.

Thomas crossed himself.

"*Very* gross," added the member who'd been closest to the scene.

"Anyway, we carried her . . ."

"*You* carried her," came a chorus.

". . . down to the trail and on down to the ranger station. There was only a volunteer on hand, with no power or phone, and she said we'd better come here, where there might be some medical help."

Oberon, torn between gratitude and rage, uttered a muddle of both. Then he said, "Thomas, how is she?"

"It sounds as if she very nearly died. But she will not, I think."

Oberon let out a little sound somewhere between a groan and a sob.

"She may have a concussion, but I can't feel any fracture of her skull or other bones. All her limbs move. She must have X-rays as soon as possible. She is bruised all over, has some cuts and scratches. We've dressed the worst, but none seem deep or dangerous. She is not comatose, her pulse and blood pressure are strong. She's just sleeping deeply, as when she arrived here the first time with you and Attalus."

Sylvanus continued his diagnosis. "Miss Cloudcroft thinks there was no bodily assault, apart from the blows." (*Rape* was not a word he ever could have uttered.) "And no serious exposure, which is re-markable, since she must have been out all night at high altitude without protection. I don't know how that could be—it nearly froze last night."

"More luck," muttered Mead, "or something."

"Oh, and one more thing," said Thomas. "Minor, but odd." They all waited to hear, as he looked around the curious faces. "Mary has a number of small red welts around her body—they look very much like fleabites."

In the general hubbub at that end of the Great Hall, no one noticed when another two forms slipped in from the farther, darker side, where the glimmer from the flames didn't reach. Thomas was say-ing, "Yes, I believe Mary will live, though I can't say whether this additional blow to her head will have any effect. But now I have a question: Who *is* this poor sister, whom I have twice examined now in piteous condition?"

"There is some question . . ." Sylvanus suggested.

"Not in her mind," Mead interjected. "She is—"

"That's Mary Jordan," came a voice from the back of the knot. Then another, similar, pitched just a fifth higher, "No, that's Mary Glanville!"

The first continued, "I recognize her from Yale." The second fol-lowed, "Yeah? Well, *I* recognize her from the home."

"Yale?" Mead echoed in perplexity. "Who said that?"

"Hi, Jim. Hi, CB, Annie. We came in a back door, I guess. We've just been listening until things calmed down and our eyes got adjusted. Hope nobody minds."

"Well, I'll be. Michael, you ol' son!" Carolinus said, giving Heap a big bear hug.

Annie's was more of a mountain lion hug. "And who's this with you?"

"This is my brother, Howard Heap. I sprang him from his digs in the big D for a couple days out in the hills. We stayed in a cabin down at Raymond where we used to go with our mom. We were on our way to Baldpate for a bite when these guys passed us at a hell of a rate and we thought we'd better see what's up."

"We were in a hurry," said Lisa.

"With good reason, it sounds like. Anyway, I'd recognize the Nordic Green Aphid anywhere, even in a hurricane, which it is out there, by the way. We just followed them and blew in in their wake. Playing hero again, huh, CB?"

"But Michael," James said, "you say you knew Mary at *Yale?*"

"That's right. She was a grad student in the Yale Divinity School last time I was back in New Haven, maybe three or four years ago, as a guest lecturer for a course George was team-teaching on Evolution and Other Creation Myths. He asked me to come speak on creationism in the rural West—it's alive and well out where I live."

"But how did Mary—" Oberon began to ask.

"Mary was taking the class. She was striking and smart and warm, I thought. We had a good talk at dinner with the Winchesters and her own prof from the D. School before I left. He was pretty cool, too—the university chaplain, an agnostic named Reverend Caskette. It was a memorable evening. Except that her husband, an economist named Max Jordan, was kind of a jerk; he kept belittling her idea for a thesis topic, as I recall."

"Which was?" asked Annie.

"Well, let's see if I can remember." He tugged his long, woolly beard as if it were a gong pull. "Yeah, of course, that's it! She was interested in Saint Mary Magdalene, and how she became a sexual scapegoat for the church, or something like that. I told her about Maggie May the butterfly and suggested that George could show it to her in the Peabody."

"Good God," said James.

"So to speak," said someone.

"We stayed in touch for a while. I got a postcard from Egypt a couple of years ago . . . and then one from Marseilles. Later I heard from a mutual friend that she was divorced, and casting about for a suitable surname; I never learned what it was. I knew her only as Mary Jordan."

"Ah—so perhaps that's why the police found no Mary Glanville after the accident," said Oberon. "Are you *sure* this is the woman you're thinking of?"

Heap regarded the reclining woman again, bending closer to examine her face in the firelight. "This is Mary, all right . . . just as striking as I remember her, even with the bandage." He shivered, in spite of the fire. "But what the hell is she doing *here*, and why did someone try to murder her, for Christ's sake?"

"She came here in our care," said Oberon, "having escaped from a nursing home in the city. She was kept there after a bad auto accident a year ago. We found her on Loveland Pass—the would-be murderer and I—after she got away."

"Right!" spoke up the soft-voiced Howard, suddenly excited. "I know about that part! I live in that in-sti-TOO-tion. But I come and go. Mary couldn't. I got to know her last year." He cleared his husky smoker's throat. "She wanted to kill herself. I told her not to—told her what my big brother here tells me, that it doesn't solve anything. It never works, anyway . . . you always come back." Howard spoke slowly, carefully, enunciating each word. Eyebrows went up at his hypothesis of circularity. "I was in a car wreck too," he said, "I know. Anyway, Mary wanted out, so I said, why don't you just go? And one day, she was gone. I was sad to see her leave, she made that place so much nicer. But she really needed to get out. Boy, did it cause a hassle around the home when she did! HAAA!" Howard roared an odd, hoarse laugh, ending on a falsetto note as he recalled the incident. "So now she's here. Wow. Wooow. Whoooo!" He spoke for everyone with that final, feral whoop.

"Wow is right," said Oberon. "Thank you both for filling us in. So now she's suffered another head injury."

"Not as bad as that Attalus cat," said Randy.

"Hush!" said Carolinus.

"So we brought her here, *much* against Attalus's will. It seems she may have been bound for here in the first place."

"Cool!" said Brian.

"Will you please keep your corks in?" CB pleaded.

"Was she interested in the place because of its name?" Michael asked. "That would accord with her studies of Mary Magdalene."

"More than that," Annie said, taking up the narration, as Oberon was taxed from the effort. "When Mary arrived here, she believed"—she glanced over at Oberon, who nodded—"she *believes* that she actually *is* Mary Magdalene, reincarnated."

"Really?" asked Michael.

"Really!" said his brother. "I knew that."

"Heavy duty," "Weird," and similar outcries emerged from the kids, whom CB could no more stifle than he could tie down a circus tent in the wind outside.

"Mary has no recollection of being Mary Glanville, except for the name itself. She's a lot clearer on the other, ancient Mary," explained Annie. "Oh! I hope her new injury doesn't make her delusions worse!"

"So who's to say it's a delusion, Annie dear?" Michael asked, surprising his friends, who knew him as an unreconstructed rationalist. "I don't believe in reincarnation as such—can't imagine any biological mechanism for it. But I do believe in separate realities.

My brother Howard here suffered severe frontal-lobe damage from a head-on with a cattle truck. His reality is a little canted away from mine sometimes . . ."

"*I'll* say," said Howard, smiling aslant, one eyebrow up almost to his scar.

". . . but it is totally true for him, as a psychiatrist friend helped me to see. His mythos about the accident, its prequels and sequels, is every bit as real in his mind as Maggie is in mine. Maybe it's the same way for Mary.

"Besides," Michael added, "lots of scholars come to relate so closely to their subjects that they virtually become them. I daresay George Winchester would love to be Charles Darwin aboard the *Beagle*. Sometimes I think I'm watching the rocks below through Maggie's eyes. Mary obviously admires the other Mary immensely. So if she has *become* her—let it be! Lucky woman to be who she wishes to be."

"And to be alive," said Thomas, silent through all of this.

"Amen," said Kate. "That goes for these guys, too."

Thomas, still a Roman Catholic, asked, "And what of Attalus? Should someone lead me up to him when the storm abates?"

"Absolutely not!" said CB. "Unless you can pull off a Lazarus, you can't help that sonofabitch. No offense."

"No offense taken. I've heard worse, even up here," said Thomas.

"Or unless somebody here has more faith than I think they do. Did you guys notice that Jesus has a lightning rod down there?" Sterling meant that crack to be for his teammates, but just then there was a lull, and everyone heard it. He blushed and sputtered, "Sorry about that."

"Worse than that, too, has been spoken here, I assure you," said Thomas. "In fact, that sentiment has been observed before. And I suspect he may need it out there tonight! In any case, when I asked if I should go up to Attalus, I was thinking in terms of administering last rites, ex post facto, and recovering his body."

"I'm not even sure I could find the spot again," said CB. "Or"—with a shudder—"that I'd really want to." The shudder spread and became a collective shiver, whether from contemplating the beastly weather beyond the log walls or from the thought of the dead monk's sodden body and shattered head running off the rocks above.

Oberon spoke. "I call for a consensus."

"But, Oberon," Sylvanus objected. "There are just the two of us here!"

"Then it should be easy, shouldn't it? I propose that Attalus be left to rot among the rocks and the ravens. Since he was both a Christian and a pantheist, that is the worst curse and the best blessing I can contrive for him. Let his body return to nature like all the rest and his tortured madness dissipate onto the pure mountain air. That should be last rites enough for anyone."

"So be it," said Sylvanus. "It seems both the loving and the just thing to do."

Thomas held his peace, and no one dared make any cracks at all. At least not for the minute of silence that no one called for but everyone observed. And then someone from the circus spoke, borrowing a line from every B movie with a body to account for:

"And the authorities?"

"For now," said Oberon, "the only authorities concerned are the rockslide rodents whose territories his corpse pollutes. Let them deal with the formalities as they see fit."

"Nicely spoken, Oberon," said Annie, "and I agree that the question is irksome—but it's relevant too. Surely the law—"

"Look—" Oberon interrupted. "Does anyone here want to drag Mary into court to relive her ordeal? Do any of you witnesses want to try to explain all this to an inquest?" For once, all three rings were still, along with the ringmaster and everyone else. "The crime is redressed. After a while, I'll notify the archdiocese that Attalus has left us over irreconcilable differences of procedure. He has no family, and no one else to worry about it."

"But what if a hiker finds him up there?" asked one of the students.

"I believe you were far off the trail, yes? Between the scavenging of ravens, coyotes, and deer mice, it is unlikely that anyone ever will. And if human remains should be found up there one day, well then, he was hunting lichens, as he was accustomed to do, and must have suffered a lethal fall. Everyone who knows what happened is in this room. Other than his, no crime has been committed, nor any injustice. I say, leave it. Are there any objections?"

Only the fire spoke. The conspiracy was sealed. And fifteen years later, some of those present would remember this decision when they heard that Ed Abbey had died and his body disappeared into the Pinacate Desert without a death certificate, his last instructions to his friends having simply been, "Lots of rocks."

"Has anyone got a beer?" asked Carolinus Bagdonitz.

40

A kind of resolution seemed to have settled over the group, who were now mostly dry and warm. Beer, brandy, red wine, cocoa, and broth were circulating along with what food Sylvanus could find. Kate sat with Mead and stroked his thunderstruck head in her lap as Annie did Oberon's. Mead, dressed now in a dry robe of the pagan brothers, lay back and let the fire's glow fill him. He thought he might sleep again. Then a new volley of lightning ignited, making him start in reaction as he never had before. He spilled Kate's wine. "Sorry," he said. "That may be a permanent condition after today."

"It's only jeans," said Kate. "It'll wash out."

"Uh, good. But I meant my response to the fireworks. Now I know why dogs go under the bed in electrical storms."

Kate thought of a related, altogether preferable response, but kept it to herself. Mead was in no state for play. That did not keep him from making the most of the proffered lap, or from loving it when Kate painted his temples with feathery strokes. If lightning is what it takes for this, he thought, hit me again.

The lightning had also served to block the glare of the headlights that shone uphill as a car turned off the highway toward the chapel. Thunder followed like the bass drumrolls in *Lohengrin*, and a dam broke overhead as an inch of rain fell on the roof of the Great Hall in thirty seconds. Or so it seemed to those mesmerized within. When, at the same instant that a fat pine knot exploded in the fire, the great lion's-head knocker came clapping down on the door three times, more than one body jerked like a tickled cricket.

A member of the field team closest to the door asked, "Should I open it?"

"Of course!" said Oberon. "Now who could this be?"

Aided by the tug-of-war wind, the heavy door swung open to reveal one large figure and one petite one in the cast firelight. They stepped into the beam of a lantern, and Mead yelped like a cat mistaken for a log and tossed on the fire. "Jesus!"

"No, just George."

"You can tell," a smart-assed field assistant pointed out. "No lightning rod."

"And Noni!"

"Hello, James. Nice dress. Who's the pretty woman?"

"Greetings, James," said George. "How are my roaches doing?"

Before Mead could even begin to reply to either or even ask himself if they were really there or just part of some strange, post-shock dream before the fire, Oberon raised his torso and issued a labored greeting. "Professor Winchester? Welcome to Magdalena Mountain. Forgive me for not standing. We've had a couple of shocks here . . . I'm delighted you could accept my invitation, and glad to meet you at last. I am October Carson."

James Mead, bolt-struck all over again, just lay back and gaped. George Winchester knelt beside October-cum-Oberon, extended his hand, and expressed concern over his present condition. Noni

Blue disappeared into a welcoming and admiring knot of young male lepidopterists. Then the door of the Great Hall burst open again as an ebullient crowd of nature monks and feminist peaceniks blew in. Fresh from the antinuclear demo, jail, and the storm, which seemed to be waning at last, the returning brothers and sisters filtered into the room. Providentially, they had stopped at a liquor store and a pizza place in Golden before the power went out all along the Front Range. One by one they were filled in on events, in varying versions.

Catherine Greenland spotted Oberon's horizontal form and came over to him. "Catherine," he said.

"Try Cybele."

"Eh?"

"You guys can't have all the fun. Now that you're finally letting the Goddess into her own Grove, we've decided to adopt the goddess names of the fritillaries. I'm Cybele, and we've got an Aphrodite, an Astarte, both a Freija and a Frigga—gave the clerk fits at the county jail."

"That's a hoot, Cybele—but how did you know those were fritillary names?"

"I told you we were going to be studying our *Peterson Field Guides.*"

"So how did it go?"

"Well. But it's a long row to hoe. We all agreed that we can imagine a day when both Rocky Flats and the Rocky Mountain Arsenal will become wildlife preserves. It might not be in our time, but we're helping it along."

"Good work. And you're joining us?"

"We are. At least for the winter. We'll see how it all goes."

"Spoken like a true Great Mother, which is what the Romans called Cybele, yes?"

"Well, I'm hardly that. But it's a pretty name, as is the English: great spangled fritillary!"

Oberon leaned back into Annie's lap and closed his eyes.

Kate got up to pee. Mead, unsteady and dizzy, standing on his own feet for the first time since electricity had taken him down, stepped outside to do the same: they'd been pumping him full of fluids for hours.

Noni intercepted him. "Ducking out, huh?" Now it was hardly raining outside, the wind down to a light gale. She pulled the door shut behind them. "Oh, James!" She embraced him around the waist, almost knocking him over, and he held her silky head against his chest.

"I came here with George because I heard you were here—I want you to come back to Gothic with me for the last of the field season and then travel with me in the mountains until we both have to leave. Will you come? I've missed you so much."

"Noni, Noni." Mead struggled to stand, and to think—to not cry and hold his pee and speak all at the same time. He was never very good at even double tasking. "No," he said. "I can't. There are things I need to finish up here."

"So I see. You jerk!"

"What . . . you mean Kate, in there? Oh, Noni, she was just being nice to me because I was hurt. I like Kate, and she likes me, but I hardly know her."

"Really?"

"Really. But you don't mean it, anyway. No holds, right? And isn't it a good thing, with you off to Cambridge?"

"You're right, I don't mean it. I was just spitting out quid pro quo and it came out sounding like *jerk*. I'm sorry. But, James, I've changed my mind."

"You're not going to Cambridge after all?"

"Yes, I am."

"Oh. So?"

"The other one. Harvard gave me a better deal."

"Wonderful! So how about you coming *here* for the duration?"

"Well . . . I've got to finish up one experiment . . . but I could come after that!"

Mead got to pee at last. Back inside, Noni took over lap duties for his juiced head. Kate had rejoined her bunch. The women exchanged looks and then winks. James didn't even try to keep up. He looked across at Oberon, who was awake, and said, "Good gosh! So you're October Carson!"

The older man nodded and frowned, as if to say "so what's it to ya?"

"I've sort of been looking for you," Mead admitted. "I've read . . . I'm curating your journals and specimens at the Peabody. I've been eager to find you and discuss *magdalena*, among other things. Imagine being so close to you all this time!"

Carson's eyes went way up at the mention of his journals. "So they're still around, are they? Yes, we must talk. We've already had quite a field trip together."

"Somehow I suspected you two would be simpatico should you ever meet," said George, "but I hadn't anticipated *quite* such electricity between you."

One of Bagdonitz's students overheard and issued the sort of bleat usually reserved for his own prof's more egregious puns. Winchester shot him a withering look, then revived him with a grin.

"Professor Winchester—" James began.

"Reverting to formalities are we, Mr. Mead?"

"George . . . I meant to tell you before now . . . hoped to find you at Gothic, but you were away . . . I've been trying to write . . ." Mead was unable to continue.

"James, I've long been aware of your defection. Steve called me for advice."

"Advice?"

"It seems a colony of giant hissing roaches somehow got loose in Kline Tower and settled into Professor Griffin's labs. Strange, none of mine were missing. Manton told me your plans to come out here; he probably thought we'd already talked." George spoke gravely, giving nothing away.

"I really am sorry . . . not for going, but for not managing to tell you."

"I cannot condone your unilateral actions, James, you know that. And of course I should have heard it from you first. This doesn't reflect very well on our mutual trust."

Mead felt called on the carpet, and rightly so, even though he was already *on* the carpet. "So . . . are we quits?" he asked.

"Certainly not from my standpoint. You handled the roaches responsibly—the beloved blabberids are fine. I would have set your mind at ease about that if I had known how to reach you. As for your choice of experiences, I can't blame you at all."

"I'm relieved. I was afraid you might not understand. So how come you're here?"

"I'm to give a lecture at Science Lodge in a couple days, if it survived this storm."

"I saw a poster for it at the lodge," said Oberon. "I wrote inviting George to visit."

"And I was delighted to accept, and for the chance to meet our most productive field collector at last," said George.

"And I hitched along," said Noni, "to see the scenery and discuss my results."

"Weird," said Mead.

"So what do you plan to do now?" Winchester asked.

"A little more here," he said. "Then back on the bus to New Haven, if you'll have me."

"I'm glad to hear it. Your charges will have missed you."

"I really do appreciate your understanding, Professor. But . . . what about Professor Griffin? Won't he be sure to cook my goose for ducking out in spite of him?"

"Quaint mixed metaphor, James, but preferable to the way your peers would probably put it. I think not. All efforts to eradicate the roaches—overseen by Steve Manton—failed."

"So what happened?"

"Frank was livid and wouldn't go near his lab. He had to take tranquilizers, and then he took triennial leave while the eradication efforts proceeded. Apparently the 'accidental infestation,' as the dean ruled it, played a major part in our good colleague's regrettable decision to accept a senior chair at Adelphi University, down-Sound."

"Really?" James asked, thunderstruck a third, fourth, fifth? time for the night.

"Really. You owe Steve two big ones, James, and if he takes any more courses from me, they'll be automatic As."

Mead let the fact settle in.

"Only"—and for this Winchester assumed an attitude and tone that Mead had heard once or twice before, which struck him by turns as ironical and enigmatic yet at the same time entirely straight—"I do wonder where those roaches originated."

Mead changed the subject. "Well, I hope Professor G. will be happier at Adelphi than I was with him at Yale."

"Quite. And the rest of us. And so, welcome back, James, whenever you want to arrive—just so it's before your committee meeting on"—he consulted his tiny blue vest diary, peering over his half-glasses and furrowing his Viking brow as Noni sneaked a look through a pass in their mountain range of shoulders—"September seventeenth. You should look forward to meeting your new committee member, Steve Kebler, a fine young wildlife biologist interested in public attitudes toward nature. He's crazy about Gothic."

"Holy cow," said Mead.

"Another rhetorical relic," said George. "Perhaps appropriate in context. Now, James, you know there really should be some consequences for your flight. You took care of the roaches, all right, but you also broke a trust. I suppose I could assign you to copy out the last paragraph of the *Origin of Species* one hundred times, but that would be more pleasure than punishment."

Mead waited for what would follow. He glanced at Noni. September 17 seemed ages away, and her face shone like Christmas.

"So," said George, "I've decided your penance should be to find me a bill-marked *Erebia magdalena* next summer to fill that gap in the collection."

Carson had been listening in. His eyes met Mead's, and the two of them erupted in laughter for no reason that anyone else in the room could possibly guess.

It had been quite a while now since anyone had shown up, and the roster seemed full. So when a woman now named Selene came back from a breather in the scoured air and announced that headlights were coming up the driveway, it came as something of a caution. When someone else reported that the car bore a state seal, all of Oberon's alarms—recently charged—went off. He struggled to his feet. When the door opened, the face he'd feared to see, that of Tonkin of the state, was absent. Instead, there was Tonkin's colleague, Dr. Ziegler, from the previous invasion, and a black woman in a nurse's dress. Oberon wanted to shut the door, but he hesitated.

"Mr. Oberon," said Ziegler, extending his hand. Oberon-Carson took it, but kept his silence. "You've got quite a party in progress— forgive us for crashing it. What's the occasion?"

"Storm, lightning, attempted murder, general mayhem . . ." Oberon replied. "Beyond that, I couldn't begin to tell you. But if you've come for—"

"Has Mary been hit by lightning?" asked the nurse, spotting Mary and dropping to her knees beside her.

"No, but *they* have!" shot someone from the BFC, and "Hi, Iris!" said Howard Heap. Iris blew Howard a kiss.

"This is Iris Empingham," said Ziegler, wearing a raincoat and a flannel shirt this time instead of a white coat. "She was Mary's floor nurse soon after the accident."

"Welcome, Ms. Empingham," said Oberon. "No, not lightning—she met with other misfortune on the mountain."

"May I look her over?" asked Iris.

"We'd welcome your opinion," said Thomas from the shadows. He had remained near Mary in the inglenook. Iris saw his medical bag.

As Iris gently palpated Mary's more obvious wounds, Dr. Ziegler spoke quietly to Oberon. "I became interested in Ms. Glanville's predicament after our unfortunate prior visit," he said. "I apologize for that. I've found little more. But recently a fisherman discovered her purse several miles down the canyon. From the still legible documents, I've been able to piece together something about her."

"Let's hear," said Oberon. Mead was listening too, as was Michael Heap.

"Well, her documents are under a former, married name, Mary Jordan. Apparently she quite recently took the name Glanville. She has a recent PhD from the Yale Divinity School, and she was supposed to report for a faculty appointment last fall at Grinnell College in Iowa. When she failed to show up, they reported her missing. As did her family, what there is of it. But everyone knew her as Mary Jordan, so our efforts to find her under the name Glanville have been to no avail."

"We too have recently learned some of that," Oberon said. "But other parts of what you say are a surprise."

"How has she been, until this mishap?"

"She became wholly articulate, if still forgetful of her past.

But she has recently been hurt in a fall, as you see. Our colleague, Thomas, a paramedic, feels she is likely all right, but she should have a full exam when possible."

Iris said, "I'd agree, from what I can tell. But there's no getting out tonight—the road is blocked."

"Which is why we arrived here so late," said Ziegler. "We had to talk our way around the state troopers at the roadblock by pleading medical emergency. They finally let us through. We barely made it, hugging the edge of the caved-in road. Won't be open till morning, if then."

"Flash flood?"

"Both ways. Big Thompson's even worse, several cars and cabins swept away. They hope to have some way out cleared by morning."

"So you didn't come to take Mary back?"

"No, not at all. I decided after we left last time that you were right. Sam Tonkin blocked me for a while, but he finally went back to Corrections and got out of our hair. We came here merely to advise Mary, and you, of what we've learned. And to offer our help."

"Mary was special," said Iris. "I knew it."

"I knew that too," said Howard.

For some time longer, happy if subdued confusion reigned in the Great Hall of the Mountain Monastery. The pizza was long gone. Carolinus and the BFC set up a sleeping bag encampment on the far side of the hall and settled in, bantering softy about the memorable day. "Brained by his own boulder," heard the cricket on the hearth. "A costly fumble." "*Incredibly* gross." Sterling started in on JC's lightning rod and the workout it got that night, when Bagdonitz told him to cut it out. "You're going to offend our hosts if you don't watch it," he said.

"Not to worry, Professor," said Abraxas the Baptist, who had overheard. "We're tough to offend. And besides, we've already worked that one for all it's worth."

A contagion of yawns overcame the assembly. Then a cry was heard from a corner, where a door opened down into a half-cellar in the stone foundation. It hadn't been used or even opened in years. "Hey, you guys!" came Randy's voice out of the dark. "Come see! There's a tunnel down here!"

41

Soon the clutter of the BFC became the snores and heavy breathing of youthful bodies spent for the day, for the season. By ones and twos (for the merger had well begun on one level and another) members of the two peaceful camps took to various corners and levels. No one felt like trading the fireside and the assembly it had brought together for a cold and solitary monk's cell upstairs. George Winchester accepted the big sofa at Oberon's request, while Oberon and Annie bedded down near Mary to keep watch over her. James and Noni took the other inglenook, and Michael, his brother Howard, Dr. Ziegler, and Nurse Iris found a quiet corner not entirely out of the fire's influence. Outside, the rain had subsided altogether. The storm drifted out over the plains and dissipated, having wrung itself out over Boulder County. Stars came out and the fire gurgled in its red and blue throat.

By midnight, peace and sleep overtook the mountain hall.

Now it is that she who has done nothing but sleep all day awakens. Mary feels her dressed head and says nothing. She arises, waking no one. Stepping softly if shakily to the door, she creeps outside, squats, and beholds the sky. From the soaked ground all around, the scents of broken vegetation, and her newly injured head and bruises, she surmises a storm and drastic events, but recalls nothing of them. Or anything else. And when she comes back to the warm hearth and gazes upon the faces of the man and woman she has been lying beside, lit by the last embers' glow, she does not know them.

Mary sleeps again. Again she wakens, and this time she has knowledge—fearful, vague knowledge of murder and persecution, and a warm, nebulous knowledge of love and safety surrounding her. Her head spins, and she sleeps once more.

The third time Mary awakens, hours later, still more is clear to her. The fire is dead, and all those around her are dead to the world. Could her face be seen, a kind of serenity might show on it such as she has never known before, crossed by flickers of uncertain intensity. No longer clad in her blue and saffron, but in soft green plush, her skin a palette of rising pinks and russet shadows, she rises. Mary stands in front of the middle window where the faintest eastern light is leaking in, faces the sleepers with deepest composure, and begins to speak:

"*Think of having no roof above us tonight: think, and shiver in your sleep. Instead, we are all warm and secure together. Last night I slept beneath cold stone, warmed by the bodies of gray beasts that crept about me, wrapping me in the mercy of their rich pelage. Tonight I slept beneath this roof, warmed by all of you.*

"*But for the safety of the stones, it could be me up there rotting on the rocks, soon to be part of pink campion and black butterfly, shrill marmot and warm pika, instead of my tormentor.*

"*Again, my rescuer was a teacher—but no ascetic this time! More like Dionysus with his band of fauns and dryads. Thank you, gentle friends. You are right to revel, to laugh. The world cries out for laughter in the dark.*

"*My oppressor had no laughter in his heart. His world was a place of stone and crust, unsoftened by human love. That his blood flowed at all was a wonder of nature. To him, all was black and white, good and evil, male and female counterposed. Oh, there is evil—but it is not black, as the butterfly whose name I have lately borrowed shows—and it is certainly not female. He, whose body rots on the rocks—forgive him. He had no idea.*

"*Seek your shelter in nature. Breast the perpetual storm outside the walls. Sway in the tree in the gale, Muir-like. Walk the flooded gutter barefoot, face the rain with no umbrella, gather the bolts to your breast with no lightning rod and no promise of salvation. Be ready to ride the river down to the sea as selfless stuff, to join the jellies and the plankton, the meconium and the mud and the mold, and to call that heaven.*"

Mary pauses, her face placid in the wan mix of starlight and dawn. She rests for a little while, drinks some water, looks out the tall window behind her to the Twin Sisters becoming visible in the gathering pallor. A woodrat, happening upon the scene unawares, runs across her feet. She jerks her tickled toes, startling the rodent, who thought he was alone here. He stamps his hind feet in cadence, gives a *cherk!* of alarm, then gallops across a dozen slumbering bodies to the attic ladder and up to safety. No one awakens or even moves, and Mary continues:

"*I might have died . . . I have died . . . or someone died. I feel that someone is dying within me now. Oh, no, don't leave . . . we're not finished!*" She stands, face against folded hands, grieving the loss of something that has been part of her for as long as she can remember. Which is not very long at all, or else forever. And then she says, "*All right, go then. Like the black butterfly, off on the wind. I'll catch up with you someday.*"

Mary faces out into the silent hall, and her sweet, sonorous voice echoes off its opposite walls like feathers. "*You, who follow Pan, Jesus, or Jehovah, Allah or Darwin: you might as well worship the warm-furred pika, or the marmot who whistles warning of maniacs on the loose among the sacred stones. Worship the black butterfly, if you must. Or a cabbage white butterfly. Or a cabbage root maggot. Or a cabbage. For God is all of these equally, or nothing at all: take your pick. A messiah would be better off coming to us as a butterfly or as a flower, able to turn water into nectar—look there for your miracles! For your holiness, if holiness is what you need.*

"Worship what you will, if you must . . . but the world needs love more than worship. In love lies the only real shelter there is, as you shall discover in the morning. And so, I wish you good night."

Mary has awakened no one, though everyone has heard every word. The cricket on the hearth stridulates, hears a muffled exclamation from the bodymound of the BFC, and then all is silence. And in the morning, everyone seems to have dreamed the same dream and remember it with unusual clarity. One member of the women's camp finds that her clothes, left beside her sleeping bag last night, are missing.

Mary too recalls a dream—or was it?—of a sweet incubus, a visitation from a great pika who enveloped her with soft black wings and softer gray pelage and made warm and tender love to her. This is what she dreams again in the warm cab of the truck that carries her south on the Peak to Peak Highway.

42

In the aftermath of the storm, rivulets of red sand ran down the road. Oberon worked the restored telephone and radio while others searched the premises. Mead and Noni, dodging downed limbs and wires, walked the highway to Magdalena Park Lodge to inquire whether anyone had seen Mary.

"James!" Mead was greeted by Marion Dever. "We've wondered how you all weathered the storm up there. We've lost some shingles on cabins and a shutter or two, but otherwise we came through okay. Your things are still upstairs. And who is this?"

"Thanks, Marion. Yes, it was quite the fireworks on the mountain. But we're all fine, considering. This is Noni Blue. She has to leave today, but she'll be back here soon for a visit. But, Marion, have you seen a lone woman on foot?"

"No, James, we haven't seen anyone like that at all. Is someone missing?"

As soon as the road opened, Mead caught a ride down to Loveland with Bonnie, the eldest of the Dever sisters, for a quick physical exam, which turned up no damage from the ground flash. Then he hired his old Rent-a-Wreck Merc and made a quick trip to Albuquerque for the promised visit, while Noni returned to Gothic with

Winchester to wrap up her summer project. In New Mexico, nothing was resolved, but at least no more storms broke. He got in an afternoon's fishing with his father. They exchanged little talk, yet their bright flies in the slanting sun seemed, somehow, like shared wishes. He left feeling flickers of hope.

When he rejoined Noni at Magdalena Park, it was in the time of gentians. The two of them spent the next days among gentians in the yellowing, reddening meadows. They found the big bluebottle ones, like those the Austrians distill for their *Enzian* schnapps, and the four-in-hand fringed ones too. They peered at minute deep indigo gentians and delft vases that don't even open. One afternoon, high up on Meadow Mountain, they discovered the last blooming arctic gentians, their deep ivory corollas speckled with navy blue. They knelt to sniff them and their four long, fuzzy petals. James wrote to his mother about them, and about Noni.

On one of the last days possible, as the lodge closed down each year after Labor Day, they accepted an offer from Patty Dever, the lodge's wrangler, to take them on a ride. They'd both grown up near horses and were fairly comfortable with them. For two hours, pony-tailed Patty led them up trails to Deer Ridge behind the lodge. The close-cropped pastures beside the willow thickets were lined with blue bands of gentians, like some herbaceous border groomed by the mountain gnomes. As the riders rose into the lodgepole forest, pale mauve asters, scarlet amanitas, and maroon-velour boletes took over the trailside.

Mead's big Appaloosa, Hercules, took the rocky path easily and compliantly. Noni rode a roan mare called Jubilee, as spirited as her name and her rider. She skittered now and then at sliding rocks loosened by the rain's pickax, but Noni managed the reins well, barely touching toe to rib now and then. All the way up, Roxy the retriever ran crazy through the fragrant damp sand and downwood, back and forth across the trail ahead. From below the summit of Deer Ridge, the three gained a view of the lodge from on high, along with the entire, unobscured face of the mountain—*that* mountain. No one felt the need to say a thing, except a blue grouse that thrummed from the Engelmann spruces, or to remark on a freshly emerged pine white butterfly spreading its new, soft wings across a spray of bristlecone pine needles to dry them in the sun. If either James or Noni thought a thing about a crisp white butterfly taking wing even as the tatty brown ones retired from the rockslides, they felt no need to share it.

Patty had an appointment for another ride, a family from Kansas eager for a gentle walk along the highway and back below Horse-tooth Park before they packed the station wagon and headed for Estes. She felt confident that James and Noni could get their mounts back safely by themselves. They'd had a good canter atop the ridge and had handled the horses well, so she left them to return on their own, in their own good time. The horses would soon be driven down to lower pastures for the winter, so they were getting in their last ride, too. Seeming to sense this, they didn't lurch toward the barn as usual when they neared the homestretch. After Patty and Roxy had trotted off, James and Noni dismounted and shared the picnic they'd packed. Then, confident that no one was near, they lay back beneath a yellowing aspen on the amber-spattered ground and crushed their own *Enzian* from the gentians with the press of their young bodies.

At first just playful, their urgency rose like a summer storm, and soon it was invincible. Shirts came off and jeans came down like leaves in a stripping wind. James's hands found the places they had missed and knew they would miss again. He licked her teeth and crushed her lips. Noni did all those things back, and a few of her own. Their abdomens found their way back together, his aedeagus found her bursa copulatrix, and they remembered why they'd thought last spring that they fit together so damned well. James rode a smooth, slow trot as long as he could, and then broke free, threw the reins to the wind, and galloped bareback to his foregone conclusion. Changing places in midstream, Noni took her own sweet time in the saddle, holding on to James's beard like a stallion's mane. And it wasn't long until she cantered on home herself.

Then Roxy found them, his cold nose on her rump making Noni jump and cry "Oh!" Patty's party had balked at the highway walk, so she decided to bring them this way after all. Always sharp-eyed for hazards, she managed to distract the kids and the dad by pointing out some coyote poop. But the sunny-haired mom saw something she wasn't meant to see between the aspens. She smiled, and remembered another time, another summer, not so very far from there.

On their last evening at the lodge before heading east, Noni and Mead brought back a mess of mushrooms from a final hike into the Indian Peaks Wilderness. They had a bucket of small, succulent golden chanterelles, a peck of firm and strangely aromatic matsutakes, and two big, otter-brown king boletes, almost free of worms, as well as a couple of meadow mushrooms from the pasture out back. They asked Marion if they might cook them up in the lodge's kitchen. Patty, a wild mushroom lover, was repaid for her kindness on the ride, and Keith, Marion, Bonnie, and Laura consented to try the native but none too familiar sweetmeats. Surprised by their savor, after her third helping Laura asked, "So if we all die from these, how will you ever know?"

"I guess we wouldn't," said James, "since we'd croak too. And you all'd go to heaven for sure, but I think our chances are shot."

"Don't worry," said Noni. "All these are tried-and-true kinds, much sought after."

"That's good to know! But seriously, will you stay in touch?" Laura asked. "We'd love to know if you learn more about all those butterflies."

Mead promised they would. Still, he was surprised a week later to receive a packet postmarked Allenspark, and he seriously hoped it had nothing to do with mushroom poisoning.

He'd wanted to introduce Noni to the joys of long-distance bus travel, but she had argued for spending those days in the mountains instead, and in the end, Mead accepted her offer of airfare east.

Now she had a week with him in New Haven before taking the train north to Boston to begin her studies at Harvard. She leaned over his shoulder at his lab desk as he slit open the thick envelope from Colorado. There were three letters inside and a short note from Laura Dever. "Dear James," it read. "These all came for you soon after you left. I hope they find you OK, and that we'll see you both back here next summer. All say hi. XOX, LD P.S. We're all still alive."

The first letter came from Albuquerque. It was a short one from his mother.

> I don't know if this will still reach you in Colorado, James, but if not it will follow you. Thank you for writing about the gentians. That caused me to have a look for myself. I didn't find any in the Sandias when I went up with your dad, but I did get into a bunch of asters. They're pretty, but damnably difficult to identify, not to mention the <u>Erigerons</u> and <u>Townsendias</u>.
>
> You know that brochure you left for your brother, about RMBL? Well, I took a look at it, and I'm thinking about signing up for Harriet Barclay's non-credit wildflower class next summer. I think they let old ladies in. By the by, don't wildflowers and butterflies have quite a lot to do with each other?

"That sounds promising!" said Noni. James hadn't tried to conceal the letter.

"Maybe," he said. "Maybe."

Helga concluded, "And since you told me about those women at Rocky Flats, I've been looking into Los Alamos. It sounds as if something similar is fomenting there. I may drive down there next week and have a look-see. Who knows? I don't think it's my style, but you'd better be ready to go my bail, just in case. Oh, and it's a good thing your father is retired. Love, Mom."

The second letter was marked "By Hand—for James Mead, please forward." After he wiped his eyes, Mead could see that it bore a familiar script. Then he remembered where he'd seen it before: the journals of October Carson. "Dear James and Noni," it read.

We're sorry we missed your departure, but we've been gone ourselves a lot since the storm. I wanted to sincerely apologize for putting you at mortal risk, James. And to thank you again for helping me look for Mary. Also for your interest in my former life, and for curating the journals, for what they're worth. I'll look forward to sharing questions about our mutual love interest, both by letter and in person when you return to Colorado next summer. Oh, and please tell George that yes, I'll be both happy and humbled to serve as external reader for your thesis, when the time comes.

Meanwhile, you might be interested in developments here. Of Mary, we've heard little, and perhaps we never will. However, a single postcard arrived, postmarked from Silver Plume, a little place off I-70 on the way to Loveland Pass. All it said was, "I am well, and I love you all. MG." I have an abiding feeling she'll be all right, come what may. Dr. Ziegler has expressed a similar conviction, though he couldn't say why he thought so. And speaking of the good doctor, he and Michael Heap are exploring options for a better situation for Michael's brother, Howard.

Our merger with the camp is moving along well, although come spring, most of the women will move down to a house that has been donated to them in Golden. The Grove will continue in one form or another, ever-evolving, I am sure. As for the monastery, Annie has decided to launch a long-held dream of hers here, at our invitation. It is to be called the Enos Mills Outdoor School.

Through close contact with the mountains, she hopes to raise a generation of—in Mills's phrase—"nature-guides," for our species and our time: citizens who won't freak out when they have a bat in the cabin—we remember your story! We all agree that this fits the Pan-Pacific ideal to a T.

Please do plan to come back next summer. Bring George and Noni if they are free, and see what we have wrought. Perhaps we can go afield together again, this time with nets in hand—on a <u>clear day</u>. You have that penance to satisfy for George, and I'd be happy to help.

I'll be here at least until then. After that, who knows? The road does have its claim.

With all the best, O. Carson

"Sweet," said Noni. "I'm so relieved to hear about Mary. I hope he's right about her. Let's go back in gentian time."

"Right," said James. "Sounds like October might hit the road again, so let's not miss him. But first in Maggie season, okay? Maybe the Fourth of July—catch the fireworks in Estes?"

Noni ignored the reference to fireworks. "Okay! So what's the third letter?"

"Let's see . . . it's from Brownie! I saw him just before our Big Night at the monastery, and he said he might have something more for me."

"So hurry, what does he say? Maybe Mary has fetched up on his doorstep."

James read it to Noni:

Dear Mead, I much enjoyed our recent visit. Thanks for dropping by on your way to see your folks. I trust you found your family well. If this missive should fail to find you still at Magdalena Park, I'm sure it will be forwarded . . .

"Da *da*, da *da*. Okay, here goes."

Most of my summer has been fully engaged among my fossils at Florissant. The other day, as I was brushing away Oligocene ash from a fine new specimen of <u>Prodryas persephone</u> (the ancestral satyr that Scudder described from these deposits—this is the first one found in a hundred years!), I was reminded of your interest in the etymology of <u>Erebia magdalena</u>. I stand by my brief postal response regarding Strecker's irreligious prejudice. But jogged by your visit, I have remembered that nagging connection that I mentioned. It speaks to the plenitude of Magdalena monikers along the Peak to Peak.

You will recall that I had two coauthors for <u>Colorado Butter-flies</u>. One, Don Eff, is a very popular amateur who works for the post office in Boulder and corresponds with lepidopterists all over the place—good friend of George's father, P. S. Winchester, in fact. The other author was the Reverend Bernard Rotger. Don is gregarious and well known among all the western collectors, but Father Rotger was not. He'd immigrated from Malta before the War and has long served in parishes in southwest Colorado, remaining isolated down in places like Pagosa Springs and forming a fine collection from that undersampled part of the state.

Bernard belonged to a lesser-known Catholic order, the Theatines. The chief object of the order was to live an edifying life—what better way, I ask you, than butterfly collecting? But his favorite saint was always Mary Magdalene—I suspect because of the alpine, I don't know. One of his brothers (by blood, not Holy Orders), Bautista, was employed as a surveyor for the Archdiocese of Denver. He was involved in siting, planning, designing, and ultimately building the old monastery north of your lodge, on Cabin Creek. Also, that handsome little stone chapel beside the highway—I know you must know it.

"Well, *sort* of," James said.

"Get on with it," said Noni, unused to Brown's old-fashioned discursions.

Mead continued. "'Well, it seems Bernard went to see his brother while he was engaged in the project. I dug up his letter about it after you left. He stayed at Columbine Lodge—same place Nabokov stayed in '47 when he went after <u>tollandensis</u> with Winchester. While there, he went out with Don Eff—I think it was the only time he ever collected in the Front Range.'"

"Where is he going with this?" asked Noni, impatient for the punchline, if there was ever going to be one. "Is all this necessary?"

"He's a storyteller," said James. "Give him time."

"'Well,'" James went on,

<u>magdalena</u> is spotty and uncommon down in the San Juans. Up north, things must have been perfect that summer because Bernard and Don had a big time with <u>magdalena</u>. In fact, he is responsible for those sentences in the book you like: "Once in a while conditions have been such that a large brood of the species is produced. Then if a collector is around he has a field day." I believe Bernard wanted to commemorate that day, and through his brother's connections, he found a way to do it.

Meanwhile, the building project had been bankrolled by a man named Oscar Malo. When it came time to commission the building and sanctify the new church, the monastery was going to be called St. Malo's and the chapel St. Catherine's, for the wife of Malo's partner and father-in-law, Denver bigwig J. K. Mullen, and for St. Catherine of Sienna. But no one knew who the heck St. Malo was, and Mullen pulled out when the chapel went over budget in those Depression times. So, seeing his chance, Bernard prevailed upon Bautista to propose a name change to commemorate St. Mary Magdalene.

Bernard never told church officials <u>why</u> that name was so suitable for the place, just that the setting resembled Mary's hermitage in the French Alps. They bit. No one raised any objection, except, as Bernard wrote, one of the young seminarians moving into the monastery, a minority of one, and too junior to count. So the change was officially made.

"Holy shit!" said James.

Noni just waggled her head in wonder.

"Wait, there's more. 'And there's more,'" he read. "'The mountain itself! I wasn't too sure about that, so I looked it up with the assistance of a friend down in Denver in the USGS, Rob Wall, who helps me find the best fossil sites on the geologic maps. It turns out that when you go back in the records of the Board of Geographic Names and check the old maps, the mountain has borne several names. For a number of years it was called Mount Meeker. That's how Enos Mills referred to it. I'll bet you could find old-timers around there who still use that name.'"

Mead flipped to the last page of the letter and continued reading.

But along about 1935, application was made to change the mountain's official name. The argument advanced on the petition claimed confusion with the town and county of Meeker on the Western Slope of Colorado, named for the pioneer Ezra Meeker. Apparently the residents of Meeker Park agreed with that complaint. Nor had Ezra's brother, Nathan Meeker, former editor of the New York Tribune, much to do with the mountain. All he did was come west with Horace Greeley in 1870 and help found Greeley's Union Colony, and later serve as Indian agent. He was killed by the Utes for plowing their racetrack and trying to make them farm. He merely increased the confusion.

"Curiouser and curiouser," said Noni.

"'Meanwhile, the chapel-on-the-rock was rapidly gaining fame as a tourist attraction. So the petitioners to the Board—get this, B. Rotger, M.A., A.I.S. & Rev. B. Rotger, C.R.—proposed a new designation for the peak: Magdalena Mountain. The hearing record contains only one dissenting testimony, from the same dyspeptic monk, who offered Mt. St. Paul as an alternative. Needless to say, Magdalena won out. Magdalena Park and lodge simply followed suit.'"

"Wow," said Mead, just "Wow." Noni nodded.

"'I thought you might find some interest in these arcane details of the area's nomenclatural provenance, James. I hope they will prove useful to you. Thanks for giving me an excuse to track them down in the rapidly fossilizing strata of my filing cabinets.

"'Good luck in your studies, and please give my regards to your esteemed professor.

"'Sincerely yours,

"'Brownie.'"

James stood stunned, the letter falling from his hand like so many wings. "So," he finally said. "It was all just the butterfly, after all."

"*Just* the butterfly?" repeated Noni, at his elbow. "Because if Mary's right, James—what else *is* there?"

AFTER

Up on Magdalena Mountain, new snow clings like the soft stria-
tions on an eland's flank. The tear-track cleft, a backward question
mark, is already cast in white again. Solifluction bands stripe the
north slope, freeze-thaw pillows the south. Pine fringes below stand
flocked, shocked by the night's surprise; and aspen leaves cling like
the last yellow scales on an old swallowtail's wing. Across the face,
every rock—each stone, all the boulders—stands out as sharply on
the new white field as the Steller's jay sweeping across the scene
shows up against the pale blue behind it. Wispy white clouds that
could be blowing locks of an old man's hair form and reform across
the mountain's brow.

Last night, Erebia sought a deeper cleft in the rocks to escape
the coming cold. But all through this end-of-summer nocturne, the
snow fell and the boulders froze. All the creatures of the mountain
shivered, departed, or perished as its stone-built face took on a rimy
glaze. Fingers of wind with sharp nails picked through the rocks to
send martens down the slope into the forest and their prey into still
deeper holes. The fingers found the big rock spiders and squeezed the
life out of them. They searched out the last green sedges and wrung
them brown.

Now, in the frosty dawn, the fluids jell in Erebia's body. Ice crystals congeal in his cells. Circulation ceases, and a butterfly dies.

Nearby, a tiny caterpillar, cowled in a sedge beneath the insulating snow, preserves the promise of another spring on Magdalena Mountain.

Those frigid fingers find Erebia's tattered husk, teasing it out from where it rests in its crevice. And on the open wind, the black butterfly sails across the rocks one more time.

ACKNOWLEDGMENTS

I must thank a number of people for their help and faithful support for this book over the years. The Devers of Meeker Park Lodge; the Ray and Jan Chu family, Mary Jane Foley, the Ron and Murt Cisar family, Ron Wahl, and many other Colorado Summiteers; the Young Colorado Feminist Lepidopterists' League (Jan and Amy Chu, Carol Bylsma and daughters Lauri and Lynelle, Josie Quick, Rusty and Molly Muller); Audrey and Jim Benedict, Gerald Hilchie, Charles Slater; Terry Chester, Francie Chew, Paul Ehrlich, and everyone at RMBL and Yale OML; and especially the late F. Martin Brown, Charles Remington, and Karölis Bagdonas, and all of the BFC. Larry Gall and Debra Piot provided critical assistance in the C. L. Remington Archives at Yale University, establishing a key date for a meeting with Nabokov. Andy Warren showed me Nabokov's Maggies in the Cornell University Collection, and Naomi Pierce in the MCZ at Harvard University.

Generous writing grant support was provided by the Raymond Chu Family Foundation. JoAnne Heron brought Magdalena back from the Wind River Range and indulged my early obsession. Sally Anne Hughes took my Saturday morning watering shift in the Yale greenhouses so I could begin the book, and Thea Linnaea Pyle saw it through many drafts. For helpful readings of earlier versions I am grateful to Harry Foster, Eve Prior, Donna K. Wright, Fayette Krause, Jan Chu, Mary Jane Foley, Boyce Drummond, David Branch, Ron Cisar, Susan Kafer, Howard Whetstone Pyle, Pat Miller, and members of my writing group: Jenelle Varila, Lorne Wirkkala, John Indermark, Pat Thomas, Susan Holway, and Brian Harrison. Jane Elder Wulff, Neil Johannsen, Mathew Tekulsky, and Peter Stekel offered valuable fellow-writers' counsel throughout.

Very large thanks to my wonderfully encouraging literary agent, Laura Blake Peterson; Patrick Thomas; Jack Shoemaker; and especially Harry Kirchner and Florence Sage, all of whose critical readings were essential to the final form. And thanks to Jordan Koluch, Jennifer Alton, Kelly Winton, Megan Fishmann, Alisha Gorder, Kathleen Boland, Miyako Singer, and everyone else at Counterpoint Press who helped to make the book and bring it into the world.

Bel's poem from Vladimir Nabokov's *Listen to the Harlequins!* is reprinted with permission from *Nabokov's Butterflies: Unpublished and Uncollected Writings,* Brian Boyd, Robert Michael Pyle, and Dmitri Nabokov, eds. (Beacon Press, 2000). The Magdalena mating sequence previously appeared in *Walking the High Ridge: Life as Field Trip* (Milkweed Editions) and in *American Butterflies.* The image of *Erebia magdalena* that appears on the title page and elsewhere came from William Henry Edwards's grand work, *The Butterflies of North America* [with colored drawings and descriptions], (Boston & New York; Houghton, Mifflin & Co. 1888). I thank John V. Calhoun and Jonathan P. Pelham for providing me with this striking image for use here, and for their splendid butterfly scholarship, which has informed, inspired, and excited me for many years.

CREATURES, PEOPLE, AND PLACES

Magdalena Mountain is a real place, with a different name. The Magdalena alpine (*Erebia magdalena*) and all the other animals and plants mentioned in these pages are real species, and I have endeavored to depict them as accurately as I can. The insect order Grylloblattodea (ice crawlers) has been shifted south of the Red Desert biogeographical barrier in southern Wyoming, but it does co-occur with *Erebia magdalena* in Alberta. The particular butterfly I've named Erebia is an imaginary individual of *E. magdalena*, but nothing in his experience should be other than plausible, given what we know of his kind. The Theano alpine's name has been changed to *Erebia pawloskii* in North America, but I've used the old name *E. theano*, as it is what October Carson would have known. Certain other places and landforms are based on actual locations, but their names have been changed if I have made up much about them.

When historical figures appear under their own names, such as Evelyn Hutchinson, F. M. Brown, Enos Mills, and Vladimir Nabokov, I have tried to be true to them and their actual activities in the book's arena of action. Most players are either wholly de novo characters (including Professor Griffin and Attalus) or composites loosely based on real people. Their names are different, and I have felt no compulsion to treat their models accurately, only kindly.

Vladimir Nabokov's connections to the place and the butterfly and to a couple of the characters (or their inspirations) are absolutely truthful; only a detail or two have been adumbrated by way of fill-in flash. However, during earlier drafts of the book I was unaware of Nabokov's personal attachment to the vicinity of Magdalena Mountain, and of his poem-within-a-novel about *Erebia magdalena*: I discovered these parallel details only while coediting and annotating *Nabokov's Butterflies: Unpublished and Uncollected Writings* (Beacon Press, 2000) with Brian Boyd and Dmitri Nabokov: a truly stunning case of convergent evolution.

ROBERT MICHAEL PYLE grew up and learned his butterflies in Colorado, where he fell in love with the Magdalena alpine and its high-country habitat. He took his PhD in butterfly ecology at Yale University, worked as a conservation biologist in Papua New Guinea, Oregon, and Cambridge, and has written full-time for many years. His twenty-two books include *Wintergreen* (John Burroughs Medal), *Where Bigfoot Walks* (Guggenheim Fellowship), and *Sky Time in Gray's River* (National Outdoor Book Award). He lives in rural southwest Washington State and still studies butterflies.